HELLHOLE
AWAKENING

HELLHOLE
AWAKENING

BOOK TWO
in the
HELLHOLE SERIES

BRIAN HERBERT
and
KEVIN J. ANDERSON

TOR®

A Tom Doherty Associates Book
New York

This is a work of fiction. All of the characters, organizations, and events portrayed in this novel are either products of the authors' imaginations or are used fictitiously.

HELLHOLE AWAKENING

Copyright © 2013 by DreamStar, Inc., and WordFire, Inc.

www.wordfire.com

A Tor Book
Published by Tom Doherty Associates, LLC
175 Fifth Avenue
New York, NY 10010

www.tor-forge.com

Tor® is a registered trademark of Tom Doherty Associates, LLC.

Library of Congress Cataloging-in-Publication Data

Herbert, Brian.
   Hellhole awakening / Brian Herbert and Kevin J. Anderson. — First edition.
      p. cm.
   ISBN 978-0-7653-2270-8 (hardcover)
   ISBN 978-1-4299-4959-0 (e-book)
   1. Space colonies—Fiction.   2. Space warfare—Fiction.   3. Life on other
planets—Fiction.   4. Fantasy fiction.   I. Anderson, Kevin J., 1962–
II. Title.
   PS3558.E617H46 2013
   813'.54—dc23

                                                                    2012038824

Tor books may be purchased for educational, business, or promotional use.
For information on bulk purchases, please contact Macmillan Corporate and
Premium Sales Department at 1-800-221-7945 extension 5442
or write specialmarkets@macmillan.com.

First Edition: March 2013

Printed in the United States of America

0 9 8 7 6 5 4 3 2 1

We dedicate this book to the many readers who enjoy our
Dune novels, as well as this original series and our other books.
Thank you for your years of support, interest, and enthusiasm,
and all of your many letters and comments.

Acknowledgments

All of our books are complicated undertakings, and we cannot do them alone. As always and more than anything, we want to express our thanks and deep love to our wives, Janet Herbert and Rebecca Moesta, who provide more support in all ways than we can possibly say.

For *Hellhole Awakening* we are especially indebted to the tremendous support from Tom Doherty, our publisher at Tor, and the editorial work of Pat LoBrutto, Maxine Hitchcock, and Emily Husain, and the support of our agent, John Silbersack. Mary Thomson provided excellent transcription support.

HELLHOLE
AWAKENING

1

The growler storm rolled over the landscape of Hellhole, a riot of static discharges and blistering wind. The electric bursts etched glassy scars along the ground, scattered pebbles and dust, and splintered a spindly tree on the edge of the spaceport landing field.

High-resolution weather satellites had observed and followed the storm as it came over the hills toward Michella Town. The colonists took shelter in their reinforced homes, protected from the planet's persistent violence. They were accustomed to the destructive vagaries of Hellhole's weather, the frequent quakes and everyday shifts in wind. By now, they knew how to survive here.

On the outskirts of town, Elba, the large headquarters-residence of General Tiber Adolphus, stood armored against the storm: The sealed window plates and thick doors held firm, and the wind moaned with frustration as it pressed against the structure. Grounded lightning rods dissipated the repeated blasts.

Standing at the reinforced window plate, Adolphus stared out at the wind-whipped landscape. During the first desperate years of the Hellhole colony, growler storms had taken a high toll, but now the fury was just part of daily existence. Static discharges exploded in the sky like weapon blasts. He saw the weather as a metaphor, an apt one.

The storm is coming. The members of his strategy session were safe for the moment, but soon a far more destructive hurricane would arrive when Diadem Michella Duchenet sent her Army of the Constellation against the upstart rebels.

Sophie Vence brought him a cup of hot kiafa to drink before the strategy meeting resumed. "This is recently harvested, our best crop yet. Another step toward providing civilized amenities out here."

He sipped the hot beverage and nodded. "Further amenities can wait until I secure our freedom."

It was here, inside the meeting room of his headquarters, that he had conspired with a select group of like-minded planetary administrators to construct their own transportation network that did not rely on the old government. And they had done it right under the Diadem's nose. Now that the isolated frontier worlds were connected by the new string-line network, they could become self-sufficient, without paying exorbitant tribute to the Diadem Michella.

Holding his cup of kiafa, Adolphus took a seat at the planning table. "The Constellation fleet will be coming—we can be certain of that. Sonjeera received our announcement more than a month ago and killed our ambassadors two weeks ago. We know Diadem Michella will respond."

"We've been preparing for this all along, quietly building up our defenses. Each day, we get more and more ready." Bony Craig Jordan, his security chief, was proud of the hodgepodge Hellhole military. A veteran from the first rebellion, he had been protecting the General for years in his exile. Now, during the rapid military preparations, Jordan managed part of Hellhole's defensive army.

"The Army of the Constellation is a lumbering beast, widespread, mismanaged, hobbled by its own bureaucracy. That buys us a little time." Adolphus tapped his fingers on the table. "Their fleet is being assembled, armed, loaded, and supplied right now—a gigantic operation for which they are ill prepared. The Diadem is impatient, but confident in her overwhelming strength. She will try to destroy everything on Hellhole, just to make an example of us." He showed strength by maintaining a smile on his face. "I would prefer not to let that happen. Therefore, we have to outsmart them—that's all there is to it."

Jordan let out a boisterous laugh that carried more velocity than his frame seemed capable of delivering. "Diadem Michella has a habit of underestimating you, sir. When she exiled you to Hellhole, she didn't expect you or our colony to survive, much less prosper."

"We can hope she's too old to learn any new lessons," Sophie said, her voice laced with equal parts bitterness and sarcasm. She had been both his sounding board and lover for years. With gray eyes and wavy dark hair, she was beautiful without relying on elaborate makeup, hair-styles, jewels, or fashions. Although she owned a house in the heart of Michella Town, she spent most of her time with him at Elba these days. Not only was it practical to have her here at his headquarters when they had war planning to do, but she also made the place feel more like a home.

As if to express frustration, a tantrum of wind hurled itself at the house, but was unable to reach the people protected within. Adolphus turned to the other strategists in the room; they still looked windblown, although they had arrived before the storm struck in full force. None of them seemed bothered by the violent growler outside.

The exiled lordling Cristoph de Carre said, "No one disagrees with you, sir, but how do we ensure it? We should buy more time." His face became angry, perhaps as he recalled the tragedies that had driven him out here. "I suggest we blow the stringline substations, cut ourselves off from the Crown Jewels, and just be done with it. It's the only way to be sure."

"That remains a final option." Adolphus frowned. "But it's a desperate one, and very costly to reverse."

"If we cut all the stringlines," Sophie said, "it'll take years to reconnect, and possibly more iperion than we have."

"But at least we'd be safe . . . ," Cristoph persisted.

"Unless it starts a civil war here in the Deep Zone," the General pointed out. If he completely severed contact with the Crown Jewels, his fragile coalition might not survive the uproar. "We can't afford the distraction."

He knew that six DZ leaders had already voiced resentment over how his decisions placed their people in danger. They had never asked to become embroiled in a vast rebellion, but they had been swept up in it anyway. Though the frontier worlds overwhelmingly wanted independence, Adolphus had forced the matter. There was no turning back. When faced with retaliation from the Constellation, he worried that those surly administrators might turn against him. For security, he had stationed extra warships—ships he couldn't spare—at those planets, ostensibly to help protect against the Diadem's incursions.

Adolphus held up a hand before Cristoph could argue further. "We have other alternatives at the moment. Planning makes the reality." The General had proved that time and again, achieving seemingly impossible military victories because he could see several moves ahead on the most complex of game boards. He expected to do it again.

Next to Cristoph de Carre, the Diadem's tall, auburn-haired daughter spoke up. "And we have our telemancy. The Constellation fleet cannot be prepared for that." Keana's voice changed, becoming more flat and formal as her inner alien companion, Uroa, took control. "This is the Xayan homeworld, too. We will use our powers to protect it."

As strange as it felt to allow Michella's only child to participate in this planning meeting, Keana Duchenet was a powerful telemancer with the Xayan memories inside of her, capable of tremendous psychic powers. Worst case, she made a potentially valuable hostage.

The growler continued to cause havoc outside, moaning and scraping along the walls of the main house. A static discharge exploded in a geyser of sparks in the General's yard. The house lights flickered, but came back on.

"No matter what, we can put up a hell of a fight—much more than the old bitch suspects." Sophie rattled off the numbers without even consulting her data display. "We've had more than a month of full-bore military preparations across the Deep Zone, and plenty more already in place. Our factories are producing metals and equipment at breakneck speed. Right now, the DZ Defense Force has twenty-one military ships, and we've armed and refitted another seventy-five at Buktu. They're on their way here now."

In Michella Town, Sophie managed warehouses full of incoming goods and a set of productive greenhouses; at the distant outpost of Slickwater Springs, she also oversaw the settlement of "shadow-Xayan" converts, human volunteers who had merged their consciousnesses with ancient alien memories. She performed her work with extraordinary skill and had become one of the largest commercial brokers on the planet. Adolphus had made her his chief quartermaster, whose job was to prepare everyone on Hellhole for the lean times ahead.

Now, ignoring the building storm outside, the General looked at all of his advisers, waited for silence. "I don't expect it'll come to an outright military confrontation. I have a plan." He smiled. "It's a matter of timing and strategic use of information. I still have many loyalists in the Crown Jewels, and some of them even work for the military. Very soon now, I expect to receive details of the offensive operation Diadem Michella plans to send against us, the exact numbers of ships and crew, as well as the precise departure date. She wants to make a grandiose gesture—which takes time. Enough time for us to prepare a trap."

Craig Jordan grinned. "A trap! Now that's what I like to hear."

"Don't cut it too close, sir," Cristoph warned.

"The General can make it happen." Sophie had no doubt in her voice.

2

Red Commodore Escobar Hallholme monitored operations in the command tower of the fleet base, gazing across the sunlit military operations that stretched as far as he could see. A blond man in his thirties, Escobar drew a deep breath, let it out slowly to quell his impatience. This was maddening. He had envisioned charging off to battle on a moment's notice, overwhelming the enemy of the Constellation, planting his flag in the history books.

Such a large military operation had turned out to be more preparation than action.

After General Adolphus's heinous act, thousands of soldiers had responded to the call, rushing to the main base on the planet Aeroc. They were the finest troops in the Army of the Constellation, with the most advanced equipment and the best training. In the name of the Diadem Michella Duchenet, they would grind this new uprising to dust and defeat the rebel General once and for all. Escobar would recapture the planet Hallholme—which was named for his father, after all—and earn his own prominent place in history, perhaps even a greater place than old Commodore Hallholme's. And why not, since he was finishing the job the old man had left incomplete.

Escobar studied the mounting tallies on an interactive admin-image in the air to his right, noted the shipments received and distributed, the materiel and personnel yet to be launched, the armed vessels arriving from other Crown Jewel planets still waiting to be installed aboard one of the giant haulers.

For weeks, Aeroc had been a beehive of activity as the massive military operation was mounted. Crews loaded upboxes full of munitions and supplies for the fleet; each day, dozens of upboxes launched into orbit, where they were transferred to the one hundred capital ships installed aboard five huge military stringline hauler frameworks. Soon, fifteen thousand uniformed fighters and support crew would shuttle up on troop transports to fill the great vessels. The fleet carried a higher than optimal percentage of officers, because every noble family wanted to claim that a son or daughter had participated in the glorious, final defeat of General Adolphus.

Yes, it was an impressive operation, yet daunting and unwieldy.

Two weeks ago, Diadem Michella had stood in the Council Hall and declared war. Because the General's announcement had taken the Constellation completely by surprise, the Constellation fleet wasn't ready.

Escobar was anxious to go. "This is too damned slow!" he said into the unit's receiver.

"We can't leave before everything's loaded, sir," the response came over his earadio. Logistics Officer Bolton Crais was a silver major in the fleet and the mission's second in command—not because of military prowess or competence, but because his wife, the Diadem's daughter Keana, remained a prisoner of the General's. "A poorly planned mission is a disaster waiting to happen."

Escobar sighed, wondering if his father had ever been forced to wait for weeks before he engaged his nemesis. The old Commodore told interminable stories, but rarely included bureaucratic details. "What excuses do you have for me today, Major? Are we at least on your *revised* schedule?"

"I'll be right up, sir. We need to talk about this."

Escobar made a sound in his throat halfway between a groan and a growl. At least the situation would advance his own military career. Having recently been promoted to the rank of Redcom for this assault, he intended to demonstrate the superiority of his skills as a decision maker and leader. If Commodore Percival Hallholme had killed Adolphus when he had the chance, the rebel General would not now be tearing apart the Constellation. . . .

He heard the machinery of the tower lift, and Major Bolton Crais stepped out, tall and slender in his gold-and-black uniform, with the silver rank insignia on his collar. Crais stepped up to the projected columns of numbers that hung in the air. "A shortage of upboxes has created a new bottleneck, sir. Our crews have to wait for the containers to come back before we can load them again. As I explained in my memo several days ago, we were forced to decommission an entire shipment of defective upboxes, all from one manufacturer."

Escobar scowled. "You're supposed to be the logistics expert. You should have tested all of the upboxes ahead of time."

Crais did not let the criticism wash over him, as a lower-ranking officer should have. "Sir, you opted not to waste time testing the new deliveries. Time was of the essence."

Escobar did not know how to direct his frustration. "Our task force is on a fast track, Major. The Diadem wants Adolphus's head delivered to her on a platter, and Lord Riomini demands the swift and efficient deployment of the fleet. It's been weeks already!"

"I understand, Redcom. You, and the Black Lord, have my apologies. Swift and efficient are often at odds, however. From the moment I became involved, I began to discover problems with the planning, not to mention unrealistic expectations. The Army of the Constellation has been weighed down with bureaucracy and nepotism for years, and the past decade of peace has made our soldiers soft and unprepared for war."

"You're not filling me with confidence, Major."

Bolton did not even seem embarrassed. "We also had a false bomb scare and had to evacuate half our ships."

He sighed. "More excuses. Has the perpetrator been caught?"

"No, Redcom. Likely one of the General's deluded loyalists causing problems."

Escobar tried to calm himself by imagining the size and power of the force he would eventually bring to bear against Adolphus. Then all the delays would be forgotten. "Once we get the fleet to the Sonjeera hub and launch to planet Hallholme, it is only a four-day stringline flight. We can wrap up this bothersome uprising swiftly enough." His words were clipped, his voice angry. "The sooner we depart, the sooner we defeat the General."

Bolton looked away. "There's . . . another snag, Redcom. The Diadem just issued a directive that we must bring back thousands of prisoners so she can hold a dramatic show trial. Our fleet has to be prepared to hold and control all those captives."

Escobar shook his head. Did she understand what she was asking? "I understand the Diadem's need for a grand spectacle, but I don't think she comprehends the difficulties of transporting thousands of prisoners!"

Major Crais was all business, completely organized. "To that end, Redcom, I requisitioned large stockpiles of a stasis drug from Sandusky so we can sedate them en masse, and stack them like cordwood if we need to. It will make the prisoner situation manageable. The last shipment of the drug should arrive from Sandusky within two days."

A delay, but not a disaster. "Yes, yes. But when do we actually launch the fleet? That's the only detail I really care about."

"Best estimate, sir—ten days."

Each answer disgusted him more and more. "A week behind the original schedule! I hope to conquer the General before he dies of old age. You're losing credibility, Major, and sooner or later your noble friends will no longer be able to protect you."

"We're loading as fast as we can, sir. Given the uncertainties of the engagement, we don't want to leave behind anything important. If we take dangerous shortcuts, we risk high casualties. We need ample supplies so that we are in a position to impose what might be an extended siege."

"Extended siege? The longer we delay, Major, the more lives we're going to lose because the General has a chance to strengthen his defenses. He's got to be expecting us. In fact, he's probably surprised that we haven't already bombarded his planet."

"General Adolphus understands the complexities of large fleet movements, sir."

Escobar grumbled as he paced the tower's observation deck. "If we struck faster, we'd likely need half as many ships to take him out."

"But we don't want to take that chance. Lord Riomini and the Diadem don't want to take that chance. Ten days, Redcom. You have my best estimate."

"And I'll hold you to it, Major." Escobar turned to the windows and watched one of the upboxes surge up its launch chute and streak into the sky. With a ripple of sonic boom, it vanished into the blue.

As Bolton Crais rode the lift back down to his office, he reminded himself that he had actually pulled strings to be transferred to this assignment. Bolton's marriage to the Diadem's daughter had never been more than political window dressing. He was realistic about that much. She had cuckolded him, flaunted her affair with Lord Louis de Carre until political backlash brought down the de Carre family. Even so, Bolton cared a great deal for Keana, though he felt more like a brother to her than a romantic hero. He worried about her, especially now that she had fallen under the spell of the rebels. And, possibly, the aliens . . .

The Diadem might have abandoned her daughter, but Bolton still hoped to rescue her. He was determined to prepare the fleet properly so Keana could be saved. On his own authority, Bolton had added many key items to the fleet manifests, just in case; to avoid criticism, he had used his family wealth to purchase auxiliary life-support equipment, medical supplies, a pair of discontinued civilian trailblazers, even a cargo of iperion, to be used in the event of an emergency. To avoid drawing notice and a potential reprimand from Redcom Hallholme, he loaded the additional equipment aboard the stringline warships in innocuously marked containers.

Theoretically, the punitive mission should last no more than a couple of weeks, but many things could go wrong, especially in such a large operation. He would not let the Redcom's impatience force him into making mistakes. Escobar Hallholme was not even a shadow of his illustrious father. Bolton was convinced the new Redcom was in over his head—and they had not even departed yet. . . .

The descending lift came to a stop, and Bolton stepped out, making his way into the military encampment. He organized his mind, monitoring all the loose ends that still needed to be tied together before the fleet could depart.

Ten more days. Even that seemed unrealistic.

3

During a decade of service, the linerunner *Kerris* had followed many stringline routes throughout the Constellation, both in the well-traveled Crown Jewel network and out to the far-flung Deep Zone. Turlo and Sunitha Urvancik flew the small ship, maintaining the iperion path that made hyperfast space travel possible.

Before throwing in their lot with the General, the two linerunners had always done their lonely work without drawing any attention. Now that the DZ had declared independence from the Constellation, though, the Urvanciks had to slip back to Sonjeera like thieves in the night. If they succeeded in this intelligence-gathering mission, they would help save Hellhole, perhaps even bring down the Diadem's government.

"And that wouldn't make me shed a single tear," Sunitha said.

Turlo saw the hard expression on his wife's face. Sunitha had large, dark eyes and dusky skin, a beauty that had not diminished as she grew older; her hair was still deep black, with only a few shadows of gray. "Nothing will bring Kerris back," he said. "But at least it might help the scars fade."

At the beginning of the General's earlier rebellion, their only son had believed the Diadem's propaganda and joined the Army of the Constellation. He considered himself a patriot. But in the war, after Kerris witnessed unspeakable things, his initial patriotism turned to disenchantment and then to outright shock. He had died a "hero," according to the Diadem's official consolation note, but Turlo and Sunitha learned later that their son had been killed in an accident caused by the incompetence of his own comrades. The Diadem's note had placed the blame squarely on Adolphus, keeping the blood off her own hands.

Now Turlo believed Kerris would applaud their decision to side with the General. If only their son were still alive, he could join them in the fight for true freedom. . . .

"I just want life to get back to normal," Sunitha said.

The stringline timer sent a signal chime through the cockpit, and the two became all business. Once they acquired the information from the loyalist spy, the General could finalize his defenses and set a trap before the Army of the Constellation came to destroy him.

Sunitha leaned forward to verify their position as space traffic increased on the outskirts of the Sonjeera system. "Need to make sure we're not too close to the planet, not too far out." All the Constellation's stringlines converged at the central Sonjeera hub, but any vessel on the interdicted Hellhole line would arouse immediate suspicion. Without giving Turlo time to brace himself, she disengaged the *Kerris* from the iperion path and they coasted in toward the capital planet.

Officially, the two linerunners had been "lost" on one of their routes, written off as dead. If they were discovered now, secretly working for the rebel General, the Diadem's torturers would make even their son's lingering radiation-poisoning death seem easy.

The best idea, Turlo decided, was to avoid getting caught in the first place.

Once the *Kerris* was off the stringline, Turlo activated the spacedrive, nudging them toward Sonjeera. He merged into the flow of traffic converging on the planet. They already had a fake ID beacon, which identified the *Kerris* as nothing more than a small cargo distributor. Nothing of interest to the authorities.

Sonjeera's orbit was crowded with transfer stations and holding matrices for cargo boxes. Some trade items and raw materials were delivered via downboxes to Sonjeeran markets, but the majority were shuffled aboard other stringline haulers to be delivered throughout the Crown Jewel worlds.

Because all Constellation travel and commerce had to go through the bottleneck, the orbiting complex was enormous. Even with the Deep Zone lines now embargoed, the hub was a hornet's nest of confusion. The disorder worked to Turlo's advantage as he received clearance and an assigned dock from a crisp, impatient-sounding woman. "We may as well use our last Constellation credits," Turlo said. "I want to pick up a case of Sonjeeran brandy. We can sell it at a premium to the DZ planetary administrators."

Sunitha raised her thin eyebrows. "Oh, so now you're a black-market trader?"

"It's more festive to have them toast their independence with something other than Sophie Vence's wine."

Turlo and Sunitha found the crowded observation bar where they were supposed to meet their contact. Panoramic windowports showed sparkling Sonjeera below, and they watched the passenger pods and downboxes drop from orbit, and stringline haulers hurtling in on the Crown Jewel lines. Watching the time, feigning nonchalance, growing nervous. When their contact was late by ten minutes, Sunitha began to perspire; she drank two servings of hot, sweet kiafa, which only made her more jittery. Turlo pretended to be aloof, despite the knot in his stomach.

A thin man with short brown hair and protruding ears sat beside them, startling Sunitha. He said in a low, conversational voice, "Been watching you. Had to make sure."

"We're who you think we are," Turlo said.

"Depends on *who* you think we are," Sunitha added, flashing her eyes at her husband.

Toying with crumbs and drops of liquid on the tabletop, the stranger drew a casual script DZ, a symbol of Adolphus's rebellion, then swept it away with the side of his hand. He leaned closer. "The General still has loyalists here, even one or two planetary leaders in the Crown Jewels. Not everybody accepts what the Diadem is doing. Tiber Adolphus isn't the only one thinking of rebellion."

The spy, Dak Telom, was a midlevel officer of the Army of the Constellation who had access to supply records and ship movements. "I came in from Aeroc yesterday. The fleet is still being readied and loaded, but they'll be launching soon. They'll converge here at the Sonjeera hub, then set off for planet Hallholme. I have the specific details—total number of ships, weapons capabilities, crew complements—and of critical importance, their exact departure time and transit information."

Turlo smiled; he could feel his pulse racing. "That's what the General needs."

"That's *everything* the General needs," Telom said. "He'd better make the most of it. We've all got a lot riding on him."

"Yes," Sunitha said. "We do."

Dak Telom removed a foilpaper packet of nuts from his pocket, carefully tore it open, and dumped the nuts into his palm. He gobbled them in a single bite and tossed the empty wrapper on the table in front of Turlo. "Take that with you." Turlo looked around for a recycler receptacle, but the spy put a hand on his wrist. He whispered, "Molecular imprinting on the inner liner. The General will know how to decode it. Use that data to keep the Deep Zone safe."

Dak Telom finished his kiafa in a single gulp and left without another word while Turlo pocketed the wrapper.

4

Although desolate Hellhole was considered the worst Deep Zone world, Tanja Hu could see that frozen Buktu was no prize either. The remote planetoid had only a gossamer-thin unbreathable atmosphere, showered by a heavy sleet of solar radiation.

All things considered, she much preferred her own lush, tropical Candela.

Nevertheless, Ian Walfor and two hundred hardy colonists had made the best of things on Buktu, even though the small world turned out to be far different from what the original probe data suggested. They had built their colony under difficult conditions and not only survived but thrived. That was what resourceful pioneers did. Deep Zone people, *independent* sorts who did not need the choke collar of the Constellation.

Every time Tanja thought of the corrupt central government and the machinations of the bitch Michella, she wanted to hurt something. Thanks to the General, the frontier worlds had finally broken free, and Tanja took great satisfaction in that. Now, if only they could hold on to their independence.

Ian Walfor's ships from the industrial yards and spacedocks on Buktu would help ensure that.

Down in the Buktu operations center, Tanja met with Walfor inside a smooth ice grotto, where a porthole field presented the black starry sky and the pocked ice field. He sidled close to her. "I brought you here for the view."

"I can get a view anywhere." She looked at him stiffly. "You brought me here to help deliver ships to General Adolphus—and also because I'm the only one who can negotiate for the stardrive engines you need."

Walfor gave her a roguish grin. "True, you can pull strings with Administrator Frankov on Theser, but my reasons don't have to be all business."

Tanja had long, inky black hair, high cheekbones, and large eyes. For several years, she had enjoyed (and diverted) Walfor's flirtations. He was an attractive man in his own way, with a weathered face and wavy black hair, and she did enjoy his company. One day she might accept his advances—when the Deep Zone was free and safe, and she could turn her attentions to romance. For now, her duty to the rebellion, and to Candela, consumed her.

She had been hardened by many difficulties and tragedies, most of which she blamed on Constellation corruption and on the Diadem herself. It was a barbaric fantasy, but she often imagined the withered head of evil Michella Duchenet thrust onto a stake; *then* Tanja could relax.

Seeing her expression darken, Walfor said, "You're beautiful when you're angry."

She drew her brows together. "Then these days I must be beautiful all the time."

He let out an exaggerated sigh. "We're all in this together. I don't know why Frankov's engineers refuse to leave Theser. They're like conceited lordlings forcing everyone to come to their court. How can they refuse to travel? Don't they trust their own stardrives?"

Tanja was also annoyed at the inconvenience, especially during a war. The brilliant Theser engineers supplied vital components, but no amount of coaxing would budge them from their laboratories inside the crater walls on Theser. Through her friendship with Sia Frankov, the planetary administrator, Tanja had arranged to get the shipments herself. She straightened, keeping her mind on the goal. "That's a difficulty we can overcome," she said. "In fact, it's not even much of an inconvenience, now that the new Candela-Theser route is established.

Trust me, it would take longer to argue with them, and we still wouldn't succeed. Leave it to me—I can round up stardrive engines for your scrap heaps."

"*Defense ships,*" he corrected. "They need to be functional, not pretty. And we've got plenty of hulks here that nobody ever noticed."

Of all the Deep Zone planets, Buktu was the farthest from Sonjeera. Years ago, the original pioneers had made the long journey from the Crown Jewel worlds, theoretically a one-way trip to a comfortable new home, where they would be far from the Constellation.

Unfortunately, the long-distance remote surveys of Buktu gave falsely positive images, and, after two years in transit, the colonists found only an ice-covered planetoid with virtually no ecosystem. Without enough fuel to return to civilization, they were stuck there. Though hardly a garden spot, the planetoid did have resources, and the determined colonists tunneled outposts into the thick ice, excavating cozy chambers where people could live. The large ice sheets were saturated with numerous exotic isotopes that could be harvested and used for FTL stardrive fuel, long-term energy sources, and containment-field systems.

Meanwhile, back on Sonjeera, the Diadem had set her sights on the many untouched planets in the Deep Zone, sending out trailblazer ships to open stringline trade routes, and to annex the worlds that assumed themselves to be independent. Also tricked by the rosy measurements from the original probe, Michella dispatched a Constellation trailblazer to Buktu. She was deeply disappointed by what she found.

When the unexpected stringline ship arrived at Buktu, reestablishing contact, the colonists were surprised and disappointed as well. They had not wanted any further contact with, nor obligations to, the old government.

After an uneasy nine years, however, not to mention great expense from the Constellation, the Diadem finally declared the Buktu route "not commercially viable." She abandoned the stringline path, announced that the Buktu colony was defunct, and commanded Ian Walfor and his people to return to Sonjeera so they could be relocated to a more hospitable place.

But the Buktu colonists refused, unanimously, and stayed where they were, even cut off from civilization. Incensed that Walfor and his people would snub her benevolent gesture, the Diadem washed her hands of these subjects—which was what they had wanted anyway. The abandoned iperion path was left to deteriorate.

Meanwhile, Walfor turned the resources of Buktu to his own advantage, using the saturated ices of his planetoid to create stardrive fuel, and his engineers built repair and reconstruction facilities for the numerous abandoned one-way ships out in the Deep Zone.

Michella didn't realize it, but the Buktu colonists had done very well for themselves indeed.

Even Tanja was surprised by just how successful the colony was. She stared through the porthole field and admired the operations. Outside on the glacier fields, large equipment trundled along the rough surface, chewing the top layer of frozen water and gases. Melters scraped off the ice and processed it into useful fuels. Bulbous tanks stored the residual fuel and stockpiles of valuable chemicals for transfer to the General's war effort.

"I'm impressed," she admitted, nodding to him. "Your operation is going to be the key to Deep Zone independence."

"That has always been my goal," Walfor said with a warm smile. "To impress you, I mean."

Tanja focused her gaze on the new fleet, all the ships salvaged from old abandoned vessels. Smaller ones landed on the frozen spaceport yard, and others circled above the planetoid, seventy-five in all. "Are they ready to launch for Hellhole? The General is waiting."

"One more day of shakedowns. Some weren't in the best condition when they arrived."

For years, Walfor's people had acquired old colony ships from across the Deep Zone. Tanja admired how Walfor had seen an opportunity. He had taken those old ships, made them spaceworthy again, and operated his own black-market fleet completely independent of the Constellation. He refused to be beholden to the Diadem's government.

"I'll ride with them on the stringline to the Hellhole hub," Tanja said. She liked to be hands-on, not an administrator who never left the office. Her uncle Quinn had been adamant about that. Quinn had taught her many things, made her who she was . . . but the man had been buried under incalculable tons of mud washed down in a monsoon.

Tanja considered Diadem Michella to be responsible for that tragedy as well. She felt a hollowness in her heart as she thought of how workers on Candela had been forced to strip-mine the unstable hills, cutting corners, working themselves to exhaustion in order to achieve the payment the Constellation demanded.

No, she felt no regret that the Crown Jewels were falling apart.

She shook the dark thoughts aside. "These new ships will greatly expand the General's defenses. I want to see his face when we come to the rescue."

"*Before* the Constellation fleet arrives, I hope." Walfor snorted. "You don't want to be there when the shots start flying."

"If I could fire shots at the bastards myself, I'd be happy to. Better still if the old bitch is aboard, but she'll never go far from her comfortable palace." Tanja's nostrils flared, and again she drew a deep breath to calm herself. The air inside the Buktu cave chamber seemed chilly and dry. "If I had the chance to wring the Diadem's neck, I'd do it. She deserves it a thousand times over."

As the planetary leader of Candela, Tanja saw too often how the decadent Crown Jewels preyed upon the fledgling Deep Zone worlds, how Michella demanded oppressive payments that nearly bankrupted the colonies, even though they had never wanted to be part of the Constellation.

For years the nobles had paid little attention to the DZ, interested only in their tribute. They didn't think the frontier worlds would produce anything of particular note, but thanks to the hard work of the settlers, the Deep Zone was on the verge of thriving. Tanja's engineers had discovered an extremely rich vein of iperion in the hills of Candela, a source of the stringline marker-material that was far more extensive than the played-out iperion mines on Vielinger. No one in the Constellation knew anything about the discovery, and Tanja had no intention of simply handing over the wealth.

Not when the DZ colonists could use it for themselves.

As she watched, two of Walfor's finished ships lifted off the frozen spaceport plain to join seven others already waiting at the newly established stringline terminus over Buktu. Tanja mused, "Hellhole isn't the only planet that needs to be guarded. I'd like a patrol force over Candela, too. If word gets out about my iperion mines, we would become a special target—"

Walfor made a magnanimous gesture, smiling as he half bowed. "For you, my lady, I'll see to it that Candela gets ships."

"Make sure everyone gets ships," Tanja said. "With the DZ connected, and protected, we can have trade like the Constellation hasn't seen in a thousand years. Now that I've got the Theser line established from my new hub, I'm launching a link to Cles as well. The more intertwined our stringline network becomes, the stronger we are, and the less vulnerable we'll be to a single point of failure." She knew full well that the Deep Zone could become a vibrant economy in very little time—provided the frontier planets didn't need to worry about an attack from the Crown Jewels.

Walfor nodded. "We'll make the old Crown Jewels irrelevant and never be driven through a single bottleneck like the one at Sonjeera." A curl of white vapor bled out of the exhaust stack of one of the huge fuel tanks lined up outside the spaceport. "I expect good terms on setting up fueling stations at your hub."

"And I expect good prices on stardrive fuel from Buktu."

Walfor smiled again. "We'll be quite a team. I look forward to working with you."

"I look forward to having the Diadem rot in hell," Tanja said. "There will be no peace until we accomplish that."

5

Diadem Michella ruled from her imposing Sonjeera palace, whose structures and ornamental gardens covered more acreage than some capital cities on other worlds. During her long—some said too long—reign, the old woman had kept the noble families in line while enriching her closest allies beyond their dreams. But her pinnacle of success was being eroded by Adolphus's outrageous new rebellion, by her own daughter's betrayal, and by an infestation of aliens that threatened to contaminate human civilization.

She needed to deal with this nonsense swiftly. Ruthlessly.

Accompanied by Lord Selik Riomini, Supreme Commander of the Army of the Constellation, Michella climbed the palace's central tower, an ornate and heavily fortified structure that included her impregnable keep and administrative offices. As they trudged up the marble steps, Michella continued the conversation, not at all winded. "My son-in-law just sent me the final schedule for the launch of the Constellation fleet. This should be a quick assault, an overwhelming victory, followed by a mop-up operation." She shook her head. "But it's taking too damned long to get going. What are your people doing?"

He was red-faced, more from being out of breath than shamed. "I expected the fleet to launch a week ago, Eminence, but don't underestimate the effort of staging and launching such a huge military operation.

I admit, it does appear Major Crais is being overly meticulous and cautious." Dressed entirely in black, Riomini took several deep breaths before continuing in a voice that carried only echoes of his usual deep and confident tone. "I think he's driving Redcom Hallholme a bit mad."

"And me as well." Michella scowled, pausing so that the Black Lord could catch up to her. "For a man so anxious to rescue Keana, Bolton doesn't seem to be in any hurry. Good thing I already consider my daughter to be lost."

Riomini sounded surprised. "Perhaps there's a chance we can still rescue her, Eminence."

Michella had made it clear that she wouldn't grieve if her flighty child became a casualty of war. "She is brainwashed by aliens, probably contaminated by those loathsome things." The Diadem shuddered at the memory of the hideous half-humanoid, half-caterpillar creature that had arrived along with the human emissaries sent by General Adolphus. When they were all killed, the alien had turned to slime. She did not regret for an instant her decisive reaction to sterilize the Deep Zone ship before the invader emissaries could unleash that awful plague on Sonjeera.

Riomini paused on the stairs beside her, grateful for the rest. "We could take one of the elevators, Eminence." Michella was annoyed that, though he was three decades younger, he had let himself get badly out of shape.

"Every stair you climb adds a few seconds to your life." Pushing on, she called over her shoulder, "If I climb enough stairs, I will live forever." She stared down at his perspiring face and shook her head. "I need you to run the Army of the Constellation, Selik. I forbid you to drop dead here."

Although she relied on Selik Riomini, she had never much liked him. Riomini fortunes had bankrolled the Constellation military, and old Lord Gilag Riomini had helped put her on the Star Throne when she was very young, but Selik was far too ambitious for her tastes. And far too anxious for her to die.

The Black Lord controlled not only his own world of Aeroc where the Constellation fleet was currently being assembled, but also the old Adolphus family holdings and the Lubis Plain shipyards on Qiorfu and the former de Carre world of Vielinger. Yes, unquestionably ambitious. The Black Lord expected to become the next Diadem, as if it were his due. True, Michella saw no real alternative among the nobles, but she didn't want him to think his appointment was assured. He had to earn it . . . and keep earning it.

Just to put him in his place, she pretended to sound sweet and concerned. "Will you be able to make it to the top, Selik?" He seemed too fatigued to catch the double meaning.

"Give me a moment." He heaved several long breaths, then continued up the stairway, using his anger to drive him to the final floor.

She watched his deliberate pace, then trotted ahead of the huffing man, taunting him. Even though the view was breathtaking—Sonjeera's rolling hills, the arboretum and parks, the fountains, the sprawling city—Michella had stopped noticing the panorama decades ago; she had other priorities.

When they reached her private office, Riomini slumped onto a settee, red faced and perspiring. He was still making excuses. "Eminence, the annihilation of General Adolphus and his rebels cannot be rushed or sloppy. We are making history. I wouldn't be too concerned about whatever defenses the General might be able to cobble together."

"He did trick me into sending his old mothballed fleet to Territorial Governor Goler, so those ships have fallen into enemy hands." She sniffed, annoyed to be reminded about the turncoat Goler. How could one of her own governors switch sides and take up the banner of a monster like Adolphus?

Riomini dismissed her concerns, too. "Twenty-one old vessels cannot match the sheer might of the Constellation fleet. If he gets desperate enough, the General might blow the stringline to the Crown Jewels, but then he'd be cutting his own throat. How would his planet survive without outside supplies? He wouldn't dare risk cutting the lifeline; his people would overthrow him in a week." By now the Black Lord had caught his breath, and his face looked less flushed.

Michella made herself a cup of kiafa from an automated dispenser, offering none to Riomini; he could get his own if he wished.

"And even if he did sever the Sonjeera line," Riomini continued, "we could travel a roundabout route via one of the other DZ worlds, then use the General's own new stringlines to strike planet Hallholme."

"Unless he cuts himself off from all of his own allies as well. And then every other Deep Zone world cuts their lines to Sonjeera, too."

"Preposterous! That is never going to happen, Eminence." The Black Lord took the initiative and procured his own kiafa. "Frankly, I am more worried that our delay will give Adolphus time to plan his escape."

Michella's eyes flashed. "Then we will hunt him down! On the run, he poses no military threat, and we can use the chase to rally my loyal subjects. People will be vigilant, they'll see his shadow under every bed or inside every closet—and that may be a good thing."

The Black Lord sat back on the settee. "I'll make a quick trip to Vielinger to inspect my iperion mining operations, and return to the Sonjeera hub in time for the launching of the fleet."

"Yes, nine days according to Major Crais," she said. "Plenty of time to tend your little business operations."

⇜⇝

That evening, Michella took an ornamented autocarriage to the bustling Sonjeera spaceport, a place of buried secrets. Although she had enough to worry about, one other matter was of great concern to her: How dangerous was the threat of contamination from those disgusting aliens? She had ordered all the emissaries killed . . . but had it been enough? How insidious was their control?

After what she had seen inside that sealed passenger pod, the caterpillarlike monster, the possessed humans, the evidence of a telepathic power that had nearly torn open the armored craft, Michella had never been able to set aside her fears despite the most powerful security measures she could impose.

Though she hated the General, Michella *understood* his military rebellion, and she knew her Army of the Constellation could crush it. But what if those hideous creatures spread their *possession* throughout her Crown Jewel worlds?

Michella prided herself on her sharp mind, her physical fitness, her absolute fearlessness. But the aliens had become a chink in her mental armor. She would not admit her fear, but it was there. She was no longer utterly fearless. What if she lost everything—her mind and her body— to the aliens through *possession*? Her own daughter had become one of them.

The Diadem stepped out of the autocarriage, ignoring the man who opened the door for her. Michella stared at the sealed hangar where the alien creature and possessed humans had been entombed in thick epoxy like an ancient insect in amber. Was it enough?

Fernando-Zairic, the half-human spokesman for the doomed group visiting her, had reveled in his own contamination. Upon his arrival at Sonjeera, he had made no secret of the fact that he wanted to spread it across every inhabited planet in the Constellation.

Even with the whole hangar structure cocooned in impenetrable resin, she kept the area under heavy guard. She could not be too careful. Her aide Ishop Heer had reported on how many human converts the resurrected aliens had already made on planet Hallholme—including Keana. Even Ishop had been duped at the time, thinking the aliens were merely a hoax. Michella could not afford such a mistake again.

Now, responding to her summons, Ishop waited for her at the edge of the guarded zone. A husky man with a shaved scalp and alert green eyes, he looked as uncharacteristically anxious as she felt. She trusted his instincts, even though he had failed her (he didn't do it often). Michella valued his skills and his loyalty. Though he was only a commoner, Ishop was adept at developing information on her political enemies, and always provided her with excellent advice.

"Don't get too close to the hangar, Eminence," he cautioned. "I don't like either of us being here. Dangerous."

"As I well know, Ishop." She could not take her eyes from the encased building, knowing what was inside. "Do you have evidence that the containment integrity is failing? Or just concerns?"

"I always have concerns. If some vestige of the alien were to seep out of this building, there's no telling how far the contamination might spread. It's in the middle of Sonjeera."

Michella swallowed in a dry throat. Ishop was the only person who truly shared her concerns about the potential horrors. He had been at her side, and the two of them had watched the dying alien dissolve into slime that oozed over the dead human converts. Michella shuddered—it had given her nightmares.

The Diadem remained standing close to the autocarriage, in case she needed to duck into the vehicle for an escape. Just coming out here in denial of her fear required a bravery she was beginning to regret.

Fastidious Ishop was even more worried than she was. "I know the creature and the converts are all dead. We watched the poison do its work. And yet I still feel an eerie alien presence lurking in the air around here."

A cold sickness twisted in her stomach, but she kept her voice calm and offhand. "Maybe we should get rid of the ship, the bodies, the whole damned hangar. Incinerate everything. Vaporize the entire spaceport."

She knew Ishop had already been pondering the question for some time. "Deep access tunnels and catacombs run beneath the spaceport, Eminence. We could excavate below the hangar, let the entire building drop underground, then pave it over and seal it away."

The Diadem frowned. "Such action would create its own risks. What if the structure broke open and the contamination leaked out? What if it spread through the underground tunnels and got into the city? Much too dangerous, Ishop."

"Seal the tunnels first."

She shook her head. "I don't like it."

He gave a reluctant nod, then raised another big concern. "We both know that the real threat comes from planet Hallholme. That's where the alien infestation was discovered. Those creatures have undoubtedly corrupted the entire population there, and Adolphus has connected the Deep Zone with his new stringlines. We have every reason to believe the contamination is spreading across the frontier worlds. We should sterilize Hallholme with all due haste—before it's too late."

In her heart Michella knew that even his paranoia did not go far enough. By now, Adolphus and all his rebels could be hybrid aliens. "And maybe we should sterilize other Deep Zone worlds as well."

Ishop was quick to agree. "Possibly even all of them."

6

At the Michella Town Spaceport, a drizzle of alkaline-smelling rain misted General Adolphus's face as he watched a sky full of ships: Seventy-five former Constellation vessels, repaired and refitted on Buktu, dropped from the main DZ stringline hub in orbit. With their landing struts down, the spacefaring vessels resembled fat beetles.

Beside him, Sophie smiled and said, "Looks like Walfor came through for us." She held up her display clipboard. "I already factored these ships into our expanded inventory. We can put up a hell of a fight now."

General Adolphus would pit his military skill against any enemy commander. He had already placed a large force in orbit to guard both stringlines—the terminus ring from the Crown Jewels and the major new hub that anchored his entire DZ stringline network. The Diadem would never expect that he could marshal so many defenses.

Even so, he knew it was only enough to delay, or at best stalemate, the Constellation fleet. Not enough to defeat it.

But if his plan worked, he wouldn't need to fight at all.

Once the Urvanciks and Dak Telom came through, he would have all the specifics to choreograph and finalize his careful plans, add all the logistical punctuation, and set the wheels in motion. . . .

When the spaceport dust had settled, the General and Sophie ventured among the refurbished vessels. They were of varying colors, some black, some silver, others garishly painted. A number of the hulls had obvious patches and dents; four looked pristine, as if they had just come off the assembly lines. Given the luxury of time, the General would have repainted them all. It was a point of military precision and efficiency to show unified colors, demonstrating that they were a unified Deep Zone Defense Force, but he could not waste the effort now. The vessels could fight; that mattered more than cosmetic appearances.

Scruffy pilots emerged from the landed ships, milling around, stretching their legs, breathing the dusty air. Ian Walfor stepped from the undercarriage lift of one of the newer ships, accompanied by Tanja Hu. While Tanja was hard-edged and beautiful, Walfor looked as rumpled as a comfortable set of clothes. He had weathered skin, wavy dark hair, and a larger-than-life personality. This man's audacious plans to run old faster-than-light ships among the DZ worlds had laid the groundwork for the General's own transportation network.

Adolphus regarded the fittings and the lines of the vessels. "Some of these ships look fresh out of spacedock."

Walfor stepped forward and shook the General's hand. "They'll get nicked up in battle soon enough. I'd appreciate it if you don't wreck too many of them."

"I'll do my best, Mr. Walfor."

Tanja Hu looked very serious, and her voice had a sharp edge, as always. Adolphus had not seen her truly relaxed in several years. "Most of these ships are ready for frontline duty right now. Six more need new stardrives from Theser, and we'll take them directly there for installation. I've got to meet with Administrator Frankov anyway."

Sophie stepped forward with her organizational clipboard. "I've worked up a list of the DZ worlds most likely to be threatened by direct Constellation attack, and the General and I have some ideas about how to distribute these new ships, but I'll want a breakdown of the total weapons complement, so I can decide how to divide them up."

"You're not keeping them here to protect Hellhole?" Walfor sounded surprised.

Adolphus gave a small shake of his head. "We know this planet is the Diadem's main target, but other DZ administrators demand defenses as well. Many of them were swept along in this rebellion without having any say in the matter. Understandably, they are feeling very vulnerable right now."

"Vulnerable . . . and unreliable," Sophie said with a quiet snort.

"They know what the old bitch will do to them." Tanja looked as if she had swallowed something sour. "Governor Goler told everyone what really happened at the Ridgetop Recovery. Once the six vessels get new engines from Theser, I'm going to place them at Candela—enough to scare off any Constellation attack ships." Her eyes flashed. "Better yet, enough to destroy them."

Sophie said, "There aren't enough ships to give each DZ world a complete defense force. We have to hope Michella doesn't hit random frontier planets just to make a point."

"As far as Diadem Michella is concerned, *I* am the point," the General said. "Her own military isn't large enough to fight a war on all those fronts. For now, her obsession with me gives the rest of the Deep Zone a certain measure of safety. From basic intel, we know she's sending a massive force here, and we're getting more details soon. That's all I need."

"I hope so, General. If you're defeated, where does that leave the rest of us?" Tanja asked.

Walfor flashed a bitter smile. "My dear, you *know* where it'll leave us. That's why we have to make sure the General doesn't fail."

"I won't fail," Adolphus said.

⁓

Sophie was still trying to accept the radical changes in her son, now that he had immersed himself in slickwater and taken on a new Xayan personality. Devon and his girlfriend Antonia had been desperate, trying to escape a horrific and tragic situation. Sophie feared she had lost her son, and Adolphus could see her obvious pain.

But he also recognized the opportunities. As shadow-Xayans, Devon and Antonia had extraordinary powers of what the aliens called telemancy, and they were now training many of their fellow converts to help in defending Hellhole.

When the two sent word that they were prepared to demonstrate the powerful defenses they and other shadow-Xayans had developed,

General Adolphus was eager to see what they could do. Despite his best efforts, the standard defenses that he could cobble together might not be sufficient, but the alien telemancy might give him an immeasurable advantage.

If the converts could learn how to combine their powers in time.

Tanja Hu and Ian Walfor joined him to witness the demonstration before departing for Candela. Adolphus led the group out to the primary shadow-Xayan settlement near a thick grove of resurrected alien red weed. More than a thousand converts lived there, united by their common alienness—all had acquired Xayan personalities from the slickwater pools. The shadow-Xayans still looked human, but their mannerisms were peculiar.

Devon-Birzh and Antonia-Jhera had brought hundreds of their trained comrades together in the center of the red-weed forest. They had used their telemancy to create an expansive clearing, driving back the vigorous foliage. Now the scarlet leaves waved in the air like kelp fronds in a sea.

Whenever he looked at Sophie's son, Adolphus couldn't help but feel sadness for how much she had lost. Devon was no longer simply the bright, wide-eyed young man she had raised as a single mother, now that he carried the weight of another entire life within his memories. But the changes were not entirely bad. After acquiring the Birzh personality, he claimed to have matured in immeasurable ways. He still had his original personality, and so much more. As lovers, he and Antonia— and Birzh and Jhera—were connected soul to soul in a way that surpassed any other relationship.

As the party arrived at the thriving red thicket at the fringes of the clearing, Devon greeted the General in an ancient voice that did not belong in such a young throat. "Creating and maintaining this clearing invigorates us and steels our collective will. This exercise helps strengthen our telemancy." He extended his hands out to his sides and gestured to the quivering barricade of fleshy red weed. The plants trembled, as if straining against an invisible barrier. Devon smiled at it. "It is a trivial gesture for so many telemancers. Let us show you that we can do much more."

Antonia was close beside him, as always. Her eyes had a sparkling, spiral sheen as she spoke of the spiritual goal of the aliens. "And as we practice our telemancy, it brings us all closer to *ala'ru*."

To the General, the Xayan push toward a higher plane of existence was mysterious, incomprehensible, but he had agreed to let them make every effort; in exchange, the aliens had not challenged the human colony, graciously telling Adolphus that his people were welcome to the world after they achieved *ala'ru*.

And they would help protect Hellhole in the meantime.

At the edge of the clearing, the leathery weed fronds waved, then parted like curtains drawn by invisible strings as two inhuman forms glided forward on rows of caterpillar legs. Like a pair of centaurs, the two Original Xayans had humanoid torsos, but from the waist down the Xayan bodies were segmented and wormlike. Their smooth heads sported large black eyes and vibrating membranes where the mouths should have been. From the spotted patterns along the soft, gelatinous hides, Adolphus identified the two female aliens named Tryn and Encix.

Although thousands of human converts had acquired Xayan memories and personalities from the slickwater pools, only three of the Originals remained alive. The big male named Lodo worked in the underground museum bunker with Keana-Uroa and Cristoph de Carre to discover and document Xayan history, but these two Originals had come out to witness the telemancy demonstration.

As the pale caterpillar aliens approached, Walfor muttered, "I don't know that I'll ever get used to seeing those things."

"Those *things* are our allies," Sophie said.

"I want to see how they can use their powers to stop a military attack." From Tanja's expression, she was already viewing the aliens, and alien-possessed humans, as an army.

Preparing for the demonstration, as ordered, Craig Jordan and a group of veteran soldiers had set up artillery pieces and explosive launchers on one side of the wide clearing. Jordan smiled. "They've improved considerably, sir. This little party will be under realistic conditions."

Sophie flashed a glance toward her son and asked the security chief, "You're using live ammunition?"

"Nothing they can't easily deflect." Jordan whistled to the soldiers, and they scurried to prepare their weapons. He lowered his voice, dismissing Sophie's concern, "Look, ma'am, if they can't stop a little problem like that, they won't be much good protecting the whole planet."

"That's still my son you're shooting at," she said.

When Antonia spoke, her voice sounded much stronger than the battered young woman who had fled to Hellhole. Jhera's voice. But her lips also quirked in a normal, *human* smile. "Don't worry about us, General. We've practiced this many times."

Adolphus nodded. "The shadow-Xayans have to be ready for a real attack."

Devon-Birzh and Antonia-Jhera guided three hundred shadow-Xayans to stand side by side on the opposite side of the clearing, a ragtag group with whatever clothes they'd brought along, including some fabrics made from the processed red weed. But they moved in a smooth, symbiotic unison more perfect than the General had seen in his best-trained troops during his original rebellion.

The shadow-Xayans showed no fear as they faced a pair of large artillery guns two hundred meters away. A thrum of telemancy hung around them, making a perceptible disturbance in the air.

Jordan did not hide his anticipation. "Watch this, sir."

Encix and Tryn simply observed this particular demonstration and did not participate. From prior demonstrations, the new converts had shown they were able to summon greater mental power than even the Originals themselves possessed—a kind of hybrid vigor. Tryn, the smallest of the remaining awakened aliens, seemed willing to add her mental powers to the maneuvers, but Encix held her companion back. Adolphus still could not read the alien expressions, but he felt that Encix—who was ostensibly the leader of the surviving Originals—was skeptical of what the converts were doing.

When Devon called out to his volunteers, his human personality came to the fore and took charge. The alien converts pressed closer together in ranks and held their splayed hands out to touch the fingers of the person on either side of them. The mental charge crackled in the air.

Adolphus and his companions stepped behind the artillery guns, out of the danger zone, and the two hulking Originals glided over to join them on the sidelines. "As they learn to combine their telemancy," Encix said, "we draw closer to the skill and power we need for *ala'ru*."

"And your race is welcome to do so," Adolphus said, "as long as you help me stop the Constellation first."

His security chief gestured, impatient. "Ready, General. Watch—they won't even break a sweat." For preparation, he ordered one of the artillery guns to fire downrange and over the heads of the congregated shadow-Xayans. As the explosive projectile soared overhead, it veered even farther away, as if it had bounced off a shield around the group.

"That was just a test." Jordan laughed and turned to the man at the weapons controls. "Now aim for the target!"

The gunner adjusted the angle of the large barrel until it pointed directly at the mass of shadow-Xayans standing in the clearing. Adolphus tensed. Even though he knew this group had practiced the same test many times, it still looked like it would be a massacre. Sophie turned pale.

But Devon himself signaled the gunner, looking confident, and the artillery piece thumped with the explosive launch and recoil. The second artillery shell hurtled toward the crowd of peaceful-looking, calm converts. But the projectile recoiled in the air, as if yanked by an invisible leash, deflected up over their heads, pirouetted in the air, and plunged down into the dense red foliage behind them. Flames and debris shot up in a rooster tail of spray, spreading across the dense vegetation; not even a crumb managed to land in the protected area.

Jordan whistled and clapped his hands. "See, nothing to be concerned about. They've practiced this daily without getting so much as a scuffed knee." The shadow-Xayans did not cheer their own victory, though, but remained in their placid rows; Devon and Antonia smiled at the head of the group, waiting for the next shot to come at them.

When the cannon fired a third shell, the shadow-aliens not only diverted the projectile, but teasingly sent it speeding back toward the small military force. Walfor yelped, dragged Tanja to safety (to her embarrassment)—but the converts deflected the artillery shell from the gunners at the last possible moment.

Adolphus nodded, impressed. He preferred careful planning, standard military maneuvers, and superior firepower, but he would not turn down a secret weapon. "Are they strong enough to shield Michella Town against a bombardment from space? Or even deflect a landing enemy fleet?"

Jordan kept smiling. "They will be."

Standing beside them, Encix bowed her smooth head and said in a begrudging voice, "They are better at controlling their psychic powers in a joint operation. Previously, they could only react. Now they can manipulate. Telemancy should not be wasted, however. Their powers would be better devoted to *ala'ru*."

"Not wasted," Adolphus said. "This could be our best line of defense."

Encix sounded dismissive. "If necessary, we will help protect Xaya against Constellation attack. Increasing the number of shadow-Xayans is our only hope of gathering enough power to achieve our ascension. But we do not have much time."

Tryn suggested, "If more humans were to immerse themselves in the slickwater, then we would have more telemancy available to defend this planet. And more converts to help us achieve *ala'ru*."

Encix agreed. "More volunteers should accept Xayan lives and personalities. So many of our people remain to be awakened from the pools."

Adolphus felt torn, especially after Devon and Antonia had surprised them by becoming converts. "The people have been encouraged," he said. "But I won't force them."

Having concluded their demonstration, Devon and Antonia bowed, then all of the converts did the same in perfect unison. A relieved Sophie ran to her son, gave him a long hug. The young man seemed stiff for a moment, then his own personality reasserted itself and he returned the embrace, but still looked embarrassed. Like a normal twenty-year-old.

Devon and Antonia said their farewells and stood shoulder to shoulder, their youthful faces raised to the sky, eyes closed. Using telemancy, they levitated themselves off the ground, arms outstretched at their sides. "We need to return to our settlement to plan the next exercise, General."

Behind them, like the finale of a well-choreographed performance, the first line of shadow-Xayans also used their joint telemancy to lift themselves into flight. Then the next row, and the next rose, into the air. With perfect timing, they all accelerated away headfirst, in formation. The shadow-Xayans streaked across the sky like a flock of large migrating birds.

Adolphus stared after them, and Craig Jordan shook his head. "I never get used to them doing that."

As the two Original aliens stood next to the General at the artillery piece, Encix grew more intense. "We have pondered the danger posed by the Constellation fleet, General Tiber Adolphus. When Diadem Michella Duchenet killed Cippiq and Fernando-Zairic, she proved that she would not hesitate to exterminate us as well as you. We cannot allow that. There is too much at stake."

"No argument from us," Ian Walfor interjected.

"We did not understand that a leader would actually do such a thing," Tryn said. "We had no quarrel with the Constellation government, but we failed to comprehend the factions of humanity. Now we see them clearly."

Sophie added in a pragmatic voice, "If you want to achieve your *ala'ru*, first you'll have to survive."

"Five centuries ago, we Xayans could not save ourselves from the asteroid impact," Encix said. "Now Diadem Michella Duchenet intends to destroy the remaining Xayans."

"And us as well," Adolphus said.

"There is a difference," Encix said. "If such an attack happens, your *race* will not become extinct. Ours will."

Tryn said, "At least some of us must be protected, no matter what happens to this world."

Adolphus tried to understand what they were asking. "Do you need to build another vault? Or seal yourselves in the existing one again?"

"This time, General Tiber Adolphus, we have another option," Tryn continued. "Previously, when the asteroid came in, we could not flee to safety. I wish to take a group away from this planet, using your stringline ships. Some of us can be far from the threat of Constellation retaliation. Will you let us establish a seed colony of shadow-Xayans on another world? At least temporarily?"

"Makes sense not to put all your eggs in one basket," Sophie said. "Some clichés hold true."

"But I thought you needed all of the converts together to grow closer to *ala'ru*," Adolphus said.

"When our seed colony is established, our telemancy should extend across space, forming lines much like your iperion paths so we can remain in contact with our people," Tryn said. "We will still be strong. And safer."

Tanja Hu spoke up, "After what I just saw, you're welcome on Candela. I'll grant you a place where you won't be disturbed, so long as you promise to come to our aid if we are attacked. I'll set it up and send for your group as soon as I return from Theser."

Adolphus was surprised by her quick offer, and Tanja looked at him, "I've got my own new stringline hub at Candela to worry about. If I can't have enough warships to protect my planet, maybe alien telemancy can do the trick."

Tryn bowed in gratitude. "We accept your offer, Administrator Tanja Hu. I will gather one hundred shadow-Xayans and accompany them to Candela, where we will remain out of danger until the Constellation conflict is resolved."

"Do it," Adolphus said.

7

Lord Selik Riomini carried himself with a pride he had earned by virtue of his position. His black-clad female bodyguards, every one a deadly killer, escorted him from the landed aerocopter; their menacing demeanor had been earned through ruthless training and fighting prowess. Like a hunting pack, they crossed the grounds of his lavish new manor house on Vielinger. The spoils of victory.

After thorough political machinations and a carefully exploited scandal against the hapless de Carre family, the Riominis had acquired the planet along with its dwindling iperion operations. He had begun to amass quite a collection: his own world of Aeroc, the former Adolphus planet of Qiorfu, and now Vielinger and the iperion mines. But it wasn't enough.

Lord Riomini had no interest in living in the old de Carre manor house, believing it too encumbered with memories of failure, so he had selected a far better location for his secondary home. Perched high on a hill overlooking a verdant river valley and forested hills, the new estate had plenty of room for a landing field and military defenses. The late Lord Louis de Carre had not worried about such things, to his misfortune. No one would ever take Vielinger from the Black Lord.

While the major iperion deposits had been excavated during the boom years when Diadem Michella created the stringline network, even the played-out mines promised to generate enormous income. As iperion supplies dwindled, the price would skyrocket, and Riomini coffers would fill to bursting.

Money led to power, and power led to money. It was a complex dance, and he was the choreographer. Riomini came from a long line of noblemen, including several Diadems, and he expected to take the Star Throne soon enough.

As he approached the high-arched entrance to the mansion, the carved goldenwood doors opened smoothly. As a precaution, he waited in the entryway with three of his female guards while the rest scurried ahead to secure the house. After they pronounced the residence safe, Lord Riomini strode inside.

Much construction progress had been made since the last time he'd visited. Ceiling murals had been crafted by the finest artists and gold filigree applied to the high moldings; only the interior wall painting and tile work remained to be done. Good. He approved of efficiency.

A woman appeared at the top of the main staircase. She wore a black uniform like the other bodyguards, except she had added a red blouse under the jacket coat as a defiant flash of color. While Gail Carrington was in his offices and homes, Riomini permitted her the eccentricity. But never on public duty.

She descended the steps with fluid, catlike movements, not like a fine lady but like a stalking predator. She had short brown hair, a lean, wiry figure, and deadly reflexes from her training. A decade ago, she'd been Riomini's lover—a most energetic and satisfying one—but he had ended the affair, with her assent, for pragmatic reasons. Complicated feelings might adversely affect her ability to protect him, and that was paramount.

Until recently, she had been the leader of his guards, but upon reaching the age of forty, she submitted her resignation, claiming that she no longer had the necessary strength and reflexes. (Riomini remained convinced she could kill anything that might threaten him.) Nevertheless, he promoted Carrington to be his most trusted aide; he wanted her close by.

Though she was no longer, technically, a military officer, Gail gave him a crisp salute. Her intense eyes were a striking shade of blue. "My Lord, I gave the job foreman a list of minor problems I found with the construction quality. They will be fixed soon."

"I have no doubt of it, but building inspections are not your duty. I placed you in charge of overseeing my iperion mines." Gail was not a miner or businessperson, but he needed someone loyal to watch over the critical resource; he trusted her ability to choose the right people around her.

"Everything about Riomini operations is my duty, sir. Every thread is connected." She led him down the corridor to his new office, modeled after his offices on other Riomini holdings; he liked the consistency. Inside, he settled into his familiar-seeming desk chair and motioned for Gail to take a seat across from him. The rest of the female guards remained outside.

"Under my careful supervision, the iperion mines have already surpassed the level of production under the de Carres. The process lines are no longer so sloppy," she said. "And the persistent accidents have ceased."

Now that we've ceased causing them, he thought. Frequent tragedies and sabotage had cast a pall of mismanagement on the de Carre family; the young lordling Cristoph de Carre had been shamed by the continual mishaps, while his father brought disgrace to the household through his ill-advised affair with Keana Duchenet. Incompetent, oblivious fools! Even without Riomini intervention, the whole operation would have collapsed sooner or later. Much better the way Riomini had accomplished the transition. Much quicker . . .

He skimmed the production figures Carrington presented. As usual, everything appeared to be in order. "That is excellent news, because iperion supplies have become even more vital to our military plan. Once our fleet crushes General Adolphus and seizes his new DZ network, we'll need to maintain those stringlines as well. Demand for iperion will double."

Gail looked at him for a long moment, letting her silence hang in the air; he knew she had something important to say, but she seemed disappointed that he didn't follow her train of thought. "The question arises, my Lord—when Adolphus created such a vast new network, how did he lay down the stringlines in the first place?"

He thought for a moment. "I presume he used his own trailblazer ships. Such craft would be easy to obtain."

"Not the trailblazers, sir, but the *iperion*. Where did Adolphus get the iperion in the first place? It certainly didn't come from here—the amount required would surpass the full output of our mines. The obvious answer is that he has some other source."

Riomini's eyes widened. "Somewhere out in the Deep Zone?"

Carrington's voice was maddeningly calm. "Fifty-four planets, all of them minimally explored. A major new iperion discovery might have given him the impetus to break away from the Crown Jewels."

Riomini's thoughts spun. It did indeed make sense. He had to inform the Diadem of this immediately . . . or not. A new supply would change the economics of the Constellation—and deflate the value of Vielinger and its current monopoly. He had to be very cautious.

"Who is administering the mines here?" he asked.

"Lanny Oberon runs the day-to-day operations, sir. He was a line supervisor under the de Carre administration. A competent, honest man."

"Do you have confidence in him?"

She considered the question. "Yes. He is the best-qualified person for the job, and he appears dedicated to the work."

He nodded. "I'm glad you have a competent supervisor, because I have another job for you, something even more important."

She lifted her eyebrows. "More important than iperion?"

"As you said, everything is connected—General Adolphus, the Deep Zone uprising, the new stringline network. Now I have to consider the possibility of a new iperion source out in the frontier. I need my own person there to investigate, and to represent Riomini interests." He nodded again, as if reaffirming his decision to himself. "You will accompany the fleet to planet Hallholme. Prepare yourself—the ships are due to depart from Aeroc within days."

Her eyes narrowed. "Red Commodore Escobar Hallholme is in charge of the operation. He is a member of your family—is he not sufficient?"

"No, he is not sufficient! Escobar is only a family member because he married one of my grandnieces, but he has his own personal ambitions." Riomini shook his head. Gail was loyal to him, and not at all interested in her own glory or advancement—which made her perfect for what he had in mind. "You will represent me, be my eyes aboard the fleet, with my full authority."

He leaned toward her, placing his elbows on the desk. "On paper, Redcom Hallholme will remain in charge of the operation. I won't take that away from him, and there's a certain historic symmetry to having the son of Commodore Percival Hallholme defeat the General for the second time. But I want you there to make sure nothing goes wrong."

"Do you have specific concerns, my Lord?"

"About victory? Not really. Given the overwhelming strength of our forces, I have no doubt that the operation will succeed, but Escobar is cocky and impetuous. He may feel a need to prove his heroism or some such nonsense. You must prevent him from making any foolish decisions that are not in the best interests of the Riominis or the Diadem—in that order. I need you to see that he is not allowed to make bad decisions in an attempt to be a hero. Take any action you feel is necessary."

Her blue eyes were bright. "Anything, sir?"

He never needed to mince words with Gail Carrington. "To be blunt, better for him to be a dead hero than a living disgrace. If he makes significant enough blunders, in your estimation, I grant you my blessing to eliminate him, so long as the mission succeeds and I succeed. I can deal with my grieving grandniece. We can say her husband died bravely in battle and decorate him posthumously. But that only works if the mission is a success."

She let out a long breath. "Understood, sir."

"General Adolphus is the greatest threat the Constellation has faced in modern times. If I can take credit for his defeat, no one will question my succession to the Star Throne. But if Escobar fails, the debacle would have the opposite effect on the Riomini family name. Worst case, we'll use Escobar Hallholme as a scapegoat to shield me."

Gail did not seem concerned. "I'll make sure nothing goes wrong in the first place, my Lord."

He smiled. "I know you will. And if you find where General Adolphus gets his iperion, then so much the better."

She stood at attention. "Your mission objectives are completely clear, sir. I will depart for Aeroc posthaste and join the fleet before the ships head off."

8

When his spies returned from Sonjeera with their vital intelligence, General Adolphus took a fast flyer out to meet them at the expanded spaceport city at Ankor. The *Kerris* had just arrived from the Crown Jewels, and Turlo Urvancik transmitted the exhilarating news. "General, we have it."

Adolphus could finally set his trap.

Diadem Michella knew nothing about Hellhole's second spaceport city; the entire installation was another one of the General's intricate secret operations. Official Constellation records listed Ankor as a distant mining outpost worked by the worst exiled convicts, a place where the rugged terrain and isolation provided more security than any number of guards. The Diadem's nosy inspectors had never bothered to make the long, unpleasant trek to the other side of the continent just to look at a few mines and factories.

So, the General managed to build his new spaceport there without the Constellation suspecting a thing.

After revealing his new stringline network, though, he had cast aside all pretenses. As DZ operations expanded, Ankor would become a bustling commercial complex. The colonists merely had to prevent themselves from being obliterated in the meantime. . . .

Adolphus arrived in a basin surrounded by stark brown-and-red mountains. Downboxes landed in large paved areas; launching gantries catapulted ships up to orbit. With a blast of white smoke and dancing orange flame, a carrier shuttle heaved itself upward and dwindled to a bright point in the sky.

Groups of evacuees waited to board the next crowded passenger pod. In the three months since he had proclaimed DZ independence, many people had fled Hellhole, fearing a disastrous retaliation from the Crown Jewels. They piled aboard stringline ships and headed to other, supposedly safer Deep Zone planets. Ever-increasing quakes across the continent also made the settlers uneasy, and even more chose to evacuate. Many of the colonists, though, did not have the resources to leave Hellhole. . . .

In anticipation of increased space traffic through the Hellhole hub, construction teams were erecting two new lodging complexes—not quite luxury hotels, Adolphus thought, but they would improve in time. Dust that had been whipped up from dry lake beds drifted in gauzy brown clouds over the basin and settled in a fine grit across the landed vessels and the walkway. Adolphus wrinkled his nose at the powdery smell in the air, alkali mixed with exhaust fumes and volatile fuels. But it was the smell of industry, of progress.

Sophie accompanied him on the quick trip, ostensibly because she wanted to inspect the distribution operations. "I've hardly seen you this week," she said as they walked from the landed flyer toward the towering gantries. "I've gone to three factories in the last two days, verifying their output, found spare parts for two retooled process lines in the weapons factories, and even visited mining operations."

"You never struck me as the stay-at-home type anyway."

"I'm not." She took his arm. "I'll make damn sure everything is ready so we can thumb our noses at the Constellation fleet when it arrives."

Of the functional ships that Adolphus had so far incorporated into the DZ Defense Force, the bulk of them remained in Hellhole orbit to guard the stringline operations, while a large number had been distributed to other key worlds. When they departed after the telemancy demonstration, Tanja Hu and Ian Walfor took the six unfinished ships on a stringline hauler to Theser for the eccentric engineers there to install new stardrives. Then, when the ships were complete, Tanja would base them at her own planet of Candela as a first line of defense. Since the

Diadem herself had decommissioned the stringline from Sonjeera to Buktu years ago, Walfor felt his own planetoid was safe enough, so he relinquished any claim on the ships he might have kept, sending them to other DZ worlds instead.

Adolphus gave Sophie a firm smile as they approached the spaceport operations building. The cubical structure was fashioned from fused silica bricks that gleamed in bright sunlight. "If the Urvanciks bring the intelligence I need," he said, "I'm confident I can prevent the Constellation fleet from bothering us at all."

At the door of the operations building, Rendo Theris welcomed the visitors. Short and muscular, Administrator Theris had very little hair on his head, just a few wisps of rusty red that stood up in the breeze. The spaceport administrator looked harried, his clothes wrinkled and smudged.

The man was not Adolphus's first choice to manage the major spaceport, but the very competent team of Tel and Renny Clovis had been lost—Renny perished when a sinkhole had swallowed up the construction dozer he was driving; the tragedy had driven a grief-stricken Tel to immerse himself in slickwater and acquire a Xayan personality.

Before Theris could open the conversation with complaints, as he often did, Adolphus asked, "Are the Urvanciks on their way?"

"Descending now, sir. Their passenger pod is en route." Theris wiped a hand across his brow, more focused on his own problems than Hellhole's desperate situation. "I need help around here, General. Ankor is understaffed, and we can't handle the increased traffic. We should beef up security, too—in case those strange ships come back."

"More sightings?" Sophie asked. "Any idea what they were or where they came from?"

Two weeks earlier, a squadron of unidentified ships had streaked in from nowhere, darting over the Ankor complex. They moved like swift recon vessels, dodging the spaceport defenses. They had transmitted no message, made no contact whatsoever, then flitted away. When he first reviewed the alarming images, Adolphus was convinced the ships were Constellation spies, but his engineering experts had never seen the design before and could not understand any vessel that could perform such maneuvers.

"Haven't seen them again—and we can be thankful for that!" Theris said with a groan. "All we need is another crisis."

As if the already flustered administrator had tempted fate, the ground began to tremble. The nearest gantry tilted, and a sealed box dangling from a cargo crane swung back and forth before it broke loose and crashed to the paved landing field. The rumbling grew louder. As the fused silica wall blocks cracked and shifted, Theris darted away from the operations building. Adolphus and Sophie ran clear of falling debris. A jagged fissure split the paved landing area, and the ground swelled, heaved . . . then fell quiet again.

As the quake diminished to silence, Theris caught his breath, struggling to control his panic. "These tremors have been increasing in intensity and frequency. Fourth one this week! Now we'll have to check the launcher alignments and repair the landing fields." He used the codecall at his collar to shout to his support technicians. "Do an inspection immediately—we have a passenger pod descending!" Spaceport personnel scrambled about to certify a section of the landing field for the Urvanciks' passenger pod.

Adolphus marched across the pavement, keeping his eyes on the fissure to assess the damage, unable to forget how the ground had swallowed Renny Clovis before his eyes. Liquid began to ooze from the jagged crack as if a water main had broken, spilling across the black, sealed surface.

Sophie put a cautioning hand on his arm. "Careful, that's slickwater."

Adolphus stepped closer to the slow, almost sentient movement of the data-charged fluid, unafraid, though he had no intention of becoming a convert.

Theris paled and hung back even farther. "This isn't the first time we've been plagued by slickwater seeps around here. Whenever we excavate new areas or try to put down deep pilings, we run into fresh leaks. We've known for a long time that a significant slickwater aquifer lies beneath the site, but the liquid seems to be swelling up, rising to the surface and causing more problems for us. We aren't able to finish expanding the spaceport until we drain it away."

Adolphus pressed his lips together. This was a serious setback that affected the future of the spaceport. "I'll send engineers to develop a plan. I'm sure they can drill down, breach the aquifer, and drain it into the basin on the other side of the mountains."

As the three of them watched, the alien fluid retreated as if by its own choice, seeping back into the ground, leaving the cracked pavement dry. "If you can get the slickwater to cooperate, sir," Theris said.

Sophie suggested, "Maybe Devon and Antonia can help?"

Hearing a rumble of sonic booms, Adolphus looked up to see the descending passenger pod. Theris used the codecall at his collar, and a flight director frantically transmitted revised instructions to the pilot, who altered course and guided the passenger pod to a new landing zone. Technicians ran across the field to wave in final positioning at an undamaged spot.

Adolphus brushed dust off the front of his shirt and stood ready as the passenger pod's hatch opened. Turlo and Sunitha Urvancik emerged, and their expressions lit up. Turlo blurted out, "General, the Constellation fleet is due to depart in five days!" The barrel-chested man pulled out a wrinkled wrapper from a package of nuts, holding it between his two fingers. "Molecular imprinting: We have here the plans of the Army of the Constellation."

Adolphus felt both relief and determination. "I've put most of our defenses in place already, but this will fill in the rest of the blanks. Now we have them!"

A stray breeze blew the wrapper out of Turlo's grasp; he and Sunitha scrambled after it, snatched it from the field, and handed it to the General. "And, sir, there's one other thing." Turlo looked flushed and breathless. "The commander of the fleet is the son of Commodore Hallholme!"

⁓

Adolphus commandeered Rendo Theris's office inside the cluttered operations building. He requested a precision surface-layer scanner from one of the spaceport techs and revealed the hidden intelligence files that Dak Telom had obtained. The General read the summaries and viewed images of the full Constellation fleet being assembled on Aeroc. He had every detail he could possibly need. It was all a matter of planning.

Turlo and Sunitha sat across the table, fidgeting but relieved. The

General studied the classified orders. "This is beautiful data. More than I could have hoped for. Our response is going to require careful timing, maybe even more precise than our Destination Day announcement of all the new DZ stringlines."

Sophie smiled. "You've done it before, Tiber."

"Yes, I have."

Sunitha Urvancik sounded hopeful. "So this is enough to help us defend the DZ?"

"Oh, better than that." He gave the two linerunners a warm smile. "In a single maneuver, we're going to defeat the Army of the Constellation— and you two will play important roles."

9

When the Diadem's fleet finally launched for the Sonjeera hub, Redcom Escobar Hallholme made certain that satellite images and ground-based cameras captured the spectacle. If this operation succeeded—and it *would*—his name was going to be as prominent in the historical records as his father's. At last, a measure of well-deserved respect. His entire career had existed in the shadow of expectations.

In a gold-and-black Constellation uniform, he stood on the bridge of his flagship, *Diadem's Glory,* which was clamped with nineteen other warships in the framework of the stringline hauler. He wished his father could have been there to observe the fleet's departure; such a gesture of support would have meant a great deal to Escobar, but the old man had bowed out, choosing to remain at the family estate on Qiorfu.

On further consideration, Escobar thought the Commodore might have done him a courtesy by staying away. The doddering war hero would have stolen all the attention from his son. . . .

"Our ships are secured in docking clamps, Redcom," said Lieutenant Aura Cristaine, the flagship's first officer. "Stringline engines are primed for departure. The five haulers are ready to leave the Aeroc terminus."

Drawing a deep breath, Escobar nodded. "I want the haulers to arrive one after the other at Sonjeera—it'll be quite a spectacle. Consider it a practice for when we sweep in to planet Hallholme."

Lieutenant Cristaine tapped her earadio. "Yes, Redcom. Each hauler pilot acknowledges."

He stood straight, hands clasped behind his back, conscious of the imagers recording every moment. "Departure is hereby authorized. We won't give the General's rebellion another day to gather momentum."

He looked out the broad forward screen of the *Diadem's Glory*, but the view was cluttered with warships arrayed in the framework. The five large military haulers began to move out from the Aeroc terminus ring, one after another, lining up on the iperion path for Sonjeera. The short trip to the Constellation's capital world would take only three hours, whereupon the officers would attend a special ceremony hosted by the Diadem: more politics, more showmanship . . . and more delays.

From one side of the bridge, not quite unobtrusive, Gail Carrington watched his every move. At the last minute, the hard-looking woman had been assigned to the flagship as a special observer, a mysterious officer of classified rank. Escobar had known nothing about it in advance, but since she was here by explicit order of Lord Riomini, he was powerless to challenge her presence. The woman's intense blue eyes observed the operations as if looking for a weak spot, filing away every detail. Escobar tried to ignore her.

Major Bolton Crais was a much easier man to ignore. Escobar had little respect for the rich nobleman with no real military experience, a man who had been blatantly cuckolded, yet didn't seem to mind! As a logistics officer, Crais's weapon of choice was a database and a calculator, and his bravery probably extended no farther than taking an unauthorized break during a warehouse inventory.

As a detail-oriented accountant and supply staff officer, the major did possess vital skills for such a large operation, but his meticulous preparations had delayed the fleet's departure for days, to no visible effect. Once the hundred ships were loaded and ready for the main thrust, Escobar had expected Crais to sit on the sidelines. Crais did not need to go on this military operation, yet he insisted on coming. The befuddled man was worried about his wife, Keana (more than the Diadem herself seemed to be), but the battle might get ugly. Escobar could not guarantee the safety of the Diadem's daughter. Those weren't his orders. Crushing the enemy was the most important thing. He hoped this desk officer would let military professionals take care of the crisis and not get in the way.

As the five haulers began the journey to Sonjeera, Escobar considered the military might at his fingertips: weapons, squadrons of fighter craft, thousands of fighters and support crew—enough firepower to overthrow the upstart General, as well as an occupation army to take over the illegal stringline hub and impose the Diadem's rule throughout the Deep Zone.

The General must know that Diadem Michella would retaliate, but Escobar doubted the rebel leader would anticipate such an overwhelming military assault. The five haulers would arrive like a thunderclap; the hundred large battleships and frigates would disengage while unleashing thousands of smaller fighter craft. An invincible, overwhelming strike!

It would be over so quickly that Escobar hoped he'd have a chance to relish the taste of victory. A faint smile curled his lips as he realized that someday his two sons would have to endure listening to *their* father drone on about his war stories. He looked forward to the day.

❧

In preparation for the fleet's arrival, all stations at the main Sonjeera hub had been vacated, and commercial traffic was placed in a holding pattern to make room. Civilian ships in the system flew about in a flurry of confusion.

Bolton Crais shuddered to think of the administrative nightmares caused by rerouting and delaying those vessels, but he supposed the chaos was Michella's way of emphasizing the sheer scope of this operation to crush her rival.

When the five stringline haulers docked at the main Sonjeera hub, Diadem Michella summoned Redcom Hallholme, Logistics Officer Crais, and for good measure the individual captains of the one hundred warships to come to the central concourse. She had planned, funded, and choreographed a send-off ceremony with nearly as much precision and enthusiasm as had been spent on the military operation itself. The invited officers wore dress uniforms and full rank insignia; Escobar Hallholme even carried a ceremonial military sword.

The old Diadem welcomed them aboard the giant station with a sweet smile and velvet voice. Bolton had been married to Michella's daughter for a long time, and he knew that beneath her honeyed exterior, the Diadem was as cuddly as a fistful of broken glass. By contrast, Keana was naïve, filled with unrealistic romantic delusions. Her marriage to Bolton had been a political match, and they had never been right for each other, although he did understand her . . . even if Keana didn't exactly understand herself.

Michella shook Escobar's hand and, purely as a formality, greeted Bolton with the same respect. "Gentlemen, today you make the entire Constellation proud."

Lord Selik Riomini stood next to the Diadem, dressed in a black uniform with gold epaulets and spangled with military decorations. He wore a serious expression on his patrician face and squared his shoulders as if competing with Michella over which of them could look more impressive.

The Diadem continued, "I call for you, my loyal commanders, to remove this scourge from our peaceful Constellation. Bring our prodigal Deep Zone worlds together into a harmonious civilization again! I declare this a day of celebration for all Sonjeera. Our citizens cheer you as their heroes."

Inside the hub's concourse, broad screens (normally reserved for displaying the arrival schedules of incoming vessels) showed crowds in Heart Square and in front of the enormous headquarters of the Bureau of Deep Zone Affairs. People waved banners, and with a curl of black smoke they burned an effigy of General Adolphus dangling head down.

During the weeks while the fleet gathered, Bolton had noted the increasingly heated propaganda. People in the Crown Jewel worlds felt the pinch as supplies and tribute payments were cut off, and Michella encouraged the unrest, so long as she could point the finger of blame at General Adolphus.

The crowds began to chant, "Strike fast, strike hard!"—a slogan the Diadem's publicity crew had developed for the operation. This war needed to be branded to stir the people's patriotism while teaching them how to think, whom to hate, and what to do when they were rallying.

The Diadem called four foppishly dressed bureaucrats whom she had assigned to this mission. "Allow me to introduce the diplomatic team that will accept the General's surrender and impose my wishes upon the defeated populace." She gestured to a jowly red-haired man. "This is

Jackson Firth, one of the official historians of General Adolphus's rebellion."

Firth bowed so deeply that he must have trained himself with regular stretching exercises. "My team and I are ready for our duty, Eminence. We will bring closure to this tragic turn of events. I understand the psychology of Adolphus better than most because I have studied him for years."

In a slow, even voice as if explaining to a schoolchild who had never heard the familiar history before, the diplomat described the chaos caused by the previous rebellion. When Firth talked, he was so soft-spoken that he nearly put the audience to sleep. Maybe he intended to lull the enemy into complacency, Escobar thought.

"My team has already developed numerous possible diplomatic approaches." He turned to Escobar with a patronizing smile. "Red Commodore, we are available for consultation in flight."

The diplomat finished without bringing his speech to any sort of climax or resolution. Bolton and Escobar both hesitated before realizing they were supposed to applaud, which signaled the crowds on Sonjeera to cheer and whistle.

Michella said sweetly, "Red Commodore, I anticipate you have prepared some remarks for the occasion of the fleet's departure?"

Escobar had not expected to speak, but he lifted his chin. "The occasion demands it, Eminence." He remained silent for a few seconds to build suspense, then drew the ceremonial sword he wore at his side, grating the blade on the scabbard. He held the unsheathed weapon horizontally, one hand on the hilt, one on the blade's tip.

"My father, Commodore Percival Hallholme, gave me this sword. Though he could not be here for the fleet's departure, he is with us in spirit. When he defeated General Adolphus the first time, who could have guessed that my father's greatest mistake would be mercy?" He glanced over at the Diadem. "The same mistake, albeit a human one, made by Diadem Michella herself when she sent him into exile rather than executing him?"

Her expression pinched at the implied criticism, but Bolton saw that everyone listening was riveted. The crowds on Sonjeera had fallen into a hushed silence.

Escobar raised his voice. "Now I take up this sword and launch another fleet against our enemy—and this time *I* will not show mercy. General Tiber Adolphus and his followers will curse the day they ever heard the name *Hallholme*." With a brisk snap, he thrust the ceremonial sword back into its scabbard and bowed before Michella. "Thank you for giving me this opportunity, Eminence."

The crowds chanted the persistent refrain of "Strike fast, strike hard!"

Michella turned to Bolton, as he'd suspected she would. "Major Crais, would you care to say a few words? You, too, have much at stake in this operation."

"Thank you, Eminence," he said. "But I am here only to see an end to this operation, and to rescue my wife, Keana Duchenet—your daughter." The words struck a chord with the crowds below, and they applauded loudly. Bolton muttered, although he was sure the voice amplifiers caught his comment, "This is not a festival—it's a military operation. Our ships are ready. We should depart with all due haste."

❧

After the speeches were done, the five military haulers transferred onto the stringline to planet Hallholme. Michella had blessed her brave Army of the Constellation, and Supreme Commander Riomini issued the official order to launch. All according to the proper formalities.

Impatient, she went to wait in the hub's private observation lounge with Lord Riomini. Here, free of eavesdroppers, they could be candid with each other. Normally, Ishop Heer would have recorded the conversation with a secret imager, but her aide had asked to remain in Heart Square, wanting to observe incognito for security reasons.

"It won't be long now, Selik. After four days in transit to Hallholme, the fleet will secure the planet and seize the illegal stringline hub."

"The General's handful of outdated ships can never stand against an entire fleet of modern vessels," Riomini said. "I don't expect it will take them long. Then we can get back to normal."

The five military haulers lumbered away from the stringline hub, gathering speed along the molecule-thin path in space. Michella tapped her fingers together and studied her rings before confessing, "I have learned a valuable lesson from this, Selik. We granted the Deep Zone population far too much autonomy, and they abused their freedom."

"That's the problem with 'rugged individualists.'" Riomini paced the lounge restlessly, completing a second circuit. "When you opened the DZ to colonization, you wanted to get rid of the rabble, send them where they could cause no harm."

She frowned at him. "Since they are obviously causing harm, that solution didn't work as expected."

The Black Lord ventured an idea. "Eminence, we should discuss the administration of the Deep Zone once this operation is wrapped up. For my role in the victory, I believe the Riomini family has earned authority over at least ten DZ planets."

She let out a grating laugh. "I just gave you Vielinger! You also have Aeroc and Qiorfu with the Lubis Plain shipyards, and you command the Army of the Constellation. Curb your ambitions, Selik."

His expression hardened. "When my uncle helped you become the next Diadem, *your* ambitions were plain as well."

She raised her eyebrows. "And why are you so confident you'll become the next Diadem?"

"Because I am the obvious choice."

"Nothing in politics is obvious," Michella said, giving an indulgent sigh. "See that your man wraps up this operation cleanly and efficiently. Afterward, we'll discuss the spoils of war."

10

With all the distraction of the fleet launch and the wild celebrations, Ishop Heer seized the opportunity. He had nearly finished his list of murder victims, which was cause for his own momentous, although private, celebration.

Of course Ishop supported the Constellation efforts to destroy the monstrous rebel General, but his family name had been ruined many centuries before Tiber Maximilian Adolphus was born. He and his assistant Laderna had business to take care of.

As the Sonjeerans watched the giant display screens, Ishop slid through the throng like a shadow. He flinched as he brushed against people, worried about what sort of diseases the unwashed populace carried. But he focused on his goal. He would bathe thoroughly afterward.

A trio of noblemen stood just ahead, regarding the screens with haughty pride. "Strike fast, strike hard!" came the chants. Only one of the three nobles mattered to Ishop.

He had memorized the list of names that Laderna compiled, descendants of traitors who had wronged his ancestors seven centuries ago; because of those people, his family name had been erased from the list of nobles, and *he* had been born and raised as a mere commoner, denied his rightful social position, many hundreds of years later. For that, an accounting must be made.

He fingered the triggering mechanism of the tiny skin-colored weapon concealed in the palm of his hand. The central nobleman, Zinn Parra, wore a fine white suit with purple collar and lapels. Golden jewelry adorned his hands and dangled from his wrists. Parra probably planned to attend a gala ball that evening.

The man would never make it, nor would his companions. Ishop had nothing against the others, except for the fact that they had chosen their friends poorly. Besides, they were in the way.

Parra had no idea what his ancestors had done to Ishop's family. In fairness, according to Laderna's obsessive research, the poor man wasn't a bad fellow, as far as noblemen went. But Ishop did not indulge in sympathy. No amount of kindness could make up for seven hundred years of damage.

In just a matter of months, Ishop would legally qualify to regain his status as a nobleman. The mandated centuries of exclusion would be over, and he could return to the fold, a lost son who had been cast out through no fault of his own. He had always known he was destined for great things. He belonged among the gentry.

First, though, he had to make the proper accounting, cross off the last names on his list. Laderna said it was a necessary step in his own healing process. How else could he sleep at night? The two of them had been so exquisitely careful in their work that no one would guess, much less prove, their involvement. . . .

When the military stringline haulers finally launched from the hub, the crowd in the square shouted brave curses against the rebels. Ishop had no love for General Adolphus. As far as he was concerned, the man could not be crushed swiftly, or painfully, enough. Ishop had seen the slickwater pools on Hellhole, how gullible people were affected by them, *infected* by them. The threat of mass insanity spreading to civilized worlds made his skin crawl.

Ishop loathed both germs and disorganization, and this alien threat was far worse than any human disease. Fortunately, Diadem Michella recognized the danger and had sterilized the disgusting alien emissary from Hellhole, along with his horribly transformed companions. The aliens would be stopped, and the Constellation fleet would handily defeat General Adolphus. Ishop could be confident in the future.

Now, first things first.

On the screens, the Constellation fleet raced away down the string-line. Zinn Parra and his two friends shared a private joke and chuckled.

With a quick, smooth motion, Ishop fired darts into their necks in rapid sequence, and then—before they could even swat at the unexpected stings—he shot a second, retractable dart into the neck of Parra, the actual target. When the dart came back to Ishop's receptacle on its gossamer thread, he had the cellular evidence for his collection. The poison would take several minutes to paralyze the three noblemen, which gave him plenty of time to slip away and find a place from which to watch.

The crowd shook fists in the air; friends and strangers clasped one another; women offered kisses to anyone nearby. Ishop dodged them all. When he reached the wide stone stairway of the Council Hall, he turned in time to see his three victims slump to the pavement, clutching their throats. Ishop hoped their bodies might even be trampled in the crush of people, which would further muddy the crime.

By killing all three noblemen instead of just Parra, he concealed his real target and made it look like a random act, maybe an assassin dealing with some feud. No one would guess that Ishop Heer merely sought restitution for an ancient crime that everyone else had forgotten.

At the top of the stairs he met Laderna Nell. From her smile he knew she had observed the full scene. Grinning, he let her take his arm as they walked away from the celebration, and he said, "Now I'm ahead of you, five to four. Not counting collateral damage, of course."

"You've lost count, boss—it's four to four." She brought a list from her pocket. "Facts are facts."

He scanned the names. "You're not giving me credit for the Duchenet family. I tricked Keana into going to Hellhole. She is removed."

"But not dead. Don't change the rules, boss."

He scoffed. "You saw the fleet that just departed. Those Constellation warships will turn Hellhole into a cinder, and Keana is already possessed by an alien presence. She's as good as dead."

"Then you should give me part of the credit. I helped you trick her into rushing off to that planet." She tightened her grip on his arm as she strolled beside him. "After all, I'm the one who found Cristoph de Carre in exile. If Keana hadn't gone chasing after him—"

"Very well, we're partners, not competitors—we can share credit."

Laderna examined the list. "By law, the time limit is up in three months, and you are allowed to present your petition for restitution to the Council of Nobles. The seven hundred years will be over."

"Setting aside Keana Duchenet, we still have three names to go," Ishop said, maintaining his focus on the goal. "Plenty of time to finish our work."

11

nside the parlor of the old Adolphus manor house—he simply could not call it *his* house, even after more than ten years on the Qiorfu estate—Percival Hallholme leaned forward, elbows on knees, enjoying the rapt expressions of his two grandsons.

"And how could you fight back after the explosion in the weapons grid?" asked Emil, the older boy.

"It wasn't just an explosion, boy—it was sabotage! One of the General's traitors had hidden on my own ship, posing as a crewman." He puffed out his chest. "So there we were, hanging in space above Barassa, our warship facing off against two rebel vessels that had enough firepower to tear us to shreds."

"If you didn't have any weapons left, what stopped them from shooting you?" Coram, the younger son, didn't understand politics, tactics, or implications; at eight years old, he just focused on details of the exciting story.

"Ah, but that was the one advantage I had," Percival continued. "Their saboteur had destroyed our weapons grid, but we caught him and confiscated his transmitter device before he could send a confirmation signal to General Adolphus. We drifted in space, gunport to gunport, ready to blow each other up—but they didn't *know* I couldn't fire!"

"So what did you do, sir?" Emil asked.

"Why, I bluffed my way out of it, of course! My first officer had shot the traitor, and he lay dead on the deck, which meant we couldn't interrogate the man and learn if there was more to the plot. But I sent a transmission demanding that the rebels surrender or we would open fire. They split up and tried to run away, but we headed after them in hot pursuit."

"But if you couldn't shoot them, what good did it do to chase them?" Emil persisted.

"I couldn't let them think I was afraid of a fight, boy! We tried to repair our weapons systems, but we had to let the enemy escape, alas. But that was only one of many battles with the General's rebels."

"Was there only one traitor aboard your ship?" Coram asked.

"We found a few others when they committed acts of sabotage. We managed to repair the ship each time, and we prosecuted every traitor we could." He shook his head. "Even today, I suspect the General still has many loyalists hidden in the Crown Jewels."

"But the General is far away," Coram said.

"We're at war with him again," Emil snapped at his brother. "That's why our father went off with the fleet—to defeat him for good."

"And your father will do a fine job of it," Percival promised, because it was what the boys wanted to hear. "You'll see him on the news feeds."

Their mother, Elaine, hurried into the room to gather the boys. "And you both will be great commanders, too, when you're old enough. You'll wear Constellation uniforms, and you'll be brave soldiers—but let's hope no one ever needs to fight General Adolphus again."

Emil sounded disappointed. "Then who will we fight?"

"There are always enemies, boys." Percival meant to sound sad, as a warning, but the boys seemed to take it as a promise.

Elaine smiled at the old Commodore. "You fill their heads with so many stories—how are they supposed to sleep?"

When Percival shrugged, a sharp pain coursed down his spine, but he kept his expression calm. He did not like to let others see his ever-increasing infirmities. With his debilitating disease he no longer felt like a hero; he was barely able to walk across the meadows and down to the Lubis Plain shipyards, much less command a fleet in battle. "If the boys are going to bed, I'm off to town to see if I can find Duff Adkins at the tavern."

Elaine scoffed. "You know he'll be there."

She was a good wife to Escobar, a military spouse who stood by her husband, raised a family, maintained a household. She was also the grandniece of Lord Riomini, so the marriage offered significant political connections, although Elaine seemed happier here at the Qiorfu estate than back at court on Sonjeera. Percival liked her, maybe even more than Escobar did.

The old man put on casual civilian clothes, swallowed a pain reliever so he could better hide his limp, and took a groundcar down to the military town that was adjacent to the shipyards. Because he and Adkins, his longtime adjutant, were both retired, and wanted to put their military service behind them, the men frequented one of the local taverns preferred by the Qiorfu farmers and townspeople rather than Constellation servicemen.

Even after the Hallholmes had been their planetary administrators for more than a decade, the locals still looked askance at the elderly Commodore. He would always be seen as an interloper here, the man who had defeated General Adolphus. The people of Qiorfu had formed the heart of the initial rebellion, and they still had fond memories of the Adolphus administration. They knew how Tiber Adolphus's father had been tricked out of his possessions, how the corrupt legal system had failed; they knew of the treachery that had caused the uprising in the first place.

Percival didn't want the forgiveness of the locals—he would never get it anyway—but he insisted on their acceptance. Perhaps in several generations the wounds would heal. Rather than gloating in his triumph or position, he treated the people with respect, greeted them rather than confronted them. Still, they didn't seem to like him much.

When he entered the tavern, conversation fell to a lull as the bar patrons looked up to watch him before returning to their own conversations. As usual, Duff Adkins sat alone at a small table. The husky man had thinning black hair, with a streak of gray on one side. He already had a large mug of local beer and a second one across from him. "I guessed when you'd get here, Commodore, so I had this ready for you. It's still cold."

Percival took the seat across from his old friend, sipped from the mug.

Duff Adkins had been the Commodore's right-hand man for much

of his career, serving as a sergeant during the rebellion and then retiring into Percival's service. Adkins had accepted punishment for one of
his friend's early unsuccessful missions. (Percival had been appalled to
learn that Adkins had planted evidence that cleared his superior of any
miscalculations.) Later, when he was promoted to the rank of Commodore and sent out to defeat Adolphus, Percival insisted on having Adkins assigned as his de facto first officer, much to the displeasure of
other officers—nobles and military scholars, people with credentials
but no experience. He had demanded to have Adkins, and he had won
the war.

Percival had dedicated the rest of his career to becoming a better
military leader and being worthy of the loyalty that Duff had shown
him. But those days were long past, and Percival was weary from carrying myths of his military career on one shoulder and his guilt on the
other.

Both men wore nondescript clothes, simple shirts and trousers like
everyone else in the tavern, but they could not hide their shared military background. It was in their blood and set them apart as distinc-
tively as if they came from a different species.

Adkins took a long drink of his beer. "The fleet should be launching
about now, Commodore. Shouldn't you be on Sonjeera, waving farewell
to your son and cheering the fleet?"

Percival sighed. He'd been invited to watch the departure of the
strike force but had declined, much to the Diadem's disappointment. He
was less than enthused about a military parade or a speech. "Maybe I
should be there, but my limp and my disease make me want to stay home.
I'd rather the public remembers me from the archival footage, not as I am
now."

Adkins responded with a sober nod. "You have been used for propaganda purposes over the years, sir. It was the right decision."

"We're retired, Duff. You don't have to call me 'sir' anymore."

He grinned. "Yes, sir."

The old Commodore leaned back, drank the sour beer. "I didn't want
to steal my son's spotlight, so I sent my ceremonial sword instead. Escobar
seemed happy enough with that." He wrapped both of his hands around
his mug and stared into it for a long moment.

Percival had watched his son closely, seen the young man's ambitions. He knew how Escobar always strove to be better, to make his own mark . . . and that often caused him to choose foolish paths and go overboard. Invariably, Percival would have to call in favors to salvage his son's reputation—all without Escobar knowing about it, or else the young man's resentment would grow greater yet. The old Commodore's legendary status already rankled his son.

Adkins lifted his beer. "Then let's hope for success, sir."

"Success," Percival said with a nod. He had sent a lengthy letter of congratulations to Escobar before the fleet departed, hoping for the best. But in his heart, he sensed that his son was in over his head.

Worse, he was sure that Escobar would underestimate General Adolphus.

12

A day into the stringline voyage, Bolton joined Redcom Hallholme, Ambassador Firth, and the three members of his diplomatic team for dinner at the captain's table aboard the *Diadem's Glory*.

The chef had prepared a feast: roast prime rib of the most tender pampered beef from the rangelands on Orsini. They had opened three bottles of Qiorfu wine from old-stock vineyards that had once belonged to the Adolphus family and were now managed by the Hallholmes. They relished the wine, not because the vintage was so fine, but because it symbolized what Tiber Adolphus had already lost.

Jackson Firth raised a glass and said in his bland voice, "A toast to our mission, ladies and gentlemen. Through a position of strength, we shall impose Constellation freedom upon the Deep Zone. My team and I have already begun discussions about the next steps to take after our powerful fleet frightens the rebels into submission." He nodded to his diplomatic companions with their frilly collars, wide sleeves, and impeccably styled hair. "We drafted firm responses to every possible thing General Adolphus could say. Be assured that we can make a ready reply no matter what he tries, so I am confident of negotiating a satisfactory settlement for the Constellation."

Bolton saw anger rise on the Red Commodore's face. "I have run simulations, too, Mr. Firth, and I don't expect him to survive the initial engagement. All day long, throughout the four days of this voyage, team after team will be in the simulators, running mock battles and setting up engagements. My fighters will be ready at the snap of a finger."

Bolton had helped to program the fleet simulators that ran the fighters through numerous military engagements. Because no actual battle had taken place in more than a decade, none of the soldiers had recent experience.

"I have been monitoring the simulations, Redcom," Bolton said. "I can present you with the scores, which may help you determine who is best qualified to command the initial attack squadrons."

"I'll look at your numbers, Major," Escobar said. "At the proper time." He turned back to the ambassador, saving most of his scorn for the useless diplomats. "Though we have five times the projected military capability of our enemy, I will not assume that he can be defeated easily. General Adolphus is demonically talented, and it's my job to anticipate any surprises." He had raised his wineglass in response to the toast, but did not yet drink. Now he faced Jackson Firth. "*Your* job is to leave the military matters to me. Once I have crushed the General and taken thousands of prisoners for the Diadem, then you can tidy up your documents and get signatures from anyone left on that planet."

Bolton sat between the two, watching the tension rise, but Firth was a professional diplomat and not easily offended. "Very good. To be better prepared, we should discuss what concessions you would like for yourself, Redcom. Perhaps a fief on planet Hallholme once we conquer it? It would seem an apt reward for your service. I am certain the Diadem would allow it."

"I have no interest in that dreadful place. It may be named after my family, but I have no fondness for it. The Hallholmes have already taken the old Adolphus holdings on Qiorfu, and I don't want to make a habit of scavenging the General's leavings."

After the dinner began, Gail Carrington appeared in her black, insignia-free uniform. She stopped beside the captain's table, saw that all the chairs were full, and waited for someone to rectify the error. Bolton summoned a steward. "Please join us, Ms. Carrington." He added uncomfortably, "I never know whether or not to salute you, ma'am."

"Pay no attention to me at all, Major."

"Beyond observing, what is your role, precisely, Ms. Carrington?" Escobar asked. "As the fleet commander, I need to know."

"You already know what you need to know. I served the Black Lord for years as one of his most skilled special operatives. When I require you to listen, I will inform you."

She took the seat brought by the steward and waited for him to set another place; within moments, the staff had adjusted to the additional person at the head table. She looked at the lead diplomat with blunt dislike. "Lord Riomini objected to your assignment aboard the fleet, Mr. Firth. He gave me instructions to watch you as well."

Firth raised his eyebrows. "My team and I serve at the pleasure of the Diadem. Lord Riomini's opinion matters little."

"He is Supreme Commander of the Army of the Constellation."

"And I believe he holds a grudge against me because I've voiced public support for Enva Tazaar to become the next Diadem. Lady Tazaar is the same age as Michella was when she took the Star Throne. Lord Riomini is too old with too much baggage."

Bolton watched the exchange, remaining silent. He had heard, in hushed discussions when no one thought he was listening (an advantage to being underestimated), that Firth himself had forwarded embarrassing evidence against Selik Riomini to the Diadem, thinking it would ruin him.

"Your talk of politics and family squabbles gives me indigestion," Escobar said, setting down his fork. "This is a military mission and we need to keep our attention on the operation, not on who might become the next Diadem."

Bolton cut into his juicy prime rib. The slab of meat on his plate was twice the size he wanted, but he understood the need to flaunt the bounty of the Constellation, the sheer quantity available on even a military vessel. "I hope the main dish is to your liking," he said, to reduce the tension. "While the ships were being prepared, I loaded enough of these beef roasts aboard that the whole crew can celebrate with a feast when we finish our operations."

And when we see that Keana is safe.

"Prime beef for fifteen thousand soldiers? I hope it comes out of the Diadem's budget," Carrington said.

"We'll take what the General has in his warehouses and feast on that," Escobar grumbled. "That seems more fitting."

"Hear, hear!" Firth raised his glass and took a long sip. His fellow diplomats followed suit.

The diplomats shared additional platters of creamed vegetables and baskets of steaming, buttery rolls. Bolton was already stuffed, but he forced himself to eat more. At last, he pushed the plate away with half of his beef remaining, just so he could pretend to enjoy the billowy dessert of jellied fruits and chocolate shavings, followed by liqueurs and cups of fresh kiafa.

In mess halls throughout the fleet, the crew received extra rations so they could be well fed and energetic for the upcoming military engagement. A fanfare of "Strike fast, strike hard!" rang out across the ship's PA system.

Bolton remembered numerous formal dinners he and Keana had attended, making politically required appearances in the Diadem's name but having few actual duties. Princess Keana had inaugurated new buildings, christened ships, welcomed minor diplomats to Sonjeera; she always looked beautiful and elegant, playing her role adequately, but she'd never been happy. Because the Constellation Charter precluded any member of the Diadem's immediate family from becoming the next Diadem, Keana was destined for a life of comfortable mediocrity, and her own ambitions had never blossomed.

Bolton didn't have the fire in his belly either, which greatly disappointed other members of the Crais family. He held a respected position in the Army of the Constellation, and was satisfied with his career. Until Keana ran off to Hellhole on a naïve errand to rescue Cristoph de Carre and to assuage her guilt for her role in ruining the de Carre family, Bolton had even been somewhat satisfied with his marriage. He'd had few expectations. He knew why Keana married him. She was certainly beautiful enough, and he found her sexually exciting—more so than she found him, apparently—but he had never longed for a passionate relationship. Keana was the one who had those romantic dreams, hence her foolish affair with Lord Louis de Carre.

Bolton had learned to live with her flings, and he had no archaic notions of "possessing" her. She probably assumed that he took lovers of his own; they'd never discussed what she'd thought was an open marriage. He didn't care what other people thought. But they talked alas, and

Diadem Michella had responded by destroying the de Carre family, driving Keana's disgraced lover to suicide, humiliating his son Cristoph, and handing over Vielinger to the Riominis.

Jackson Firth raised his wineglass again and exclaimed, "To the Diadem!"

The others echoed the toast and drank.

On impulse, Bolton said, "For Princess Keana. May she return to us safely."

The response to his toast sounded just as enthusiastic as the other one; Bolton realized that the diplomats were only interested in continuing to drink. They lost count of the bottles of wine.

After the tedious dinner, Escobar Hallholme returned to his command quarters, the largest cabin aboard the flagship. He needed to get away from the yammering diplomats. Upon reflection, he respected Bolton Crais for turning down a chance to grandstand at the Sonjeera hub. The Major was right—this was a military operation, not a pageant. They should be focused on the mission, not on premature celebrations.

This very flagship was the one that Commodore Percival Hallholme had flown in the Battle of Sonjeera, in which he had roundly defeated General Adolphus. Now upgraded, the *Diadem's Glory* would once again lead the Constellation forces to a decisive victory.

He looked at the ceremonial sword mounted on its stand, a reminder of the faith his father had placed in him. Escobar intended to make a fine accounting of himself. Though he didn't yet understand what level of authority Gail Carrington wielded, he knew she reported directly to the Black Lord. It was possible that she even had the power to boost, or destroy, Escobar's military career.

Though he had endured years of having his superior officers and training instructors compare him to Percival Hallholme, Escobar had worked hard to succeed in his own right. But no matter what he did, regardless of the skill with which he commanded his troops, some believed Escobar had no real talent and that his promotions were due only to nepotism.

In public, he was cool when people rhapsodized about the old Commodore's exploits, but here in private, Escobar reviewed his father's memoirs and studied the battles Percival had fought. He learned from the tricks the old man had used when he won, as well as the mistakes he had made when he lost.

Early in his career Percival had bungled two high-profile assignments, including an uprising on the Crown Jewel worlds and one out in the Deep Zone. But because he became General Adolphus's primary nemesis during the rebellion, Percival's history had been whitewashed. A legend could do no wrong. To his credit, the old man seemed embarrassed by his legendary status and preferred to live in obscurity on Qiorfu.

Using the library screen on the bulkhead wall, Escobar called up images he had watched countless times of the General's formal surrender aboard this flagship. A battered-looking Adolphus with reddened eyes and sunken cheeks had presented himself to Commodore Hallholme after a tense standoff in orbit. Even though the rebel ships far outnumbered the Diadem's forces, a wily (and desperate) Percival Hallholme had pulled out his last trump card—numerous rebel family members held hostage aboard the Constellation ships, who would become victims if the rebels opened fire. The General hesitated at the crucial last instant, but Percival did not. The Diadem's ships fired at point-blank range, dealing a crushing blow to Adolphus's fleet. General Adolphus had called the act dishonorable; the Diadem had called it a stroke of genius.

Either way, the war was won for the Constellation.

Escobar stared at his father's image on the video record. The stoic Commodore showed no smugness at his victory. Some staff officers made catcalls as Adolphus walked forward to surrender, but the Commodore commanded them to respectful silence. The defeated rebel leader came alone in his disgrace, although he'd been allowed to bring ten staff members as an honor guard. Adolphus chose to face the brunt of shame and failure by himself. He stood stony and silent as the Commodore plucked the symbols of rank from his uniform. The General's own followers had fashioned the pins and insignia for him.

"Tiber Adolphus, I strip you of a rank that means nothing. Your rebellion is over. May peace forever reign across the—"

Adolphus interrupted him. "I gave you my word that I would surrender, and I have done so, but I did not promise to help you make speeches. I request clemency for my men and women. They followed me in good faith to the best of their abilities. My failure here is no reflection on the quality of their service."

"I accept your surrender," the Commodore said, "and I grant your soldiers clemency and shelter. All those who foreswear violence against the Diadem will be taken into custody temporarily, for eventual safe release."

Escobar's father had gotten into trouble for that particular promise, because Diadem Michella had wanted to execute many more of Adolphus's followers as an example. But the great war hero, riding high on public acclaim from his victory, had neutralized her vindictive plans.

Now, having reviewed the historical record, Escobar vowed not to make any such foolish, open-ended promises.

A signal at the door interrupted him, and Escobar allowed the visitor to enter. "Sorry to interrupt, sir," Bolton Crais said.

Realizing he had left his father's biography and the General's surrender on his screen, Escobar quickly shut them off. "How can I help you, Major?"

Bolton nodded toward the screen. "Studying your father's exploits?"

"Preparing for our imminent ceremony of accepting Adolphus's surrender." He realized his voice sounded terse. "It will be a historic event. I want it to be worthy."

Bolton stood looking uncomfortable. Escobar doubted he had any inkling of how to fight if it ever came down to personal combat; the nobleman had not been bred for such things, did not belong aboard a battleship. To a certain extent, Escobar respected him for insisting on participating in this mission for his wife's sake, though the man must feel terribly out of his depth. As a man who was in a political marriage himself, Escobar wasn't sure he would have tried to save Elaine if she'd cuckolded him and run away to join an alien religious cult. . . .

Looking uneasy, Bolton said what he had come to say. "After our dinner conversation, sir, I felt the need to reassure you. While I may not have the same combat skills you possess, I swear to do my best to make this operation a success. I have reviewed the complement of officers aboard the fleet. You have a valid concern that we carry a great deal of—how shall I put this?—*deadweight* in the command structure. I can help you streamline that, should it become necessary. We could quietly assign important operational duties to the most competent staff, regardless of rank or family ties, while we give showy but irrelevant jobs to lackluster personnel. We can do it subtly enough that they will never realize what's happening."

Escobar found the suggestion amusing. "I always considered *you* to be one of these lackluster officers, Major Crais."

"Then I hope to convince you otherwise, sir."

13

Five substations marked and stabilized the iperion path from Sonjeera to Hellhole, and Turlo Urvancik knew them all. Over the course of their career as linerunners, he and Sunitha had stopped at each station many times for regular servicing operations. The substations collimated the quantum "breadcrumb" path through space, defining the route so that the ultrafast stringline ships did not go astray.

Now he and Sunitha had to blow up two substations, with precise timing. Destroying the target was easy, but doing it with enough finesse to snare the hundred Constellation warships—that was more complicated, and a lot more exciting.

Thanks to the intelligence data from the Constellation spy, General Adolphus knew exactly where and when to strike, and the Urvanciks had taken position well ahead of the oncoming attack fleet. The success of the General's vast scheme to create a secret stringline network across fifty-four DZ worlds already proved his grasp of tactics and timing. Compared to that masterstroke, this mission was far simpler—but still the Urvanciks needed to do it right.

The five substations were evenly spaced across the vastness of space between the Crown Jewels and Hellhole, with Substation 1 nearest to Sonjeera and Substation 5 closest to the opposite end. With Sunitha piloting, the *Kerris* arrived at Substation 3, in the middle of the iperion line.

After setting up the proximity charges, Turlo climbed back inside the airlock of the *Kerris*, fidgeted through the decontamination procedure, and removed his spacesuit, wiping sweat from his forehead. The proximity fuse here at Substation 3 would be triggered by the passage of Escobar Hallholme's attack fleet. Moments after the warship-laden haulers hurtled past, the explosives would destroy the substation and sever the stringline from behind. Traveling at many times the speed of light, the Constellation fleet wouldn't even realize what had happened in their wake.

To avoid unnecessary and expensive damage to the line on the Sonjeera side of the substation, Turlo and Sunitha had placed silent, stealth-coated anchor buoys, which they could locate when necessary. The stringline would not lose its integrity, but the Constellation fleet would never be able to find it.

The delicate iperion in the rest of the stringline segment would dissipate, and Escobar Hallholme's fleet would have no path to follow, thus their hyperfast engines would be useless. No going back.

Turlo took a deep breath of the ship's recycled air. "Ready to head on to Substation 4, my dear," he called over the intercom as he removed the gloves and disconnected the life-support pack.

Sunitha said, "We still have twenty hours until the Constellation ships are where we need them to be."

"Just anxious to have the job done." He walked into the cockpit, where his wife was completing her calculations. She accelerated the *Kerris* down the stringline path before he finished donning his jumpsuit. They would be a day en route to Substation 4, which was plenty of time.

Turlo and Sunitha merely had to destroy Substation 4 before the fleet got there. That would close the other end of the trap. Then the Diadem's great military force would be cut off, both ahead and behind, stranded in space, far from any planet. . . .

When the *Kerris* reached the cluster of spheres, antennae, and solar-power collectors of Substation 4, Turlo dispatched another series of stealth buoys, as he had done at Substation 3. The virtually undetectable signal markers would help repair crews find the ends of the iperion path and reconnect the segment—when it came time for that.

"The DZ doesn't need anything from the Crown Jewels," Turlo said. "Personally, I would've just cut the line and lived with the consequences."

"That's why he's the General and you're just a linerunner," Sunitha said.

"Ah, but I have you. So I'm better off."

Since they had enough time, Turlo removed all the viable spare parts from the station. By the time he was finished, the linerunner's cargo hold was crammed with power packs, chemical tanks, and salvaged pieces of equipment that could be put to use in other substations.

"It's a Deep Zone mentality," Turlo said to her.

She nodded. "Use all your resources, and don't waste anything."

He looked at the schedule, then at the chronometer on the bulkhead. "We know the fleet was scheduled to depart from the Sonjeera hub more than two days ago, and they should be triggering the proximity fuse at Substation 3 any time now."

"We're at least a day ahead of them," Sunitha said, "but there's no reason to wait. Get this done. I want to see an explosion. Let's open one of those bottles of Sonjeeran brandy that you smuggled aboard."

"I sold them all!" Turlo said.

"No you didn't, you kept one in your private cabinet. I already found it."

He'd wanted to surprise her with that. "You shouldn't go looking through my things."

"*Our* things. And I never doubted for a minute that you would keep one bottle for us."

Sunitha retrieved the brandy and a pair of crystal snifters, perfect for sipping the expensive drink. As the *Kerris* drifted near the substation, the two took their seats, each holding a snifter. Sunitha glanced at her husband. "Ready?"

"I'm ready."

She activated the explosives, and the substation erupted like a bright star, spreading hot shrapnel in all directions. Turlo whistled in approval, but Sunitha said, "It would have been more spectacular if you hadn't drained all the fuel tanks."

"It was still effective."

Putting the *Kerris* into radio and sensor silence, they settled back to wait so they could verify their success to the General. Turlo said, "I wish we could see the expression on Escobar Hallholme's face when he realizes his fleet has been cut off."

14

As soon as Tryn had gathered a hundred shadow-Xayan volunteers to set up a new seed colony on Candela, General Adolphus accompanied the strange group of hopefuls to the Ankor spaceport. He knew it would be a few more days before the Urvanciks returned from cutting off the Constellation fleet. All the pieces were in motion.

Sophie Vence's assistant manager had arranged for two cargo aircraft to land by the main shadow-Xayan settlement. Adolphus marveled at the twisted free-form buildings and the ever-spreading red weed.

Though a storm was brewing at mid-continent along their flight path, the pilot and the weather experts deemed the risk acceptable. It would be a bumpy ride over to Ankor, but Adolphus did not delay moving them out. He'd had bumpy rides before.

Undulating forward on her soft, stubby caterpillar feet, the Original alien swiveled her smooth face toward Adolphus. Tryn's oversize eyes reflected the sky, and her mouth membrane thrummed, forming discernible human words. "If the weather grows too severe, General Tiber Adolphus, our telemancy can carry the craft safely across the sky."

The ranks of shadow-Xayans ascending the ramps appeared calm and confident. Most wore placid expressions, although some of the human personalities shone through; a few whispered with excitement.

"I'd prefer it didn't come to that." Adolphus followed the exotic alien into the cargo hold. Though he knew Encix best among the surviving Xayans, he had grown familiar with Lodo and Tryn as well. While Encix had a hard and determined edge to her personality, Lodo exhibited an identifiable sense of humor. Tryn was the quietest of the three and the smallest in stature, even somewhat shy, although Adolphus realized he was anthropomorphizing. How quickly he had grown accustomed to their strangeness, accepting their bizarre body shapes and their incomprehensible history.

It was not difficult to remember that *Diadem Michella* was the hated enemy, the inhuman creature that had to be eradicated. These Xayans were his friends and allies.

When the group finished filing aboard, the two large vessels lifted off in a blast of dust. The General rode with Tryn in the large cargo bay, and they peered out through the windowports at the landscape of this blasted planet.

As the aircraft lifted off, Adolphus noted the bright, mirrorlike pools of slickwater and the ever-expanding camp for the human volunteers who wanted to immerse themselves. He had left Sophie there to manage the new arrivals, and a new group was due to arrive at Michella Town that afternoon. "More and more people are coming, immersing themselves in slickwater. They're afraid of the Constellation fleet, and they believe Xayan personalities and powers will help protect them."

"We all believe that," Tryn said. "Do you not?"

He responded with a skeptical frown, though he doubted the Xayan could read human expressions. "If you were convinced of that, you wouldn't be evacuating a hundred of your people to Candela."

"It is simply a . . . safeguard." Her facial membrane thrummed, and retractable feelers emerged from her forehead to wave in the air, as if questing for the truth. "Our separate colony will be analogous to the museum vault, which survived the asteroid impact. This is no less."

Adolphus knew that if his stringline trap worked, then most of the fears would be moot.

As the craft flew along, he could see the scarlet splash of alien red weed, like a bloodstain across the valley. Even with the details of the landscape blurred by haze and stirred dust, he saw swatches of red, blue, and turquoise that indicated the spread of vegetation—more plant life than he had previously seen. "This planet seems to be softening its mood."

"Xaya is part of us, and it is awakening, as if a planetary spring has returned," Tryn said. "With so many of our lives and memories restored from the slickwater, it builds the charge in our racial psychic battery. All of us have begun generating the telemancy necessary to achieve *ala'ru*."

As the two cargo aircraft soared across the landscape, winds buffeted them, jostling the passengers inside. The pilots had to gain altitude to fly over the turbulent system. As if in silent agreement, the shadow-Xayans crowded in the cargo hold closed their eyes and concentrated. Adolphus felt a unified thrumming in the air, and a cone of stillness surrounded the two distressed craft. Then he felt a lurch as the aircraft accelerated.

The pilot yelped and spoke over the intercom. "General, sir, I'm not doing this!"

The shadow-Xayans continued their synchronized concentration. Tryn remained calm. "We will arrive at Ankor spaceport safely, and with all due speed."

Adolphus responded to the pilot. "I think we're in good hands." A huge static discharge leaped up from the storm clouds and surrounded them in a ball of electric blue light, but the telemancy deflected the blast and dissipated it into the air. He watched the ease with which the danger had been shunted aside. He muttered to himself, "Diadem Michella doesn't know what she's up against."

Tryn agreed. "No, she does not."

An hour later, when the two cargo craft landed at Ankor, he descended the ramp next to Tryn. Rendo Theris hurried out of the operations building, staring at the sluglike body of the Original Xayan. Adolphus smiled at him. "You look as if you've never seen an alien before, Mr. Theris."

"I haven't, sir." The spaceport administrator reached out his hand in a tentative greeting, then withdrew it, not sure whether he wanted to touch the supple hand extending from Tryn's torso. "Administrator Hu has already sent her stringline ship and an escort for the new colony. She says she found a suitable place for the shadow-Xayans on Candela."

"Administrator Hu is very efficient like that."

Persistent quakes had continued over the past several days, but not enough to damage the spaceport structures. The General's expert engineering team was already studying the unstable ground beneath the spaceport; they had drafted a plan to drain the slickwater aquifer into an adjacent basin, but they had not yet agreed on the specifics. Theris was eager to continue his spaceport expansion, but not until he could be sure the alien liquid would not interfere.

Overhearing them with her sensitive membranes, Tryn said, "Do not damage our slickwater database. The Xayan civilization is contained within."

"The slickwater survived an asteroid impact," Adolphus said. "Our construction machinery isn't likely to damage it." He looked around him at the bustling complex. "Ankor is the center of Hellhole's commerce now—our new capital. Besides, once you achieve *ala'ru*, the slickwater won't matter anymore, correct?"

Tryn considered. "True. After *ala'ru*, the Xayan race will be gone, and we will have no further need of this planet."

As shadow-Xayans filed out of the other cargo craft to stand around the landing area, Adolphus was surprised to recognize one of the men. Rendo Theris spotted him at the same time and called out, "That's Tel Clovis! Has he come back to take over his duties as Ankor administrator again?" Adolphus heard a hint of hope in the man's question.

"No, Mr. Theris. Tel is one of them now. He's going to Candela."

Theris sighed as he regarded the lanky man who walked in casual lockstep with the other alien converts. He nodded. "He looks good, though. Happier . . . or at least at peace. Last time I saw him, he was so distraught—I was afraid he'd kill himself after what happened to his partner."

Adolphus had been worried about that as well. "He surrendered in a different way."

Her antennae vibrating, Tryn said, "He seized hope and took a new chance." The Original lurched forward on her caterpillar feet, urging the General and Rendo Theris to follow.

Tel Clovis saw them coming and gave a pleasant smile. "You've done well with Ankor, Mr. Theris." He spoke in his old voice, but with a softer, calmer presence.

Although Tanja Hu had promised to nurture the new colony in exchange for telemancy protection, the shadow-Xayan colonists carried cases of alien artifacts with them, preserved items that Lodo, Keana-Uroa, and Cristoph de Carre had removed from the subterranean museum vault.

"We brought the original writings of Zairic as well as our recorded history, some Xayan poetry, and music," Tryn said, sounding exuberant. "It is what we need to make our colony whole."

The General looked at the artifacts with interest. "Are you sure we can't use anything here to defend Hellhole?"

"Everything is of use," Tryn said, "if one knows how to use it."

"That's not very helpful," Adolphus said. "I was hoping for weapons technology." Even with his detailed scheme, he never stopped thinking of alternative plans, just in case.

A lean and energetic woman emerged from the Ankor operations building dressed in a trim, comfortable uniform that was part jumpsuit and part business attire. She had short brunette hair, dark eyes, and a pointed chin. A well-behaved ten-year-old boy followed her; his brown hair showed a prominent cowlick. The woman's manner was crisp to the point of brusqueness. "General Adolphus, I am Bebe Nax, aide to Administrator Hu. She sent me to fetch the new colonists." She glanced at Tryn but showed no alarm at the alien form, nor did she seem bothered by the shadow-Xayans. "It'll be different, I admit, but I'm not one to judge."

The silent boy stood at her side, keenly interested and unable to tear his gaze from the Xayan. Bebe remembered her manners. "This is my adopted son, Jacque. He's never been away from Candela, and I want him to see and learn as much as possible."

The General extended his hand. "Welcome, Jacque."

"Thank you, sir." The boy seemed more in awe of him than of the alien. "I've read about your rebellion."

"And I made sure he read the *correct* history, too," Bebe Nax said. "Not the Crown Jewel propaganda."

"If only everyone in the Constellation would do the same," he said.

Bebe looked at the group, mentally counting and assessing the space they would need aboard the transport. "We can ferry these people up twenty at a time in a passenger shuttle. I'm ready to go as soon as they are."

"We are ready." Tryn twitched the retractable feelers on her forehead.

"I support your goal, you know that." The General paused, thinking of the telemancy powers he had already seen. "Just don't ascend yourselves and vanish on me before we defeat the Diadem and ensure peace."

15

At midmorning, Sophie stood near the shimmering slickwater pools, reservoirs of preserved alien memories. Her lightweight blue-and-gold jacket—a gift from the General—carried insignia of the Deep Zone Defense Force, and she wore it proudly.

While awaiting an aerocopter filled with a group of eager, and nervous, new arrivals, she saw continuing construction activity as workers framed another lodging structure on the west side of the property near the landing field.

This "resort" was the site of the original discovery of slickwater, where Fernando Neron had stumbled into the strange pool and emerged with a full-fledged alien personality and memories from the planet's supposedly extinct race. After Hellhole cut itself off from the Crown Jewels, tourists from these worlds stopped coming, but increasing numbers flocked in from the DZ itself, people curious or determined to bring back the Xayan race and use newfound alien powers to help defend Hellhole. Thousands of shadow-Xayans already lived nearby in their own settlement.

To accommodate all the visitors, many of whom stayed for days before they could summon the courage to plunge into the slickwater, Sophie had arranged for tents, cabins, and larger lodgings. On a boardwalk that encircled the nearest of the three pools, Sophie surveyed a new group of volunteers pausing at the edge of the strange, viscous water. As she watched, one of them slipped into the pool, splashed, remained submerged for a very long time, and then rose to the surface with a changed, beatific expression and an eerie shimmer in her eyes. So many visitors had come to Slickwater Springs that she no longer tried to keep track of them; she had enough trouble remembering her own staff.

An office aide named Marie Cluré hurried up to Sophie, her steps sounding on the boardwalk. She had never summoned the courage to immerse herself in the pools, but had proved invaluable in managing the flow of visitors. Now she carried a printout of a high-res image. "I thought you should see this, ma'am! Observation sats detected something unusual out on the prairies to the north—a fresh expanse of wild, fernlike vegetation. It wasn't even there on the survey a month ago. The growth is unbelievable. Like the whole plain was reseeded and watered."

Mystified, Sophie looked at the image. "I've heard of patches like this cropping up all over." Several months earlier, one of her scouts had discovered the explosion of red-weed growth, a resurgence of life to the devastated landscape. This new outburst of vegetation had appeared within the space of a few weeks.

"We'll investigate it later," she said, "when we don't have to worry about the Constellation fleet."

With the General's declaration of independence, fear and tension had spread across the DZ. By now everyone had also heard the real story of the massacre on Ridgetop, when the Diadem had brutally retaliated against a frontier colony that had dared to defy her. The rebels knew what could happen to them unless they defended themselves, and some believed that the best line of defense was for them to gain access to Xayan telemancy.

Governor Carlson Goler had recently led a rally on Ridgetop, calling for volunteers to immerse themselves in the Hellhole slickwater, and a new group had just arrived via stringline. As the volunteers disembarked from the landed aerocopter, Sophie went out to greet and reassure them. For the most part they were strong young men and women, with a few hardy-looking older colonists. Regardless of their current physical condition, the slickwater would heal and strengthen them. By coming here, they had already agreed to join the Deep Zone Defense Force.

A man in his thirties, Rolf Jessup, told Sophie he was their unit commander, though they wore no uniforms. Jessup had a presence about him
that she found appealing, an intensity and intelligence in his eyes and a
confident way of carrying himself. He would become a different person—
even stronger, she hoped—once he acquired a Xayan companion personality.

Jessup gave her a firm handshake. "We're not much to look at, ma'am,
but every one of us will give you as much dedication and fighting spirit as
you could want. And we won't lose this time."

As the manager of Slickwater Springs, Sophie frequently encouraged visitors to acquire Xayan personalities, but she felt like a hypocrite.
Though she had seen wonder and satisfaction on so many faces, she
would never plunge into one of the pools herself. She still struggled to
accept the changes that had occurred in her own son. Devon was the
real reason she had left their Crown Jewel home of Klief and come to
Hellhole, to give him a new start—but she hadn't expected this. She
hadn't expected to *lose* him.

"He *is* still here, Sophie," Adolphus had said when she expressed her
concerns. "But he isn't the same."

"I know. He's tried to reassure me—and I can convince myself rationally of all the benefits he says he's enjoying from Birzh—more than he
ever had before, more memories, a wealth of ideas, mental powers." She
realized she was just repeating the words Devon had told her, as if trying
to convince herself. "He's achieved and experienced an existence that
he could never have dreamed of in his normal life." She drew a deep
breath, shook her head in dismay. "I see flashes of the old Devon,
but . . . he's not nearly as close to me anymore."

"He and the shadow-Xayans may save us all."

Now, as two new converts emerged from the slickwater, dripping
wet, the liquid oozed off them and returned to the pool. They stood
together, changed, amazed, *strong*. Sophie forced herself to congratulate
them.

⸙

Returning to Elba that afternoon, she found Devon and Antonia in
the General's parlor. The slender, brown-haired young woman sat at the

piano, picking at the keys with an expression of intense concentration on her face.

Sophie knew that Devon had been smitten with the girl from the moment she took shelter in their warehouse during a growler storm. Now the two were not just lovers, but were connected with a pair of alien personalities who also loved each other.

Devon perked up as his mother arrived, and sounded like his old self. "Come listen—Antonia is about to play a special song."

Plinking the keys, Antonia said, "My mother was an excellent pianist and taught me how to play. My Xayan counterpart is also a musician, so Jhera and I decided to combine our skills. A duet like there's never been!"

Antonia's old life on Aeroc had been idyllic and luxurious, until it all came crashing down when a sadistic boyfriend murdered her parents. She had fled to the Deep Zone to escape him . . . but even Hellhole hadn't been far enough.

Antonia-Jhera looked up from the piano, turned her shimmering eyes toward Devon, and played a few more notes. "Listen . . ."

As she grew more comfortable, Antonia entered a sort of trance, playing faster, adding familiar melodies with an unexpected counterpoint of music constructed on an entirely different set of mathematics. The composition started out lovely and haunting, a simple tune that became more energetic and complex as she immersed herself in it, then slowed and wound back to what it had been, then took an entirely different and equally complex route into another high-energy variation of the underlying melody.

Antonia kept exploring tributaries of the core music, then returning. From the distant look on her face and the spiral shimmer in her eyes, Sophie knew the alien Jhera was fully immersed in the performance. The hypnotic swirl of notes and tones seemed impossible from a piano, and the sound resonated throughout the parlor.

It was a concerto of sound different from anything Sophie had ever experienced. Hearing it, a flickering of images filtered into her mind, and her head filled with frightening but indefinable shapes. Instinctively, she wanted to flee the parlor, but just as she became conscious of her panic, she felt the opposite and sat back down, as if the music drew her back, welcoming her and wrapping its soothing notes around her in a comforting blanket of sound that contrasted sharply with the preceding sounds.

She looked at her son, who also sat transfixed. Seeing the love for Antonia in his eyes, Sophie began to cry. Maybe it was the music, or maybe it was her own heart.

16

While some Deep Zone worlds were rugged places fit for only the hardiest settlers, most were attractive in their own ways: untamed, with vast landscapes to explore, untapped resources, and far from the stifling Crown Jewels. Tanja Hu had no desire for any other world besides jungled Candela, but she could understand why her friend Sia Frankov loved Theser.

The planet had a wide-open landscape forested with spiny succulents, and was rich in minerals. Numerous ancient asteroid strikes had left deep and lush crater valleys, and the largest bowl provided a comfortable, sheltered habitat for Theser's capital city of Eron. Moisture tended to settle in the lowlands. Low cloudbanks watered the agricultural fields that thrived on the porous soil of the crater floor. The city itself was built in terraced layers of the steep crater walls.

After passing through Tanja's new stringline hub recently installed above Candela, she and Ian Walfor transported the six rebuilt warships along the direct path to Theser. Ambitious, Tanja had made the new iperion route a high priority. Her people had finished it at breakneck speed, and a trailblazer ship was already laying down a second line from Candela to Cles. She expected that in due time her world would become a major DZ commercial center.

Sia Frankov was a like-minded woman, and she and Tanja often got together on their respective planets, sharing a drink of the local alco-holic specialty, plotting their dreams, negotiating commercial alliances, anticipating a bright future for the Deep Zone. Tanja wished the damned military preparations would stop interfering with her commer-cial ambitions, but she also wanted to humiliate Diadem Michella after all the bitch had done.

Walfor used a powerful tractor ship to drag its towline of vessels that required stardrive engines from the Theser engineers. He seemed to en-joy operating the huge and unwieldy vessel so he could show off his pi-loting skills for her. Sitting next to Walfor on the command deck, Tanja smiled as she watched how smoothly he did it. And she would let him show off for her. Someday, they would be able to enjoy peace and she could think of romance; for now, she had to remain focused.

The cluster of vessels landed inside Eron's massive crater. When ready, the six refurbished warships would return to help defend Candela.

It would have been far more efficient for the reclusive engineers to leave Theser, bring new equipment to Buktu, and work there, but they were adamant homebodies. Although Frankov was also frustrated by her recalcitrant workers she merely rolled her eyes the last time Tanja mentioned it. "I have tried, Tanja. But they are brilliant, and I've fi-nally accepted that they won't travel. It's just the price I pay for their genius."

Tanja wanted to see the strange engineers and deliver her ships to them, but she had another reason for coming to Theser as well. As part of her deal to share stringline costs with Sia Frankov, Tanja had agreed to take a difficult political prisoner off the administrator's hands and keep her on Candela for safekeeping.

When the Deep Zone broke away from the Crown Jewels, three of the Constellation's five territorial governors had been on Sonjeera and thus were cut off from their assigned worlds; Governor Goler from Ridgetop had thrown in his lot with the rebels. The last recalcitrant governor—a woman named Marla Undine—had been arrested on The-ser and remained a political prisoner. But Sia Frankov didn't know what to do with Undine and did not like having such a dangerous captive.

Tanja, though, had her own ideas.

As she and Walfor stepped off the ship at the bottom of the crater, a thin, elegant-looking woman in a business suit greeted them. Sia

Frankov was accompanied by officers and soldiers of the Deep Zone Defense Force in blue-and-gold uniforms.

"I was afraid you wouldn't be able to land all those ships at once," Frankov said. The wind in the bowl of the large crater whipped her long reddish hair. The Theser administrator gave Walfor a flirtatious gaze, then looked down the line of vessels that he had so smoothly set down, one after another.

"Barely broke a sweat," Walfor said.

Tanja gave her friend a quick, warm embrace. Frankov said, "Would you like an early lunch?" By local time, it was late morning, with Theser's sun only partly visible through a mist of low clouds above the crater.

Walfor grinned, but before he could agree, Tanja pressed, "We'd like to meet with the spacedrive engineers without delay. Could we have these ships moved to the fabrication center?"

"It's always business first with you, Tanja," Frankov said with an indulgent sigh. "If the Constellation withered away and left you without an enemy, you wouldn't know what to do with yourself."

"If the Constellation withered away, I would find plenty of other things to do."

The Theser administrator instructed one of her officers to have the ships moved, then she led her guests away from the spaceport. "But you still have to eat, and there's no reason you can't enjoy it. I know what kind of food you like. I already alerted the engineers that they have priority work, and I've had my chef prepare a nice meal. No delays, and no rudeness either. See? Everybody's satisfied."

Tanja forced herself to relax. "Sorry to sound so impatient, but I need to get Candela's defenses in place. Every day, I expect—" She felt herself flushing, her muscles tensing. For all the terrible things the Constellation had already done, Tanja knew she had not yet seen the depths of what the Diadem might do. "I will be glad to have Governor Undine under my control, as a hostage and a bargaining chip." She caught herself. "But I have no intention of bargaining."

Frankov interrupted with a hard smile. "And for me it will be a relief to get rid of Undine. I can't thank you enough for taking over as her host."

"Host? That sounds a little more pleasant than what I have in mind."

Frankov brushed the comment aside with a flippant laugh. "I'd rather not hear about it. Once you take the governor away from here, the Constellation won't have any reason to pay attention to Theser. *You'll* be in their sights, and I'll have nothing to worry about."

Walfor let out a snort as he walked between the two women. "You're both expecting the Diadem to react rationally."

"For security, we should just blow all the stringlines to Sonjeera," Tanja grumbled. "Get it over with."

Frankov chuckled. "And be cut off from the Crown Jewels for years after this little squabble is settled? I think not. *I* intend to act rationally, even if no one else does."

"We can do without the Constellation," Tanja insisted.

"Of course we *can*, but I'd rather not."

After a quick lunch in the administrative banquet room, Frankov led her visitors to an all-terrain roller for climbing the steep road up the terraced slope of the crater wall.

The vehicle kicked up a cloud of dust as it switchbacked up an incline toward buildings that looked like a complex of monasteries. For arcane reasons the Theser engineers considered the crater sacred. *As long as they get their job done and the ships finished,* Tanja thought.

She and Walfor followed Frankov into the laboratory citadel. Tanja saw dirty couches and tables that had not been cleaned for a long time; no one sat behind the reception desk, but she didn't expect anyone to be there. This structure had been built by the old territorial government—an exorbitant expense paid for by draconian tribute demands—and it did not fit the personalities of the stardrive engineers. Nevertheless, they had sprawled into the unclaimed administrative space.

When no one came to greet them in the cavernous, dusty foyer, Frankov marched through a doorway in search of someone while Tanja and Walfor waited. And waited. They'd been through this irritating routine before. Not a very efficient way to fight a war! Now that she had her direct Candela-Theser stringline, she no longer needed to travel to this planet via the Hellhole hub, thereby saving days on each trip, but the planet-bound engineers still made the process needlessly difficult. Frankov claimed that she and Tanja would laugh about it one day, when all the turmoil was over.

Tanja couldn't visualize when it would ever be over.

Finally, Frankov returned with a group of eight very tall men. Their hair was uniformly black, and their eyes pale brown. They wore gray jumpsuits smudged with dust and grease. The spacedrive engineers were all said to be from the same family, raised in a crater-rim settlement several kilometers from the city. They looked different from other Theser settlers; Tanja wondered if it might be due to inbreeding. The isolated specialists had gaunt faces and paunchy bellies.

"We don't have much time for this," said one of the men in a gravelly voice—Jaluka Vobbins, the only one who ever spoke with visitors.

"We know your time is valuable," Walfor said in his best diplomatic voice.

"As is ours," Tanja added. "There's a war on." These inflexible but brilliant scientists were the only way to get new stardrives in time, and the General needed the additional ships to bolster DZ defenses. She bit back her irritation and said, "So we would appreciate your help. General Adolphus has . . . requested . . . that you install new engines on the six vessels we just delivered, as soon as possible, so they can be stationed as defense ships."

Vobbins looked sourly at his companions. "We already have projects in the works. New experiments."

Tanja rolled her eyes in frustration, and Walfor spoke up, wearing a congenial smile. "An invasion from the Diadem would interrupt those projects permanently. And if you are all killed in a punitive action, then we'll never get those ships. So if you don't mind?"

Vobbins looked alarmed. How could the engineer be so oblivious to what was going on in the Deep Zone?

Sia Frankov said mildly, "They have a very good point, Jaluka."

Vobbins looked at the other engineers, who nodded. "Very well, we choose to accept the request of General Adolphus. Now we shall return to work." He bowed slightly, then turned his back and left, followed by the others.

"Maybe they're following Sia's example and acting rationally," Tanja muttered with a trace of sarcasm. "For a change."

❧

Frankov drove the roller down the switchbacks to the city prison, a formidable structure at the base of the crater. "I expect you'll find Governor Undine as unpleasant as I do," Frankov said. "You are welcome to her company."

Fiercely, and naïvely, loyal to the Crown Jewels, Governor Undine had refused to accept the new reality in the Deep Zone. When General Adolphus had unveiled his DZ stringline network and declared independence, Undine tried to rally the people of Theser, demanding their continued allegiance to Diadem Michella. But Adolphus supporters had been laying the groundwork for years, and the Deezees loathed the oppressive Constellation. Planetary Administrator Frankov had arrested Undine and locked her away so she could no longer interfere. The people of Theser applauded the decision, since Governor Undine was not well liked among the frontier people she scorned.

Undine was held in a cell within a maze arrangement of other cells delineated by a combination of metal bars and advanced electronics. "Theser has little need for maximum security prisons, but I took all the precautions I could," Frankov explained.

"I doubt she could make a prison break," Walfor said.

Frankov did not laugh off the comment. "I couldn't be sure. Governor Undine has important contacts back in the Crown Jewels, and I didn't want her thinking she had any chance of being rescued."

Tanja saw the dour former governor sitting on a hard bench inside a yellow electronic containment field. The woman looked arrogant and bored, and Tanja felt an immediate antipathy for her: no compassion, only contempt. Marla Undine symbolized the excesses and corruption of the old government, the oppression of the DZ settlers. "I doubt anyone misses her terribly," she said, making sure that the prisoner heard her.

Undine glanced at them, then looked away. "I don't talk with traitors. Unless you've finally come to your senses and decided to free me."

Tanja spoke to her friend, rather than addressing the prisoner, "Don't worry, Sia. We'll find suitable quarters for her on Candela. She is no longer your problem."

Undine refused to rise from her seat. "You have no right to hold me. I don't recognize your authority."

"What you do or don't recognize is irrelevant," Walfor told her. "General Adolphus approved the transfer. We're moving you to a secure location."

Tanja grew impatient. "Secure, but not necessarily comfortable. If you won't come with us willingly I'll have you stunned, and we'll haul you to Candela in the cargo hold."

Glowering in defiance, Undine rose to her feet and went with them.

Sia Frankov let out a sigh of relief. "Thank you, Tanja. Someday I'll return the favor."

Tanja continued to stare at Marla Undine, seeing her as the symbol of all the damage the Constellation had done. "My pleasure," she said in a tone that implied no joy at all.

17

The Constellation fleet was less than two days from planet Hall-holme along the hyperfast stringline when alarms rattled through the ships.

Red Commodore Hallholme was already edgy; the passage seemed interminable, and he just wanted to get on with the fight. He was down in the simulation chambers watching a squadron of fighter pilots go through a mock bombing run in a scenario with General Adolphus entrenched on the ground in his Elba fortress. A second group of fighters completed a training mission, this time fighting—and winning—a space battle. Even though the simulation gave the General twice as many war vessels as he could possibly have, the Constellation fighters seized the new DZ stringline hub with very little effort. Victory after victory.

Major Bolton Crais had accompanied Escobar into the simulation nerve center, where the wall of segmented screens looked like a giant fly's eye. Taking notes, Bolton identified crewmembers who made imaginative responses and noted their names. On the training screen, attack squadrons flew together in a bombing run like a well-coordinated swarm of hornets. Imaginary explosions flashed and sparkled while curls of smoke rose into the sky, leaving only a black crater where the rebel General had thought he was safe.

Just as the trainees scored a complete victory, however, the *Diadem's Glory* lurched. Gravity spun from the horizontal deck to the walls, then back again like a wild pendulum. Sparks flew from control panels while foul-smelling smoke spurted from burning circuits. The lights went dark, then flickered back on at half strength. In some of the sim-chambers, the doors sealed and locked, trapping the soldiers inside. After a five-second delay, alarms droned throughout the PA system, drowning out the cheery loop of patriotic music.

Thrown to his knees on the deck, Escobar scrambled to regain his feet and his dignity. His gaze latched onto Bolton Crais. "What the hell was that, Major?"

"I've never experienced anything like it, sir."

A fresh-faced young squadron leader crawled out of a sim-chamber, blinking in alarm. "Is this part of the exercise?"

A second fighter appeared beside him. "No, it's real. The General must have launched something against us."

"This is not part of the simulation," Escobar said in his command voice. "We're still two days away from the target, so I won't give General Adolphus credit until I know what happened. Major Crais, come with me." They took a tube lift and emerged onto the bridge.

Lieutenant Aura Cristaine was the officer on duty. She rose from the command chair. "I've been in contact with the stringline pilots high up on the framework, Redcom. All five haulers have disengaged from the stringline. Emergency measures activated."

"Mechanical problems? On all five haulers?" Escobar was aghast. "How could anything go wrong? We're just following the stringline."

"Still checking, sir." Lieutenant Cristaine looked harried. A few wisps of her straight brown hair had escaped from her regulation pinned-back style. She moved from station to station, looking at reports. "We lost the iperion path, and our haulers are drifting loose."

Bolton's brow furrowed. "At our speed of travel, if we broke loose from the stringline, we could have gone the length of a solar system before emergency deceleration stopped us."

"Get Pilot Dar on the channel now," Escobar said. "I want an explanation."

The communications officer signaled the pilot of the giant hauler framework. During the emergency deceleration, two suspended warships had broken free of their docking clamps and tumbled out of the frameworks into space. In only a few seconds they had drifted hundreds of thousands of kilometers apart. Mayday signals came in from the two lost ships as they tried to find their way back to the stringline haulers. Cast loose, the five haulers had spread far apart as well. The comm channels lit up as numerous captains demanded explanations. Escobar muted them all until he had answers himself.

Finally, the pilot of their stringline hauler appeared on the screen. Suri Dar was a stocky old woman who rarely left her chamber atop the framework. She lifted both her hands, adding frantic birdlike gestures to her words. "If I had an answer for you, Redcom, I'd tell you," she said, before Escobar could ask. "Automatic systems kicked in. Something happened after Substation Three. We just passed where Substation Four should be, but . . . it's not there. The stringline just ends. We're off the damned iperion path!"

"How can a substation not be there?" Escobar said.

Bolton lowered his voice, leaning closer. "The answer is obvious—General Adolphus destroyed it. He severed the line after all."

"That bastard!" Escobar said. Before the fleet launched from Sonjeera a fast drone had verified the integrity of the stringline—only a few days ago. "How could he cut himself off from the Crown Jewels? And right now?" He glowered at Crais, quick to cast blame. "Of course, since we took weeks to load and dispatch our fleet, he had plenty of time." Escobar turned back to the screen. "And what does this mean, Pilot?"

Dar sat back, her wrinkled face like a prune from which too much moisture had been extracted. "What does it *mean*? You know how stringline travel works, sir—without an established iperion path we can't use our superfast engines. We'd be flying blind at suicidal speed. Without the stringline, your hundred ships would have to disengage from the hauler frameworks and use regular faster-than-light spacedrives to get to Hallholme."

Escobar clenched his hands, drew a deep breath. "FTL would take too long."

Bolton said, "A couple of months, give or take, depending on where we are. But we don't have near enough fuel to make that passage with FTL engines. It's not an option."

Gail Carrington spoke up, startling him. She had been so shadowy and silent, he hadn't even noticed her standing on the bridge. "I'm not surprised the General did this, although I am disappointed. With his own DZ stringline network, he can still reach Sonjeera via some other Deep Zone world—unless he's blown all fifty-four lines."

"He would never do that!" Bolton cried.

"No reasonable man would. But that doesn't answer the question." Escobar turned back to Suri Dar. Unlike the skilled fighters he had just watched in the simulation chambers, stringline hauler pilots were little more than train engineers. They traveled back and forth along the clearly defined iperion lines, and the routes never varied. They did not maneuver; they could not go anywhere except forward and back. Therefore, the job did not attract exceptional applicants.

"And what do you suggest we do, Pilot? What are our options?"

"Options? If there's no stringline, we damn sure can't go forward. We'd get lost, or destroyed. It's as if they've blown up a bridge across a canyon."

"We do have the navigation records," Bolton said. "We know the time when we lost the stringline, and we should be able to calculate backward, retrace our steps, and find out where Substation Four was located. If we can't find the path ahead, then we head back and pick up the Sonjeera end of the stringline."

At the very suggestion, Escobar watched a dark cloud cross Gail Carrington's face. He was annoyed, and said, "What good will that do us, unless we want to go home with our tails between our legs?"

Bolton's voice remained calm, although it contained an edge of strain. "Offering options, sir, as you requested. It would give us a baseline point. Right now we're drifting in the middle of nowhere. When we pick up the line again, we'll know where we are, and we can reassess our situation from there." He brushed a hand across his face and eyes, hiding a glint of sweat—or a tear? "Believe me, Redcom, I want to get to Keana as soon as possible, but we could very easily get lost and never make it."

Escobar realized he had a point. "Very well, that seems like a reasonable decision. Pilot Dar, contact the other four hauler pilots, coordinate your data, and project where we fell off the iperion path. We'll find our way back to the original line."

The old woman sounded dubious. "All right, sir. We'll try."

He did his best to hide his annoyance. "I didn't order you to *try,*
Pilot. I ordered you to *do it.*" He switched off the codecall screen.

Half an hour after the first alarms, Jackson Firth and his diplomatic
staff hurried onto the bridge. "Red Commodore, brief us on what's happened." Even with the emergency, the four diplomats had troubled
themselves to don full finery, as if the team expected to be called to
negotiate the General's surrender. "Were we attacked by rebel ships?"

"No, Mr. Firth. The stringline has been cut. We're stranded here for
now."

"Then we must call an immediate meeting," Firth said. "We'll gather
input and discuss our best course of action."

"I will determine the best course of action," Escobar said.

"Excellent." Firth smiled. "Shall we set the meeting for one hour,
then?"

18

Diadem Michella was in a good mood—likely a temporary one, but even so it was a rarity in the past two months, since the recent troubles with Adolphus.

She and Lord Riomini sat in the viewing stands of the palace arena, both in formal state dress. Though the Black Lord was at least three decades her junior, Michella noticed signs of age and stress—and *weakness*—in his demeanor; she could see his face beginning to sag. With Michella, on the other hand, the years made her look *majestic* (or so her advisers told her).

The Diadem's most magnificent horp geldings pranced in front of them, wearing tall headdresses adorned with feathers in the colors of the various ruling noble families. The spirited, long-necked horps looked like a cross between a horse and a giraffe, and the Diadem had a monopoly on breeding them; the animals were just one of her many sources of income, and a symbol of her prestige. Their riders wore an assortment of militia uniforms, all for show, though they seemed particularly puffed up by their appearance.

Though they applauded at the appropriate moments, she and Riomini paid little attention to the festivities. Even in wartime, the social and political requirements continued. "We still need to make plans for the Constellation-wide celebration," she said, "as soon as we can announce the utter defeat of the DZ rebels."

"We could always burn General Adolphus in effigy," Riomini suggested.

"I would prefer to burn the actual man. While he's still alive."

Riomini leaned back thoughtfully, keeping his gaze on the performance below. "People do have a way of dying around you, Eminence. Your brother Jamos when you were just a child, then your husband mere months after Keana was born. And your sister vanished. How is she these days?"

"Every family has its unfortunate situations. I assure you Haveeda is perfectly well cared for, in a quiet place where she can spend peaceful days, untroubled by painful politics."

"I'm happy to hear that." Obviously, he didn't care in the least. Michella was reminded, though, that she needed to visit Haveeda soon. Her sister was always a good sounding board, someone in whom she could confide.

The Diadem and the Black Lord offered occasional waves to the riders and dignitaries while continuing their private discussions. "By this time tomorrow, our fleet should begin crushing Adolphus," Michella said with a smile. "Another problem solved."

Riomini grunted. "Our ships will dispense with the General's defenses within a day or two, but don't expect word for at least a week." He seemed distracted by something below.

Michella's smile faded as two white geldings emerged from an arena gate pulling a carriage full of nobles and ladies. Instantly, she recognized the colors of the Crais family. The elaborate carriage approached her box and came to a stop. She identified the elderly parents of Bolton Crais, along with two of his younger brothers and their wives. The wrinkled Madam Crais carried a white bird in her hands, and she released it into the air.

It was an unusual show, which the audience appreciated. Michella saw that the bird carried a parchment in its talons. Well trained, it flew up to the Diadem's box. Her guards rushed forward, but too late to do anything if the white bird posed some sort of threat.

Useless protectors, she thought. *Poorly disciplined.*

By contrast, Lord Riomini's female guards moved forward in a blur to shield their master with their own bodies; Michella noted they did not seem concerned with protecting *her*. The white bird dropped the parchment on her lap, then flew off, as if released from its duties.

Michella unrolled and read the parchment, then burst out laughing. It was a birthday message for her, wishing her great happiness—a preemptive communication, because the day was still several weeks off. The note also promised a valuable gift to be delivered to her palace, a chest full of rare jewels mined on Noab, the primary Crais holding. As Riomini's bodyguards withdrew, Michella waved her appreciation to the noble family in their carriage below.

Riomini said in a low, troubled voice, "Your security could be improved, Eminence."

"And your *generosity* could be improved, Selik." She read the congratulatory note again to flaunt the value of the gift of noaby jewels. "How much have you shown me you want my endorsement? How much is being the next Diadem worth to you?"

With an annoyed sniff, he said, "It's a blatant overture from the Crais family to place a member of their family on the Star Throne."

"Of course it is—noabies for nobles. I've always liked their sales presentation, and the Craises are a powerful, well-respected family. But who do they offer as a candidate? *Bolton* as the next Diadem? Hmm, my son-in-law *is* younger than you are, and more easily managed. . . ."

"And far more lackluster. Bolton Crais is not a leader. You can't honestly be considering—"

"The Constellation has had lackluster Diadems before. Besides, my successor is chosen by a full Council vote. All members of the Duchenet family are out of consideration."

"Don't be coy, Eminence. Your support carries a huge amount of weight."

She gave him a sweet smile. "Which is why I must be absolutely certain before I bring my influence to bear. A valuable gift like this is an inventive gesture." Michella fluttered the small written message. "But I already gave the Crais family a great boon by letting Bolton marry my daughter, and that hasn't turned out well. I don't think I owe the Craises anything more."

Out in the stadium, ten colorfully adorned, long-necked horps galloped in a circle, while the riders held out flapping pennants like rip-ping rainbows.

"You *do* owe my family, Eminence."

"Yes, I would not be on the Star Throne had it not been for Riomini influence." She continued to toy with him. "On the other hand, Enva Tazaar has been making a good case for herself. Energetic, likable, full of fresh ideas."

"Enva Tazaar! She's just a child—and an *artist!*" He made the word sound pejorative.

"She's thirty-one, and her aerogel sculptures are masterpieces, if the prices she charges are any indication. She gave me one of them, and I keep it in the palace." Actually, she kept it *hidden* in the palace; she found the free-form, modernistic shape puzzling and disturbing.

"I've seen her sculptures, Eminence, and they are ugly."

She couldn't disagree with him. "As is this one, but it doesn't matter. Art is one of the things that separates us from barbarians like Adolphus."

"Let me have the sculpture," Riomini said. "My bodyguards will use it for target practice. Enva Tazaar could use a lesson in humility."

"Don't let her fool you. She's been ruthless in quashing unrest on Orsini after Lord Azio was murdered."

"That loathsome man deserved to be murdered several times over, and painfully each time," Riomini grumbled.

"Yes, I know your feelings toward him. What would our government be without its tension? Nevertheless, I do not plan to surrender the Star Throne to anyone—at least not soon." Michella gave him an enigmatic smile. Riomini was right, to a degree, but she would never admit it. She needed to keep the Black Lord on edge, making him feel he still had to prove himself. Her tactic was already having an effect, because the Black Lord looked incensed, and worried.

With a determined sniff, he said, "I'll become such a war hero that the people will put me on the Star Throne by acclamation."

"And how do you intend to do that?" She could tell he was planning something.

He smiled. "Adolphus richly deserves the punishment he gets, but the rest of the Deep Zone worlds are just as culpable in this uprising. The Deezees defied you, and they need to serve as an example. We must show any other restless populations the consequences of defying Son-jeera. We can do more—*I* can do more." He chuckled. "After all, why should Redcom Hallholme hog all the glory?"

Good, she thought, he sounded anxious to demonstrate his abilities. "And what exactly do you have in mind, Selik?"

"Years ago, you commanded the Ridgetop Recovery to deal with a small group of intractable settlers. . . ."

"Don't remind me of that traitor Governor Goler," she snapped.

Riomini was so enthused he half rose from his seat. "Forget about Ridgetop! This will be the *Deep Zone* Recovery. Let me take my own battle group and scorch a frontier world. Returning the breakaway plan-ets will be my gift to you."

She nodded, pleased with his initiative and drive. "Yes, that would trump a chest full of noaby jewels. Bring me your battle plan as soon as you have it."

Anxious to make his preparations, the Black Lord left the stadium even before the final horp demonstrations. "Wars are for heroes, after all," she said to herself as she watched him depart.

19

On Ridgetop, the excavators discovered the first skeleton, and then twenty more within two days of digging. A thin rain turned the excavation into a slimy, muddy mess. Tasmine, Governor Goler's gray-haired housekeeper, looked disturbed, but she couldn't tear her gaze away from the dirt-encrusted bones.

Although he had known about the Ridgetop massacre for some time, Carlson Goler felt sickened to see evidence of the crime. He stood next to Tasmine, watching the grim volunteers sift through the dirt. He could not comfort her over the tragedy the Diadem had inflicted upon the original colonists here.

"It was raining that awful day, too," Tasmine said. "I was roaming the hills, far from the settlement, to gather seedcones and mushrooms. I had just climbed a rock outcropping at the top of a ridge, and I remember the view, the mists rolling in from the low valley, the goldenwood groves shimmering even in the rain.

"The Diadem's ships came down, and they were different from the trading vessels we usually saw—these were battleships. Their attack craft streaked across the sky, crisscrossing in search patterns, and I ducked out of sight. I remember that their vapor trails in the sky made a pattern like a grid." Her gaze was far away as she relived every smell, every sound, of those nightmares. "Then the soldiers burned the town and shot everyone they could find. Even from far away, I heard the screams, the gunfire, the explosions. Oh, how I wanted to run, to find my sister and be with my neighbors. I longed to go and help, to fight those monsters, to *do something.*"

"If you had tried to fight them, you'd have been killed, too."

"I've reminded myself of that countless times, but it doesn't make the guilt go away."

At the mass burial site the diggers used rakes and brooms, careful not to damage the skeletons. One of the muddy workers spoke up. "We can count them, Governor, but we'll never be able to identify them."

"We'll honor the victims," Goler said. "That's our point here. Tasmine helped me reconstruct many of the names from her own memory."

She said, "How could I forget?"

The twenty diggers were lumberjacks who usually cut down stands of goldenwood, shearing off the curling metallic leaves and packaging the lumber. Now that they had stopped shipping tribute cargo back to Sonjeera, the lumberjacks didn't need to work themselves to exhaustion. Goler had already begun negotiations to provide goldenwood supplies to other Deep Zone worlds through the new stringline network.

Back when he was the territorial governor, Goler ostensibly worked for the Diadem, but he'd had only a lackluster career. His sympathies had always leaned toward the rugged colonists rather than decadent, noisy Sonjeera. Of the five territorial governors assigned by the Bureau of Deep Zone Affairs, only Goler chose to live out on the colony worlds; the others had plush dwellings on Sonjeera. His fellow governors had treated him with little respect or interest, thinking him unremarkable.

The colonists on the planets he supervised hadn't much cared for Goler either, seeing him as the Diadem's lackey; Tanja Hu actively disdained him. They gave him little credit when he tried to mitigate the Constellation demands, when he asked to lessen the unreasonable tribute payments, when he requested emergency aid following the mudslides on Candela.

Though Goler was not an ambitious man, he did have a strong sense of rightness. Over the years Tasmine had grown to trust him, eventually shocking him by revealing the truth of the Ridgetop massacre, which had long been covered up by the Diadem. Even before knowing the General's secret plans, Goler had begun to turn against the corrupt government. He allowed Ian Walfor to continue his black-market shipping runs, which were strictly forbidden by Constellation law; he doctored or inflated shipments to ease the tribute burden; and he tricked the Diadem into sending him Adolphus's old warships for peacekeeping efforts—the ships that now comprised the core of the fleet defending Hellhole.

When he learned of the new stringline network, Goler immediately realized the implications, saw which way the wind was blowing, and decided to throw in his lot with the rebels. He slept well at night, knowing that he had finally given his support to something he could believe in. . . .

For now, he had to get this grim duty out of the way. He realized the importance of preserving history, making sure everyone knew the atrocities Diadem Michella had committed. If Tasmine hadn't survived that day, no one would ever have known.

"I watched three children run into the goldenwoods," Tasmine continued, "but the soldiers had thermal trackers. They found the children and shot them down." Her eyes glistened with tears. "And then there was a teenage boy who had helped fix my fence—he climbed a high goldenwood tree to get away. The soldiers set a fire around the base of the tree, laughing as the flames rose up. The boy had no place to go, and finally the smoke and heat made him fall to his death."

Goler looked at the old woman. "How did you get away? If they were so thorough, how did they miss you?"

"While gathering herbs, I found a large burrow made by a Ridgetop badger. When I saw the soldiers searching the hills to finish the job, I crawled as deep inside the burrow as I could go, worming my way out of sight. I had seen administrative officers using record tablets in the settlement, keeping a tally of the people they killed, so I knew they would be thorough." Her voice hitched.

"But covered with mud, tangled in among the roots under the tree, their thermal scanners didn't detect me. I could barely stand the smell. Ridgetop badgers stink, and the burrow was full of old filth . . . but it saved me. I emerged when I couldn't stand it anymore."

The old woman shrugged her narrow shoulders. "Missing only one person out of a colony of hundreds—they must have assumed it was a counting mistake, either among the bodies or of their initial records.

They gathered up the corpses, counted them again, and threw them here in a mass grave. Afterward, I lived in that burrow for days, eating the seedcones and mushrooms I found, drinking rainwater. The Constellation soldiers razed the whole town, covered up the mass grave, and cleared the area so a fresh group of colonists could start over, with no hint of our colony."

"All clean and tidy, so the Diadem could pretend it never happened." Goler lifted his chin, raised his voice for all the excavators to hear. "But we won't forget, and we won't let the rest of the Constellation forget. You have changed history, Tasmine."

The old woman looked embarrassed. "All I did was survive. But you, Governor"—her lips curved upward in a smile—"you might not think you're a hero, and I know you never intended to be, but you're changing history as well."

"I'm just doing what's right."

"Sad, isn't it, that choosing to do what's right is enough to make you a hero."

The decayed bodies were falling apart, the bones held together by the remnants of tendons and scraps of muscle tissue. As the drizzle increased, the workers laid each corpse on a canvas rectangle, spreading them out with as much respect as possible. Each skeleton had approximately the right number of parts, and each had a prominent skull, though Goler wasn't sure that the individual pieces belonged together.

The rain stopped, and the clouds parted to show a patch of blue sky. The sunlight warmed the damp hills, and mist began to rise through the goldenwood trees. Tasmine's face remained wet. "I don't know that we're going to survive this rebellion," she said in a quiet voice, "but we can finally be honest. There's no point in keeping secrets. It's time to honor the dead . . . our friends, neighbors, and relatives who died at the Diadem's hand."

Goler called for the lumberjacks to stop their work. "We'll make this place a memorial to all those who died here. We'll erect a tall goldenwood plaque and inscribe the names of those who died so that these victims are never forgotten."

The lumberjacks were covered with mud, but they were smiling. Leaning on brooms and rakes, they looked at him with something he had not seen much of before—admiration. "Cheers for the governor!"

one called, and others took up the cry, adding to it, "Cheers for Tasmine and the governor!"

Goler was deeply moved, but he could not help but wonder how many similar memorials would have to be made before this war was finally over.

20

They finished the entire bottle of brandy. Turlo and Sunitha played games, enjoyed a slow meal, made love . . . and waited.

They knew with a high degree of certainty when the five military haulers were due to pass these coordinates. With the stringline cut and the iperion dissipated around the blown substation, the haulers would career off the path. Moving at hyperluminal speeds, they would cover an immense distance and stray far from where they expected to be. It all depended on how swiftly the hauler pilots reacted to being off-stringline and brought their great framework vessels to a halt.

The Urvanciks needed to find them, so that General Adolphus had his verification.

"This is going to be a good day," Sunitha said. She noted the coordinates where they had left the silent marker buoys to anchor the last segment of stringline back to Hellhole.

"Keep running quiet, no sensor signature," Turlo said, "but leave our own detectors open. When those haulers get disconnected, they'll squall like a baby with diaper rash."

The Constellation fleet—one hundred fully armed ships with fifteen thousand crewmembers—were gung ho and intent on fighting their sworn enemy. But they would fall flat on their faces.

After the time had passed, they combed over their own sensor records and found a tiny blip that indicated when the fleet had flashed by, traveling much too fast for any normal detection. "They've run off the rails and gone off into the void," Turlo said. He considered opening their second bottle of expensive brandy, the one he had hidden well enough that even his wife didn't know about it, but they needed to be at their peak alertness.

Still, it was a damned long time to wait.

Five hours after they detected the first flicker in the sensor traces, panicked transmissions began to come over the comm. "Looks like they overshot by several light hours," Sunitha said. "A few billion kilometers past Substation Four."

"Do you think they'll ever find their way back to the right point?" Turlo asked.

"Not likely. Why would they carry the precise coordinates for a substation that they could easily detect . . . until it was blown up?" She grinned. "They'll have an approximate location, and we know they'll try to find it, but I'm thinking of finding a needle in a haystack the size of a solar system."

Turlo locked in the coordinates of the fleet's frantic transmissions, and Sunitha accelerated the *Kerris* toward the position. In sensor silence they approached the stranded ships, drifting in without any engine noise or thermal output, coming just close enough so that their long-range imagers could spot the huge ships drifting aimlessly.

Exactly as expected: five military stringline haulers loaded with numerous battleships. Sunitha took plenty of images. "The General might want these for his scrapbook. Now let's go deliver them."

Most of the buildings in Michella Town were eyesores, and this factory was no exception. Initially constructed as a cavernous warehouse for rare export minerals for the Diadem's tribute payment, Sophie Vence had converted the facility into a manufacturing plant for rugged vehicles. Now the General joined her on an inspection to see how the machine lines had been retooled to create military equipment.

To defend Hellhole, he had ordered twenty unmanned weapons platforms to be assembled as an orbiting picket line against the Diadem's warships; so far, twelve had been deployed as sentries over the planet. The remote-operated launchers would be much smaller targets than the large guardian battleships, but could strike unsuspecting Constellation vessels.

In addition, by sending blueprints and advice via stringline drones, Sophie had coordinated the conversion of ten additional factories on other DZ planets, so those worlds could take a hand in defending themselves.

Sophie had installed a supervisory station in the warehouse rafters, and the window-encircled enclosure doubled as her office. From the high perch, Adolphus scanned the main-floor assembly lines and two levels of storage mezzanines. He heard the whir and click of the machines, watched as conveyors carried components to the eight weapons platforms being assembled.

At the moment, though, he was far more interested in the Urvanciks' report. Turlo and Sunitha looked pleased as they presented themselves, and Adolphus reviewed the grainy extreme-range images.

"Marooned, just as you planned, sir," Turlo said.

Sophie smiled. "You've bought us a reprieve, Tiber."

"More than a reprieve—victory." He looked at the two linerunners. "You're certain Substation Three blew as well?"

"As certain as we can be, General," Turlo said. "As soon as the haulers rushed past, it should have automatically detonated. The fleet is trapped in the segment between the substations, cut loose. They have no stringline, and they'll never find the unmarked end of a molecule-thin path in all the volume of interstellar space."

Adolphus tried to maintain his professional demeanor, although he wanted to sweep Sophie into an ecstatic hug. "A job well done—and that takes care of our immediate worries. With weeks of breathing room, we can put much more significant DZ defenses in place." He smiled. "The Diadem is already defeated, even if she doesn't know it yet."

"But what do we do about those ships?" Sophie asked. "I'd love to add them to our DZ Defense Forces, but they won't surrender without putting up a hell of a fight."

"Maybe not right now." Adolphus turned away from the factory line below. "We'll let time and fear do our work for us. The fleet can't reach Hellhole, and they can't get back to Sonjeera. According to the intel, they have over fifteen thousand crewmembers, including a great many nobles and midlevel officers. Their warships were loaded in a rush for a mission they expected to last ten days, and they can't possibly have enough supplies and life support to last for more than a few weeks."

Realization dawned on Sophie's face. When her eyes sparkled, she looked ten years younger. The constant strain and uncertainty had made her appear careworn and tired, but now she was again the fresh-faced woman who had brought her young son to Hellhole, ready for a new start.

Adolphus went on. "Even if they had the fuel aboard—very unlikely—it would take them three months, by my guess, to crawl to Hellhole, and at least five months to go back to Sonjeera. So we wait, while they sit alone and isolated in space, let them start to feel hungry and desperate. I don't want to give them hope too soon—they need to feel completely defeated before we round them up."

He looked at the Urvanciks, who seemed to relish the prospect, and continued, "After a few weeks their supplies will be mostly gone, life support failing. Thousands of crewmen will have lost hope. That's when I'll come in with all my ships and accept their surrender. They will know it's their only chance. We won't have to fire a shot."

Sophie laughed. "We'll add another hundred fully armed warships to our own fleet."

"Exactly—*and* remove them from the Army of the Constellation. We weaken them and strengthen ourselves at the same time. The tables have already turned."

21

The mood aboard the Constellation fleet rapidly devolved from exuberance to confusion, then disappointment. They had set out to crush General Adolphus—strike fast, strike hard!—but now that the path had vanished from beneath them, the soldiers were bewildered. After a vague announcement of the delay, military music played over the intercom.

On the bridge of the *Diadem's Glory*, Escobar rested his elbow on the padded arm of the command chair, chin in hand, and stared at the starry view. A hundred warships, an intimidating force . . . but going nowhere.

Gail Carrington stood next to his command chair—much too close, as far as he was concerned. When she spoke, her tone conveyed criticism rather than useful advice. "You must find a way forward, Redcom. Sitting here accomplishes nothing." She was always watching him, breathing down his neck, reacting to his every movement with disapproval. He couldn't recall her ever relaxing.

"I'm not *sitting* here, Ms. Carrington. I am planning our next move. In order to 'find our way forward,' we must follow the stringline, one end or the other. Until then, we can't proceed." Escobar shifted in his seat, feeling like a failure. "Lieutenant Cristaine, it's been six hours. Any word from the scouts yet?"

"They've crisscrossed the vicinity of Substation Four, sir, but they have not yet reacquired the iperion path. Sensor logs give us the exact coordinates of where we went off the line, so we anticipate they'll stumble on the severed terminus, given enough time. We are still searching for the substation itself."

Escobar shook his head in dismay. "Given enough time . . ." Once they found the substation, they could anchor themselves and reassess. But he didn't want to *reassess*. He was a leader. He should be decisive. The son of Commodore Percival Hallholme couldn't dither and bite his nails.

Gail Carrington was watching.

Bolton Crais stepped through the sliding metal doors, preoccupied and shaking his head. "I used my authorization to request that the ship-wide intercoms silence that patriotic music. It seems awkward to play a cheerful anthem when we're just hanging here in space."

Escobar's lips drew together. "Thank you, Major Crais. I should have thought of that detail myself. No need for ironic reminders."

Bolton focused his attention on the Redcom, ignoring Carrington. "I've also ordered the pilots to continue their simulation drills—in fact, I've increased the frequency of the training, to impose a sense of urgency. Everyone is convinced this is only a temporary setback . . . for now."

"It *is* only a temporary setback," Escobar said.

Near him, the comm-officer touched her earadio, then turned to the command chair. "Redcom, one of the scouts located the substation! It's destroyed—sabotage, no doubt—but he did find the intact stringline that leads back to Sonjeera."

The bridge personnel cheered. Sounding relieved, Pilot Suri Dar transmitted from her isolated chambers on the hauler framework. "At least now we can go home safely." Her voice rang out across the bridge.

Escobar chided the stringline pilot. "Have all five haulers regroup at the ruins of Substation Four and await my orders. Major Crais, I want to see you in my office." He forced himself to add, as if taking medicine, "And call the diplomats so they can participate in the discussion." He looked at Gail Carrington. "You're welcome to join us as well, Ms. Carrington."

She said, "I don't need your invitation."

Within an hour, the five haulers had rendezvoused at the ruined substation. Escobar hosted a small meeting with the door closed. Carrington looked hard and aloof, Bolton seemed worried, while Jackson Firth was full of ideas, none of which were practical.

Escobar began the meeting. "General Adolphus has cut the stringline, and we cannot proceed to our target as planned—at least at the moment. We need to find an alternative way to complete our mission."

"We have the route back to Sonjeera, but that does us no good," Carrington said. "Better if we find the *other* end of the severed stringline so we can go forward to planet Hallholme."

Escobar said, "We had precise data on where we fell off the iperion path, so we could backtrack to the substation—and even that took us half a day. With dissipation, the outbound end of the stringline will be much more difficult to find."

"Then we do the difficult thing," Carrington chided.

Bolton had already pondered the situation; he offered his advice before anyone else spoke. "If I may suggest another alternative? Even if the *direct* stringline to planet Hallholme is cut, we still have a roundabout way to get to the General—and to Keana. We could return to the Sonjeera hub and relaunch our fleet to a different Deep Zone world—say, Ridgetop or Candela. Once we overwhelm and secure the rebels there, we commandeer the General's own DZ stringline network and proceed to Hallholme. We'll approach from his flank, where he won't expect us."

"Unless the General has blown all the direct lines from the Crown Jewels," Carrington said.

"The DZ cannot survive without help from the Crown Jewels! That would lead to mass starvation and hardship," Jackson Firth said, then allowed himself a smile. "Hmm, but should that happen, we would be welcomed as saviors by the time we arrive."

Carrington said, "Supreme Commander Riomini has no intention of waiting that long. We must resolve this situation."

Escobar felt the weight on his shoulders. "I have no desire to bring the fleet back to Sonjeera, Major Crais, even if only to launch again for a roundabout assault. It would be embarrassing. We would appear to be returning in defeat."

"But it may be the only way to win," Bolton said.

Escobar could already imagine the catcalls and the ridicule, a sharp contrast to the fanfare that had feted them when they departed: "Strike fast, strike hard!"

Jackson Firth brushed at his collar. "At the very least, now that we've found the return stringline, we must dispatch a message drone. The Diadem needs to know of this setback so she can alter her expectations accordingly. We should wait here for her orders."

Escobar leaned forward to skewer the diplomat with his dark gaze. "I am in command of this fleet, and I make the decisions."

Firth bristled. "Diadem Michella needs to know! We're already delayed."

Bolton pointed out, "It will take days for a message drone to reach Sonjeera, and days more to return, not counting however long the Diadem takes to formulate her response."

"We can't wait that long!" Frustrated, Escobar turned to Carrington, who sat brooding, offering no help whatsoever. "Ms. Carrington, feel free to make suggestions."

"I have yet to hear any plan that I am willing to endorse. I can state without reservation, however, that Lord Riomini would oppose having his glorious fleet return home without firing a single shot, stymied by a juvenile effort to impede our progress."

The diplomat actually raised his voice. "I insist! The Diadem must be informed."

Bolton added, "A discreet message drone with a coded report would be an acceptable alternative to having all our ships return to Sonjeera. The news could be kept quiet—I doubt the Diadem would want to advertise the setback. And in the meantime, we keep searching open space for the outbound end of the stringline. We might get lucky and resolve the problem before we receive a response."

Escobar was flustered, but he needed to make a decision, and that sounded like the best alternative. "Very well. We'll anchor our five haulers here and send a private message back along the stringline. The Diadem and Supreme Commander Riomini must be informed. We can finesse the phrasing, make it a mere informational report, a courtesy message so that the Diadem can update her plans. This is *not* an admission of defeat."

"I can word it properly, sir," Firth said with inappropriate brightness. "My team can be finished within the hour."

"Glad we can get some use out of you, Mr. Firth," Escobar said while thinking otherwise. "In the meantime, I fully expect that somebody aboard will devise a viable solution before we receive a response from Sonjeera."

"Or," Carrington said, "we could just find the other end of the stringline and be on our way."

Escobar ended the meeting and returned to the bridge, where he sat in his command chair and tried to look important. Everyone kept glancing at him, and he could read their thoughts, sense their anxiety, disappointment, and disapproval. They expected more from the son of Commodore Hallholme. To be honest, Escobar expected more from himself.

Once they sent the message drone racing back to the Crown Jewels, he felt the urgency increase. Anxious to solve the problem on his own, rather than let the Diadem give him an answer—or a reprimand— Escobar held private meetings with his engineers, who were also at their wits' end. On impulse, he made a fleet-wide announcement, guaranteeing an extra six months' pay and a personal citation from the Diadem (he was certain he could convince her of that, once they succeeded) to anyone who could offer a solution.

In the ensuing hours, Escobar received numerous submissions of ideas, which his bridge staff vetted. A few suggestions were innovative, but most were ridiculous and poorly thought-out. Although it helped morale to maintain optimism, Escobar worried that they weren't taking the situation seriously enough.

⤜∽⤏

The message drone returned in only two days, far sooner than expected. Even under the highest stringline acceleration, it could not possibly have traversed the distance to the Crown Jewels and back in that time.

Perhaps Lord Riomini had sent another fleet behind them, which was currently closing in. The message drone might have been intercepted and returned. . . .

"A second fleet is not likely, sir. It took us weeks to prepare, load, and launch," Bolton said as the two men went to inspect the recovered message drone. "They could never have dispatched another battle group in only a few days."

As soon as he looked at the returned capsule in the receiving bay, Escobar's heart sank. "This is ours, still sealed." Using the command code, he accessed the interior and found their own message inside, unread. "Why did it bounce back to us?"

Bolton checked the travel log. "It got only as far as Substation Three." He swallowed hard. "The stringline was cut from that end as well."

"Both ends of the segment are severed?" Escobar said. "We're cut off? How did the General do that?"

"With careful planning. Now we can't go forward or back."

Escobar's throat was dry. "General Adolphus has stranded us."

22

The underground museum vault on Hellhole remained a mysterious, terrifying place for Keana, even though she shared her mind with the Xayan leader Uroa. His alien memories were elusive, explaining little to her; the chamber was filled with secrets and haunted by ancient alien spirits.

Working alongside the Original alien Lodo, the team of human investigators had spent several months combing through the countless stockpiled treasures—relics, bits of technology, stored knowledge, and cultural landmarks. The General had placed Cristoph de Carre in charge of the effort, to guide the engineers and experts.

Carvings and designs adorned the rock walls, and teams of xeno-archaeologists and scholars studied them, with Lodo's assistance. It was the work of years, probably decades, to compile even a perfunctory *inventory* of the miracles stored here, much less catalog and understand them. She saw the artifacts around her, small containers and decorative items as well as exquisite little jeweled creatures made of shaped stone and silver and gold. The alien designs meant nothing to Keana as she viewed them with her own eyes, but Uroa's presence identified the patterns.

"One day we will be able to share the lost Xayan history," Cristoph said, "but at the moment we have more pragmatic concerns. Our priority is to identify some scrap that might be converted into a weapon or defensive technology."

Lodo swayed his humanoid torso from side to side. "Most of the Xayan race was focused on cooperation with a common goal, striving to achieve *ala'ru*. Why would we need weapons?" His caterpillar body moved in a wet whisper of motion.

Keana detected a hint of avoidance in Lodo's answer, and words surfaced in her consciousness from Uroa's personality. He spoke through her voice: "This vault holds secrets to be unlocked, Cristoph de Carre—and some of them may be dangerous."

Though they had worked closely together for weeks, ever since Keana had awakened from her coma, Cristoph remained awkward around her because of the unwitting part she'd played in the downfall of his family. She had fundamentally changed after her immersion in the slickwater, and was no longer the flighty, self-centered woman who had drifted through a privileged life. Fortunately, there was a war to distract them while they cobbled together a relationship.

Now, though, he perked up at her comment. "Dangerous? Could they be useful as weapons?"

"The answer is the same," Uroa said. Though Keana strained to see deeper into her mental companion's thoughts, she could find no clearer answers.

Lodo cautioned Uroa, "We discussed the possibilities in Xayan convocation. Encix advised against the use of inappropriate power."

"I sided with Zairic," Uroa said, "and Encix did not lead my faction. She always was difficult."

"And you always were careless," Lodo replied. A hint of humor? Or a stinging rebuke? Keana could not tell.

Each time they arrived in the vault, strange lights and shapes accompanied them like spectral escorts, wavering and crackling in the air, vanishing and reappearing like wisps of colored smoke. Several dropped from the tunnel ceiling in front of Keana's face, as if recognizing the presence of Uroa within her. As always, she felt a tingling sensation on her face and arms when the luminous afterimages touched her skin, but she knew the manifestations were harmless.

In the vault's large central chamber, five sarcophagus chambers had held the preserved Originals while they waited for centuries, clinging to the vanishingly small chance that someone would eventually discover them. Only five Xayans had survived the asteroid impact, but Allyf had died during the centuries of stasis, Cippiq had been murdered by the Diadem, and Tryn had departed along with a hundred shadow-Xayans to form a seed colony on Candela. Now only Lodo and Encix remained on Hellhole. *Xaya.*

Back at the height of their former civilization, the Xayans had never ventured beyond their own planet. How could they rely on such infinitesimal hopes? Though previously Uroa had shared his memories and thoughts with her, now she heard only silence.

After hours of intriguing but ultimately fruitless searching, Keana and Cristoph followed Lodo back out of the tunnel to the guarded opening in the side of the mountain. The other engineers and archaeologists continued their cataloging work, but Keana was losing hope that they would find any miraculous solution before her mother sent a massive retaliation—and she knew her mother would strike as soon as she was able.

Fortunately, Devon-Birzh and Antonia-Jhera worked with the thousands of shadow-Xayans to practice their telemancy as a defensive measure. And General Adolphus had his own traditional military plans.

From her interactions with the Originals, Keana knew that Encix was willing to save the planet, but only in order for the Xayans to achieve their racial ascension. Encix did not seem overly concerned with the safety of humans for their own sake. Were the Originals just using the hybrid vigor exhibited by the shadow-Xayans to achieve what *they* wanted? Although she was merged with Uroa, and felt his longing for *ala'ru* as well, Keana vowed not to abandon the human colonists on Hellhole.

Guards and observers remained outside the entrance to the museum vault, ready to use lethal force to prevent any Constellation spies from discovering the existence of the Xayan chamber. As Keana and her companions stepped out into the open air, one of the sentries whistled to draw their attention, but not in alarm.

"Over there!" The sentry pointed to a rolling cloud along the ground in the valley below.

Keana heard a distant thunder of noise, and she and Cristoph climbed to the lookout shack on top of a knoll. "A storm?" she asked.

"A *herd*," said the voice of Uroa inside her head.

The sentry handed Keana a set of distance lenses. When she adjusted the focus, she could see a charging line of four-legged animals, like bison, moving across the valley floor, stirring up dust, razing the native vegetation in their path. She caught her breath. "So many of them! But where did they come from?"

"They are native to Xaya." Lodo gazed out at the moving mass of animals and spoke the name of the creatures, a strange, incomprehensible word that vibrated through his face membrane.

Uroa provided Keana with his own memories of large herds of these creatures on the verdant plains of old Xaya, majestic beasts that moved together.

Beside her, Cristoph and the sentry were both awed into quiet reverence. The large animals plunged on, like a wave sweeping across the prairie. "They're magnificent!" Cristoph said. "But those creatures should be extinct. The asteroid killed all large animals How could they come back?"

"There have been previous sightings of individual animals," Keana pointed out. "Recently. Why now?"

"Many signs are apparent," Lodo said in a mysterious, distant voice. "This planet is awakening."

23

Once she learned the Constellation fleet was stranded and helpless, Sophie could finally catch her breath and get down to the real work. Surviving on a frontier world required austerity and careful planning, but she was convinced that the Deep Zone no longer needed anything from the Crown Jewels.

As Hellhole's emergency quartermaster, she made a point of inspecting foundries, mines, even an explosives factory out in the bleak mountains. She had started construction on two new greenhouse domes, and assisted the farmers in providing fertilizers and hardy seed stock. At times, she felt like a watchful mother to the planet. . . .

Handing Adolphus sheets of account records, she said, "Even without enemy battleships breathing down our necks, our hardest challenge will be surviving the next few months. We're laying in harvests and stockpiling preserved food, receiving deliveries from other DZ planets to fill in the gaps. We'll have to scrape by on what we have, but we're in good shape . . . under the circumstances. We can do it." She lounged against his desk. "Want to come with me? I've got a delivery for Armand Tillman."

Adolphus had spent two days in his offices at Elba reviewing the images of Escobar Hallholme's fleet, sending the victorious announcement to other planetary administrators. He ordered the sixty ships in orbit to remain on alert and perform constant drills, and he test fired the weap-ons platforms in place.

Now he looked up at her and smiled. "Good idea. I need to thank him for the steaks he sent over—and for the meat that'll feed our sol-diers during the crisis."

Armand Tillman was a prominent, resourceful businessman who had expanded grazing lands and provided insulated shelters so that his herd thrived even in the rigorous environment. Recently, he devoted his ranch output to the Deep Zone Defense Force.

Heading out to the open range on the fringe of Michella Town, their aerocopter traveled through the milky-gray sky of a dissipating smoke storm. Sophie saw the pasturelands and agricultural fields that Tillman nurtured with automated irrigation and fertilizer systems. On Hellhole, where a new agricultural matrix had to be laid down on the scoured landscape, cattle manure proved almost as valuable as the meat itself. Sophie's greenhouse domes in Helltown produced large amounts of fruits and vegetables, but once open-field farming was established, the crop yield would increase by orders of magnitude, provided the plants sur-vived the frequent storms, electrical discharges, and dust clouds.

The aerocopter landed near the livestock nursery building, and the noise of the aircraft brought Tillman to the doorway. He waved, and Sophie shouted through the dying engine noise as she stepped to the ground. "The stork has a delivery today. You're the proud papa of some kids—goat kids. We brought two hundred embryos."

Grinning, Tillman pointed out to his pastures where his cattle were grazing. "Beef isn't enough?"

"Goats might not produce the best-tasting meat, but they're hardy animals for a tough environment, providing good milk and cheese," Adolphus said as he opened the back of the aerocopter to remove the sealed cases. "More food for the troops."

Before Hellhole cut itself off from the Crown Jewels, Sophie had been using backdoor contacts to obtain shipments of equipment, sup-plies, and special items, including a case of goat embryos, ready for incu-bation. Tillman was a cattleman, but he would diversify his herd if called on to do so.

"I paid for these embryos myself," Sophie said. "No charge to you, so long as you keep supplying the military at cost."

Tillman helped them carry the embryos into a temperature-controlled room. "Doesn't do me much good to make a profit if the Constellation fleet levels our settlements and arrests the survivors."

"We may have taken care of that problem," Adolphus said with a smile, then explained how he had circumvented the attack.

They passed glassed-in enclosures where cattle embryos were grown and nurtured in successively larger tanks. In small pens, Tillman's handlers tended newborn animals that were so young that they were uncertain on their feet. "Once we have a large enough artificial herd with sufficient genetic diversity, we can let nature take its course," he said.

They strolled outside, where Tillman pointed to fields of hardy alfalfa and grasses. "When they're ready we'll release the animals into the pastures to fend for themselves, breed, increase their numbers." He scratched his sideburns. "They can be happy until they're called to serve—or should I say, *be* served."

Several of Tillman's ranch hands began shouting and pointed to the south. On the horizon, Sophie spotted an ominous cloud coming toward them over the dry hills, looking like black static. "What the hell is that?"

Tillman squinted through a distance lens, then handed it to her. "Nothing good. Looks like millions of locusts. Never seen anything like that around here before."

The General frowned. "Hellhole infestations don't tend to be pleasant."

The ranch staff began running. Tillman hurried toward a gate as alarm bells sounded. Workers streamed out of the facilities, powering up all-terrain rollers to start driving the cattle to shelters.

A blond, bearded foreman shouted orders. A strong gust of wind slammed the nearest gate shut, and Sophie pulled it open, her hair blowing. After the all-terrain roller had passed through the gate, she and the General climbed aboard as Tillman raced out into the grazing lands.

Tillman and his crew chased as many of his cattle as possible, driving them into runways that led to large barns. Sophie kept watch, saw a few outlier insects whipping in the air overhead. She had heard Devon's stories of the cannibal beetles that had shredded an entire settlement of religious isolationists.

As the buzzing, blurry swarm swept toward them, the General shouted, "That's enough, Tillman! We've got to get to shelter ourselves."

"Half of my herd is still outside!"

"And you can rebuild it with the other half—but not if the bugs eat you."

The locust cloud descended upon the buildings, and Tillman roared the vehicle inside one of the barns; Sophie leaped out before it had come to a stop and ran to the door controls as a few last cattle ran into the shelter. The thick doors rolled down and sealed in place as the buzzing outside grew louder. Inside the enclosure, the panicky cattle lowed and milled about, bumping against gates and walls.

Sophie and Adolphus joined Tillman near the sealed windows, wiping sweat and dust from their faces. "We don't even know if those insects are a threat," she said, hardly convincing herself. The tension grew as the insect swarm fluttered over and around the ranch, and they could hear the bellows and squeals of the remaining cattle stranded outside the shelters.

Sophie watched the swarm of colorful and delicate insects flitting about like butterflies. The bugs landed everywhere, settling on the cattle and crops, covering everything like a blizzard with brown and yellow wings.

As the nervous ranch hands whispered, Adolphus said, "They remind me of mayflies on Qiorfu."

Tillman shook his head. "A swarm like that, hatching all at once, moving across the landscape. They look innocuous—maybe we got lucky."

"Any creatures that survived the aftermath of the asteroid impact aren't generally innocuous," Sophie said. "We still need to be careful."

The ranch foreman came up to Tillman, "Should I go collect a few specimens for the xeno-biologists back in Helltown?"

"Stay inside until they're gone," Adolphus said. "I wouldn't be quite so optimistic yet."

The straggler animals outside clumped together for protection on the far end of the pastures. The butterfly creatures continued to alight on them, but apparently without biting or stinging, since the cattle seemed unperturbed. They watched the slow, hypnotic tableau for more than an hour, and Sophie began to relax, her concern replaced by a sense of wonder.

When the butterfly creatures finally flitted into the air, they rose in a graceful swoop, like a migrating flock, and moved on. The colorful cloud was gone as quickly as it had arrived, flying off toward the hills in the distance. Adolphus suggested waiting another fifteen minutes, just to be sure, and then they ventured outside.

A few straggler insects swirled around the barn buildings before following the rest of the swarm toward the horizon. Ranch hands wore gloves and scooped up some of the sluggish bugs, sealing them in specimen containers.

As Tillman walked around the main buildings, he examined the structures and grounds with a dawning grin on his face. "I don't see any damage."

"Maybe we did get lucky," Sophie said.

When they were finished with the inspection, Tillman went to his roller and swung himself inside. "Better round up the loose cattle and check them out," he shouted over the engine noise. "You two want to come along?"

She and Adolphus climbed into the spare seats. Out in the pastures, the stranded cattle were becoming anxious, as if in pain. Sophie saw no reason for the animals to be skittish, but as the vehicle pulled up, she realized that the cattle hides were covered with blisters that grew visibly larger. The cattle lowed in pain and fear.

The General held up his hand. "Don't get any closer, Tillman."

With a lurch, the rancher halted the vehicle at a safe distance and stared. "What's happening to my herd?"

He'd barely spoken the question before the cattle hides erupted, the festering sores bubbling and boiling. The blisters burst open to reveal millions of grublike larvae crawling over the agonized animals.

He prepared to swing out, but the General held him back. "No, those butterfly things laid eggs everywhere." The swarming grubs began devouring the cattle, tunneling inside the bovine bodies, releasing a hideous stench. The animals staggered and collapsed, rotting where they fell.

"It's so fast!" Sophie said.

Adolphus got on the roller's codecall to contact the other ranch hands. "We need to get flame guns, burn the carcasses, torch the whole pasture before it spreads!"

Looking ill, Tillman swung the roller around, keeping his distance from the collapsing cattle. "Retreat to the barns!"

Before they could round up the fuel and flame guns and rush back out to the infestation, the larvae had devoured the carcasses and completed an astonishingly swift metamorphosis. While Tillman's ranch hands approached the pasture with their equipment, another flock of the colorful butterfly insects rose from the shreds of dead cattle, testing their wings. The new swarm flew off, following the breezes to other feeding grounds. . . .

Sophie swallowed hard and stared out at the dead cattle, the battered grazing lands. "It's hard enough to prepare for war against the Constellation. But the planet is fighting against us, too."

24

With the doors sealed, Bolton sat at the boardroom table, listening to the private brainstorming session with the Red Commodore, Gail Carrington, Jackson Firth, and the fleet's two best stringline engineers.

The five military haulers had been stalled in space for six days now. Crew morale had plummeted. Though the Redcom had twice given rallying speeches across the fleet-wide intercom, he had offered them little reason to hope. The search continued for the end of the outbound stringline that would guide them to Hellhole, but so far they had no luck.

When Carrington spoke, Bolton flinched at the vehemence in her voice. Until now, Lord Riomini's observer had watched, but made few comments, and she surprised them all by unleashing her ire. "You were placed in command of this operation, Red Commodore. You carry the expectations of the Constellation as well as the personal support of the Diadem herself. Your ineffectiveness reflects badly on Supreme Commander Riomini—and I cannot allow that. In a crisis, a true commander does *something,* even if it's not the right thing. You have done nothing, Redcom, nothing at all."

"I'm holding this meeting to weigh our options."

"You're moving too slowly!"

Escobar spoke in an acid tone. "Thank you for your opinion, Ms. Carrington. Perhaps you would like to present me with a miracle solution?" He stared at her, and she stared back. Bolton could smell the tension around him.

"Find the other end of the stringline," she demanded, "the one that leads to planet Hallholme. It's out there, somewhere. Take risks. Venture farther. Obviously, it isn't here, so we need to range wider, expand the search across a greater volume of space." She gestured to the two engineers, who huddled down in chairs on the side of the table as if wishing they could be invisible. "The alternative is to sit here and rot."

"Or starve," Bolton muttered.

"Chances of finding the other end of the stringline are small, Redcom, but it is possible," said the thinner of the two engineers, whose hair was pure white, though he did not appear to be old. "Based on the location of Substation Four, we can make projections."

"But there is some risk," said the other engineer. "The substation was destroyed at least six days ago, possibly seven. Without the collimation anchor, the iperion concentration close to the severed ends will have dissipated. Finding a trail that is only a molecule thick in all this open space is very unlikely."

"A small chance is preferable to no chance," Carrington said.

"But if we wander from our position, then we truly will be lost," Bolton pointed out. "How will rescuers find us?"

Carrington didn't try to hide her anger. "There are no rescuers. The stringline segment is *severed* behind us! The Constellation could never reach us without some sort of specially outfitted long-range ship. We can't expect any help from Sonjeera. We have only ourselves."

"What about General Adolphus?" one of the engineers suggested.

Gail Carrington glowered around the room. "The success of the mission is paramount, but *failure* is not acceptable under any circumstances. Better that we are lost without a trace than captured by the enemy. We cannot allow these ships to fall into the General's hands."

Escobar sounded defeated. "So we expand our search, keep our scouts wandering the emptiness 'round the clock in hopes of blundering onto the stringline?"

"As each day goes by, we'll have to range far because of the continuing dissipation of iperion," said the white-haired engineer. "If you want an expanded search, it would be best to disperse the five stringline haulers to cover as much volume as possible. Equip our fighter craft with detectors, send them out to comb space in ever-widening circles. Given enough time and ships . . ."

"Can't we just draw a straight line to planet Hallholme?" Escobar asked. "We know where the path *should* be."

"Not a valid assumption, sir," the engineer said. "Substations rely on gravitational curves, ripples in space-time to route the iperion path for the most efficient stringline travel. With Substations Three and Four gone, the existing iperion line could have wandered far afield."

"We are between systems with no landmarks," added the second engineer. "We're already marooned. If we don't find the stringline in our search, the effort could put us in a far worse situation."

Escobar laughed at that. "Worse? If we just sit here, we will surely die. A small chance is better than nothing."

Noticing the change in the Redcom's mood, Bolton said nothing. He saw merit in Escobar's caution as well as in Carrington's more aggressive position. Out here in deep space, in an unexpectedly disastrous situation, there were no easy answers.

Gail Carrington did not look satisfied. "After cutting the line, General Adolphus must think he's safe. But if we locate the stray end of the stringline, then we can crash down upon him." Her hands clenched into tight fists. "And make him pay for his crimes. I would like to bring the General's head to Lord Riomini myself."

"First we need to find the stringline," Bolton said. His stomach fluttered. He thought of Keana, how he had been a poor husband, doing a miserable job of watching out for her. When they'd married, he'd been aware of her naïveté and impetuousness. Bolton believed he had a solid head on his shoulders, while the Diadem's daughter often went off on flights of fancy, embracing causes but not really knowing what to do with herself. In a way, he had found it endearing; he was not a perfect man either.

After he learned that she had been trapped, and possibly brainwashed, on Hellhole, he wanted to be there for Keana, to save her and show her that he still supported her. Now, however, it looked as if he himself, and all the members of the Constellation fleet, were the ones who needed saving. . . .

"Then we range as far as necessary and devote all our resources to the search," Escobar said. "We've got to find the path."

25

Ten days should have been long enough for Sonjeera to hear at least an initial report. Knowing the old Commodore's son, the Diadem expected Escobar would have been quick to crow about his victory.

Michella did not like to wait for anything. As a child, she had been impatient and easily frustrated over trivial matters, anxious to receive a toy or a favorite dessert. She wanted everything right away, and that was how she felt now.

Nevertheless, not even a Diadem could overcome the laws of physics. Stringline travel was extremely fast, but not instantaneous. Four days for the Constellation fleet to reach Hallholme, and four days for a message drone to return. But she had already allowed two extra days. Escobar Hallholme, or at least Bolton Crais, should have been more attentive.

At this very moment, she imagined that the attack force was consolidating its hold on planet Hallholme; they should have captured or killed General Adolphus and seized the new DZ stringline hub. Her loyal soldiers were probably rounding up the thousands of hostages she would punish here in a massive show trial.

But she hadn't heard anything.

Selik Riomini met her out in the palace horp stables where she was feeding the animals. Unable to disguise his concern, he said, "The fleet had explicit orders to send us an initial report upon their arrival. Gail Carrington is always more reliable than this."

His female bodyguards remained outside the stable doors to give them privacy, but Michella had no doubt they were eavesdropping. The new lead bodyguard, Lora Heston, perked up when Riomini mentioned Carrington's name. Sound-enhancer implants in her ears? Probably.

One of the horp stallions stretched its long black neck over the railing to gobble an apple from Michella's open palm, then snorted for another. The impatient creature reminded the Diadem of herself, but she was not amused by its behavior.

"Nothing should have gone wrong," she said with a sour frown, "but this is General Adolphus. Are you sure Redcom Hallholme was sufficiently prepared?"

"I'm sure he did not underestimate the General, Eminence." The Black Lord was careful to stay back from the animals to keep his dark uniform unsoiled. "Yesterday, I dispatched a message drone to demand information. As soon as I hear any word, I will inform you."

The horp continued to pester her for another apple, but she pushed his round snout away. She hated not knowing what was going on. To distract herself, Michella reached into a bucket for another apple, ignored the black stallion, and moved to the next stall to give the treat to a white horp broodmare. This animal was her favorite, because the mare demanded nothing, merely waited while Michella fed her as much or as little as she wished. In the other stall, the black stallion made importunate grunts.

"On to other business, Eminence." Riomini brought out a sheaf of documents. "As we discussed, I developed a punitive strike on another Deep Zone world, which will serve as a warning to the rebels." He spread the papers out on a bale of hay that served as a makeshift table. "I also have electronic files, if you prefer."

"Just give me a summary." She had already decided to let him do as he wished, give him a chance to prove his heroism and leadership abilities to the Constellation. Either way, Michella would benefit: Based on his own performance, Selik would crown himself the next Diadem or remove his name from consideration. "And which planet have you chosen?"

"The most opportune target is Theser, as explained in my plan."

"Theser?" She looked at the documents, read a summary of the attack plan, and flipped to an astronomical chart on the next page. "Quite an obscure frontier world."

"Everything in the Deep Zone is obscure, Eminence." He smiled. "I have already begun gathering my strike force, twenty-three warships, two military stringline haulers."

"Don't waste Constellation resources on grandstanding."

"Necessary insurance, Eminence—not grandstanding. Theser is the best choice for several reasons. The planet is a kind of technological oasis, a source of innovation and engineering advancement. Those high-tech industries might be vital to the General's plans. And Theser is holding one of your loyal territorial governors as a political prisoner."

Michella tried to remember the names of her Deep Zone governors and which one had gone astray. "Who?"

Even Riomini had to check his notes. "Marla Undine."

"Undine? Oh, I had almost forgotten about her. Yes, rescuing her would make for good propaganda. Yes, we can claim our strike is in response to the governor's illegal arrest. By all means, grind Theser into dust. This whole mess should have been over by now."

After yet another day with no word from the Constellation fleet, the Diadem was significantly worried. The public had begun to whisper about what might have gone wrong, so she issued instructions for continued patriotic rallies, asking her citizens to pray for the troops engaged in battle.

When Riomini arrived at her private chambers, she could tell by the gray cast to his features that he bore grave news. "I know why we have heard no word, Eminence. The stringline has been severed. Planet Hallholme is cut off from Sonjeera."

She fumed. "And what of our fleet? Are they returning?"

"No sign of the five stringline haulers."

"Do you think Adolphus is responsible?"

"No, for the simple reason that the substation wasn't destroyed until *after* our fleet had flown past. The General would never have been so sloppy."

She felt agitated. "Our warships are still on their way, then. They can hammer the enemy defenses, even if they can't send a message home right away."

"My thoughts exactly, Eminence. The General *will* be defeated." He fidgeted, as if expecting her to change her mind. "However, this makes my attack on Theser even more critical. Not only will we punish another rebel world, but we can also seize the Theser stringline terminus and ride the General's own network to planet Hallholme. From there, we will reinforce the Constellation fleet."

She could see the eagerness in his eyes. "But if you take so many ships, won't that leave the Crown Jewels poorly defended in the meantime? The Army of the Constellation will be stretched too thin. Now that Deep Zone tribute payments have dried up, we may see some unrest here as well. It's a time for strength."

"Not to worry, Eminence. I will bring in all the reserves from the Lubis Plain shipyards." She could see the eager flush on Riomini's face. "We cannot let this opportunity slip through our fingers."

She knew he was right. "Very well, Selik. When can you be ready to launch for Theser?"

He answered without hesitation. "Immediately. Of course."

26

shop Heer stood in the busy air terminal building with his bookish-looking assistant, reviewing details before they each left on their next assignment. So much to do, another assassination, as well as tedious paperwork.

His family's seven centuries of legally imposed banishment from the noble ranks would end soon, and he had to make certain to take care of every detail. He had his lists, and could always count on Laderna Nell. Such an efficient woman. Though he found it unnerving sometimes when she took brash actions on her own without telling him until afterward, he did not usually disagree with her decisions.

When Laderna first discovered the ancient criminal insult that had ruined and stripped Ishop's family, she had eliminated the first person on their list of assassinations—Lady Opra Mageros—without even asking him. Once Ishop learned the details from the moldy historical archives, he fully supported her plans, and together they relished working their way through the list.

Sometimes, Laderna was so attuned to him, he felt as if she could read his mind. Knowing her feelings of attraction toward him, he had allowed himself to become her lover—in a celebratory sense, whenever they crossed another name off the list. Somewhat gangly, Laderna had red hair and a long neck, and she drank too much kiafa, which made her frenetic and edgy at times. She was not the sort of woman he considered attractive, but she had an earnestness that he found appealing.

However, her increasing feelings for him were becoming disturbing. And now when he looked into her brown, almond-shaped eyes, he detected a softness toward him.

"Be careful on this mission, boss," Laderna said. "I wouldn't want anything to happen to you."

Surely she knew their relationship was all business, despite the sex? She was intelligent enough to understand all the intricate clockwork of the overall scheme and not allow silly schoolgirl emotions to wreck the smooth-running machinery.

The two of them stood out of earshot of the spaceport crowds, near a ventilation fan that provided a background drone. "Watch yourself, too." He let a smile play around his mouth. "Genealogy can be dangerous work."

That morning they had made love in a secondary office that he maintained on a backstreet. Now, to wish her luck as she departed, he gave her a lingering kiss. When she walked away, she looked back and smiled, then strode across the terminal building to board a shuttle.

He was heading out on his own assignment, murdering a member of one of the three remaining families on the list. Laderna had wanted to join him in the task, insisting it was her turn, but she proved so much better at meticulous research than he was. And although she could kill people when necessary, he was better at it than she was. Each of them had a particular set of skills.

During his years of service to the Diadem, Ishop had grown comfortable with murder whenever it was necessary. So far, Michella had asked him to eliminate five troublesome political and business rivals, and with Laderna's help he had murdered eight others for his own purposes, crossing one name after another off his list.

Those victims were personal, descendants of the nobles who had stripped the Osheer family of wealth and prominence. Seven centuries did not make the wound any less raw to him, even though he would soon be allowed to reclaim his noble title.

Justice had been a long time coming, but he and Laderna were almost finished with their list. First things first.

Ishop completed his task without complications, as usual. He had plotted the careful "accident" of a dropped sheet-crystal windowpane onto the unsuspecting businessman Tann Ciarli. Ciarli wasn't much of a noble; his family's influence had waned significantly from when they had participated in the ruin of the Osheer family in the distant past. The man also beat his children, according to reports.

Ishop had hoped for a well-choreographed spectacle, with the toppling sheet crystal decapitating Ciarli, but the sharp pane had tumbled in the air and broken in half, making a butchered mess of the victim. Not the finesse he would have liked, but a success nevertheless.

When he met Laderna at the redstone townhouse they shared, her eyes shone as she presented him with her discoveries as well. He found the archival details far more interesting than the story of killing yet another guilty noble.

"Plenty of colorful details, boss," she said. "It really helps paint the picture of your ancestors' tribulations, how they were caught up in political machinations, lost the game."

Since learning of his family's long-ago disgrace, Ishop had become fascinated by his history, wanting to learn more details about why they had been exiled to the backwater Crown Jewel planet Ogg. Heading there to study civic records, Laderna had sifted through old files, reconstructed the history, connected the dots, and now proudly presented him with the full story, including names and dates of the people involved, the failed attempts to thwart schemers that had taken everything from the Osheer family, the alliances and trumped-up legal documents and court cases that stole Ishop's heritage.

"In hindsight, boss," Laderna said, "your ancestors were naïve, didn't safeguard themselves against their enemies. I think they were surprised when they were buried under the avalanche of plots."

Ishop read the new report: A group of treacherous nobles had gathered valuable planetary assets for themselves, then conspired to manufacture false charges against Lord Elman Osheer. Sensing a plump fruit for the picking, they had brought about Elman's disgrace, maneuvering the Council into issuing a censure that stripped his family of noble titles for a period of seven hundred years, while they divided up the spoils.

Now certain descendants of those traitors were losing everything as well, thanks to Ishop and Laderna.

His own ancestors might not have been ready for the web of treachery that destroyed them, but he was smarter than that. And more determined.

The destruction of the Osheer family bore disturbing parallels to what he himself had recently perpetrated against the de Carre family, as ordered by the Diadem. Louis de Carre had been distracted and incompetent, a fool in a world full of predators, much like Lord Elman Osheer. Lord de Carre had already been destroyed by the schemes and sabotage of the Riominis—he'd lost his wealth, his planet, his honor; his son had been exiled, the whole family ruined—and yet Michella commanded Ishop to murder the poor fop as well, to make it look like a shameful suicide. Was that really necessary?

Ishop had the blood of de Carre on his own hands, and he didn't like it very much.

He shook off any disturbing echoes of guilt. Ishop had his own honor to uphold, and the situation was now reversed. Since he was not a commoner after all, he had to start acting like a noble, with noble actions.

In the meantime, to make everything neat, tidy, and satisfying, he had two more people to kill while he was still a "commoner."

And one of them was a Duchenet. . . .

27

Back on Candela, Tanja Hu worked at her office in the harbor city of Saporo, waiting for the Theser engineers to finish installing engines in the six warships that would defend her planet. She found her administrative work much more difficult without her assistant, Bebe Nax—a catalyst, a rudder, an organizer, a sounding board, and a good friend. Now that Bebe devoted her energies to fostering the shadow-Xayan seed colony out near the iperion mines, as well as managing the mines herself, Tanja rarely saw the woman.

Over the years of her service, Bebe had been a devoted, detail-oriented person. Tanja had hired other assistants, but none had worked out as well; the woman could do the work of three. Now, frustrated with details that her other employees let slip through the cracks, Tanja flew her own aircraft out to the iperion mines. She needed advice and, most of all, she just wanted to see Bebe.

As usual, the two women greeted each other with hugs. Tanja regarded the small, feisty woman with a sigh of relief. "Please tell me the mines and the shadow-Xayan colony are running smoothly." She needed something to be going well, without unnecessary complications.

Bebe's dark brown eyes glittered when she replied. "I wouldn't have it any other way. How is Jacque doing?" Bebe had placed her ten-year-old son in a dormitory in Saporo where he could continue his education.

"As of last week he was doing well at school. I think he'd learn just as much from being around you, though."

Bebe's eyes misted over. "Tell him I'll come to visit as soon as I can get away. I miss him." Tanja kept herself so focused on the Constellation threat that she sometimes forgot that other people had personal lives. Bebe proved to be a good reminder for her.

As if to set aside thoughts of the boy, Bebe gestured toward the newly built settlement on a wooded hillside near the mining operations. The buildings consisted of alien telemancy-formed structures mingled with standard prefab housing units.

Tel Clovis walked up from the small settlement and joined the two women. He served as an intermediary between the shadow-Xayans and Bebe. "We strive to prove ourselves useful here, Administrator Hu. We have been practicing our telemancy to protect Candela, and to prepare our race for *ala'ru*." He guided them toward an arrangement of the exotic, free-form buildings. "Come, this might interest you."

The alien structures had smooth architectural lines, supposedly identical to old Xayan buildings. The caterpillar form of Tryn moved among the structures, accompanied by shadow-Xayans who gathered in the center of the colony. Tel Clovis smiled, a strange and placid expression that cut through his persistent aura of sadness, and before Tanja could ask what he intended, the new alien-form buildings uprooted themselves and lifted into the air. The clustered shadow-Xayans were airborne, too, and the levitating structures began to spin, slowly at first, and then faster until they became a blur. In a matter of moments the floating settlement vanished entirely, and then the blur came back into view, the free-form buildings spinning slower and slower, until they settled down to the ground again.

"Interesting," Tanja said. "But what purpose does it serve?"

"Maybe to demonstrate their abilities?" Bebe suggested.

"It was an experiment with a specific objective," Tel said as the slug-like Original alien approached, accompanied by two shadow-Xayan companions.

Tryn bent her humanoid torso atop the caterpillar body in an awkward attempt at a bow. "That was an effort to connect with the others back on Xaya. We can link minds across space through telemancy strands, somewhat like your stringline paths. We must remain joined with the rest of our race for harmony, and all of us keep building toward *ala'ru*."

Tanja knew how the human converts clung together, almost like a hive mind. "It must be difficult to be so far from the other shadow-Xayans."

"While you were away on Theser, we had a few problems," Bebe said. "Five of the new colonists panicked at being away from their own world—they levitated themselves back to the spaceport and tried to commandeer a stringline ship. Before Tryn could bring them under control, they injured two security personnel, using telemancy to hurl objects at them. Fortunately, things have quieted down considerably since then."

"All five are now contributing members of the colony," Tel Clovis added. "But I also feel the loss of being so far away. Renny's memories remain somewhere in the slickwater pools back on Xaya."

Tryn said, "In the demonstration you just witnessed, my shadow-Xayans enabled me to feel the auras of Encix and Lodo, as well as the thousands of other shadow-Xayans gathered back home . . . but we must continue to train, and advance. The stronger we become, and the more Xayan memories we reawaken from the slickwater, the greater our chances of ascension."

"We help you, and you help us." Tanja placed her hands on her narrow hips. "Protect the Deep Zone from Constellation attack, and you're welcome to do your *ala'ru* afterward."

"That is our intent," Tryn said. "We have given our word." The Original turned and glided back toward the settlement.

⊸⇝

Since Tanja had traveled out to the distant location, Bebe Nax led the planetary administrator on a full inspection tour of the nearby iperion mines.

After leaving the small shadow-Xayan colony, they stopped at a small office building just outside the main shafts. Iperion production continued at a substantial pace, with shipments regularly dispatched to the stringline hub at Hellhole and distributed throughout the DZ for line maintenance. Tanja needed her own iperion supply for the linerunners establishing new routes from her Candela hub. The decentralization would benefit the Deep Zone, giving all frontier worlds the freedom to establish their own trade relationships.

The two women entered Bebe's temporary office and made tea in a kitchenette. Tanja asked about the intransigent Governor Undine; on her specific instructions, the political prisoner was being held under appalling conditions in a nearby swampy area, the mudflats that marked a devastated town. After all the suffering the Constellation had caused here, Tanja did not feel guilty about making this midlevel figurehead miserable. She relished the images of the squalid, disgusting holding cell.

Bebe, though, was uncomfortable about what she had done. "You did give me specific instructions to make her suffer, but . . . Governor Undine is a recognized representative from the Constellation. Are you sure this isn't being too extreme?" Here, in private, Bebe spoke to her as a friend rather than a formal assistant.

Tanja sniffed, feeling all her bitterness toward the corrupt government. "Extreme? Hardly. Don't forget the people of Puhau, buried under meters of mud because of what the Diadem forced us to do." She could not drive away the memories of her uncle Quinn, who had been the first manager of these iperion mines, before Michella's greed for more and more tribute shipments killed him by forcing the unsafe mining practices. "Governor Undine can be uncomfortable until General Adolphus tells us what to do with her. I expect we'll use her to send a message to Sonjeera."

Bebe nodded. She had made her point and accepted the response. "I'll make sure Undine causes no problems. And I'll keep the iperion mines running smoothly. Just a matter of attention to detail."

Tanja sipped her steaming tea. "What would I do without you, Bebe?"

"You'd govern less effectively."

They traveled from the admin office to the iperion mines, where they encountered four grave-looking guards manhandling a male prisoner whose head was bloody and bandaged. One of the angry guards looked up, recognized her. "Administrator Hu! We caught a spy taking images in one of the airshafts of Mine Four."

Tanja stood in front of the battered man. He had very short black hair and a stubble of beard. His small eyes darted around like a caged animal's as he avoided her gaze. The Diadem would have rewarded a spy extravagantly for information on the secret Candela iperion mines.

"Taking souvenir pictures?" Tanja asked, her tone dripping acid. "An odd place for a tourist." The spy made no excuses for why he had been in a highly sensitive, unauthorized area. In disgust, she turned to Bebe and said, "Use any method necessary to loosen his tongue. Find out if he's caused any sabotage, or if he has any cohorts."

Bebe looked determined. "I'll move it to the top of my list of things to do."

28

By now Redcom Hallholme has surely realized his dire circumstances," Adolphus said to Sophie as they stood outside on the porch at night. The stars above Elba looked infinite and full of possibilities. "The Constellation fleet will try to find their way back to Sonjeera, but that won't work. In another week they'll begin to panic. Two more weeks, and they will have lost hope." He smiled, visualizing the five isolated stringline haulers filled with thousands of crew. "I intend to give them enough time to know they are completely defeated—and then our fleet will go in and round them up. Three weeks is a long time when you're stranded out there."

He felt more relaxed than he could remember in a long time. "Meanwhile, we've got nothing to do but wait—and I plan to take advantage of the opportunity. I've been exiled on Hellhole for more than ten years, and I will no longer abide by the Diadem's terms. It's time I left this planet. The symbolic gesture is important."

Sophie agreed and slipped close to hug him. "Where will you go?"

"Ridgetop, I think—to visit Governor Goler."

"I've heard the goldenwood groves are marvelous," Sophie said. "I want to see them for myself. In fact, I want to see all of the Deep Zone, now that we're free. We can—"

"I promise we'll visit those places together, Sophie—after this is over. For now, I have another matter to take care of. Once we capture the fleet, the Diadem will have to capitulate. I intend to have Carlson Goler negotiate a Deep Zone accord with the Crown Jewels. He seems like the most appropriate liaison."

"And while you're gone," Sophie said with a long sigh, "I am going to see Devon."

‹❧›

It did not seem possible for the peculiar red-weed forests to grow so swiftly, but the lush foliage surged forward faster than the telemancy could drive it back from the growing shadow-Xayan settlement. The first chaotic growths had appeared shortly after the discovery of the slickwater pools, and recently, according to satellite imagery, dozens of similar infestations had sprouted in isolated, unpopulated valleys across the continent. Hellhole seemed to be burgeoning.

For months, as the numbers of converts swelled and more Xayan memories were awakened, the settlement thrived; nearly three thousand shadow-Xayans lived amid oddly geometric alien structures. Accompanied by a watchful and cautious Encix, Devon-Birzh and Antonia-Jhera continued to organize large crowds of shadow-Xayans, guiding them through exercises to increase their cooperative telemancy and to move closer to their sacred racial goal.

It was the second session of the day. They had been training against typical ground and air attacks that might be expected from a traditional invading fleet. On undulating caterpillar legs, Encix glided among the shadow-Xayans, watching the activities with her large black eyes, but speaking little.

Now Devon-Birzh guided a wave of telemancy from the hundreds of volunteers, creating a wall of wind that rose into the sky. Devon said, "That should be enough to deflect a squadron of attack fighters."

Encix expressed no admiration. "Continue to build your mental strength. The shadow-Xayans have already equaled or surpassed the Originals' powers of telemancy, but you are far stronger when one of us joins you. Time is short. Stretch your power. Improve faster."

Although he allowed Birzh to take over his mind during the actual use of telemancy, now Devon's own personality came to the fore. "We're preparing to fight side by side with General Adolphus. Look at the progress we've already made."

Encix swayed back and forth, and her expression was unreadable to Devon, even with help from his own alien personality. "There are other reasons to hurry."

Antonia took Devon's hand and gave him a warm smile. "Let's show Encix what we can do."

As always when she touched him, Devon felt his pulse quicken, and his fused mind reached out, linking with the thoughts of his numerous shadow-Xayan companions as they built a collective energy. Encix acted as a catalyst to increase the mental output, channeling the whirlwind of telemancy. . . .

With a pang, he wished his mother could witness these demonstrations again. Though she tried to hide it, Sophie Vence remained saddened that he lived among the shadow-Xayans. Devon wanted to convince her that he had gained so much more with the infused memories, abilities, and passions of Birzh. And his counterpart's love for Jhera was the perfect complement to his own love for Antonia. His mother had accepted what he said and claimed that she understood, but she remained worried about him; she had sent a message that she would visit on the following day, just to spend time with him.

After growing up here, Devon had never been afraid of Hellhole, though he respected the planet's dangers. The *challenges*. Early on, while he was just getting to know Antonia, he had taken the battered girl under his wing and explained the local hazards to her. He had been so young before he met her, so eager and innocent . . . but now, with the double vision of alien lives and loves inside them, he and Antonia were never separate.

Birzh had increased Devon's courage as well as his understanding, and the prospect of ascending to a higher plane, joining an entire race as it evolved, expanded his hope. For the first time in his life, Devon felt that he could do something really significant.

Yet, when the Xayans finally achieved *ala'ru*, Devon wasn't sure that he would accompany them in the sacred ascension, or if the Birzh personality would abandon him . . . leaving him as a mere human again. Birzh either did not know or would not tell him the answer, and Antonia said it was the same with Jhera. Just walls of silence, leaving unanswered questions.

Now, as the practice group exerted their telemancy, drawing upon the strength of Encix, Devon noted that the more he pushed his mental powers, the more Birzh seemed to recede and allow him to dominate. His human part added fuel to the Xayan part, which made them far stronger together.

In earlier demonstrations, the group had faced off against conventional artillery fire; this time, the challenge would be different. His mother would have been horrified at the risk, but Devon had no qualms.

Hearing the sound of engines, the shadow-Xayans looked up to see four fast aircraft. The approaching fighters shot flashes of orange as j-palm rockets burst overhead in a blossom of liquid fire. An inferno of burning chemicals poured down on them.

The telepathic energy level intensified as more humans took greater control of their hybrid minds, creating an invisible defensive shield. With an inner calm, Devon watched the raining sheets of flame ripple off the protective field. Guiding the telemancy, with Encix's participation, Devon-Birzh gathered the incandescent j-palm and squirted it back up into the sky like a geyser with such speed and focused intensity that it created a sonic boom. Another psychic nudge, and he was able to launch it all the way out into space.

Through the thrumming telemancy, he sensed a slight disturbance coming from Encix, though he could not determine the reason. Feeling exhilarated rather than exhausted, Devon relaxed while Antonia pressed close against him. In his thoughts, he heard the voice of Birzh, "You did well."

"*We* did well."

❧

The next morning, the awakening sun was still low in the sky, and the air was cool but gritty on Sophie's face. Wearing khaki clothing, she and Devon rode in an open-air track vehicle that rumbled along dirt roads.

Though she enjoyed every moment she spent with her son, trying to hold on to what she remembered of him, the young man was especially quiet today. She wondered what he was thinking, knowing he maintained a constant running dialogue with his alien companion.

As a young man, Devon had longed to go fishing on Klief, and when the first trout ponds opened on Hellhole, she had promised to take him. For years she had repeated the promise, always assuming there would be time. Ever resourceful, the young man had even taken a makeshift pole out to streams near Michella Town to fish, but he'd caught only strange and inedible aquatic slitherers, spiny native creatures that fought and thrashed until he severed the line. That wasn't real fishing!

Now, even though Devon had changed beyond measure, she wanted to make up for all the disappointment. Their fishing gear was in the back of the vehicle.

Sophie guided them along the bumpy road to the local fish hatchery, telling him about the holding ponds full of fingerlings. Growing up on Hellhole, Devon had become an expert on the geology, the weather, the plantings in the greenhouses, the native creatures that had survived the devastating impact. He loved science. Now he listened while she discussed the water-quality problems due to the intrusion of sulfur and trace selenium into the ponds.

With a flash of his old personality, he seemed interested and glad to spend time with her, but he was also distracted to be away from Antonia and the other shadow-Xayans. Sophie leaned closer as the vehicle lurched over a rut in the road. "We'll enjoy this, Devon," she insisted. "We need this time together."

The vehicle rumbled past outdoor runways for yearling fish, water-filled tanks that were covered by roofs to keep native predatory birds from feeding on them. Off in the distance, Sophie saw the main hatchery building and the half-built learning center where tourists and schoolchildren would be brought to learn about the hatchery operations. Someday.

When she stopped the vehicle at one of the fishing ponds, Devon's interest perked up. The lake was well stocked with warm-water trout in a natural environment. Along the pond's shore, pale blue succulent trees provided shade for fishermen. As the vehicle came to a stop, Sophie saw a man and a boy on the far bank, fishing together. Her heart ached when she saw the two. Devon hadn't had a father to do that with him.

She could have been a better mother to him. When the boy was only ten, she'd whisked him away to the Deep Zone—and from that point on, the day-to-day difficulties of establishing a decent life in the rigorous environment had required most of her attention. Now they faced a war, which placed many demands and anxieties on all citizens of Hellhole. Time had slipped through her fingers. She regretted that her son had never enjoyed a normal childhood. Even worse, with Birzh living inside of him he had no normal adult life either.

The previous night while Adolphus prepared for his trip to Ridgetop, she had worked long hours to catch up on her summaries and delegated tasks. Now, for half a day, while the weapons factories worked smoothly, while ships patrolled space around the planet, while the shadow-Xayans continued their drills, Sophie set everything else aside, determined to spend time with Devon.

In a flash of his old personality, the young man sprang from his seat and retrieved their fishing gear from the back of the vehicle. Sophie was glad to see the childish delight in his blue eyes. "I'll set up our poles, Mother."

Sophie's feelings were more than just the regrets of a busy mother. She needed reassurance that his human personality remained intact and strong. Glancing at Devon, she could see the alien shimmer and faint spirals in his eyes, but his occasional comments and expressions gave her hope that she was actually sitting beside *Devon* now. She wanted just a few hours with her son, her only son. Relenting, Birzh had granted him full prominence, although their personalities were so interconnected that Sophie had trouble distinguishing one from the other.

She smiled as she watched him prepare the poles, and when he caught her watching, he smiled back—the warm, pure smile she remembered so well from his childhood.

"Birzh finds this interesting," he said. "The Xayans eat by grazing over native vegetation on the ground. The process of catching food, especially out of the water, is strange to them."

"I'm glad we're able to entertain him," Sophie said.

"Actually, we're educating him."

They fished from the bank for more than an hour, sharing a snack and a drink, although they got nothing more than a tentative nibble on their hooks. Devon laughed often, and kept changing the lures and bait on their lines, trying different options. When he was younger, he had read extensively on fishing techniques, constantly daydreaming about the sport.

took so long for us to spend this time together," Sophie

ould have done it years ago."

been busy with important things. I understand a lot more now."

"You never complained," she said. "You've always been a good son, and I'm really sorry."

"No need for apologies. Today makes up for it all." He kissed her cheek. Yes, this was the familiar Devon. He *was* still there inside. "But don't be sad, Mother. I need you to understand that Birzh has gained as much from *my* memories as I have gained from him. I take a lot of pride in letting him relive some of my favorite meals from years past, as well as what you did for me on my birthdays, the time I hid from you in the greenhouse domes, and the first time you tried to sew me a shirt."

She gave an embarrassed chuckle. "I was never meant to be a seamstress, darling, but you wore that shirt anyway."

"And the first time you let me take the Trakmaster controls, and when I tried to bake you a holiday cake."

Sophie rolled her eyes. "That cake was a disaster as bad as the asteroid impact."

"The mess I left in the kitchen was a true disaster." Then after a long pause he added, "I am different now, though."

"I know," she said.

"But I'm still Devon, and I still have human feelings. I know you've been worried about me, and I don't blame you for that—but I don't regret for one minute what's happened to me, or to Antonia. I've already experienced more wonders than I could have wished for in ten human lifetimes."

She felt tears well up in her eyes. "Just don't go too far away from me."

"I haven't, and I won't."

On the opposite shore the other boy hauled in a big, energetic trout, and held it high like a trophy. Neither she nor Devon caught any fish, but it didn't matter. Sophie had not come out here looking for fish; she'd come here looking for her son—and she'd found him.

When they packed up to go back, Devon said, "I had a great time with you, Mother. I love you."

"I love you, too," she said. "More than I could ever put into words."

29

Far afield. Adrift.

Despite the growing sense of unease throughout the Constellation fleet, Escobar Hallholme tried to avoid feeling like he was lost. Everybody aboard could sense it as the numerous ships ranged in ever-widening search spirals, trying to locate the molecule-fine iperion line. They spread farther apart, expanded their hunt.

And found nothing.

Though Escobar laid out a plan to sweep the emptiness, crisscrossing the open volume, by the end of the first week the efforts had an increasingly frantic edge. The five military haulers stayed within an hour's light-distance from one another to remain in emergency communication. The warships detached from each hauler framework and ventured out to comb empty space, their iperion detectors extended.

"It's not so easy to find a stringline." Jackson Firth sounded as if he had just realized it.

"No one ever said it would be easy, Mr. Firth." Escobar hated to be reminded of his failure. No, not failure, he corrected himself: *setback*. He did agree with Gail Carrington about the need for this search, and as soon as he found the outbound iperion line again, no one would regard this as a failure anymore. He was determined to turn the situation around, which would make the eventual victory taste even sweeter.

Before the pedantic diplomat could make further comments, Escobar said, "Lieutenant Cristaine, any report from the other four haulers?"

"Reports, sir, but no success. The search continues."

The diplomat sounded annoyed. "I will not be dismissed, Red Commodore. For the first days of this expedition, I ignored your insulting comments, your obvious disapproval of me and my team. You told us that we were irrelevant until you completed your part of the mission. Well, I'm waiting, sir. Do your part of the mission so that I may perform my own valuable work."

"Thank you for your advice, Mr. Firth," Escobar said, his irritation plain. "I'll consider it carefully." He wanted to strangle the man. "Now kindly leave the bridge so that I can do my job, as you demand."

The diplomat left, indignant, but clearly satisfied to have scored a point. Escobar sat back in his command chair, noticing furtive glances from other members of his bridge crew before they went about their business again.

As each day passed without locating the stringline, the iperion was dissipating further, decreasing the chances of the line ever being found again. By now his search effort had probably taken them a great distance from the severed stringline, but he bullishly insisted on going ahead. Finding that route was their only chance. Even if they located the opposite end of the stringline segment, they could not go back to Sonjeera; Carrington had made that clear, and his own sense of honor refused to let him to consider it an option . . . not that they could pursue it anyway.

And so the haulers pushed ahead and wandered farther afield, following Escobar's orders. As everyone else was surely thinking, his heroic father would never have given up.

As his frustration increased, Escobar was plagued with homesick thoughts. At his wedding to Elaine Riomini, he had paid little attention to how beautiful his new wife was, or her personality, or whether their interests were compatible. The marriage forged an alliance between the Hallholmes and one of the most powerful bloodlines in the Constellation. It brought his family into the ranks of nobility. Escobar could not have wished for more. And when Elaine turned out to be pleasant enough, and on good terms with her powerful great-uncle, those things were unexpected benefits.

The wedding had been a sparkling, extravagant affair, with hundreds of guests from across the Crown Jewels; neither Escobar nor Elaine had ever met most of them. Her dowry had been enormous, and the wedding gifts alone added up to more wealth than Escobar had ever seen in his life. Intricate golden eggs, ornate wire-frame sculptures, jeweled towels, and bottles of wine so old and so valuable that no one would ever consider drinking them.

They were married in the vineyards of the old Adolphus estate. Though he would have preferred a ceremony on Sonjeera, Escobar realized it was a good symbolic way to twist the knife, should the exiled General ever learn about it.

He still hoped to groom their two sons into prominent members of the military. After defeating General Adolphus, Escobar had expected to claim administrative responsibilities over one or more Deep Zone planets, to supplement his family's wealth and influence.

He had never dreamed that he and his entire fleet would get *lost* in deep space, and that the General would trip him and make him fall flat on his face.

⟡

The numbers didn't lie.

Despite his noble blood and impressive marriage, Bolton Crais was little more than a glorified inventory specialist. Militarily speaking, he wasn't much. Now his stature had risen even when he didn't really want it to; he was a mathematical fortune-teller, able to see the future of the stranded fleet. And it was frighteningly grim.

Bolton sat alone in a small observation blister on the top deck of the *Diadem's Glory*. The framework of the stringline hauler blocked part of his view, and the other warships crowded in docking clamps made him feel claustrophobic, but he stared out at the swatch of stars through the gaps. The fleet was in the middle of nowhere, cast adrift like rudderless sailing ships after a storm, with no hope of finding their way back to civilization.

Bolton had dimmed the lights in the observation blister as he tried to think of a solution, but the numbers were as implacable as the laws of physics. He had arranged the inventory himself. He knew their food supplies, fuel levels, life-support capabilities, energy reserves, and the number of crewmembers.

They could not survive for long.

Escobar Hallholme interrupted him from behind, making Bolton jump in his padded observation chair. "We need to find a way out of this, Major Crais."

"I didn't know you were there, Redcom."

"I'm not here with an entourage or fanfare." Escobar lowered his voice, as if there might be eavesdroppers. "Is it as bad as I think it is?"

Bolton got up from his seat. "I'm afraid it is, sir. When we loaded the ships on Aeroc, I included more than the recommended supply buffer, and I took contingency measures with equipment and personnel—but even factoring in unforeseen difficulties, I never prepared for a lengthy operation. The fleet should have resupplied after we seized planet Hallholme, and we expected the Constellation to send ships full of occupation forces later on, via the stringline." He shook his head. "I have gone over the numbers, run models using the most extreme initial conditions. There is no possible way we can survive more than six weeks, maybe eight at the outside under strict food and water rationing."

Startled, Escobar said, "I don't plan on staying here six weeks, Major. We need to find an alternative before that."

"I agree, we *must*. But what? With the stringline cut, our haulers can't go anywhere. Our warships do have standard FTL engines, but there's not enough fuel to take them to planet Hallholme . . . and that journey would still require almost three months, so our people would be dead before the ships arrived. Or we could try to head back to Sonjeera with standard engines, but that would take a minimum of *four* months under conventional power."

"I shouldn't have mocked you for your conservative estimates when you were loading the ships." Escobar straightened. "On the other hand, if we had left sooner, we might have arrived before the General could blow the stringline."

"Our only option now is to wait to be rescued," Bolton said. "We must tighten our belts, reduce our life-support requirements and power drains . . . and hope we can last until someone comes for us."

Escobar stared out at the stars. His voice carried a machete edge of anger. "And who would rescue us? General Adolphus? I would not allow that!" His voice became quieter. "When we left Sonjeera with all that fanfare, I was certain we'd wipe out the rebel vermin in their filthy nests, and we would do it quickly. Now it appears we were overconfident."

"Hubris," Bolton said. "It may be that we have only two choices left: die, or let Adolphus rescue us. From a practical standpoint, he will want to commandeer our ships. Neither option is heroic, but it's what we have."

⌘

Each time the crews went to the mess halls and saw their meager rations, they were reminded of the "temporary austerity measures" that were supposed to see them through this crisis.

On the bridge of the *Diadem's Glory*, Escobar stared out at the starry expanse. He felt a dull knife in his stomach—tension and anxiety for now, but soon it would become the ever-increasing ache of hunger. Ten days ago, he'd sat at the captain's table enjoying a feast, eating too much prime rib, opening too many bottles of wine.

As the son of Commodore Hallholme living on the Qiorfu estate, Escobar had never wanted for anything. When he was growing up, he had thought nothing of sending away his dinner plates with half the meal untouched. Any morsel that didn't meet his fancy went into the waste processor. It was quite different now.

If they didn't find the stringline soon, the Constellation fleet would be in no condition to attack General Adolphus.

"Redcom, there's an emergency message from one of the search frigates," Lieutenant Cristaine said. "Some sort of a struggle aboard."

"Play it!" he barked.

At first, the communication bursts were peppered with shouts, cut-off sentences, and weapons fire. Finally, a haggard-looking man—Captain Felix Noorman—appeared on the screen. "Redcom, my crew staged a revolt. We have thirteen dead—seven in the actual conflict, and six mutineers whom I summarily executed. I saw no alternative, sir."

Escobar started to respond, but the comm-officer told him, "There's a forty-five-minute signal delay, sir."

Captain Noorman continued his report. "Tensions have been high. Our seventh search pattern found nothing, and when we received a fleet-wide report of null results, twenty crewmen broke into the armory, killed the guards. Apparently they believed with fewer people aboard they could ration our food and fuel and use the FTL engines to make it to another star system."

"That's preposterous," Escobar said under his breath. "Pause the transmission." The report cut off as he rose from his command chair. "I'm going into my ready room. Pipe the rest of the signal in there. And I want to send a coded transmission back to Captain Noorman with explicit instructions."

"Other ships in the fleet have already heard the broadcast, Redcom," Lieutenant Cristaine cautioned.

Escobar silently cursed Noorman for revealing too much. The man should have kept his report classified. The Army of the Constellation had not operated on a wartime footing for years, and service in the military had been an exercise in self-aggrandizement for noble families with extra sons and daughters. Discipline had fallen apart, making the fleet a private club with fancy uniforms and large military ships.

As he walked to his ready room, Escobar said, "Broadcast my orders to the entire battle group. I am imposing strict, complete radio silence. All transmissions are to be sent on a coded band, reports to be made directly to me here on the flagship. *I* will choose which information to disseminate fleet-wide. This isn't an entertainment network. This is a vital military operation."

He thought of another tack that would impress the crew. "General Adolphus cut the stringline. For all we know, his spies could be eavesdropping on our transmissions. Any crewman who does not maintain silence per my order will be subject to court-martial."

Feeling the stunned quiet behind him on the bridge, he sealed the door of his ready room, activated the codecall screen, and replayed Captain Noorman's full report. He then composed his own message, keeping his voice hard and stern, knowing it would take the better part of an hour before his transmission reached the frigate—a transmission that contained fictitious information or, at the minimum, conjecture.

"Captain Noorman, listen to me very carefully. The mutineers aboard your ship were loyalists of General Adolphus. Somehow they infiltrated our fleet, intending to sow fear and destroy morale. We will institute a plan to root out any further traitors among us. Your loyalty and dedication to the cause is appreciated—not only by me, but by the Diadem and Lord Riomini."

He closed the message, coded it, and transmitted. Better to create a scapegoat, find another shadowy enemy to blame, but he knew that wouldn't last long. He could only pray that one of the scouts found the iperion path soon, but that thread of hope grew thinner with each passing moment.

30

The air had never smelled sweeter, the sunshine never looked brighter. General Adolphus turned his face up to the open skies of Ridgetop and drew in a long breath. He savored the moment and closed his eyes without even moving away from the landed passenger pod, just drinking in every tiny detail. The shimmering leaves of Ridgetop's goldenwood trees danced in a faint breeze, twinkling as they reflected light. The sounds were like faint wind chimes.

After more than a decade of exile, this sensation of freedom, of being able to get away from his hellish planet, was euphoric. Only his ancestral home on Qiorfu could have pleased him more.

After the heady moment, he stepped away to meet Governor Goler. He didn't focus in on the smells of the pavement, the hot metal from the descended pod, or the sounds of fuel trucks and crews unloading the shuttle. He just relished being somewhere other than Hellhole.

Goler interrupted his thoughts. "I can't believe this is your first time off-planet in eleven years, General." The lanky, dark-skinned man smiled, basking in Adolphus's enjoyment.

"I was honor-bound by the terms of my agreement," he said. "Yes, I had the wherewithal to slip away any time I wanted to. I could have taken on a new identity, escaped to a much more pleasant world—like Ridgetop." The breeze picked up among the hillside groves. Oh, how the goldenwood sparkled! "But if I broke my word, then I would truly have been defeated. I waged my rebellion against the cynical dishonesty of the Crown Jewels. I stood for something different. I accepted the terms of my exile and, unlike the Diadem, I'm not a cheat or a liar."

His neck and shoulders tensed at the mere thought of how Michella had betrayed him, but he forced himself to relax. "I can see why you chose to keep your main residence here, Governor, rather than back on Sonjeera. This is a beautiful world."

"My people like it," Carlson Goler said. "Even better now that we're free."

The General enjoyed a long, slow exhale. "Yes . . . freedom."

Because he had made this trip on impulse, he did not expect, nor want, any fanfare or formal reception. Even though the Constellation fleet had been hamstrung and now drifted helpless in the middle of nowhere, he wouldn't launch any DZ-wide victory celebrations yet— not until he rounded up the lost ships, forced Hallholme's surrender, and incorporated the fleet into his own Deep Zone Defense Force.

But in a few weeks . . .

Every day since unveiling his new stringline network, he had made significant progress in unifying the frontier worlds, but there had also been tragic deaths: the Original alien Cippiq, the shadow-Xayan leader Fernando-Zairic, all of the optimistic emissaries who had gone to Sonjeera to win over the Diadem but had paid with their lives. The losses deeply saddened Adolphus.

Creating the new stringline network had also been burdened with regrettable costs. When traveling from Hellhole to Ridgetop, he rode on what he had christened the "Ernst Packer Memorial Stringline," named for the brave pilot who had died while laying down the iperion path to connect the planets. And before that, his best friend Franck Tello and the brave fighters who had died because of Commodore Hallholme's treachery in the Battle of Sonjeera. . . .

Yes, the price of independence from the Constellation was high, but necessary, and he did not like to count the cost.

Adolphus sneezed, his eyes and nose irritated by something in the air. Embarrassed, he tried to look dignified, but Goler just chuckled. "Sorry, General. Plenty of tree pollens here that you're not used to. Don't worry, my housekeeper has local remedies—you'll feel fine in a while."

The territorial governor's A-frame house had a magnificent view of the steep goldenwood-covered hills. His old servant, Tasmine, made them a fruity tea with a bitter aftertaste. The old woman urged the General to drink up nevertheless. "Priniflower," she said. "Do you good." He soon felt his congestion clearing, his eyes becoming less scratchy.

Adolphus knew Tasmine was more than a household servant. She had told of the massacre the Diadem's troops had imposed on Ridgetop, and her chilling tale had rallied many of the DZ worlds against the corrupt Crown Jewels.

Governor Goler showed Adolphus a polished rectangle of fused goldenwood planks the size of a coffin lid. Names had been laser-burned into the wooden surface, line after line, in a list of martyrs.

"These are the original Ridgetop colonists murdered so that the Diadem could make way for a more cooperative colony. Tasmine was the sole survivor."

Respectfully, Adolphus read each name to himself, running his gaze down the list. Finally he turned to the old housekeeper. "Thank you for your bravery."

"We'll erect this as a memorial on the mass grave site, which we just excavated." Goler ran his fingers down the names. He seemed anxious. "General Adolphus, I've risked everything to throw in my lot with you. Ridgetop is ready to fight for the independence of the Deep Zone. Scores of our people have volunteered to join your shadow-Xayan teams to help increase the telemancy defense . . . but do we really stand a chance? I have faith in you, but the Diadem already defeated you once."

"The rules have changed since then," Adolphus said. "And so have the odds. If we must destroy every connection and isolate the whole Deep Zone from the Crown Jewels, we'll do so. But I'd much rather live in harmony with the rest of the Constellation."

"The Diadem's pride is going to be the greatest obstacle," Goler said.

Tasmine looked as if she had swallowed a pebble. "The bitch would tear civilization apart rather than concede anything to you, sir."

"She won't have any say in the matter," Adolphus said. "We've rendered a large portion of her fleet ineffective, and she can't fight fifty-four separate battlefronts with her remaining ships. Before long, I'll have their fleet commander hostage, with their ships turned over to us. Then we'll have Michella Duchenet over a barrel."

"I'd rather have her head on an executioner's block," Tasmine muttered.

"Diadem Michella is old, and it's time for her to retire," Goler said. "For more than a decade, people have been calling for her to surrender the Star Throne to someone else. The nobles are circling like hungry predators, and she can't last long. If you captured most of her fleet, that'll be her death knell."

Adolphus ran his fingers along the column of names etched on the goldenwood memorial. "That's why I need you, Governor. It's the main reason I came to Ridgetop."

He looked surprised. "What do you need from me, General?"

Adolphus glanced at Tasmine, but the housekeeper showed no intention of leaving them in private. Goler said, "I trust her, sir. She kept the secret of the Ridgetop Recovery longer than I would have imagined possible."

The General allowed himself to relax. "It's my military training." He took a sip from his second cup of priniflower tea, nodding to the old woman, then focused on Goler. "I want you to be my liaison. Travel back to the Crown Jewels and deliver our terms—our *ultimatum*. Diadem Michella Duchenet must step down from the Star Throne, and I want a guarantee that the Crown Jewels will cease all hostilities against the Deep Zone. Every one of our stringlines to Sonjeera has been mined, and we can blow the substations whenever we like. Use your political connections, Governor. Michella won't listen, but someone among the nobles will. Make the case that we are willing to be independent from the Crown Jewels, for better or for worse. If the Diadem sends any ships to attack our worlds, then we'll cut ourselves off completely, simple as that, and no bluffing about it."

Goler looked very pleased. A lantern-jawed man with heavy eyes, he had always seemed a bit of a misfit, not liked in the Crown Jewels and not entirely trusted on the eleven frontier planets he administered.

Tasmine hurried off to answer a signal at the door to the governor's residence, leaving them alone for a moment, and Adolphus saw that Goler had tears in his eyes. "I'd be honored to do as you ask, sir. I've never been a soldier, but if I can negotiate peace terms, we'll have saved countless lives."

Tasmine returned from the foyer with a packet in her hands, her brow furrowed. "It's from one of the black-market couriers," she said. "A small ship just arrived by stringline from Orsini, slipped through from Sonjeera and came here." She glanced at Adolphus. "It's for the General."

"Then why did it come here?" Goler asked. "Who knows he's on Ridgetop?"

"They don't, exactly. They wanted you to take him the message, Governor. When I told the courier that General Adolphus was already here, he nearly fell over." She chuckled.

"Well, I've saved you the trouble of delivering it," Adolphus said. "What does it say? Why would anyone from Orsini contact me?"

Goler took the packet and used his thumbprint to unseal the security tab. "Shall I open it?" Adolphus nodded, and Goler removed the document, skimmed it. "It's the crest of the Tazaar family. From Lady Enva Tazaar herself."

Adolphus placed the name. "The daughter of Azio Tazaar, new ruler of Orsini. She's an artist, correct?" Tazaar was one of the more powerful families; not quite as important as the Riominis, but on a par with the Crais family and the Hirdans. What could she want from him? He had never met the woman.

As Goler and Adolphus read the document, the governor drew in a quick breath. Adolphus was amazed to see the bold proposal; it was so unexpected and blatant it rang true. Tasmine pressed close, eager for the news.

"Lady Enva wants to be the next Diadem," Goler said aloud. "She has done the same math and come to the same conclusion as we did. The best way to thrive is for the Deep Zone and the Crown Jewels to cooperate."

Enva Tazaar's letter was like a business résumé and proposal for a commercial alliance. She suggested, quite reasonably, that Diadem Michella was the roadblock to resolving the conflict. Lady Tazaar offered her assistance to remove the Diadem internally on Sonjeera; if General Adolphus threw his support behind her as the next occupant of the Star Throne, she would promise a solid and smooth transition, not only nonaggression with the breakaway worlds, but also a commercial alliance that would strengthen both governments.

"I do prefer coexistence to mutual destruction," Adolphus said. "This is quite a surprise—assuming it's not a trick."

"It is a very interesting offer," Goler said, "but I don't know if we can trust her. Enva Tazaar might not be the worst of the lot, but she's as bad as most of them."

"I like the part about the Diadem being taken down," Tasmine said.

The General knew the old servant had every reason to despise Michella, but he couldn't let such reflexive hatred color his decision. "I won't respond just yet. Once I announce that we have the Constellation fleet, then our bargaining position will be infinitely better."

31

Percival Hallholme was not an expert vintner, but he did enjoy walking the rows of rootstock vines that undulated along the Qiorfu hills. His enemy's father, Jacob Adolphus, had been a skilled winemaker from the time he was a young man, and had planted several varieties of grapes. His firstborn son Stefano had been much less interested in the craft, while his other son Tiber went off to the Constellation military academy—and ultimately became the most determined foe of the Constellation.

Percival was glad to be making wine at the old Adolphus estate again.

Some new planetary administrators would have erased every mark of a defeated enemy, but Percival refused to sink to that level. He had studied the Adolphus family history as if it were his own, and he left the hallmarks intact, despite Escobar's grumblings. Percival knew the former administrators were well liked here on Qiorfu.

After his victory, the old Commodore hadn't had any choice but to accept the confiscated Adolphus holdings from the Diadem as a reward for his military service, but Percival refused to rule this planet with an iron fist. Not only was that ruthless and immoral, it was also exhausting, and he was retired now. He just wanted a quiet life. The things Diadem Michella had forced him to accept in battle had made him callous, and although his gestures here on Qiorfu did little to assuage the guilt he felt for what he'd done to General Adolphus, he was finished with making compromises when it came to his own honor.

Under the warm afternoon sunlight, the old man knelt to inspect a cluster of hard green grapes, which would ripen over the ensuing weeks. Finding blight on one bunch, he looked closely from vine to vine and saw that the rot was spreading. These hardy vines had thrived for a century, and he couldn't allow the disease to spread. He marked the row and section, making a mental note to call an agricultural specialist right away. Percival didn't recognize the particular blight, but if necessary he would uproot and burn this entire row to keep it from spreading to the rest of the vineyard. Another hard, but necessary, decision.

He heard a rustle of leaves, then giggles and the youthful shouting of high-pitched voices as his two grandsons hid in the vineyard, calling out as they tried to find each other. Emil played grudgingly, thinking himself too old for the game; Coram giggled and did a poor job of concealing himself, though he was small enough to duck under the vines or climb through the wires where his brother could not go.

Percival heard his daughter-in-law calling out, "Father, are you out there?"

He raised his voice and waved his hand. "The boys are over here, Elaine." Then he saw she wasn't alone. His daughter-in-law hurried between the rows of vines leading two uniformed Constellation officers, one officious-looking man wearing a colonel's insignia and—somehow more intimidating—a narrow-faced young woman in black, with short dark hair, eyes like a bird of prey's, and a threatening muscularity that her garb could not conceal. One of the Black Lord's personal bodyguards. He straightened to attention out of reflex, though he outranked both of these visitors.

Elaine looked tense and worried. "Father, these officers are here to speak with you. They have a private dispatch from the Diadem herself."

Percival's heart fell. "Something about my son? I told him not to underestimate General Adolphus."

Crashing through the leaves, his grandsons bounded toward him. Coram collided with his grandfather, and Percival grabbed the boy's shoulders to steady him. Both children were laughing, but they fell silent when they saw the strangers.

The man in the colonel's uniform said, "We have a private message for the Commodore's ears only."

Elaine gathered up the boys, obviously fighting back tears. "I should hear it, too."

"I'm afraid not." The female bodyguard brushed a clump of pollen fuzz from her black uniform. "The Diadem gave strict instructions. This message is eyes-only for Commodore Percival Hallholme."

Elaine looked as if she intended to argue the point, but Percival gestured her away. "We'll all know the answer sooner if we let these officers speak, Elaine. Please take the boys back to the main house." Frightened, she led her now alarmed sons in a brisk march along the rows of grapes.

Percival remained standing stiffly as he addressed the visitors. "So this isn't a social call. I should remind you that I am retired, have been for a decade."

The female bodyguard introduced herself as Lora Heston in a harsh and gravelly voice, as if her vocal cords had been damaged; the colonel identified himself only as "Ricketts." Colonel Ricketts withdrew a sheaf of official papers from his breast pocket. Percival could see the Duchenet stamp and the Star of the Diadem embossed on the seal. "Commodore, the Constellation is once more in need of your services. Diadem Michella is hereby reactivating your commission."

Ricketts handed over the papers, and Percival accepted them with great reluctance. "As I said, I am retired." His protestation impressed neither of the two visitors.

Heston lowered her voice, though they were alone in the vineyards. "This is not common knowledge, sir, but the Constellation fleet sent against the rebel General Adolphus . . . There have been difficulties."

She had his full attention now. "What difficulties?"

"Not for us to say. The Diadem will brief you in full. She requests your presence on Sonjeera immediately for an important tactical meeting."

"Has the fleet been captured or destroyed? What's happened?" Percival insisted. "Any word about my son?"

"We have no further information for you, sir," Colonel Ricketts said. "Our instructions are to take you to Sonjeera immediately."

Percival could tell it was not a request. His shoulders slumped. "I request that my adjutant, Duff Adkins, accompany me. He has given me valuable advice for most of my career."

The colonel deferred to Riomini's bodyguard. Lora Heston showed no reaction at all. "Your adjutant may join us, provided he is ready to depart immediately."

"He'll be there," Percival said. "I need two hours to gather my uniform and pack."

"We leave in one hour, Commodore," said Colonel Ricketts.

He sighed, knew it was no use arguing. "As with any mission, I shall operate within the designated parameters."

⸎

In the private wing of the old manor house, in the suite set aside as Percival's own quarters (because Escobar didn't want the old man hovering around more than necessary), the Commodore unlocked the wooden cabinet where he stored a part of his life that he had intended to keep locked away.

Shelves lined the interior. On one of them sat a polished silver plate bearing his rank clusters, the enameled metal bars and gaudy awards that made him look like a peacock when he wore them. Though he had never desired the accolades, the Diadem had thought to keep him happy by awarding more medals. The cabinet smelled musty, the contents sealed away as if in a museum case. His old uniform hung there, vacuum-sealed in polymer film, gold and black with wide sleeves, thick cuffs—a costume entirely unfit for combat. Lord Riomini's bodyguards would never wear such a ridiculous uniform that would inhibit their freedom of movement.

Percival unsealed the polymer wrap and pulled out the uniform blouse. He ran his fingers along the fabric, then examined the jacket, the braid, the stiff epaulets. He had not played his military role in a decade, although the Diadem pestered him to attend her festivals and receptions as a living legend, a showpiece as her daughter Keana had been. But Percival Hallholme was no decoration, and the Diadem had already used him more than he'd expected, or *wanted*. And he had to live with it.

One of the last times he'd worn this uniform was to accept the surrender of General Tiber Maximilian Adolphus, after defeating his nemesis with a threat—a *bluff*, actually—to slaughter thousands of innocent hostages.

Even though he was defeated, at least the General had a clear conscience. Percival could never erase that moment of personal dishonor, though he was the only one who seemed troubled by the choice he'd made. Now he resented being called back into service—he had already done many things that went beyond his moral boundaries. The Constellation's lack of integrity, the win-at-all-costs attitude, sickened him. Honor was like a crystal goblet—even if broken only once, it was still broken.

Moving stiffly because of his chronic limp and sore muscles, Percival changed into his old uniform with painstaking thoroughness, straightened the lapels and sleeves, fastened every tab. Many aged officers grew fat and lazy in retirement, but he was pleased to see that the clothes still fit. He pinned on his medals and stood before the mirror, where he used a trimmer to groom his bushy muttonchop sideburns: charcoal gray fading to white. Nevertheless, he still cut a dashing figure, much like the propaganda images after his victory. Those portraits hung in every governmental hall on Sonjeera. Someday, his image would probably appear on a coin.

He emerged into the manor house's main room. When Elaine saw him, she caught her breath. "That looks very impressive, Father! It's straight out of the history loops." He had told Elaine only that the Diadem wished to consult with him and that he needed to leave within the hour.

The two boys were playing soldier with makeshift guns; Coram had built a fort out of furniture, while Emil tried to find a way around his brother's defenses. But they halted, amazed to see Percival in his uniform.

He maintained a brave face for his daughter-in-law and grandchildren. "It helps put me in the mind-set of what I need to do. Escobar might need a little assistance, and I'll be happy to give it."

A loud pounding came at the door, and before Elaine could open it, Duff Adkins burst inside, his eyes bright. Over his shoulder, he carried a worn duffel that looked lumpy and hurriedly packed. "What's the emergency, sir? I've thrown some things together as you instructed, but you weren't specific. What do you mean, we're going to Sonjeera?"

"The Diadem calls," Percival said.

The aide sized up the Commodore in his pristine uniform, then swallowed hard. "I was afraid it would be something like that, sir."

Percival nodded. "We've been called back to duty."

32

Bolton Crais had a suggestion, a last-ditch hope, but he was hesitant to discuss it with the Redcom. The fleet probably would not survive long enough to see the idea succeed, but if he couldn't convince Escobar of its merits, they would have no chance whatsoever. The brave fleet that had launched with such high hopes would vanish, becoming nothing more than a cluster of ghost ships lost in the void, filled with the skeletons of starved, frozen soldiers.

He would have preferred to speak with Escobar privately, but Gail Carrington had to be party to the decision, and Bolton wanted Lord Riomini's spy on his side. He invited them both to his private quarters Knowing that the anxious crew watched their commanding officers with ever-growing suspicion, he didn't want to call attention to the meeting. After he had sealed the door, Bolton said, "I have a way to get us to planet Hallholme."

"Let's hear it," Carrington said.

"What I have in mind will take a minimum of two months—if it works at all."

"Two months?" Escobar cried. "You said our supplies and life support would never last that long!"

"They may not, but we certainly won't survive unless we try something."

"Better to be lost without a trace than to fail for everyone to see," said Carrington. "We cannot give General Adolphus any sort of victory."

Escobar sat in the chair at Bolton's desk, placed his elbows on the desk, rested his chin in his hands, and looked at him. "Let's hear your plan, Major Crais."

"When I loaded the fleet ships at Aeroc, Redcom, you were skeptical about my added precautions. I don't mean to pat myself on the back, but the additional supplies I included may be sufficient to keep us alive long enough . . . provided we take extreme measures."

"Yes, you've reminded me of your foresight several times, Major. I'll give you a medal when we get back to Sonjeera, if that's what you want."

Bolton had no patience for that nonsense. "Non sequitur, Redcom. I am merely laying the groundwork to tell you something more. I also brought along an old trailblazer ship with a load of iperion, on the chance we might need to make stringline repairs."

Escobar frowned. "I signed all the paperwork myself—no trailblazer was on the manifest. Where did you hide it?"

"I used a clause in the orders, sir, that each officer is allowed to bring aboard a certain amount of personal property at his own expense. I used my own funds to store it in the cargo bay alongside our fighter craft."

"I don't like deception, Major," Escobar said. "Although I should congratulate you, since this now gives us some glimmer of hope that we might complete our mission."

"Or just survive," Bolton said. "We have strayed far from where the iperion path is likely to be located. We are badly lost. But that trailblazer can fly from here to planet Hallholme and lay down a new stringline path—like a corps of engineers cutting a new trail through a jungle. Once the iperion path is marked, we can use our stringline engines again and complete the trip in a day."

"And how long will the trailblazer take to reach its destination?" Carrington asked.

"Two months, by my estimation, and the rest of our ships would have to remain here by the new terminus. We hunker down and wait."

Both Escobar and Carrington reacted with stunned silence. When the silence grew too long, Bolton added, "You did ask for ideas, sir, no matter how unlikely they might seem."

"We'll do it," Carrington said, as if she were in command. "That plan doesn't preclude us from finding another solution in the meantime. Our search for the severed stringline can continue, but at least we'll have a second chance in the works."

Escobar threaded his fingers together, clenching and unclenching his hands. "But how are *we* to survive for two months? Just sitting here? We're already feeling the hard realities of rationing. We never expected supplies to last that long."

"Make no mistake, Redcom, our situation will get much more difficult," Bolton said. "In fact, I'm sickened to think of the measures we will be required to take for those two months—and not all of us will survive."

Carrington sounded enthusiastic, even optimistic. "But those who do survive will be able to *complete the mission*. We can defeat General Adolphus after all."

Bolton nodded, glad that she supported him, although her priorities were not the same as his.

❧

The five military haulers had regrouped at an arbitrary point in space. They had wandered great distances in their ever-expanding hunt for the lost stringline, and now they were far from the former location of Substation 4. This would be a new anchor point, a terminus for a last-ditch iperion route. Now their fate rested on a lone trailblazer ship laying down a new path of quantum breadcrumbs all the way to planet Hallholme before fifteen thousand crewmembers perished.

Although the futile-seeming search for the severed outbound path continued, the stringline haulers and the hundred warships would power down, conserve energy, wait in silence, and pray. Navigation teams had scanned space, checking and double-checking the coordinates to the destination system. It was a simple enough navigational calculation, Escobar knew, drawing a straight-line path to Hellhole, taking into account any intervening star systems. Escobar would not allow any stupid mistakes. More and more it looked as if they had only this one chance, this one way out.

Bolton Crais's surreptitious trailblazer had been removed from its storage dock in the hangar of the *Diadem's Glory*. As soon as he looked upon the distinctly different design of the ship, Escobar wondered how the rest of his crew could have been fooled . . . but the official paperwork had been signed by Major Crais, and soldiers were trained to follow orders, not ask questions.

The Redcom applauded Bolton because he had been efficient and cautious, although he also resented the quiet and unprepossessing man because he had thought of things Escobar hadn't! A mere logistics officer, a military *accountant*—a nobleman who couldn't even keep his own wife from straying; Bolton had only been permitted to join the expedition because Escobar did not have the political clout to deny him.

In their situation now, though, Escobar had a grudging respect for the man. While Gail Carrington gave him stern stares and the other officers wore unspoken accusations on their faces, Bolton did not heap blame upon him. Obviously, the man's priority was to complete the mission, to save the ships and crew aboard the Constellation fleet. Escobar had begun to think of Bolton as a reliable sounding board whose opinions were valid and well considered—a counterpoint to Carrington's unforgiving harshness.

Bolton had spent hours loading supplies aboard the small trailblazer, inspecting each package, tallying the food, water, and energy packs the pilots would need for the harrowing two-month journey.

Ten pilots had volunteered for the dangerous mission, and all had undergone thorough medical testing, but it boiled down to two men. The blood chemistry of Sergeants Francone Zabriskie and Arbin Caron showed that they were more resistant to iperion poisoning than any of the others. Cramped for months in a small vessel, so close to the shielded stockpile of the toxic stringline marker material, at least one of them had a chance of surviving.

Escobar summoned Sergeants Zabriskie and Caron to the flagship's hangar for his final briefing. These men were loyal, soft-spoken, competent pilots. Each seemed pleased that his name had been chosen from among the volunteers'.

"You're the most qualified pilots for the job," Escobar had said, without further explanation. Guiding a trailblazer along an obvious path did not require any exceptional expertise. "I hope you're both under no illusions. This will be a very difficult assignment."

Zabriskie, a compact, olive-skinned man, shrugged. "Sitting in a cockpit for two months doesn't sound any harder than a pitched battle, though my butt will be awfully sore by the time I get there."

"If our food and life support lasts that long, we'll complete the trip, sir," Caron said. He was the smaller of the two, a fortyish man with a lined but youthful face.

Bolton held an electronic clipboard, all business. Together, the three inspected the boxes of packed rations, the water tank, the sealed recycling cabinet. "This should be sufficient nutrition for both of you. We can't spare this level of rations here on the fleet, but if anyone needs to be fully fed, it's you two. By recycling everything, maintaining your calm, and not burning any unnecessary calories, you should survive the journey."

Sergeant Zabriskie skeptically assessed the cramped ship. "How would we burn unnecessary calories even if we wanted to? What are we going to do, dance? There's no room to move. In fact, we won't be able to stretch our arms and legs until we empty those food containers and compress them."

Caron snapped to attention. "You can count on us, Redcom. We'll lay down the iperion and you'll have your stringline."

"Gentlemen, the Constellation depends on you. This fleet depends on you. And *I* depend on you."

"Yes, *sir!*" both pilots said.

And Escobar heard the words of his father inside his head. So often the old Commodore had droned on with his interminable war stories, tale after tale full of anecdotes and bits of unsolicited advice. "A good commander must have a healthy balance of optimism and pragmatism Issue the necessary orders and *believe* that they will work."

The Commodore's shadow loomed over the fleet now, although Escobar was sure that even the legendary Percival Hallholme would have been at a loss for a solution in this case. . . .

Moving with uncharacteristic speed, dressed in his fashionable and completely impractical clothes, Jackson Firth rushed into the hangar. "Red Commodore, I understand you're about to send a direct expedition to planet Hallholme? I insist on accompanying the trailblazer pilot. I can serve as the alternate."

Escobar would have laughed at the suggestion if it hadn't taken him completely by surprise. "I'm afraid that's not possible, Mr. Firth."

"Nevertheless, it must happen. If this is the first ship to reach the Hallholme system, there is every chance the General's forces might intercept it. I must be there to establish diplomatic contact, to speak on the Diadem's behalf."

"Request denied, Mr. Firth," Escobar said.

The diplomat glowered. "I did not express it as a request, Red Commodore. In diplomatic matters, my rank supersedes yours."

Sergeants Zabriskie and Caron looked at the foppish diplomat and frowned. The thought of being cooped up in such a small craft with a third person was impossible. Firth's request was absurd.

Bolton Crais came to the rescue. "I'm sorry, Mr. Firth, but this is not a matter of choice, and it's not a diplomatic matter; it's a military survival matter. It's simply not possible for you to accompany the mission. There isn't sufficient room in the vessel to carry an additional person, much less the food, water, and life support required. And you haven't been given the medical clearance for long-term iperion exposure. Even though the stockpiles are shielded, they still leak. Besides that, constant manipulation is required in laying down the markers in space, resulting in even more exposure."

Firth blew air through his lips and looked at all three men as if trying to determine if they were tricking him, then relented. "Very well, but I will write a formal diplomatic dispatch for the pilots to carry. If they have any contact with General Adolphus, this will serve as your template for negotiations."

"Yes, sir," Sergeant Zabriskie said, after getting a nod of approval from his Redcom. "I will handle it very carefully." Satisfied, Firth departed.

Caron grumbled under his breath, "I'll be so bored by the end of two months, I'll probably be reading every word on the food wrappers."

Bolton cleared his throat. "Redcom, we should not delay. Two months from now, every minute might make a difference."

"Agreed," Escobar said. "Prepare for departure, sergeants. I'll make an announcement to the fleet."

⤙⤚

From the bridge of *Diadem's Glory*, Escobar and Bolton watched the trailblazer drop out of the hangar bay. The stringline engineers had already constructed a temporary anchor point for this end of the new stringline.

Using the navigation coordinates programmed into the trailblazer's cockpit, Sergeant Zabriskie set course for the Hallholme system while Caron signaled the bridge. "All lined up and ready to depart. Iperion deployment systems are optimal, fuel tanks loaded, engines check out, course set. Wish us luck."

Escobar broadcast across the hundred ships in their docking clamps, "All our hopes and prayers go with you, sergeants. Have a safe and swift voyage."

"See you all in a couple of months," Zabriskie said, then activated his FTL accelerators. The trailblazer launched with a shimmering blur while strains of military music played across the fleet intercom.

A round of cheers went up from the bridge crew. Gail Carrington stood trim and silent beside Escobar and Bolton, all of them staring at the point in space where the trailblazer had vanished.

No one could see the new stringline, but once the iperion breadcrumbs were strung from here to planet Hallholme, the military haulers could cross the final distance in a flash. The hard part was waiting—and surviving—until the trailblazer marked the route.

Bolton leaned close, lowering his voice. "Redcom, while the crew is upbeat, this is the best time to impose the next stage of our extreme rationing and conservation measures. They'll accept it now."

"Very well, Major. You have new recommendations for me?"

Bolton had an electronic clipboard in his hand. "I've run the numbers and I warn you, it'll be hard. Many will find my additional safeguards appalling, perhaps even impossible, and we can't do it all at once or they will revolt."

Escobar frowned. "What do you mean, 'not all at once'?"

Bolton looked dismal, and swallowed hard. "I'm afraid we've only discussed the first phase of what we have to do."

33

Deep underground, Cristoph and Keana-Uroa disembarked from the shaft crawler and entered the museum vault for another day of searching and cataloging. Lodo was already there, working with the human team members and their shadow-Xayan assistants and advisers. Even after centuries entombed there, the Original alien rarely left the subterranean chamber.

Although her mental companion Uroa had informed Keana of old frictions among various Xayan groups, particularly between Zairic and Encix, Keana generally liked Lodo's personality. Among the surviving aliens, he had the most congenial demeanor, and a sense of humor, instead of the edgy hardness Encix exhibited.

Long ago there had been divisions in the Xayan race, political and spiritual disagreements as their combined mental power approached the critical *ala'ru* point, rifts that grew more acute in the last months before the asteroid struck.

With their world's imminent destruction, the factions had argued over the best way to survive, and those wounds remained five hundred years later. Now, as the numbers of converts increased, adding human abilities to Xayan telemancy, their race had a very real likelihood of being able to ascend after all.

"We can feel the growing telemancy that will enable us to make the evolutionary leap," Uroa said inside her mind. "The shadow-Xayans have a greater potential than the Xayans ever did."

"Let's see what they've discovered today," Cristoph said aloud, unaware of the silent conversation in her mind. "By stranding the fleet, the General bought us time, and I don't plan to waste it. We've got to make this planet secure."

Following him and Lodo, Keana-Uroa dodged one of the illusory, glowing shapes that floated in the air. A crackle of energy snapped past her ear. Uroa continued in her mind, "Encix and I have different philosophies, but we both agree on our ultimate goal—ala'ru."

Over the next hour, as Keana continued to study the relics in the chamber, pondering the items already cataloged as "unknown" by the archaeologists, she spotted a black artifact composed of smooth nested curves resting in a high alcove. Uroa flinched at the sight of it and tried to drive her attention elsewhere, but Keana forced her eyes back and stepped toward the black artifact. "What is this?"

"An archaeological object of great importance," Uroa said in her mind, and his voice also came from her throat, as if Keana had asked and answered her own question.

Lodo glided up to her, "It was discovered outside by a group of human colonists, who subsequently perished. We store it here, but it remains unidentified."

"What is it for?" Cristoph asked. "What does it do?"

"Unknown," Lodo said. "It survived the asteroid impact—or it arrived on this planet afterward."

Cristoph retrieved the artifact from the alcove. It was half a meter long, lightweight and smooth, and seemed to swallow light while reflecting random sparkles, like the escaping images of lost stars. "Devon Vence and Antonia Anqui brought this back from a ruined camp of settlers."

In her mind, Uroa said in a silent, internal thought, "Even Encix and Lodo do not understand that artifact. They are afraid of it, and so am I. It may be an important key to the past and to the future."

Lodo spoke up, "Encix, Tryn, and I came to the vault together in an attempt to unlock the object's secrets, without success. We should not disturb it further."

Lodo took the artifact from Cristoph and returned it to the high alcove.

The other objects in the museum vault were fascinating as well, but not so enigmatic. Keana had spent days identifying the preserved relics from Xaya's glorious past, using her Uroa half to explain to the archaeologists the exquisite miniature figurines of exotic alien animals, original species that had been made extinct after the impact. She examined a favorite little figurine, a goatlike, winged animal with webbed feet. The species had been erased, unless something brought it back in the planet's reawakening . . . like the vast and mysterious herd of grazing creatures. In her mind, Uroa shared images of the living animals from his memories.

Beside her, Lodo used two crystalline cubes in his fingerlike protrusions to create and display numerous images from Xayan history—great crowds of sluglike aliens squirming, swaying, practicing their collective and individual powers under the leadership of Zairic and Uroa. Keana saw lovely and graceful buildings the Xayans manifested and maintained by telemancy, which were constantly shifting in subtle ways, as if evolving.

Suddenly the stone floor of the vault shook and vibrated as tremors built from deep beneath the surface. She felt Uroa's alarm and pain inside her mind as the shock wave shifted and stabbed deeper, like a spasm in Hellhole itself.

In the high alcove, the black object vibrated, and emitted a humming sound. The ancient images vanished like a historical record gone offline, and as the tremor increased, the black artifact hummed louder, and began to glow a deep purple.

Keana felt a strong psychic connection with Uroa and Lodo, a sharp agony piercing their thoughts. Cristoph was startled as the seismic upheaval cracked the walls and ceiling, but the telemancers joined their efforts to hold the vault stable and prevent the cracks from spreading.

Gradually the upheaval subsided, and the mountain stopped shaking. Cristoph climbed back to his feet, brushing dust from his shirt and his hair. He looked around to make sure the quake was over. "We need to check the seismic reading. That was a major shock."

"A very ominous sign," Lodo said, agitated. "The planet is restless." His translucent skin had an odd, sickly sheen.

"It continues to awaken," Uroa said, through Keana.

Even after the tremors faded, the black artifact hummed louder, growing to such an intense noise that bolts of pain rippled through Keana's mind, deafening Uroa's presence. Before she could cry out, the obsidian object fell silent and clattered to the ground.

"Did that artifact trigger the quake?" she asked, hoping for an answer either from Lodo or from Uroa. "Did it cause the tremors somehow?"

"Or did the quake awaken *it*?" Cristoph added.

Neither of the aliens replied, and Keana sensed that Uroa simply did not know the answer. But she also felt a blank silence in his presence, as if he were withholding something from her.

34

When General Adolphus returned from his trip to Ridgetop, he felt energized, already victorious—and it was time to deliver his ultimatum to the stranded Constellation fleet.

Sophie met him in their quarters at Elba and gave him a coy smile. "Before we depart, I have something you'll need."

"We?"

She lifted her chin. "You're not leaving me out of history. I intend to be at your side when we capture the Constellation fleet." She went back to the bedroom closet she had claimed as her own. "I've been waiting for the right time." She brought out a wrapped hanging garment and held it in front of him.

Sitting on the bed, the General raised his eyebrows. "A new ball gown to dazzle me? You don't need that, Sophie."

She snorted. "I'm not a woman made for fine gowns. This is for *you*." She unsealed the covering and pulled away the wrappings to reveal his dress uniform from the rebellion, which she had cleaned and meticulously restored. "This was the actual jacket you wore during the surrender ceremony. Time to use it for a better purpose now."

Adolphus touched the deep-blue jacket sleeve, the coppery buttons. "I was stripped of everything." He peeled the jacket off its hanger and held it up. The garment had a slight chemical odor, from insect repellants that had been used. "Amazing—how did you find this?"

"After your trial, your personal possessions were sealed in a vault, but not forever." She smiled. "It took my agents the better part of three years to track it down. Did you know there's quite a market for collectibles from your rebellion?"

"I thought the Diadem had outlawed the sale of rebellion memorabilia."

"She did. This was one of the last items the government sold—officially."

"I see." He shook out the jacket, beamed with pleasure.

"You should wear this when you capture Escobar Hallholme's fleet. I've been waiting for the right time to give it to you."

"You make me feel stronger, Sophie." His voice was thick with emotion—uncharacteristic of him even when they were in private. "You've always been a bulwark of competence and common sense. I depend on you to keep things organized—you're as much a commander of Hellhole as I am."

She stood behind him as he slipped his arms into the jacket and pulled it on over his broad shoulders. Kissing him on the cheek, she said, "And I'll always be here." She stepped in front of him to inspect the garment, straightened the lapel and collar. "It still fits."

He tugged down at the front, fastened the buttons across his waist. "Perfectly."

⁖

To build a significant force that would intimidate the crumbling Constellation fleet, Adolphus recalled ten more battleships from Deep Zone planets, in addition to his sixty armed vessels guarding Hellhole. One of those was his old flagship, the *Jacob*.

Yes, the flagship seemed a fitting place to accept the surrender of the Constellation fleet.

Turlo and Sunitha Urvancik had verified that the five stringline haulers were indeed stranded, and all those warships had been cut off for weeks now. According to the intelligence report his spy had provided, the fleet carried fifteen thousand people and only enough supplies for a few weeks without reprovisioning. Soldiers could survive on reduced rations, but by now they would be hungry and anxious. He didn't expect Escobar Hallholme to surrender immediately, but Adolphus would arrive with an impressive fleet of his own, issue his demands . . . and wait.

Adolphus wore the restored uniform as he stood on the *Jacob's* bridge. His ships would ride the iperion path out to the severed end of the stringline at Substation 4. Long ago, Percival Hallholme had stripped the rank insignia from his shoulders, but now they had been meticulously restored. His original general's stars had been handmade anyway, just like his army and his rebellion.

More than a decade ago, he had lost only because Commodore Hallholme threatened to slaughter thousands of innocent family members. But winning the war had erased all stigma of the cowardly act from his old nemesis. Official records now called Percival Hallholme's gambit an acceptable trick.

Victors were able to write history as they chose. As soon as he captured the stranded Constellation fleet and took all the soldiers prisoner, General Adolphus would write his own history. In preparation for seizing the Constellation fleet, he had reviewed the historic records of his own surrender, just for the turnabout. He hoped the junior Hallholme had done the same, so the younger man would know the proper formalities.

During that last face-off over Sonjeera, Adolphus had been so certain of his impending triumph. This time, he would not make the mistake of underestimating his opponent, would not be surprised if Escobar attempted treachery as his father had done before him. Another Hallholme, cast from the same mold.

Adolphus's ships streaked down the stringline away from Hellhole. Sophie paced the bridge of the flagship, the only person not in uniform. Security Chief Craig Jordan served as the *Jacob's* first officer, and most of the crew came from the pool of veterans who had voluntarily followed him into exile after the end of the rebellion.

"Are you planning a firefight, Tiber?" Sophie asked. "Or is this just going to be a dull trip like the last time I went to Sonjeera?"

"Depends on how hungry they are. We have seventy ships, fully armed and fueled, with a skilled crew at the peak of their abilities. I'm confident we're a match for the Constellation fleet anyway, but I plan to stay out of range. I'd rather not damage our ships or theirs—I plan to use all of them." Feeling some pride, Adolphus considered himself a master of details, a watchmaker on a military scale. "Mr. Jordan, keep our commanders on high alert. Be prepared for anything as soon as we arrive at the end of the stringline. This needs to be a flawless operation."

"Yes, General." Jordan was pleased to be in a position of authority aboard the flagship, and he had been performing his duties well. The man had served for years at Elba, monitoring household security, keeping the General safe, always alert for any assassination attempts staged by Diadem Michella. Adolphus had a habit of recognizing talent, and of rewarding good, loyal people.

"Another hundred warships and five military haulers added to the Deep Zone Defense Force." He leaned back in the command chair. "We'll be secure at last, Sophie."

She laughed. "We already feel secure with you in charge, Tiber."

An hour before they were scheduled to reach the cutoff point, which the Urvanciks had marked with silent buoys, Adolphus ordered his fleet to decelerate. He experienced an awkward sense of déjà vu aboard the *Jacob* as he recalled that last intense clash above Sonjeera, eye to eye with Commodore Hallholme on a transmission screen, waiting for the other man to blink, but blinking himself.

This time it would be different.

Sophie adjusted his collar. "You need to look perfect for history, Tiber. Not a single hair out of place."

After they had dropped below lightspeed, they disengaged from the stringline and headed into the large volume of space near where Substation 4 had been destroyed. When they wanted to find the stringline again, Adolphus would activate the line of marker buoys.

The General sat forward to study the starry field as they cruised ahead. "All weapons active. Prepare to open fire, but only on my command . . . and only warning shots. Let them see how many ships and weapons we have. By now they should be weak and starving."

"They'll also be desperate and unpredictable, like cornered rats," Sophie pointed out.

"Make sure we keep our distance, Mr. Jordan."

"We have to find them first, sir."

Adolphus had prepared a speech, wording his ultimatum carefully.

He would take Redcom Hallholme and all his commanding officers into custody, and neutralize the Army of the Constellation. It had to be a historic address.

Jordan extended a sensor net, searching for the five stranded string-line haulers. "We should be able to locate them in a few minutes, sir."

"They'll be there," the General said. "Worst case, we may have to follow the stringline segment back to the other end where it was cut off at Substation Three. His anticipation built, and Sophie squeezed his shoulder.

But when they arrived at the cutoff point, they found no Constellation warships, nor stringline haulers, nor any sign of the fleet.

"Send a scout down the stringline segment," Adolphus said, trying not to show his concern. "We'll wait here. Continue the search." His voice was rough, but he knew better than to let any doubt enter into his tone.

But the scout ship raced down the severed stringline segment and came back, finding nothing. No emergency log cylinders, no SOS markers, no indication of the Constellation fleet.

"Where the hell did they go?" Adolphus said. "Where *could* they go?"

35

andela had no more than a few hundred thousand inhabitants, most of whom lived in and around Saporo. The rest of the planet was sparsely populated, with only a few villages and mountain mining towns within aerocopter range of the harbor city. The landscape was a vibrant frontier, full of possibilities.

Due to steady rainfall year round, the hills were lushly forested, with mudslides and miserable conditions during the monsoon season. Even so, compared with more rugged DZ worlds, Candela was a paradise, and Tanja Hu did her best to manage the populace, considering them her responsibility.

Candela's future looked much brighter now that the people were no longer forced to pay oppressive tribute to the Diadem. Tanja would much rather pay Sia Frankov's engineers exorbitant prices for the six recommissioned warships, which had just arrived from Theser via her new direct stringline. Those six armed vessels should be sufficient to stave off any Constellation harassment, if the Diadem poked around for other weak points.

Tanja relished the prospect of telling Governor Undine about the new guardian ships, though she doubted the Diadem's lackey would accept that the Deep Zone had won—and deserved—their independence. She accompanied Bebe Nax in an aerocopter out to the Puhau mudflat.

All that remained of the once-thriving village was a bug-infested, soggy swamp—the Constellation's fault. It was the perfect site for a squalid makeshift prison complex, and a tiny measure of the suffering Diadem Michella had caused. It would be good for Governor Undine's soul.

Bebe had asked to bring along ten-year-old Jacque, so that he could better understand the fight for independence and why the harsh treatment of enemies was necessary. The boy needed to see the price of their freedom, she said, and Tanja agreed.

Jacque wrinkled his nose as they entered the main building. "It stinks in here."

"A prison isn't supposed to smell like blossoms," Bebe said.

Tanja could not conceal her own distaste for the squalid conditions, but she was more sickened by what Undine represented. "What stinks most is how the territorial governor sided against us."

They had attempted to interrogate the prisoner, but Undine refused to speak. Tanja doubted the former governor possessed any useful information, anyway. Marla Undine had spent most of her time in fancy offices at the Bureau of DZ Affairs on Sonjeera. A bureaucrat. It had been her misfortune to be on Theser for a regular but unnecessary inspection when the General cut off the Deep Zone.

A burly guard led them down masonry steps to a dank cell, where the foul odor was even stronger. While the corridor remained dry, brown water covered the cell floor.

"The water pools here in the low part of the prison," the guard said in a matter-of-fact tone. "Leeches slip in with the contaminated water. Nothing we can do to keep them out."

Undine lay on her bunk, wide-awake and haggard. Tanja looked through the heavy gray mesh around the barred cage and said with false cheer, "Good morning."

The governor looked at them with an angry expression. Her skin was sallow, her long black hair matted, her clothes filthy. But the woman's pride, oddly, appeared intact, manifesting itself in cool sarcasm. "Good morning, Administrator. Sorry I'm not more presentable, but you should have told me you were coming. I would have showered and asked the maid to tidy the quarters."

Tanja had hoped to see her broken and miserable. "I brought good news. Candela just received a new force of defensive ships to protect us against the Constellation. You'll be much safer now, without having to worry about becoming an unfortunate casualty if the Diadem's warships should attack here."

"The Diadem would never allow harm to come to her official representative."

Undine swung her bare feet onto the floor and splashed through the brown water to the toilet. She pulled up her dress and sat down, as if to insult her captors. While sitting on the toilet, she yanked leeches from her legs and tossed them at Tanja, but the slippery black things bounced off the mesh and plopped back into the standing water.

When she flushed the toilet, it gurgled and back-flowed onto the floor, then made bubbling noises. She looked up at Tanja with a dark smile, resisting the dehumanizing conditions. "Let me know if you need to use my bathroom, Administrator." Back at her bunk, Undine wiped her feet on a towel and sat with her back against the wall, propping her feet on top of the stained blanket.

The prisoner's flippant resistance made Tanja's anger flare. Being back at the Puhau site, where Uncle Quinn lay buried under the muck, had reopened the wounds and grief. "Do you understand what was here at one time? Good people worked frantically around the clock to meet the Diadem's tribute demands—and the hillsides came roaring down. All because of the Constellation's greed."

Undine was not impressed. "Easy to blame the Crown Jewels for your poor safety procedures and incompetence. When the Constellation fleet comes to crush Candela, you'll be held responsible." She sat straight, summoned her pride. "I am the territorial governor, loyal to the Constellation. I demand the rights of a diplomat under law."

"You *were* the governor. Now you're food for leeches," Tanja said, and a black sludge of anger rose up in her, making her want to strangle the woman, just to erase the smug expression from her face. "We've kept you alive. That's as far as diplomatic courtesy goes."

Meanwhile, Jacque stared wide-eyed, intent on the conversation.

Bebe added in a more formal tone, as if to counter the reckless edge in Tanja's voice, "The Deep Zone no longer has any diplomatic ties or agreements with the Constellation, Governor. Eventually, we may work out terms for your return to Sonjeera, but I wouldn't count on that any time soon."

"Make yourself comfortable here," Tanja said. "And think about all the corpses buried in the mud beneath you." She drew a deep breath and hardened her voice further. "A Constellation spy, however, is another matter. We caught a man trying to take images of classified operations. Fortunately, we apprehended him before he could slip any of his information back to Sonjeera."

Undine's sarcasm vanished. "What happened to him?"

Tanja smiled and looked at Bebe's adopted son as she spoke. "This is war. His actions could have caused the deaths of millions of people, maybe even the collapse of our Deep Zone alliance. We sent him up to the stringline terminus in orbit, as he wanted . . . then we ejected him from the airlock." She shrugged. "I hope his frozen body doesn't become a navigational hazard. Or maybe he burned up in the atmosphere like a meteor."

Governor Undine said, "You're all barbarians."

"I'm glad you think so." Tanja turned to leave. "It means you've been paying attention."

36

As Lord Riomini's strike force approached Theser, he put on a gold lapel pin with the shield insignia of the Riomini family. Ready to command the retaliation, he recalled his glory days during the first rebellion, how he had assembled the Army of the Constellation against General Adolphus. Those had been heady times! Since then, the Diadem's fleet had become bloated and without purpose, but he was beginning to feel the old energy again.

Even in those days, Riomini had never personally drawn blood, never killed anyone in close combat. From his desk, he had ordered bloody attacks, executions, and assassinations, but that had been like a business operation. As he stood there in his formal black uniform, he had watched his enemies die before him, seen their eyes go blank. He was familiar with death, but he liked to keep himself at a comfortable distance.

Now Riomini was leading the largest mission he had ever attempted personally: twenty-three advanced warships loaded aboard two large haulers heading out to the Deep Zone. General Adolphus had cut his own stringline, denying Redcom Hallholme's fleet a way home, but Hellhole was by no means safe. Nor were the other rebel frontier worlds; the Black Lord would prove that at Theser.

As planned, the military haulers arrived at the stringline terminus over Theser and disengaged from the iperion path. All his warships dropped from their docking clamps and fell into attack formation, just like the many drills they had practiced.

Riomini addressed his captains over the codecall system. "Strike fast, strike hard!" It had become a favorite saying of his, an effective war slogan, and he had ordered his propaganda wing to disseminate it throughout the Constellation.

In this punitive onslaught, the fighters knew there would be no prisoners taken, no negotiations, no surrender—only shock and terror, no time or opportunity to flee. Theser was already a dead world, although the population did not yet realize it.

"As you command, my Lord," said his operations officer beside him on the command bridge. Lucinda Ekova had too many moles and red splotches on her skin to be attractive, and her body was solid rather than shapely, but she had an excellent mind that was capable of rapid assessment. Riomini trusted her military judgment.

Other officers stood at their consoles, monitoring the warships as they descended like valkyries toward the heavily cratered surface. He heard the steady buzz of low, competent conversation, saw the interplay of multicolored diagnostics, smelled the excitement in the air.

"First off, dispatch four ships to capture the stringline terminus to the DZ network," he said. "I want it intact so we can move on to planet Hallholme."

Once he dealt with Theser, his soldiers would be even more enthusiastic, having tasted blood. He would send a report back to Sonjeera—as Redcom Hallholme should have done—and then he would take his assault fleet on the General's own stringline.

First things first, though. Followed by the other warcraft, the flagship dipped and accelerated down toward the crater city of Eron. No need to hide, no requirement to give a warning. There were no rules. Riomini planned to bring the images back to the Crown Jewels for wide play across the newsnets, and everyone would see his prowess, patriotism, and worthiness to be the next Diadem. The blood and bones of the Theser rebels would buy him the Star Throne.

Eron came into view, distorted by the thermal bow shock of heated air from their descent. The attack force arrived so unexpectedly that Administrator Frankov could not even contact her defenses. As the city dwellings, administration buildings, and industrial facilities came into range, Riomini ordered his warships to dispatch incendiary bombs that would turn the densely populated crater bowl into a furnace.

Lord Riomini broadcast, more for the historical record than for any effect it might have on the doomed people below, "In the Diadem's name, we are here to secure Theser for the Constellation and punish those who have committed treason against the lawful government."

The first wave of incendiaries ripped through the city like an incandescent flood. The open codecall speakers filled with shouts, screams, and pleading from below, but no word from Administrator Frankov. He had pinpointed her governmental center from archival images, and had issued strict instructions that her offices be left intact until the end. He wanted Frankov to witness the destruction of everything around her.

Before he could bask in success, however, an urgent message interrupted him. "My Lord, we surrounded the illegal stringline terminus ring, but . . . sorry, sir. There was some sort of self-destruct mechanism. Station personnel there blew it up before we could take control."

His throat went dry. "We need that terminus to get on the DZ stringline!"

"They sacrificed themselves, sir. The explosion took out all personnel aboard, four of their own ships, and . . . and two of ours."

Riomini's pulse pounded in his ears. Quick access to Hellhole was gone, not to mention two of his warships. So much for a perfect, clean operation. "Submit yourself for a reprimand at the end of this operation, Captain." He drew two deep breaths, then focused his attention on the flames below. Releasing his anger, he said, "Commence second bombing run."

As the explosions continued, the comm-officer said, "My Lord, Administrator Frankov is on the codecall. She begs to speak with you."

"Let her watch the flames a little longer. I want her to hear more screams."

To the people on the ground, the incendiaries pouring down on the city must have looked like Armageddon. Several ships tried to lift off from the crater floor, but the Constellation forces shot them down before they could gain altitude. So many bombs rained down into the crater that nothing could survive down there.

And nothing did.

The fires melted or vaporized everything in their path, swept across the ground in a manifestation of the anger Diadem Michella felt toward the Deep Zone rebels. No discussion, no pity, no remorse—just the eradication of everything on Theser. The smaller settlements around the cratered planet didn't matter; he would advance on them in due time, at his leisure. Theser would be no more than an afterthought in the universe. . . .

After a ten-hour blitzkrieg, at the dawn of a new day, the Constellation fleet landed in smoldering Eron, and Lord Riomini disembarked. The air smelled of burned buildings, roasted scrubtrees, and charred bodies, the detritus of life and industry that no longer existed.

His own shuttle set down halfway up the rim of the crater, where the bombardment had left a section of buildings untouched: Sia Frankov's admin center and the laboratories of the spacedrive engineers.

"It's time to call upon the planetary administrator," Riomini said. "I wonder what she'll have to say for herself."

"Does it matter, sir?" Lucinda Ekova asked.

"Not in the least."

He accompanied Ekova and a force of his guards up the blackened slope to where a group of shocked and wailing people stood outside the remaining buildings. He recognized the thin, red-haired Sia Frankov from her dossier photos, as well as a group of the tall, inbred spacedrive engineers.

He did not see Territorial Governor Undine; if the political prisoner hadn't been held in one of the surviving buildings, then Undine was already a martyr, an example of the barbarity of the Deezee rebels. The Black Lord didn't really care.

Frankov looked so broken and devastated she could barely summon outrage. "I presume you are here to take my engineers prisoner, Lord Riomini? You didn't need to destroy everything to get to them. We . . . we would have surrendered them to you."

He chuckled. "But surrenders are so heartrending. I have no interest whatsoever in your engineers. We have plenty of our own, and we can always train more if we need them."

One of the engineers took a step forward, his face contorted in rage. Riomini gave a quick hand gesture, and his accompanying bodyguards shot all the scientists in a barrage of weapons fire, splattering blood on Frankov.

To her credit, the administrator did not cringe, though she could not conceal her trembling. "So it's me you're after? That's a great deal of trouble for one prisoner." Frankov swallowed hard.

"Oh, I have no intention of taking you prisoner. I just wanted to save you for last." He was delighted to see her eyes widen in surprise before Ekova fired two quick and precise shots—one in each eye.

Surrounded by bodies, Riomini raised his arms. "On to Sonjeera! We return victorious!" It was an incomplete victory, but he would put a spin on it to minimize the loss of the other stringline terminus.

37

While riding aboard the passenger pod from Qiorfu, Commodore Percival Hallholme had polished his shoes and fiddled with the colorful ornaments of his numerous medals. During the six-hour journey, he had played card games with Adkins, and both men avoided the issue at hand.

Finally, after their third round (Adkins lost all three), his old friend threw down the polished playing cards. "So what do you think the Diadem really wants, sir? Why has she summoned us to Sonjeera, and why wouldn't they give us a full briefing en route?"

Percival did not let himself grow perturbed. "We'll find out soon, Duff."

After delivering their orders to the Commodore, Colonel Ricketts and Lora Heston chose to sit in separate compartments of the passenger pod, isolating themselves from the two men. Adkins considered it an affront. "Not a very warm welcome. Why are they avoiding us?"

Percival understood, though. "They don't want to have to deal with questions that they're not allowed to answer."

"It doesn't mean they have to be rude," Adkins said. "They could have joined us for a game or two. We'd have more fun with four players."

Percival picked up the cards and dealt another hand. "We know why we were summoned to Sonjeera—the Diadem wants my help against General Adolphus."

Adkins wasn't convinced. "She already sent a whole fleet to take care of the matter. Isn't a hundred ships enough?"

Percival looked at the cards in his hand. "We both know that General Adolphus poses more of a challenge than others expect. Escobar may be in over his head."

Adkins glowered. "So she wants us to clean up her mess."

"The Diadem wants us to follow her instructions, Duff. And since she reactivated our commissions, that is exactly what we're going to do."

❧

With Duff Adkins marching crisply at his side, the Commodore returned to the Diadem's palace. Both of them wore their old uniforms, which Percival much preferred to the new designs. They strode past the chamber guards and functionaries, chins held high, gazes forward, as if this were a training drill; Percival had taken enough painkillers to mask the ache of his limp. He had never expected, nor wanted, to come back here.

The floor was so polished that the reflected lights from above shone like pools of sunshine. His military boots sounded like gunshots in a precise rhythm that was echoed by his adjutant's steps as they walked in tandem. Moments later, the sergeant at arms saluted and regarded the old military hero with a measure of awe.

Percival presented himself. "Commodore Hallholme reporting to the Diadem, as ordered."

"This way, sir."

Diadem Michella Duchenet appeared flustered as she sat at her immense desk, her gray hair arranged in a bun, her face powdered, her expression haggard. She had been engaged in a private meeting with her shadowy assistant Ishop Heer, whom Percival had seen in the background of many formal images, as if he didn't like to be caught by the news media. She glanced up, saw the Commodore, and a smile split her face, like a small seismic event.

"Ishop, leave us. I have business with Commodore Hallholme."

The furtive assistant gathered papers, appearing to keep every piece in order; Percival thought the man had predatory eyes. "If you allow me to stay, Eminence, I could provide suggestions."

"I said *no*, Ishop. Leave us alone." Looking annoyed, the man scurried away.

"Eminence, this is my adjutant, Duff Adkins," Percival said. "I value his advice. If you intend to give me new orders, I ask that he be allowed to stay."

The Diadem's voice was honey-sweet. "Of course, Commodore. I rely on your judgment—and I need it now more than ever. The Constellation is in crisis, as you undoubtedly know, but the general public does not understand the magnitude of treachery General Adolphus inflicted on us."

Percival stood at attention with Adkins at his side, equally formal. The Diadem waved her spidery ringed hand. "Please sit, *sit*, both of you! This isn't an army review." Adkins pulled out a chair for the Commodore and took a seat himself. Both looked intently at Michella.

Percival spoke up. "Eminence, your representatives provided no explanations. Is there news of my son Escobar? By now he should have had sufficient time to subdue the rebellion."

"According to the plan, he *should* have. Unfortunately, his fleet has gone missing. Five fully loaded stringline haulers, one hundred battleships, and your son—they've all vanished without a trace."

Percival tried to cover his alarm. Missing? "Do you think the General captured them?"

"We don't know yet, but the stringline to planet Hallholme was severed, which prevents us from obtaining more information. Initially we thought—we *hoped*, perhaps—that a substation had blown by accident. But on further investigation, we feel that it was intentional. Our scouts have located anchor buoys in place on our side of the blown substation that keep the stringline from wandering. We know it wasn't anything the line builders originally installed, so that madman Adolphus had to do it."

"We're not dealing with a madman, Eminence," Percival said carefully. "He's operating under a well-thought-out plan."

She grimaced. "Our scout drones have found no trace of our fleet along the entire segment of the path, and they're still looking in space around the blown substation, and beyond. The five military haulers have been cut off somehow. I pray that they were able to continue to planet Hallholme and complete their mission. Regardless, your son has not managed to send word back."

Concerned, Percival looked at Adkins, then ran his thumb along his chin, pondering. "As a defensive measure, it would have made more sense for Adolphus to cut the stringline *before* the fleet moved, which would have forced Escobar to return to Sonjeera. But if our fleet had already passed before the substation blew, then the General would have ensured his own defeat by trapping them on his side of the stringline. It would have been like locking a vicious attack dog in the room with him." He raised his eyebrows in a sudden thought. "Unless he cut the stringline in two places and trapped them out there."

The Diadem paled. "That would have required extremely careful timing. And very thorough information of our plans."

"We are dealing with General Adolphus, Eminence." Percival tapped his fingers together. "What does Lord Riomini have to say about this?"

"We have too little information to make a full assessment. Meanwhile, Commodore, I called you back to duty because your son's fleet represents a significant percentage of our military. Those hundred warships are more than a match for anything the Deezees could cobble together. So what has the General done to our task force? Where are they? I'm counting on you—fix this! Find me answers. Rescue the lost fleet if necessary and come up with an alternative way to capture General Adolphus, crush the rebellion. If anyone can do it, you can." Anger made her voice rise.

Percival's thoughts spun. Escobar had always been overconfident, not satisfied with a slow route to a successful career. He didn't believe he had to earn it, and yet he resented any suggestion that his promotions were due to having a war hero for a father.

Nevertheless, Escobar was his only son, and Percival would have to save him from himself—and defeat General Tiber Adolphus in the process.

"You ordered me out of retirement for this, Eminence, but Lord Riomini commands the Army of the Constellation. He should be involved closely in any military planning. Perhaps he should lead this operation?"

"Don't you worry about the Black Lord," Michella' said, trying to sound sweet, but there was a brittle snap to her voice. "He is currently engaged out in the Deep Zone. He's not back yet from his mission to Theser."

Percival raised his eyebrows. "Theser? What is he doing there?"

"That's not your concern right now. I place my confidence in your abilities because I believe you're the only one who can defeat that awful man. I should have put you in charge of the fleet in the first place. When everyone thought Sonjeera was lost in the last rebellion, you stopped Adolphus in his tracks—I only wish you'd blown him up in orbit during the attack. That would have solved a lot of problems."

"He surrendered, Diadem. I was honor bound to take him alive and grant safe passage to his crew."

"As you say," she responded, not sounding the least bit convinced. "But we would have suffered far fewer headaches if you'd finished the job then and there." She sighed. "But I bear the blame for giving Adolphus a second chance. By sending him to a hellish planet, I thought he would perish, but in the back of my mind I was allowing him to redeem himself. But neither of those things have happened, and he's a threat once more."

Percival maintained a neutral expression, though he could sense Adkins stiffen next to him. He knew full well that Diadem Michella had sabotaged vital shipments to General Adolphus in the colony's early years. She had meant for the DZ colonists to fail, and many of them would have died if *Percival* hadn't surreptitiously slipped in additional supplies. Adolphus did not suspect that his secret benefactor was also the man who had defeated him. Nor would he ever know.

Michella leaned forward with an earnest expression. "I implore you, Commodore—find a way to defeat General Adolphus one more time."

Feeling the stiffness in his legs, he rose from his chair and gave a formal bow while Adkins snapped to attention beside him. "I need to look further into the matter and verify details, Eminence, but I may already have a plan."

Adkins reacted with surprise. "You do, sir?"

The Diadem did not look at all startled. Obviously, she had expected no less from the old military strategist and commander. He looked at his good friend and smiled thinly. "I always have a plan."

38

After Sergeants Zabriskie and Caron departed in the trailblazer, the initial rush of optimism faded aboard the stranded fleet. Over the next two weeks, their morale drained like a slow, deflating air leak.

Bolton huddled in his private cabin, using only one dim light to conserve energy. He wore extra layers of clothing, but could not shake the bone-chilling cold that permeated the *Diadem's Glory*. The medical specialists and life-support technicians had run detailed calculations to determine the optimal temperature for the ships, a balance between conserving energy and lowered metabolism, but not so cold that the personnel burned excessive calories just to keep their bodies warm.

Hunger was a constant ache in Bolton's stomach, as well as in his mind. Four weeks since they'd been stranded . . . and at least six more before the trailblazer could complete the new route to Hellhole. Then their ragged ships could finally plunge into enemy territory.

As belts tightened and the soldiers shivered and complained, crew-members balked at Bolton's draconian requirements, particularly the nobles who had bought their commissions and were administratively excused from rigorous basic training and planetary survival exercises. Bolton caused an uproar when he suggested—and Escobar agreed—that the leaders symbolically take even smaller portions than the soldiers under their command. The nobles still assumed that, because of their family connections, they could have their feasts, wines, and desserts, that they were somehow exempt from the austerity measures.

Some had been caught trying to steal food or hoard supplies; to his credit, Escobar doled out punishments for the infractions, regardless of the family names of the guilty parties. Bolton was no survivalist cut out for hard times and long periods of deprivation, but he did understand realities, especially when he compiled the charts himself.

Despite the increasing complaints, no one could refute his numbers or offer a better plan. He had run the calculations based on irrefutable assumptions. Most external systems had been shut down, leaving the five stringline haulers quiet and cold. The Redcom continued to hope for a miraculous alternative inspired by hunger, fear, and uncertainty . . . but so far no suggestion had been worth pursuing. The scout ships continued to search for the old iperion path, but with the fleet now clustered around the new terminus ring, they were limited in how far they could range. So far, nothing.

Throughout the fleet, engineering squads modified and expanded recycling units, closing loops and improving efficiency so that 95 percent of energy, water, and oxygen went back into the system. Bolton was able to add a little more time to their numbers, but not enough that anyone rejoiced.

He was confident they weren't going to suffocate or die of thirst. Under extreme circumstances, engineers could chemically extract water and oxygen from the standard fuel tanks, since the ships weren't flying anywhere. He also calculated that the fleet's power cells would last longer than their food supplies. But food . . . tomorrow would mark the third week of reduced rations.

Two more attempted mutinies had been quelled aboard smaller ships. The crews were hungry all the time, and uncertainty sharpened their tempers.

Bolton knew the situation was about to become much worse. By his calculations, he had no choice but to press hard for a second, even more difficult phase.

Though the trailblazer had been gone for only two weeks, the desperate crew kept watch every day, hoping for rescue. Some even secretly hoped that General Adolphus would find them—better to be well-fed prisoners than to die out here.

When one crewman tried to send out a broad-spectrum distress signal from the *Diadem's Glory*, Gail Carrington raced to the comm-station in a blur of motion. The young man squawked in indignant surprise as she grabbed the top of his head and jerked his chin up. From somewhere she produced a small dagger that Bolton had never seen before, and she neatly slit the man's throat.

Escobar leaped out of his command chair in protest. The rest of the bridge crew cried out in disbelief. Carrington shoved the dead man off the duty chair and onto the deck. "Your orders are perfectly clear," she said to all of them. "*Anyone* who attempts to contact our enemy is our enemy. I will send a self-destruct signal through this fleet before I let General Adolphus get his hands on these battleships!"

She looked at the Redcom as if daring him to challenge her. Finally, Escobar nodded. "Yes, we should reiterate the orders by courier from ship to ship." Pale and sickened, he looked at the dead crewman lying in a pool of blood on the deck. The young man still wore a startled expression. "I believe you've made your point, Ms. Carrington."

⌘

For energy efficiency, the crews aboard the smaller frigates came aboard the larger battleships and shut down the other vessels. Consolidating the personnel wasted less power and life support, although the crowded conditions raised further concerns about unrest.

When Bolton brought his latest set of numbers to the Redcom, he knew that his conclusions were irrefutable, direct extrapolations from the data, checked and rechecked. "Unless we take even more extraordinary measures, we'll all be dead at least a week before the trailblazer can possibly return."

Escobar's face sagged as he wondered what was next. Carrington stood there, ubiquitous and judgmental. "It's obvious," she said. "We must eliminate extraneous personnel so that our food and life support lasts long enough for a core group who can complete the mission."

"Like you eliminated my comm officer?" Escobar grumbled.

Bolton recoiled. "I have a different idea." He had not expected Riomini's watchdog to be so blunt, but he was glad she'd blurted out her outrageous suggestion; by comparison, his idea would sound far less extreme. "We need to sedate a large portion of our crew. Keep them tranquilized for extended periods of time with very low metabolic requirements. That will reduce our overall food, air, and water consumption, which will allow us to stretch our nutritional supplies."

"But we have thousands of crewmen," Escobar said. "Fifteen thousand. How could we possibly keep that many in comas for the next six weeks?"

"Remember, the Diadem wanted us to bring back a large number of prisoners. I loaded aboard stockpiles of the Sandusky stasis drug, and because this is a military operation, we have extensive sickbay facilities with other means of long-term sedation. We should take volunteers first, ask who's willing to sleep through the worst times ahead. If that doesn't generate enough names, then impose a lottery." Bolton stared at both of them and wondered if he looked as haggard as they did. Probably. "Understand, we've got to cut down on our consumption—dramatically." He extended his electronic pad, but neither Carrington nor Escobar needed to verify the numbers.

"We should make the choices," Carrington said. "How many would volunteer for forced sedation? Not enough, I'd say."

"Let's give them the option first," Escobar said. "We already know what it's like to feel constant hunger, know the tension. It's going to get worse. Some might find it preferable to sleep through it until we're all saved."

Or dead, Bolton thought.

Escobar continued, "If we try to sedate thousands by force, you can bet the crew will turn on us."

Though skeptical, Carrington said, "All right, Redcom. We'll try it your way first, and institute other means if necessary. The more people we tranquilize, the fewer who will be conscious to fight us when we have to impose more."

Bolton knew they might have to place all but a skeleton crew into induced comas—provided they had enough of the Sandusky stasis drug and the people to administer it, and cooperative crewmembers willing to be forced into sleep. Even at that, they would eventually run out of food, air, and water. . . .

After Escobar distributed a message requesting volunteers, they were disappointed by the first few hours of uneasy silence. "They're still grappling with the magnitude of our crisis," Bolton said.

Then one squadron of fighter pilots unanimously volunteered, deciding to stick together. "We won't be needed until we arrive at planet Hallholme," said their flight commander. "We could all use a good rest before we face the General. Wake us up when it's time to fight." The flight commander put an optimistic face on his decision. The eighteen squadron members stood together, and Escobar thanked them.

In the flagship's sick bay, doctors administered the stasis drug, which dropped the squadron members into peaceful, dreamless comas. From ship after ship, more volunteers came forward, more than five hundred the first day.

"Not nearly enough," Carrington said. "Not by an order of magnitude."

Jackson Firth and his three diplomatic comrades joined the command crew in their meeting. Firth seemed pleased that the Red Commodore was taking decisive action. "Perhaps that first squadron was onto something," Firth said. "If we tranquilize all our fighter pilots who won't be needed until we reach the planet, that would be a substantial number of personnel—and they do eat a lot of food."

"The reason we have so many fighter pilots, Mr. Firth, is because this was meant to be an overwhelming military assault," Escobar pointed out. "You are right, though—we don't need them until we arrive and begin the operation." A cruel smile crept over his face. "And you raise another significant point, sir. *Your* team will not be needed until *after* we defeat General Adolphus. The diplomats are clearly nonessential personnel at present, so I am pleased to accept you and your staff as additional volunteers."

Firth and his four team members reacted with indignation. "We were assigned by the Diadem herself. We are not expendable!"

"I didn't say you are expendable," Escobar corrected. "But we don't need your services *at present*. Your consumption of vital food and life support is indefensible. Therefore I happily accept your offer."

As Firth searched for words, opening and closing his mouth, Gail Carrington said, "It's a worthy gesture."

Seeing that they would force him whether or not he agreed, the diplomat tapped his pudgy fingers on the tabletop. "Very well. Dozing off for a few weeks does seem like a convenient alternative. You are confident the trailblazer ship will make it in time?"

"I have complete faith in my pilots," said Escobar.

Carrington seemed bright and cheerful for a change. "Mr. Firth, let me escort you and your team to the medical center. I'll make sure you are comfortable and are granted the best available beds."

"Thank you, Ms. Carrington, thank you," said Firth. He looked quite ill at ease. "Do you think we could have one more meal before we're sedated? To give us energy during the long sleep?"

"You won't need it," Carrington said. "Trust me."

⌘

The following day, Bolton reported with a sigh, "We still need more. Our next step will be to specify nonessential personnel, then impose a lottery system. Within the next two days, we've got to have five thousand troops no longer consuming food and air." He looked at them all. "The sooner we take care of this, the more food and energy reserves we'll have for when it matters most. In fact, I wish we had done this a week ago."

"We still have to survive for a minimum of five more weeks," Escobar said.

"Six weeks is more realistic." Bolton looked down at his data, but he could not deny his own assessments. "We need to drop down to a twenty percent crew complement, if any of us is going to survive. . . ."

Later, by the time Carrington called the Redcom and the Major into the flagship's sick bay, it was too late for them to do anything. The men hurried into the medical facility, and Bolton immediately saw that the life-support monitors were flatlined, the alarms silenced. The entire diplomatic team was dead.

Dr. Hambliss, the chief medical officer on the flagship, stared at Carrington in disgust and horror, but she seemed unaffected, even proud. She crossed her arms over her chest. "They're out of our way now, Redcom. The longer we wait to make harsh decisions like this, the more people will have to pay the price. They were an unnecessary drain on our resources." She held an emptied syringe in her hand.

"I saw her kill them," said Hambliss, "in cold blood, while they were sleeping and helpless."

Escobar's eyes blazed. "You injected them with poison?"

"Not necessary," Carrington said. "Just an air bubble in each of their carotid arteries. But don't worry about them. They were a useless waste of resources. I've heard you complain about them numerous times."

Bolton found it difficult to breathe. He knew that Lord Riomini despised Jackson Firth because the diplomat had inflicted political damage on him by throwing his support toward Enva Tazaar. He wondered if the Black Lord had instructed Carrington to look for an opportunity to eliminate Firth. He said in a low, husky voice, "When word of this gets out, we'll have riots across the ships."

"That's why it won't get out," she said. "Place the bodies in cold storage. No one will ever know—unless and until we get through this."

Dr. Hambliss straightened his shoulders. "I refuse. I will not condone murder."

"You will keep silent about this." Carrington's voice was like a bladed weapon. "The deed is done. When I boarded these ships back on Sonjeera, I was under Lord Riomini's orders to do *anything* necessary to make the mission a success." She swept her gaze across Escobar and Bolton, then the doctor, as if daring them to make further objections.

Bolton swallowed hard. "I . . . I will adjust my numbers accordingly. May I suggest that we quietly dispose of the bodies out in space before anyone knows?"

Ever hard and practical, Carrington pressed her lips into a colorless line. "Best if we don't do that. Times may get hard enough that we'll need the extra protein."

39

General Adolphus couldn't recall the last time he'd felt so unsettled. He was a master of juggling the pieces of a large plan, coordinating and choreographing the efforts of his countless loyal followers. Managing more than fifty links of his new DZ network, ensuring that all the trailblazers arrived at virtually the same time, across vast swaths of space, was a mind-boggling challenge, and he had done it.

With the information provided by his loyalist spy, he knew exactly the strength and timing of the Constellation fleet sent against him, and the Urvanciks had verified that they were off the stringline and trapped in empty space. As planned. Stranded in the middle of nowhere with dwindling supplies and no iperion path to follow, they had no place to go.

And yet, they *had* gone . . . somewhere.

With the *Jacob* parked in orbit over Hellhole while the Urvanciks and ten other scouts searched the last known coordinates of the stranded Constellation fleet, Adolphus pondered his alternatives. He pored over the data, desperate to discover where he had gone wrong, which reports might have been false. The Constellation fleet *had* to be out there!

Suspecting a trick, his scouts maintained radio silence while searching. Perhaps Escobar Hallholme's fleet lay in hiding—but they had left Sonjeera more than a month ago, and the crew should be desperate, low on supplies and life support.

Where were they? He didn't trust them. His plan had seemed so simple and foolproof—cut the stringline and bottle up the Diadem's warships, then wait for them to weaken and surrender. The simplest kind of siege. But now he realized he had been overconfident. Adolphus wondered if he'd been duped, if he had underestimated the son of Percival Hallholme. It was driving him mad with frustration.

While Adolphus pondered his next move from his flagship, Sophie had returned to the surface to notify the shadow-Xayans and the Originals that they might need to rely on telemancy defenses after all. Weeks ago, the General had been sure he'd bought Hellhole a reprieve, but now he wasn't so certain.

The linerunner *Kerris* returned to the Hellhole hub with their report. "We just came back for a quick reprovisioning, General," Turlo said. "The other nine scouts are still combing their grid patterns. No luck so far."

Sunitha produced a datapack that chronicled the hunt for the lost Constellation fleet. "We're covering an ever-widening volume, but I don't think they're out there, sir. Five big haulers, a hundred ships—we've picked up no distress signals, no radio chatter."

"No wreckage either," Turlo said.

His wife shrugged. "But if they wandered off into the weeds, if they used their FTL to head away in some random direction . . . well, they could be anywhere."

Turlo looked away, obviously disturbed. "When we blew up the substations, sir, we were happy to help you snare the fleet . . . but we didn't intend to impose a death sentence on all those soldiers."

"Our son used to be a Constellation soldier," Sunitha added.

"You didn't do it. They chose their own death sentence." Adolphus recognized his stinging tone, took a deep breath, and added in a quieter voice, "I didn't mean for it to be a death sentence either. We intended to capture the fleet and negotiate in a civilized manner for the soldiers' eventual return to the Crown Jewels. They weren't supposed to die." He felt sick at this failure. He straightened, and looked hard at the two linerunners. "Keep in mind that if those ships had reached Hellhole and completed their mission, they would have slaughtered hundreds of thousands."

He looked down at the search datapack in his hand, but knew the information would tell him little or nothing. "I'll have my experts scan this. Maybe we can detect some ion trail or exhaust residue."

"Yes, sir." Turlo did not sound convinced.

Adolphus's heart felt heavy. It was a victory, but not one to be proud of. Militarily speaking, he had counted on adding those hundred captured warships to his DZ Defense Force. And he had looked forward to forcing the son of Commodore Hallholme to surrender to *him*, bringing events full circle. He had not meant to condemn all those soldiers to death.

"Keep looking," Adolphus said. "They've got to be out there."

40

"Now we can celebrate," Ishop said, feeling triumphant, yet somehow disappointed at the same time. "That's the last name on our list."

He had lived for the better part of a year with the driving goal of crossing off one victim after another, nobles marked for death by the seven-hundred-year-old stain in their familial blood.

And now it was done. He and Laderna had worked together on the scheme to kill Priema Vuarner, a well-choreographed performance: The chandelier had glittered and twirled on its long tumble down from the domed ceiling in the museum of culture. Sweet Priema had been standing on the podium to accept an award for her exceptional contributions to animal welfare issues. The man presenting the award saw the chandelier falling and dove out of the way, but Priema Vuarner's foot was mysteriously and inexplicably stuck on the floor of the stage. An odd thing. Her body had positively *sparkled* after the crash, studded with so many shattered fragments of crystal. . . .

Now he and Laderna smiled at each other in the elegant dining chamber of Edwond House, the old townhouse that Diadem Michella had given him in gratitude for his faithful service. For the celebration with Laderna, he had changed into a stylish tuxedo with tails . . . the kind worn by noblemen. Now there were no impediments to the full enjoyment of his restored heritage.

In two months' time he could formally be inducted into those heady ranks. Now that the requirements of personal revenge had been taken care of, Ishop could work on cultivating a new polished demeanor. He no longer needed to slink in the shadows doing Michella's dirty work. He was a *noble*!

The two of them were alone in the historic room where Edwond the First, the Warrior Diadem, had held his cabinet meetings. Such a room seemed appropriate for the occasion.

"We can celebrate finishing the list, if you like, boss, but don't forget we still have a loose end," Laderna said, dampening his victorious feeling. "We still have to cross off a Duchenet name."

While it rankled Ishop that the Diadem's daughter might still be alive, Keana was possessed by a hideous alien entity and trapped on a planet marked for sterilization. Surely, that was worse than death!

He frowned. "Keana is gone—no need to drag this out, with our own deadline approaching. She's as good as dead, so I claim success." Maybe Laderna enjoyed the quest so much that she didn't want it to be over. He, too, felt let down from the emptiness after a completed task, but he had grander dreams to pursue now, plans to make for his future. "It's just a technicality."

Laderna sounded stern. "A technicality is what denied you your heritage for your entire life, boss. You're as much a stickler for detail as I am." She paused, as if an idea had just occurred to her, but he knew she must have thought of it earlier, then worked it over in her thoughts, prodding and testing it. "We do have an additional option. We could always find *another* Duchenet to kill."

"Not the Diadem. Killing Michella would be foolish. Or do you mean some distant cousin?" He frowned. "That wouldn't be the same."

"Doesn't the Diadem have a sister?"

Ishop drew in a quick breath. "Haveeda! But she's been hidden away for years, completely out of the public eye."

"So were these documents, but I found them. No reason we shouldn't look for her. Once we start a task we need to finish it."

"Very well, snoop around to see if you can find where she's been all these years. But it'll be a moot point as soon as the Constellation fleet levels Hellhole. The rebels will all be dead, and who would bother to count the corpses and identify body parts?" He poured chilled champagne into a pair of tall crystal glasses. "You and I have more important matters to occupy our time."

The compulsion to finish what he had begun was strong, but it was not a sufficient reason to delay his next step. He had to begin preparing his presentation to the Council, in which he would formally claim his title. He had marked the date on the calendar, but then decided to add two extra days. It had been seven hundred years, after all—no sense in being impatient. It didn't seem *noble*.

He replaced the champagne bottle in the ice bucket, rattling the ice cubes. A smile curled the edges of Laderna's mouth as she sipped from her glass. "I'm definitely in the mood to celebrate." She glanced toward the anteroom with its comfortable chairs and a settee, a place for noblemen to relax after a sumptuous meal. "Shall we go in there? We've commemorated each victory, and this should be the best so far." Her brown eyes flashed at him, and he felt his willpower melt. Ishop decided to indulge his assistant, rewarding her for a job well done. He took special care to show his gratitude for her in every possible way and position.

Afterward, Laderna lay beside him on the sheets, her head propped on one hand. Ishop finally had a moment to think, and he let out a long sigh. "That was a very nice way to conclude our relationship, a defining moment to end this stage of my life. Now I'm ready to emerge as a fullfledged nobleman, like a caterpillar becoming a butterfly." He yawned. "I wonder if I should change the family name back to Osheer, just on principle, or continue to call myself Heer."

He expected her to be pleased for him, satisfied with the part she had played in his victory. "Oh, we are far from finished, boss. When your formal title is restored, you're required to marry a noblewoman, otherwise all our work would be for nothing. That'll be the next step."

This was a pleasant surprise. He had expected that she might be foolishly jealous and forget to look at the big picture. But this was *Laderna*, utterly reliable and devoted, serving *his* goals, facilitating *his* advancement. And they were bound together by the crimes they had committed. Certainly, he could count on her.

Even naked on the bed, she was still within reach of a datapad. She rolled over and called up a new list to show him. "I have been studying acceptable candidates, based on their planetary wealth and political influence. Personally, I'd feel better if we settled on an ugly crone, but I won't be that petty."

He was surprised that she had suggested it. "You already thought of this yourself?"

Laderna's smile had a hard edge. "After what we've been through, our relationship doesn't have to be over. I'm looking at how to gain what you really want. Isn't that what we've been working toward? As a team? Once you become a nobleman, I didn't expect you to marry me. I do expect gratitude, however."

He swallowed in a dry throat. "And you shall have it. When I regain my rightful title, you'll be there."

"But out of sight," she said. "I already have it planned out for us." She extended the list, called up images. "What do you think about Enva Tazaar? She's quite attractive, and could bear enough noble heirs to solidify your lineage."

He put on his trousers and torn shirt. "All right. Let's have a look at the advantages and disadvantages of Enva Tazaar."

41

Among the twenty Crown Jewel planets, a stringline passage could be made in a few hours, a day at most: a short enough time that with sufficient planning and well-distributed excuses, even the Diadem could slip away on a private mission without the rest of the Constellation knowing. Not even Ishop Heer, who seemed to have eyes everywhere.

Though she was Diadem of the entire Constellation, Michella still had family obligations. She visited Haveeda as often as possible, though not as often as a sister should.

For the journey to Sandusky, she boarded a thin, new-model ship that could operate independently, and expensively, without being taken aboard a much larger stringline hauler. The streamlined vessel saved a full hour in the typical passage, which made it easier for Michella to keep her secret. Besides, as Diadem, her time was valuable.

During the passage, Michella remained in the sealed-off forward section of the ship reserved for special passengers. No one knew her identity, no one could track her movements. She shared the vessel with only one other passenger, a portly nobleman who made regular business runs between Sonjeera and Sandusky. Even though she wore a disguise, she made sure she had no contact with him.

During the passage, Michella remained isolated, glad to snatch a few moments of peace. For years, she'd had to deal with Haveeda, obligated to keep the unfortunate woman safe and protected, in a place where she could cause no further problems or make any accusations against Michella. Though it had been so many decades since the "suspicious death" of their brother Jamos, Michella doubted anyone would care. Still, she had no time for family scandals of any kind.

Keana had caused her own set of problems—worse ones, perhaps, and not so easily dealt with as Michella had dealt with Haveeda. Unreliable family members! She wished she could just oust them all like unsatisfactory Council members and get a set of new ones.

Her daughter had been flighty but willful, petulant in her refusal to accept her role and meet her minimal obligations. Keana had her embarrassing affair with Louis de Carre, which had been taken care of in a politically expedient way. Then running off to Hellhole in a silly gesture to find de Carre's son had been another maddening example of her stupidity. Worse, she had become an obvious pawn of General Adolphus and his revolutionary plans. But worst of all—to *allow* herself to be possessed by those hideous aliens, to give her body to that slime, the mental domination of an inhuman creature!

Michella's skin crawled. Even though she had never cared much for her disappointing daughter, the thought of the flesh-of-her-own-flesh so completely contaminated caused panic to wash over her. Who knew what other powers those creatures exerted? The infestation was a far more insidious threat than a mere political rebellion. Her stomach twisted, as if the contamination reflected back through her daughter, penetrating to *Michella,* crawling into her womb. . . .

She gasped and caught herself from crying out. She had dozed on the long passage. Now her heart pounded, and she felt sure this was more than her imagination. She had always been coldly rational, a leader who shouldered the weight of countless planets. She had never imagined she might have to deal with an alien invasion.

By contrast, the annoyance of her intractable sister was a trivial matter.

Sandusky was one of the smaller Crown Jewel worlds, sparsely populated, known for thriving biological research and isolated laboratories. If she were discovered on one of her secret trips there, Michella could always claim to be inspecting a classified project, perhaps a nerve agent to be turned against the Deep Zone rebels. Better still, she would set Sandusky researchers to work on the question of the dangerous aliens on Hellhole. Yes, she had plenty of reasons to go to Sandusky. No one would guess that this was where she had hidden Haveeda.

The Sandusky researchers also performed behavior-modification experiments on research subjects that Michella happily provided from her political prisons. Among their promising avenues of inquiry, they sought ways to selectively erase a person's memories; so far, though, they had not shown enough success that Michella was willing to let Haveeda return to a productive life. She doubted, in fact, that her sister would ever leave Sandusky—some risks were too great. Michella had no trouble living with her guilt.

After the streamlined vessel arrived at the Sandusky terminus ring, Michella rode a separate shuttle down to the surface, where she had arranged her own private transportation.

Her sister was kept in an isolated sanitarium, which was constructed of a rare, vivid green marble from local mines. The historic facility featured white columns and statues of famous Sanduskan scientists. It was a lovely place for poor Haveeda.

Guided by a lab security escort, Michella found her way to the echoing research chamber on the second floor. She found it disconcerting that only children worked in the facility, boys and girls wearing starched white lab coats and characteristic magnifying goggles that were used to examine specimens.

The oldest worker was a slender teenage girl with short blond hair, who approached Michella with a respectful bow. "Eminence, your sister's condition is unchanged, and stable."

"Thank you. I'd like to visit her for a while." The teenager guided her through an electronic barrier that slid open and then closed behind them.

When they finally reached the familiar heavy vault door, the girl bowed again and opened the door with a breath of frost and cold vapor. "I will leave you alone with your loved one now."

A clear glass tank stood in the center of the room. Michella stepped inside the vault and heard the door close behind her, but her attention was on the preservation tank. She stood over the container and wiped the sparkle of frost from the curved surface. Haveeda lay inside, frozen in her body as well as in time. Her sister's eyes were open and unfocused, as if made of glass.

It was for the best. Haveeda was no longer plagued with nightmares; she no longer threatened to expose Michella's embarrassing childhood crimes. But she was still alive.

"I told you I'd take care of you," Michella said. "And no one bothers you here." And Haveeda was no longer a threat.

The Diadem studied the younger woman's face with its passive, locked-in expression. Haveeda looked to be in her early thirties, the age at which she'd been frozen. She had been preserved for so long that Michella could still see glints of what Haveeda had looked like as a child . . . when the girl had the misfortune of witnessing Michella kill their brother Jamos. She had pushed their brother out of a tree, happy to watch his head strike a rock, more fascinated than frightened by the hollow cracking sound and all the blood. Michella had never forgotten what her brother looked like in death, the staring, empty eyes.

Haveeda's eyes looked like that now, but she was not dead. "I just come here to say things I could never reveal to anyone else, things I couldn't even discuss with Ishop," Michella whispered. "It's liberating, and you're *such* a good listener." Her voice was laced with sarcasm, but carried an undertone of sincerity.

After the murder, Michella had threatened her sister that if she ever revealed what had happened, she would slip into her bedroom one night and bash her head with a rock, just like Jamos. Haveeda had been terrified of her sister, growing into a skittish, nightmare-haunted woman. Eventually, Michella found it much more convenient just to keep Haveeda preserved like this, where the Diadem didn't have to worry.

Michella slipped on a cryo-glove and reached through a small access port in the tank. When the sealing mechanism grew snug around her arm, she probed forward and grasped Haveeda's frozen hand resting on her waist.

"You understand why I had to do this, don't you? So much is at stake at very high levels, and you could jeopardize it all. You do understand that, don't you?"

Haveeda couldn't answer, and that was how Michella preferred dealing with her sister. "Of course you do. Remember when you thought you saw me push our brother . . . but you were just imagining things. As

soon as your memories are repaired, we can wake you up. In the meantime, enjoy your beauty sleep."

Though Michella's voice was calm and soothing, she did not feel
that way inside at all. Most of her life she had been furious at Haveeda
for causing all this trouble. At least this one problem had been solved,
neatly and efficiently.

The Diadem withdrew her gloved hand and stepped away, then on
impulse she kicked the frozen canister, releasing her frustration. It might
have been kinder to kill her sister, but Michella was hardly ever in the
mood to be kind.

42

Warning the other DZ worlds to watch for a sneak attack from the Constellation, General Adolphus called all the planetary administrators to Hellhole for an urgent summit meeting. At this point, he hoped Escobar Hallholme's fleet was merely lost, but he was wary of another unexpected strike.

With his growing concern, Adolphus had half a mind to order the frontier worlds to blow their stringlines and cut themselves off from the Crown Jewels. That was the safest alternative, the only way to be certain, but many of the administrators would be reluctant to take such a radical action. On some worlds, he might even face a civil war.

As the representatives arrived over the course of several days, depending on how swiftly stringline transports could carry them to the Hellhole hub, his staff prepared the largest conference chamber at Elba, and Sophie gathered data from her various factories and installations to give a full summary of the Deep Zone defenses.

Carlson Goler arrived from Ridgetop wearing the fine business suit he had reserved for formal high-level meetings when he was the territorial governor; now he looked every bit a dignitary—a liaison between the Deep Zone and the Crown Jewels. General Adolphus noted that Goler's posture was straighter, his shoulders squarer, his lantern jaw lifted in a demeanor of confidence.

Three of Adolphus's original coconspirators—Eldora Fen from the planet Cles, George Komun from Umber, and Dom Cellan Tier from the small, low-gravity world of Oshu—arrived together and immediately began unofficial strategy sessions in the conference room. The discussions grew more heated as additional representatives arrived over the following day.

George Komun was impatient to get down to business. He sat several places down the table from Adolphus. "Every day I'm away is a day my planet could be overrun by the Diadem's military."

Dom Cellan Tier let out a snort. "Who would want Umber? It's a rock."

When the man looked indignant, Eldora Fen added in a sarcastic voice, "This is the Deep Zone. The Constellation labeled all our planets worthless until we gave them value."

"Candela was never worthless," Tanja Hu said. "The Diadem is only interested now because we declared ourselves independent."

"She is interested because we've cut off all tribute payments," Governor Goler said. "We've hurt her in the treasury, and in her pride."

Looking a bit scruffier than usual, Ian Walfor took a seat close to Tanja. "The Diadem gave up on Buktu years ago and left us to rot. I've been thumbing my nose at her ever since she abandoned our stringline, and she hates the fact that my people survived just fine without her."

"We'll all survive just fine," General Adolphus said.

All but one of the fifty-four anticipated planetary representatives were crowded inside Elba for a day of strategy discussions. Adolphus noted that the only one not present was Sia Frankov from Theser. Though he was reluctant to start formal meetings until everyone had arrived, he needed to get started. From the head of the conference table, he launched the session with an optimistic statement. "In the long run, the future is bright."

"Except for the black hole in our way," Sophie added, taking a sip of steaming kiafa.

On the wall behind him, Adolphus displayed a graphic of the five military haulers that had launched on a beeline to subdue Hellhole. "Let me explain what *should* have happened to the enemy fleet." The planetary leaders responded with anxiety, but the General raised his voice to get their attention. "We severed the stringline in two places, which should have cut them off with no way forward or back. We verified that they were indeed stranded—but when we went to take them captive, they were gone."

"Where does one hide five huge haulers?" Eldora Fen asked.

"Interstellar space has plenty of places to hide," Ian Walfor said.

Prior to this official meeting, General Adolphus had received another summary of the search patterns run in the vicinity of the severed stringline, and nothing had turned up. No sign whatsoever. The linchpin of his straightforward victory was the neutralization and capture of a significant portion of the Diadem's fleet.

"Those ships are *gone,* taken out of the equation, one way or another," Adolphus said. "A disappointment for me, a crippling blow for the Diadem. She might not have the support of the nobles to launch another significant offensive against the Deep Zone." He recalled the secret overture Enva Tazaar had made, asking for his support in overthrowing Diadem Michella. "There are already signs of strain within the Crown Jewels, and Michella Duchenet may face even bigger threats from within."

Sophie refilled her kiafa cup and passed around one of the insulated ceramic pots. Some delegates nibbled from the refreshments on a long buffet table against the wall. "We need more information," she said. "If any of you have contacts slipping in and out of Sonjeera, we need reports from them. We need to sense the mood of the Crown Jewels."

"We *need* to know where that damned fleet is!" said Ian Walfor. "If this is some sort of a trick, and they suddenly show up, we have a real problem."

"If they found the stringline to Hellhole, we'd have known about it," the General said. "Obviously."

"We're still vulnerable, General," Walfor insisted. "Even if that fleet is really lost, and even if the Diadem has political problems, she can still mount another attack, using one of the other stringlines into the Deep Zone."

"Even the DZ worlds with the best defenses have only a few token guardian ships in orbit," said Owen Lassen from Teron.

Dom Cellan Tier grumbled. "I still say we should just cut all the stringlines to Sonjeera and be done with it."

"But that would isolate the whole Deep Zone from the Crown Jewels for years, no matter what happens," said Maria Delayne from Nephilim. "No turning back. I can't support that." She was a long-haired beauty who looked twenty-five but was actually three decades older than that. Since many people from Nephilim had a youthful vigor beyond their years, rumors had spread that Nephilim possessed a secret fountain of youth, an exotic trace chemical in the water or the air that kept people young. Delayne never denied such rumors, and her planet welcomed the many colonists who went in search of the secret.

"If we sever those lines, I doubt we'd ever reconnect with the Crown Jewels," Walfor said. "They couldn't rebuild the connections, even if they could afford the expense. Their Vielinger mines are almost played out, and soon the Constellation won't have any more iperion."

"My mines have plenty of iperion," Tanja said. "Once they make peace with us, we can sell the Crown Jewels as much of the stuff as they want."

General Adolphus went to a window near his chair, stood looking out on the grounds of his estate. "If we cut all those lines and isolate ourselves out here, think about the time required to restore the system, ten years at a minimum. And the stupendous *cost* could bankrupt the Deep Zone." He turned back to the projection on the wall, showing the missing Constellation fleet. "No, I prefer to keep the stringline cuts as a last resort, a Rubicon we're not yet ready to cross. We need to show strength and solidarity here."

Tanja said, "The Buktu shipyards are refitting as many military vessels as possible, adding them to the DZ Defense Forces. We get more impregnable each day. In fact, I just placed six battleships over Candela to protect my new stringline hub. Ian Walfor is ready to deliver more ships to Theser so that stardrives can be installed." She glanced up, looking around the room. "Where's Sia Frankov?"

"No word," Sophie said. She had coordinated all the arrivals, made sure the representatives had transportation and places to stay in Michella Town.

Goler spoke up, "*Threatening* to cut the lines should be sufficient to get the Diadem's attention. Let me go to Sonjeera immediately as your representative. I'll tell her we want peace, but on our terms."

The General shook his head, returned to his chair. "That was my initial plan, after we captured the enemy fleet. Circumstances have changed, now that all those ships have vanished."

Goler's eyes brightened and he leaned forward, spoke in a conspiratorial voice. "But, General, Diadem Michella might not *know* that the situation has changed. The stringline was cut—and if her warships disappeared en route, how does she know we don't have them?" He looked at Adolphus and grinned. "I can try to bluff her."

"You're taking quite a gamble if you expect the old bitch to behave rationally," Sophie said. "With her tribute payments gone and growing unrest in the Crown Jewels, she's hanging on by the tips of her claws."

Goler said, "If I issue the threat in a public forum on Sonjeera—say in a broadcast instead of privately in her offices—the publicity should force cooler heads to prevail. I can then demand a meeting in the Council Hall to discuss our peace terms."

Tanja Hu gave a crafty smile. "And we have her loyal Territorial Governor Marla Undine as a hostage. She might be a useful bargaining chip."

The General nodded slowly, pondering if Goler would be able to convince Michella. He did, however, welcome the opportunity to pass a covert message to Enva Tazaar that he would consider her offer of an alliance.

"All right, Governor. Go to Sonjeera with my blessing. I won't have it said that I didn't try every possible avenue for a peaceful resolution."

By the end of the daylong meeting, Adolphus was concerned that no one had heard from Sia Frankov. Before accompanying Tanja Hu to Candela, Walfor said, "I'm due to retrieve another load of spacedrive engines, General—twelve more for the warships we're refurbishing at the Buktu shipyards. I'm going to Theser on the direct stringline from Candela, so I'll find out why she isn't here."

Adolphus thanked him. "Good. Report to me as soon as you talk with her. It's difficult to win a strategy game when I don't know the positions of all the pieces on the board."

43

During his normal trips to Sonjeera for the Bureau of Deep Zone Affairs, Governor Carlson Goler had always traveled in a passenger pod carried aboard a large stringline hauler. Now, on his mission as the new DZ ambassador, he rode aboard a much smaller ship that had been outfitted from one of the old colony vessels. As he spent the passage in the rear while two pilots guided the vessel along the embargoed line from Ridgetop to the Crown Jewels, Goler felt like a celebrity being chauffeured.

He knew his diplomatic immunity could be tenuous. By tricking Michella into delivering twenty-one serviceable military ships to Ridgetop—ships that were now part of the DZ Defense Force—he had deceived her. By siding with General Adolphus he had betrayed the Constellation, and by exposing her massacre of the original Ridgetop colonists, Goler had turned many restless populations against her. His stomach knotted as he thought of how vindictive Michella Duchenet could be.

The journey took the better part of four days, and he had time to plan in detail how he would face Michella and present his case. Few others in the breakaway Deep Zone worlds knew the old woman better than Goler did. Even when he was her territorial governor, she had never respected him much, but Goler still hoped he could make her listen . . . or if not Michella, then maybe someone on the Council.

Enva Tazaar had already begun circling the old leader like a vulture, the boldest noble to do so, but Goler knew there must be others in the Crown Jewels who would be happy to see a new Diadem on the Star Throne. Goler decided he would make surreptitious overtures to Tazaar on the General's behalf. *Someone* had to see reason.

In her first clandestine communication, Enva Tazaar had provided a means for Adolphus to respond to her. Goler carried a coded message for her, recorded, condensed, and disguised as an innocuous-looking advertisement. Although he knew he would be closely watched as soon as he made his presence known, one of the two pilots should be able to find a way to slip the advertisement into a mail packet for dispatch to the Tazaar holdings on Orsini.

In the meantime, Goler would bluff the Diadem and the Council that Adolphus *had* captured their fleet and was prepared to cut every one of the Sonjeera stringlines out to the DZ. He would demand that they accept peace terms. Any rational person would see that there was no logical alternative.

The pilots called over the intercom, "We've begun our deceleration, Governor Goler. We should arrive at the Sonjeera hub within one hour."

When Goler thanked them, his voice sounded strong, although his heart leaped into his throat. "As soon as we're in communications range, send out our identifier beacon and announce that I am an official representative from the Deep Zone and that I request an audience with the Council. As soon as you have everyone's attention, transmit our message on the open bands so the Constellation government and the general population can hear what we have to say."

In the broadcast, he provided information on the secondary DZ stringline network, including enough hard data to convince the Diadem that the frontier worlds no longer needed the Crown Jewels. The Deezees could be quite self-sufficient without any connection to the stagnant old planets, he said, and they were quite willing to cut the stringlines if provoked into doing so. Goler then went on to provide a summary of the vital materials and supplies that came from the Deep Zone—all of which would vanish permanently if the rebels cut themselves off. The Diadem and her advisers already knew these details, but Goler's broadcast would remind the general populace of how much they had to lose. He finished his message by demanding to meet with the Diadem and the Council of Nobles.

Goler knew all too well what had happened when Fernando-Zairic and the alien Cippiq had gone to speak with the Diadem. Now, even if Michella killed him, too, at least his message *would* be delivered.

"Judging from the amount of codecall traffic, we've already caused a stir, Governor," the copilot said. "It'll be a hornet's nest by the time we pull into the hub."

"I expected nothing less. And you both have your own mission. Any questions?"

"Leave that to us, Governor. Meanwhile, you tackle the old lady and the Council."

Goler leaned back in the seat and concentrated on breathing in and out, in and out, but a state of calm eluded him.

⤬

A swarm of the Diadem's guards intercepted the ship as soon as it docked at the Sonjeera hub. Goler instructed his pilot and copilot to remain inside the craft as he emerged from the hatch, both hands raised. Upon seeing thirty armed soldiers, tense and ready to open fire at the smallest provocation, he gave them a smile of wry amusement.

"An impressive show of force," he said, "but I assure you General Adolphus has not managed to hide an entire invasion army inside this small diplomatic vessel. I already broadcasted my credentials and stated my purpose."

"We have orders to take you into custody," said the guard captain.

Goler did not find that surprising—Michella had a penchant for dramatic overreaction. Imagers were capturing every moment of this event, but whether the Diadem allowed it to be broadcast was another question entirely.

"I see, Captain. Well, I wouldn't ask you to disobey orders. Meanwhile, kindly inform Diadem Michella of my arrival and ask her to schedule my address before the Council as soon as possible." He paused, then added mysteriously, "The General's offer has a time limit."

The guard captain seemed uncomfortable, but he commandeered the next shuttle to the capital city. Under heavy security they escorted Governor Goler to the Constellation's main spaceport, then took him in an unmarked vehicle, still heavily guarded, to a large and imposing structure—which was not the Diadem's palace or the Council Hall.

It was the Sonjeera prison.

❧

Goler didn't have long to wait. Since his own diplomatic ship had already broadcast a widespread message, his presence on Sonjeera was not a secret. It was well-known in the Deep Zone that many people here remained sympathetic to the General and his failed rebellion.

Some of the most influential Sonjeerans openly admired how Adolphus had kept his network of colonies alive under trying circumstances, and how he had remained honorable and heroic throughout. Despite more than a decade of the Diadem's devastating propaganda, an increasing number of people did not believe the "official" story. Lately, with unrest brewing, Michella Duchenet seemed a far less favorable alternative than others who might lead the Constellation. Without question, Enva Tazaar had seen that as well.

Goler remained in prison quarantine, watching as doctors in decontamination suits came into his cell, which baffled him. Despite his indignation, they took hair clippings, skin scrapings, and blood samples by force.

"We must prevent any alien infection," a physician said. "It's possible you were exposed, and we need to make sure you haven't been contaminated." From the terseness of the doctor's voice, Goler saw that his protestations would do no good, so he held his tongue. The fears these people exhibited were very instructive, though, and wheels began turning in his mind.

The pilot and copilot of his craft had been questioned and were held at the Sonjeera hub, but Goler was hopeful they would still find a way to dispatch a message to Enva Tazaar.

Within five hours, the door guards announced that Goler was to make himself presentable for the formal Council meeting. By now, he expected that the public uproar had grown in his favor—and although the Diadem surely dreaded what the General wanted, she could not ignore his offer to negotiate peace. She had little choice but to listen to Goler.

Diadem Michella presided in the Council Hall, sitting on her Star

Throne and gazing down at the horseshoe-shaped arrangement of seats crowded with noble representatives. For generations, families rose and fell, fighting over the same twenty Crown Jewel planets like drowning fishermen struggling to hold on to a life raft. By opening the Deep Zone to colonization, Michella had eased that pressure, providing a dumping ground for disaffected heirs, disgruntled nobles, and ambitious investors and visionaries. Now General Adolphus had cut off that pressure-release valve and left the old-guard nobles reeling.

Carlson Goler had not been able to make much of himself in the entrenched Constellation system. As territorial governor, he'd had few responsibilities except to fill out the proper forms and see that the tribute payments were sent on a timely basis. The Diadem never expected him to have a backbone, and now he had surprised her.

Goler stood straight and walked forward as if *he* were the one in command, an important visiting dignitary. And he was. He marched down the central aisle of the great hall, with the nobles looking at him; some sneered, while others regarded him with grim interest, as if he were on his way to an execution chamber. At least the Diadem did not make him shamble forward in shackles, like the disgraced and defeated General Tiber Adolphus.

He stopped in the speaking circle and faced the Star Throne. The old woman leaned forward to glower at him. "Governor Carlson Goler, you were our trusted territorial governor, assigned to represent and enforce our wishes in the Deep Zone. Yet, you abandoned your sworn oath."

Goler forced himself not to flinch. He had hoped for a more neutral beginning, but Michella had already launched her attack. He responded calmly, "Eminence, I represent the free Deep Zone planets and bring an offer of terms from General Tiber Adolphus."

Even though they all knew this from the general broadcast he'd made, his words still sparked a susurration of whispered comments and grumbling complaints. He scanned the faces of the nobles and spotted the blonde Enva Tazaar in one of the seats. The noblewoman was quite attractive, and her expression was not unfriendly. Glancing from face to face, Goler noted others who might be sympathetic, but he doubted if they would speak up on his behalf.

The Diadem's anger flared. "Tiber Adolphus is an exiled criminal!

His rebellion is an illegal action. We have sent the Army of the Constellation to end the disturbance. They will defeat the General and crush this uprising."

Goler watched her expression carefully, and then he gambled. "Truly, Eminence? Just where is your fleet now? I came here from planet Hallholme, and I assure you General Adolphus does not seem defeated to me. Are you certain your fleet is safe and sound? Where is it?"

Michella rose from the Star Throne as if to intimidate him, towering down from the high dais. "I demand to know what you have done with our ships! How dare you take hostages?"

So, Goler had his answer, and he continued his bluff with even more boldness. "Your hundred warships didn't have a chance. General Adolphus has his own powerful fleet to protect against any military incursions from the Crown Jewels, and we also have certain . . . alien allies, the original inhabitants of the planet they called Xaya. Their psychic weapons are unlike anything you or your military forces have ever encountered."

The Council Hall erupted in an uproar of angry shouts and threats of retaliation, but Goler continued, even more confident now. "The General charged me as his official ambassador to deliver this message: The Deep Zone does not want war with the Constellation. Although he could easily conquer the Crown Jewels, he has no intention of doing so—on the condition that you cease all hostilities against the Deep Zone. Be forewarned: Any force launched against any DZ world will meet the same terrible fate as Escobar Hallholme's fleet." He paused. "Can you afford to lose another hundred warships and their stringline haulers, Eminence?"

Silence held for a long, uncomfortable moment. Michella tried to sound brave and commanding. "I don't believe you. You're bluffing."

Goler shrugged. "You're welcome to try an attack. See what happens. We have already placed explosive charges on the stringlines leading from Sonjeera to the Deep Zone. The General will blow those lines without hesitation, if you don't abide by the peace terms he demands."

Michella's face reddened despite the powder covering her cheeks and forehead; she didn't seem to hear or care about the angry muttering in the hall that grew to a loud crescendo. "Go back and tell Adolphus to do it! Cut off your lifeline to civilization—and I hope you all wither and die out there!"

Now the voices were even louder. One of the lords, whom Goler knew as Tanik Hirdan, bellowed loudly enough to cut through the hubbub. "You cannot take such a precipitous stance, Eminence. The lords will vote you down."

"I am the Diadem, and I will veto your vote," she snapped back.

Lord Ilvar Crais stood up. A wheedling man who tried to be conciliatory, he always had his own interests foremost in his mind. "If the stringlines are destroyed out to the Deep Zone, it will take many years or decades to reestablish them, and at enormous expense. If we have enough iperion at all! We cannot allow such an irrevocable act unless there is a tangible and immediate threat to the Crown Jewel worlds."

Lord Hirdan continued to bellow, "And if we did send trailblazer ships to establish a new stringline to replace the one that is damaged, what would stop the General from blowing up the terminus ring again? Are we to post guard forces in deep space? At what expense? If they want to cut us off, they can always cut us off. Don't provoke them, Eminence!"

Goler stood listening to the debate, not needing to say anything else. After his bland career, it felt remarkable to be the fulcrum of such vital events. Finally, he said, "General Adolphus is expecting your reply. Shall I return to Hellhole and inform him that the Constellation agrees to a cooling-off period, with no further hostilities? If no further aggressive action occurs, we will open discussions about commercial treaties and the restoration of regular trade."

Michella's voice was filled with acid. "No, you may not take such an answer to the General. In fact, you will not give him an answer at all." She sat back on the Star Throne and summoned her personal guards. "Arrest this man and return him to his cell in the Sonjeera prison."

Goler barely heard the buzz of alarm from the Council as he protested, "Eminence, I am an official ambassador under diplomatic immunity."

But the Diadem would not budge. "I don't recognize any government in the Deep Zone. They are only rebels and traitors, and should be treated as such. And *you* are the worst form of traitor."

The guards grasped Goler's arms, and he didn't struggle, because it would only make him look like a fool. As they escorted him away, he held his head high.

44

Lord Riomini's attack ships returned from Theser in a great flurry, and he made no apologies for disrupting traffic at the main stringline hub. The two military haulers arrived, and his warships disengaged from their docking clamps so they could fly in around the capital planet in an impressive space parade. Even though the Black Lord made no triumphant announcement about his mission, rumors flew.

When all those ships appeared above Sonjeera, Percival Hallholme's first assumption, and hope, was that some portion of his son's fleet had made its way back home. But he quickly saw that these were not the ragtag scraps of a retreating battle force. Lord Riomini looked proud and victorious when he disembarked and took his bow. Now, at least, Percival would learn what the Black Lord had been doing on Theser.

Within the hour, Diadem Michella summoned the Commodore for a private meeting. Duff Adkins helped him dress in his faded old uniform again. His limp had worsened over the past several days, due to stress, and now the familiar outfit felt out of place with its stiff, uncomfortable fit. Since retiring on Qiorfu, Percival had grown accustomed to loosefitting overalls while he worked in the vineyards or visited the taverns. The uniform matched his discomfort at being called back to duty. . . .

He donned his gold-and-black officer's cap and gathered up the plan documents he had sketched out for his alternative move against Tiber Adolphus. Michella had demanded miracles from her Commodore, and it was his obligation to deliver them. Now he could also present his plan to Supreme Commander Riomini, who was a far more experienced tactician than the old Diadem, although he had blundered in his analysis of what must have happened to Escobar's fleet.

Percival was escorted to a private war room, an echoing chamber with enough seats for thirty advisers and subcommanders, but the room was occupied by only Diadem Michella and Lord Selik Riomini, who sat at a long, mirrored conference table. When Percival walked in, fighting his limp, Riomini gave him a respectful smile. "Commodore Hallholme, I am delighted to see you back with the service. We need men of your caliber in the fight. I appreciate your insights."

Percival spoke with clipped, formal words. "I have returned to service, sir, because my son is missing. When the Diadem called me back, how could I possibly refuse?"

"Indeed, indeed. Not to worry—we are well on our way to wrapping up this mess. I just struck a grand blow against Theser that puts the Deezee traitors in their places." The Black Lord actually sounded a bit *shy* around him, as if in awe of the legendary hero. "Once General Adolphus learns you have joined the efforts against him, he'll capitulate immediately!"

Percival removed his cap and took the seat the Diadem offered, on her immediate left. "I doubt that very much, sir."

A refreshment platter was mounded high with enough fruit, pastries, and small sandwiches to feed a squadron. Neither the Diadem nor the Black Lord had touched any of the food. Percival wasn't hungry either.

The projection screens on the walls were now gray and blank. The Diadem looked toward the screens, unable to hide the excitement in her voice. "Show us what you've done, Selik. Do you think Theser will be a sufficient warning to the rest of the rebels?"

"Definitely a warning, Eminence, and much more than a shot across their bow. Whether they'll heed it . . ." He spread his hands on the shiny table. "They have been unreasonable before."

The Diadem reached over to pat the Black Lord's hand. "We'll throw a grand celebration appropriate for your victory, and you'll be feted throughout Sonjeera. I believe that's what you were after?"

Riomini seemed satisfied. He smiled at the old Commodore. "I wanted to demonstrate that I am the most viable candidate to be the next Diadem."

"*One* of the viable candidates," Michella said.

Riomini activated the screens, and panoramic video images of destruction covered the walls of the war room. Even with Percival's past war experience, the fiery obliteration numbed him: curls of smoke, burning homes, charred and contorted human bodies sprawled in macabre disarray.

Riomini spoke as if delivering an earnings report to a board of directors. "On the journey back from Theser, my media crew compiled these images, selecting only the highlights, but there's much more if you'd like to see it."

The Diadem glanced at Percival to gauge his interest. He quickly said, "I have the gist of what happened there. Was Theser given fair warning of the attack, a chance to capitulate? Did you issue them an ultimatum and demand their surrender?"

Riomini frowned. "That wasn't the point, Commodore. The point was to demonstrate the cost of the Deep Zone's continued defiance."

"I see. And how does obliterating Theser help us reclaim my son's lost fleet? It's possible—even likely—that this violent act will merely escalate the conflict rather than resolve it. What if General Adolphus decides to retaliate?"

"Why, then you'll stop him, Commodore," the Diadem said. "Find a way to defeat that horrible man and retrieve our lost ships. That is the reason we brought you out of retirement." She nodded slightly in deference. "If Lord Riomini and I could do it ourselves, we would have left you on Qiorfu."

"I appreciate your confidence, Eminence."

Michella folded her hands together on the table. "I'm anxious to hear your own plan, whatever it is, so we can move forward as soon as possible. I assume you've brought a presentation for us to review?"

The Commodore cleared his throat and spread his documents on the glistening table. The Diadem's mention of Qiorfu made him wish he was back home. In a normal military career, even if he hadn't retired, he could have become a highly paid administrator, managing a depot or a department. He could have entered politics, or he could have become second in command of the Army of the Constellation. He could have managed the Lubis Plain shipyards.

Instead, he had to be a hero again.

"Here is my suggestion." He showed a full spiderweb map of the Sonjeera hub and all the radiating stringlines: one set extended from Sonjeera to the twenty close Crown Jewel worlds, while another set radiated from Sonjeera to the distant Deep Zone worlds. "We know that the direct iperion path to planet Hallholme has been severed, and presumably General Adolphus has captured or at least stranded our fleet. According to Governor Goler, the General booby-trapped all direct paths from Sonjeera to the Deep Zone and will blow them if he feels threatened. That sounds plausible." He turned to Riomini but did not speak until he was sure he could control the frustration in his voice. "Given what just happened on Theser, I wouldn't be surprised if he exercised that final option right away."

On the network map, Percival drew his finger along the line to Ridgetop, another one to Candela, and took his time tracing the iperion path to Theser. "Once the substations are blown, we can't reestablish those routes unless we lay down an entirely new iperion line, and we have neither the time nor sufficient iperion to do that. No, we must get to planet Hallholme by some other route." He sat back, regarded his listeners. "One of the lines, however, is not shown on this map—and I propose we use that route to strike the rebels. A back door, so to speak."

"Which line isn't shown?" the Diadem asked. "How can our maps not be accurate?"

"*This* one." Percival traced his finger across open space to a tiny dot, a remote and insignificant DZ planet. "This is Buktu. The route was decommissioned, but it *exists*. The stringline was abandoned in place years ago, on the Diadem's orders, not destroyed."

Michella said, "But that line hasn't been maintained. No iperion path maintains its integrity for that long, not even if substations remain in place."

"That's what the conservative safety standards say." Percival scratched his muttonchop whiskers. "But I'm convinced that the abandoned stringline could still be a viable option—although a risky one."

Excitement tinged Lord Riomini's voice. "We have to take risks. That's the only way we'll defeat the rebels."

"But what do we gain by going to *Buktu?*" Michella frowned as she studied the map intently. "Who cares about a poor, out-of-the way planetoid? Even Theser was more significant."

"It's a *way in*," Percival said. "I don't propose an assault like what Lord Riomini did at Theser. We'll overwhelm and capture the facilities, taking prisoners as a matter of course, but most importantly, we'll capture the terminus ring. That would be my primary objective. Once we have access to the new DZ network, my assault force can travel directly—and unhindered—to planet Hallholme."

He pulled out old historical records, ancient library texts from millennia ago, long-forgotten accounts from humanity's origin. "General Adolphus is fascinated with primitive military history, and he clearly models himself on the ancient commander Napoleon Bonaparte of Earth."

Michella and Riomini gave him blank stares. "No one remembers anything about ancient Earth," the Black Lord said.

"In order to understand the enemy, I familiarized myself with the history of the period. In the century after Napoleon, I found records of an innovative military strategy used by Lieutenant Colonel T. E. Lawrence, who led a fighting force across a supposedly impassable desert to capture a strategic target called Aqaba. That city was undefended from the desert side, because they never dreamed an enemy could possibly approach from that direction.

"I propose to do the same here. Though the quantum path will be diffuse and likely damaged, and we'll have to pick our way carefully by sending trailblazer scouts ahead to lay down additional iperion where necessary, I believe we might be able to make our way into the Deep Zone and strike General Adolphus from his undefended flank. *Buktu.* Getting there will likely take weeks rather than days, but we can do it."

"There's no longer any rush, Commodore." The Diadem seemed energized, pleased at the idea. "So long as it works."

"This is a military operation, fraught with uncertainty, but I will do my best to succeed."

"Thank you for your honesty, Commodore." Michella exchanged a glance with the Black Lord, then said, "Your plan is approved."

45

Ian Walfor ran the remote Buktu industries, but he was also a restless man and left much of the day-to-day work to his deputy, Erik Anderlos. They had converted the operations on the frozen planetoid to building and refurbishing space vessels from a scrap yard of parts he had collected over the years. For a long time Walfor had also run slower black-market routes among the nearby DZ worlds, but now that the frontier planets were networked via stringline, the opportunities seemed limitless.

After leaving the General's meeting on Hellhole, Walfor accompanied Tanja Hu to Candela—a pleasant world by any measure—and from there he met up with one of his fellow Buktu workers, Hume Keats, at Tanja's new hub. Together, they would ride the direct line to Theser with a shipload of essential war equipment and supplies that Administrator Frankov had commissioned, as well as several new ships that required stardrives.

Even in these times of uncertainty, Walfor could see the potential of so many new trade agreements. First, he needed to find out why Frankov had not attended the emergency meeting. If something was wrong, General Adolphus needed to know about it.

Tanja gave him a quick kiss before she departed on the shuttle down

Brian Herbert and Kevin J. Anderson

to Candela, but she was gone in the passenger pod before he could make sure it hadn't been an accident. Keats raised his eyebrows and had an amused expression; Walfor felt his face flush. He hurried his copilot aboard the waiting framework hauler from Buktu, which carried a dozen full-size ships due to receive stardrives.

The cockpit sat atop the framework, a Spartan chamber with only enough room for two people, and a small sleeping area in a private cabin. Keats took the first sleep shift, claiming indigestion from something he had eaten during his brief stop on Candela, although Walfor knew the man occasionally suffered from space sickness. As soon as their ship headed away from the new Candela hub, he let the copilot crawl into the small bunk.

Walfor did not mind traveling alone. Years ago, when the pioneer ships first arrived on Buktu, he had been only a third-level deputy. The expedition's leader, Captain Vondas, was in despair when he saw the miserable, cold planetoid, which was not at all like the initial probe had predicted. Later, once the Diadem's stringline reconnected Buktu to the Crown Jewels, Vondas had turned over command and fled back to Sonjeera on the first transport.

Ian Walfor had dived into the Buktu problem, though, deciding to make sweet juice from the sour fruit he found there. Although the cold planetoid wasn't the most scenic spot in the Deep Zone, he recognized rich opportunities there. While the colonists might not be able to go for strolls in forests or meadows, they did have everything they needed. Since the Buktu colonists had intended to be self-sufficient all along, they'd brought plenty of supplies, efficient hydroponics systems, greenhouse domes, and a great deal more.

Although the slow, long-range pioneer ships were designed to be discarded once they reached their destination, Walfor knew there was nothing wrong with them mechanically. They could be refurbished, refueled, and dispatched again. His first expedition was to send a scout off to Candela, a two-month journey with the slow engines. Negotiating an agreement with the ambitious new administrator, Tanja Hu, the scout had purchased abandoned colony ships that were hanging empty in Candela's orbit for decades, and then flew the vessels back to Buktu, where they were refitted and added to Walfor's long-range fleet.

Soon he had ventured farther, making deals with other DZ administrators; he even used the official Constellation stringline through Sonjeera to work his backroom deals. As salvage operators, his people continued to gather disused ships, repair and refuel them, and put them back into service—all in secret from the Constellation.

Years later, when the Diadem discontinued the unprofitable stringline from Sonjeera to Buktu, none of his people complained. They didn't feel abandoned; they felt left pleasantly alone, which was, after all, what they'd wanted in the first place. . . .

Now, as the hauler reached the small temporary terminus ring high above Theser, a timer sounded in the cockpit. Awakened by the sound, Keats emerged from his cabin, rubbing his eyes. "Are we there?" His long, braided hair was unkempt from a restless sleep.

Walfor decelerated, coming in on the night side of Theser. "No response from the terminus ring. Seems to be a stringline problem."

Keats yawned. "Sometimes Administrator Frankov gets lazy."

Tapping additional controls, Walfor activated his broadband detectors to receive transmissions from the planet. Now that they had dropped off the stringline and assumed normal speed, he expected to be flooded with the chatter of a bustling world. "Anybody home? This is Ian Walfor, coming via Candela. I have the ships you commissioned. And we need stardive engines. Hello?"

"I don't hear anything," Keats said. "Something must be wrong with our receivers."

"Not detecting any ships at their other terminus either," Walfor said, scanning ahead. The second terminus orbited close to the planet, anchoring the iperion line that extended back to Hellhole.

Walfor couldn't believe what he was seeing on the screens. "No signal ahead at all. There's diffuse iperion in orbit—wait, the Hellhole terminus ring is offline! Well, that explains why Administrator Frankov didn't attend the meeting."

As the ship coasted in toward Theser, Keats was the first to say, "It's not offline—it's *destroyed*. The stringline has been cut." He looked ill, and it had nothing to do with his reaction to food or space travel.

Despite their repeated transmissions, Theser maintained disconcerting radio silence. Through the night sky they flew over the largest crater city of Eron, but it was now an entirely *dark* city. "No lights, no transmissions," Keats said. "I don't like this at all."

Walfor received no response to his numerous codecalls. "We've got to go down there."

Leaving the hauler's cockpit, they made their way to a small personal shuttle locked in a docking clamp. The craft dropped toward the surface without any guidance from the Theser transport authority.

They flew low over the crater city before dawn, illuminating the surface with powerful beams of light—but they saw no standing structures, only the charred remains of what had once been a vibrant city. No sign of life, just slag piles of wreckage.

Halfway up the terraced wall of the crater, where the laboratories of the eccentric spacedrive engineers had once stood next to the government administrative center, Walfor spotted a pennant fluttering in the night breeze. A prominent marker that was meant to be found.

A black Riomini flag.

46

Rigorous conservation measures and drastic rationing had made a significant impact on the crew of the stranded Constellation fleet. A month had passed since the trailblazer had departed. At least four more weeks to go.

Scout ships continued to comb space from the huddled stringline haulers, tightening their search patterns for any indication of the lost iperion path. Escobar Hallholme was desperate, convinced the fleet had wandered far afield of where the severed stringline must be. Though their hopes had dwindled, finding that connection seemed like their *only* hope unless Sergeants Zabriskie and Caron were successful. If a scout ship somehow, miraculously, blundered onto the iperion trail, they would all be saved far sooner than the trailblazer could ever reach Hellhole.

Instead, the search blundered into something else. One scout raced back to the stringline haulers, sending a tight, secure codecall signal. "Redcom! We've opened fire!"

Escobar snapped to attention on the bridge. "Comm, respond. Who opened fire? Are you under attack?"

After the communications officer established the link, the female scout pilot said in a breathless voice, "It was one of the General's ships, sir. A spy vessel searching space—possibly looking for us! They pinged my ship and recognized that we were part of the Constellation fleet. I responded with a fusillade, Redcom." She looked haggard, but grinning on the screen. "Blew them out of space, hopefully before they could expose our location to the enemy!"

Escobar rose to his feet, feeling relief at first and then deep disappointment. Reprimanding the pilot would do no good now. So, Adolphus was indeed searching for them. Carrington had been correct that they could not allow this giant military force to fall into the hands of the enemy . . . but that might have saved his crew from long, cold starvation. They could have been rescued by the General's scout, but that chance was gone now.

"No need to return to the flagship," Escobar responded. "Stay out there and continue the search."

More than 70 percent of the crew, over ten thousand soldiers, had been placed in induced comas and connected to the barest minimum of life support. Seven of the one hundred warships were little more than tightly packed coffin units, their ambient temperatures reduced to deep cold where the sedated volunteers (some willing, some not) were stacked like cordwood.

But it wasn't enough.

"We have four more weeks, at least, before the trailblazer ship can reach its destination." Bolton kept his voice low in Escobar's office adjacent to the flagship's bridge. "Given the number of crew still awake and burning calories, we have maybe half that time. We need to speed up the sedation process."

Escobar looked haunted. "Once we reach planet Hallholme, we can take over all of the General's supplies. In the meantime, hunger will give the soldiers an edge to fight harder."

"They won't be in any fighting condition, Redcom. I'm talking about *survival*. You can already see the effect—not just the hunger, but the constant tension." The majority of crew walking the decks had a jittery, skeletal look, with sunken cheeks and shadowed eyes—and there had been more than sixty deaths from fights, starvation, and other causes. "We need even more of them unconscious, though we have very little of the Sandusky stasis drug left."

Escobar knew that Gail Carrington had been more aggressive, pushing people to take the sedation option, but her demands had only intensified the brewing unrest, angering the crew and making them even more intransigent. Perhaps if she provided a good example . . .

Considering this, Escobar led Bolton out of his ready room. "Come with me."

The flagship's bridge looked empty, with only essential crew at their stations. Lieutenant Cristaine, his first officer, had volunteered for sedation near the beginning of the crisis, in the third group. She'd done her duty with bravery, and now she slept peacefully. Escobar looked around, then spoke in a hoarse voice. "Have a dozen of my personal security troops meet me on deck five, midship. Afterward, I'm calling all watch commanders for a private discussion. Triple guards on the armories—this next step isn't going to be easy."

Escobar and Bolton took a lift down to deck five, where they joined the guards. The Red Commodore said, "We'll need to put down another two thousand crewmembers over the next few days. Isn't that about right, Major?"

"Yes," Bolton said. "But why the guards?"

Escobar drew a deep breath. "Because Gail Carrington will be the first of our new volunteers, and I don't think she's going to like it."

⸎

Escobar had made his choice, and though it gave him a sick dread and resignation, he did not doubt it was the right decision. A *command* decision. Gail Carrington had put forth the argument herself, though he doubted she would abide by the logic now that it was applied to her.

Even as conditions got grimmer, he couldn't get over his revulsion at how she had so casually slit the throat of the flagship's comm-officer, simply because he had attempted to send a distress signal . . . or at what she had done to Jackson Firth and his diplomatic team, killing them because they were "an unnecessary drain on our resources." Her dark violence had spilled over, and now the paranoid scout pilot had destroyed one of General Adolphus's searchers, who could well have saved them all.

Though Escobar had not particularly liked the stuffy diplomats, they did have a defined role that he could understand. If everyone's worth were judged by their usefulness to the fleet, most of the extraneous noble officers would never make the cut. They consumed the fleet's food and life-support resources, yet did not improve the odds of victory. They were deadwood, and the mission would be better off if they *were* dead.

Carrington, though, had no defined role at all. She had disapproved of Escobar's actions ever since the fleet's attack plan had gone off the rails. She had criticized him silently as well as vocally. And he still didn't know why she was here, except as some sort of internal spy. Because she came under the aegis of her master Lord Riomini, Escobar had no choice but to accept her aboard the fleet.

Now, however, each person aboard the stranded ships mattered. A human being could live as long as a week without food, but every member of the crew had been on reduced rations for the past month. They had no reserves. They couldn't last on any less.

Yes, Gail Carrington would have to do her part.

Like Escobar, Bolton Crais was uneasy about what they had to do to her now, so they brought along twelve armed guards and Dr. Hambliss, who had been so appalled by Carrington's murderous actions in the sick bay. He clutched a sedation syringe with a full dose of the Sandusky stasis drug, and was ready to use it.

Carrington answered the signal at her quarters. She looked annoyed by the disturbance, and her expression did not soften when she saw Escobar and Bolton at the door. When she noted the security guards in the corridor, she coiled herself like a spring-loaded weapon. "What is this?"

"Further extreme actions have become necessary," Escobar said. "Thank you for volunteering to join the sedated and set an example for the remaining members of our crew."

Her eyes narrowed. "I refuse. I'm an official representative of Lord Riomini. You have no authority over me."

"On the contrary, as Red Commodore I have authority over every person in the fleet, and I have given the order for you to be sedated. Doctor?"

Hambliss uncapped the syringe.

"I refuse," she said again. Her eyes were on fire. She looked dangerous.

Escobar gestured to the guards. "Please assist Ms. Carrington in the completion of her duty."

Two of the burly guards entered Carrington's quarters, and her movement was so swift that Escobar saw little more than a blur. With hooked fingers, a vicious blow, twist, and yank, she tore out the first man's larynx, then jerked him the rest of the way inside the cabin while she grabbed for the second one. A pile-driver blow in the center of his forehead, between the eyes, crushed the top of his nose. Blood spurted out his nostrils. As he lifted his hands to defend himself, she grabbed his hair, yanked his head down, and brought her knee up into his chin with a loud snap of his neck.

Escobar knew that Carrington had been one of Riomini's most deadly bodyguards, and even though she had retired because she felt her reflexes had slowed, she remained superior to these armed troops.

Before Escobar could order the other men forward, they charged through the doorway. Carrington fell into a defensive stance and used the bottleneck of the cabin's entrance to her advantage. She crushed a man's kneecap with a stiff kick, then sent him sprawling into two other guards who lunged for her. While the guards shouted as they pressed forward, Carrington remained eerily silent. Like a small army using the advantage of a narrow pass, she kept fighting, never surrendering, as if sure that Escobar intended to murder her outright. Now perhaps that was exactly what he would have to do.

She killed two and crippled three more before the guards pushed their way into her quarters by sheer force of numbers. Finally, they succeeded in slamming her down on the deck and holding her there. Dr. Hambliss rushed forward and, not bothering with any finesse, jammed the needle into her neck.

The sedative took hold within seconds, but Carrington continued to struggle, her energy dwindling until she finally collapsed, unconscious. Taking no chances, Escobar said, "Strap her down and bind her wrists. I don't trust her to stay sedated as long as she should. Doctor, watch her closely."

Bolton suggested, "We should put her aboard one of the storage ships where she can't cause any more trouble."

"She's already caused too much trouble." Escobar was sickened to see the four dead men sprawled on the deck, as well as the injured. She had tossed his best soldiers about like clumsy puppets. "I loathe her, but if I had a thousand fighters like her, General Adolphus would have no chance."

"We might not live long enough to face the General," Bolton said. As the dead and injured were carried away, he looked pale.

Fighting off his anger, Escobar inspected Carrington's quarters, which she had previously kept locked. She would never have allowed him to study her records, her private communications, but now he took advantage of the vulnerability. He needed to find out what her mission was.

The woman had few possessions, only three changes of black clothing (all identical), but no secret stockpile of food or energy cubes, as he had half expected. He did, however, discover her private journal, a logbook in which she wrote reports for eventual transmission to Lord Selik Riomini.

Over the course of their voyage, and the weeks stranded here without the stringline, she had documented and distorted every one of Escobar's missteps, his bad decisions, his failures to act, all without suggesting how she might have solved the various problems.

Escobar felt a chill when he discovered Carrington's original orders— a private letter from Lord Riomini himself.

Escobar's wife, Elaine, was Riomini's grandniece, and through her family connections his military career had been enhanced. To a great extent, the Black Lord had been his benefactor, and Escobar was pleased to accept command of the fleet sent against the rebel General. He had considered it his due, a celebration of their powerful families, the Riominis and the legendary Hallholmes.

But now he learned that Gail Carrington had been sent to watch over him and ensure that this all-important mission succeeded. Her orders were ominously explicit: If Escobar was about to fail, she was to kill him so that his incompetence could cause no further damage. As an aside, Riomini promised that he would take care of Elaine and her three sons, and that he would do his best to portray Escobar as a war hero, to save face.

As Escobar read the secret orders alone in Carrington's quarters, wide-eyed and sickened, Bolton Crais came up so quietly that he jumped. The logistics officer looked over his shoulder at the document. "Is it what you expected, sir?"

Escobar swallowed hard. "Yes, Major, I'm afraid it is."

"What should we do with her?"

"I'd like to process her into food to sustain the troops," Escobar replied, intending it as a joke, but the words were flat and awkward. "I don't know, Major. At least she's out of our way for now."

He handed him the letter.

47

The General and Sophie Vence traveled to the Ankor spaceport, where troops boarded a shuttle to launch up to join the orbiting defense fleet. It was a cloudless day, already warmer than usual, with the greenish sky tinged in yellow.

While General Adolphus kept sixty ships and twelve unmanned weapons platforms in orbit to protect the main stringline hub, he dispatched as many ships as he could spare to other Deep Zone planets; now that Hellhole was cut off from Sonjeera, the other frontier worlds were likely targets for the frustrated Diadem's wrath. A strike force could try to capture one of the DZ terminus rings as a back door to Hellhole, but all the planetary administrators had mined their terminus rings, which would be blown before an invading fleet could be allowed onto the iperion paths. By now, though, Governor Goler would have issued his ultimatum and explained the consequences to the Crown Jewels.

Adolphus always had other plans, fallback positions, secondary defenses, but he had placed most of his hope on the gamble that he could snare the Constellation fleet before it arrived. Now, not knowing where those ships had gone, he had to place his resources to defend Hellhole. Many colonists were building their own bunkers to survive an aerial bombardment, if it should come.

He vowed not to let that happen.

A great alien race had been wiped out on this world, but Adolphus refused to view that as a foreshadowing of the fate of his own colony. He considered the loyal people who followed him, who believed in him so completely. Diadem Michella had assumed this hellish world would destroy him, but she had not accounted for his pioneering spirit or personal drive, nor had she counted on the strength of character of those who gathered around him.

Rendo Theris looked harried and distraught, as usual. By now, Adolphus placed little stock in the man's frantic complaints. Theris managed the Ankor complex well enough, but he seemed to operate best in a condition of perceived urgency. "General, the primary landing fields are stable, but the tremors are constant. They build day by day. You need to send seismic engineers out here to do something about it."

"That's not a problem specific to the spaceport, Mr. Theris. We've got monitors across the continent, and the largest quakes are centered around the impact crater. A major one occurred two days ago."

"We've even felt them out at Slickwater Springs," Sophie said. "We've always had to prepare for quakes."

Theris shook his head. "Just because it's worse someplace else doesn't mean it's not a problem here. We've reinforced the buildings, kept everything as stable as possible. Each major tremor disturbs the slickwater aquifer, which causes major delays and damage here—"

The General frowned. "I thought my engineers had found a solution. Aren't they due to drain the slickwater into another valley?"

"Yes, sir. They've drilled cores, completed acoustic mapping of the strata beneath Ankor, and developed a plan. We're just waiting to bore down and install sufficient explosives so we can divert it all away. Then the slickwater will stop causing so many headaches, and the spaceport can thrive." Theris's glimmer of optimism lasted only a few seconds, though. "Unless the Constellation fleet arrives and attacks us after all. It's just one damn thing after another."

"It's Hellhole," Sophie said with clear sarcasm. "Didn't you read the brochure?"

The loaded troop shuttle was sealed on the pad, Ankor personnel completed a standard countdown, and the craft accelerated into the sky, all completely routine.

Then keening sirens began to sound. Alarms went off from the operations building, and spaceport personnel rushed to emergency stations. Theris's eyes nearly popped out of their sockets as he looked skyward, but Adolphus didn't see anything. "What is it?"

"Incoming ships—unidentified objects. Could be an air raid. Maybe the Constellation fleet arrived after all!" The administrator scrambled toward the main building, but the General and Sophie both beat him to the door.

"If it's the Constellation fleet, we should have gotten warning from our defense ships in orbit," Adolphus said.

Sophie pointed to the sky. "It's not the Constellation—we've got visitors again."

A squadron of copper ships streaked across the high olive-green clouds, flying in a peculiar, squared-off formation. The mysterious vessels swooped lower in the atmosphere, racing along in complete silence. The troop shuttle continued to climb, but the workhorse vehicle had little maneuverability. The strange ships circled it, whirling around and dodging the craft, like a flurry of wasps.

"They didn't attack last time," Theris said, but his voice carried little hope.

"Get all satellite eyes on them," the General said. "Track where they're going and what they're doing. I want to know what those ships are."

As if bored, they dropped away from the ascending shuttle and flitted around the basin with the launching pads and landing fields.

The spaceport's sentry craft took off from the field to give chase, but the coppery ships outran all attempts to catch them. The unknown visitors took abrupt turns but remained in perfect formation. Two of the Ankor fighter craft took potshots at them, but the formation split up and regrouped, unconcerned about the weapons.

As quickly as they had appeared, the unknown ships shot straight upward and sped away into space. The General stared after them, but they were gone in a matter of seconds. The troop shuttle, unmolested, continued to rise until it became no more than a bright dot.

Inside the operations center, harried-looking technicians ran from screen to screen. "They scanned us again! The burst overloaded some of our systems."

"Did the shuttle make it safely?" Sophie asked.

"The intruders didn't interfere with it," the tech said.

Rendo Theris went to one of the screens himself and called up satellite images, scanning across the continent. "Fortunately, thanks to our defenses, we have enough eyes up in orbit this time. Reports are flooding in. Those ships were first detected over the main impact crater, and then they buzzed Slickwater Springs."

"I've got a lot of people out at the pools!" Sophie looked from Theris to the General. "Is everyone all right?"

Theris played the satellite records. "They didn't spend much time at Slickwater Springs, just did a close surveillance, then headed to a valley midcontinent—not near any of our operations. Thankfully!"

"What's out there?" the General asked. "Let me see."

Theris projected images, pinpointing the site that had interested the strange ships. The isolated valley was another of the hot spots of alien vegetation, a profusion of weeds and ferns that had appeared so suddenly between the last satellite mappings. Adolphus leaned closer, studying the map. "What's special about that valley? Mineral deposits?"

"Nothing that I can tell, sir—other than all the vegetation."

"Somebody needs to go out there to take a look." Sophie straightened. "Maybe the shadow-Xayans will know. I'll take Devon and Antonia with me."

48

As a political prisoner on Sonjeera, Governor Goler had expected more hospitable treatment. Traditionally, the prison cells for arrested, disgraced nobles were almost as luxurious as their estate houses. The fact that Goler was relegated to an austere room with few comforts showed the Diadem's disdain for him.

But he took no great insult. He didn't need to be pampered. After all, of the five territorial governors, only he willingly chose to live out in the Deep Zone. He kept himself happy with what Ridgetop had to offer, and he'd get by well enough here, too. He had never liked the overblown extravagance of Sonjeera anyway.

Goler thought of how Tasmine had hidden in a badger burrow while the Diadem's soldiers massacred her fellow colonists. If his housekeeper could endure that, he had no right to complain about this cell.

He had formally requested to speak with an attorney, per Constellation law—and his request was denied without explanation. He had been kept isolated from outside news reports. By his count, he'd been incarcerated for six days, but he knew not to trust his sense of time; his keepers could try to disorient him by resetting the light-and-dark cycle in the windowless chamber.

As time dragged on, he wondered if one of his brothers would be allowed to visit him. They might be upset because his disgrace cast a shadow on their own aspirations—but so far no one had come. Maybe the Diadem had given strict orders denying him visitors. Or maybe his brothers didn't care.

He obtained stationery and penned statements for the media as well as letters to be delivered to nobles among the Crown Jewels. The guards dutifully accepted them, but he received no replies. Goler knew none of the communiqués would ever be sent, but as a trick of his own, he added odd phrases to his sentences and planted unusual words, sure that the Diadem's code-breakers would agonize over the actual meaning and attempt to decipher the secret codes—all of which were nonsense.

He steadfastly refused to give details about the missing Constellation fleet other than to imply that General Adolphus had captured the warships. In her obvious anxiety, the Diadem's imagination would fill in the blanks.

Goler took comfort in knowing he had completed his mission, and by now most people in the Crown Jewels would have heard Adolphus's offer of terms. Outside, he hoped that the pilot or copilot had managed to slip the coded message to Enva Tazaar. History would respect him for his strength, and what he did now was exceedingly important. He only hoped he didn't have to become a martyr to achieve his goal.

When his cell door opened and a passive-looking food server brought lunch on a tray, Goler said, as he had many times before, "I demand diplomatic courtesy. I am an appointed ambassador, and you have no right to hold me here."

"The Diadem says otherwise," said the guard at the door.

"Then I wish to send a formal petition back to the Deep Zone."

"Request denied. Enjoy your meal."

The thin, brown-haired server was dressed in the gray uniform of a prison employee, not a prisoner on work detail. The man averted his eyes as he placed the tray on a small table that doubled as a desk. He moved Goler's papers aside to make room.

The meal was a bland-looking affair of ground meat, starchy lumps that might have been dumplings, reheated vegetables, and a small pile of withered-looking sournuts, each the size of his thumbnail. The man made a point of looking at him, then said in a quiet voice, "Enjoy the sournuts, Governor."

The innocuous comment alerted Goler. Sournuts had always been his favorite treat here on Sonjeera, but someone would have had to dig deeply into the records to learn that fact. The nuts were not often served, because they were considered too pungent for the popular taste.

"Anything would be a welcome change from the regular flavors," he said. "Thank you."

The guards noted nothing suspicious, but the server met Goler's eyes in a furtive glance. A feathery thrill raised goose bumps on Goler's skin, and he fought down any visible reaction. The server departed, while the guard remained at the door. Goler said wryly, "Are you going to stare at me, or can I eat in peace?"

"I've got my own lunch to eat." The guard sealed the door, and Goler remained seated. His heart was pounding. He didn't know what he was supposed to do, or if he had misinterpreted the man. General Adolphus had many loyalists here in the Crown Jewels, but Goler had no way to contact them. Had they gotten into the prison somehow?

He scanned the food, sure someone must be observing his every movement through hidden spy cameras. He took a bite of a chewy, bland dumpling, then ate some of the ground meat. He found no message hidden beneath the pile of sournuts.

Casually he picked up a nut, tossed it into his mouth, and bit down through the bitter crust. He ate a second one. This one was juicier, and made his lips pucker. He had always enjoyed sournuts, especially as a child. His mother had once told him that if he ate too many, his face would take on a permanent grimace.

When Goler bit down on a third nut, he felt an unfamiliar crunch, with a metallic undertone. He froze, afraid he would cut his mouth. Then tiny circuitry implanted in the sournut sent vibrations through his molars in a precise pattern that thrummed through his jaw, attuned to his bone structure. Words echoed inside his skull, which he heard clearly in his ear canals, but they were audible to no one else in the room.

"Governor Goler, this message is from Enva Tazaar. Because the Diadem controls the prison, it is not possible for me to free you, but you can still send me an answer." She spoke in a rapid-fire fusillade of words, and he realized that the small word-transmitting device implanted in the sournut probably had a limited capacity. "If General Adolphus is amenable to my offer of an alliance, provided that we remove Michella Duchenet from power, then cross your utensils on the plate when they are to be retrieved. If the General does not wish an alliance, then leave them to the side. I already have plans in place, and I can move quickly. Once I'm on the Star Throne, you will be granted amnesty, and the Crown Jewels and Deep Zone can begin to—"

Her words cut off as the message device was exhausted. Goler chewed and swallowed to destroy any evidence. Meticulously, he ate the rest of the ground meat and dumplings, then finished the remaining sournuts, contemplating what he had heard. When he was finished, he crossed the utensils over the top of the empty plate and waited for the tray to be retrieved.

⁓⁓

Something about the man who delivered food to Governor Goler alerted Ishop Heer. Ishop's suspicions were easily triggered—that was why he did his job so well—but he took no chances.

By habit, he'd been keeping an eye on the Sonjeera prison. He had been in these dank corridors many times doing the Diadem's business, much of it behind closed doors with the security eyes deactivated.

In this building, he had killed Louis de Carre, who was more of a fool than a threat. That had been messy work, made to look as if the man had committed suicide by slashing his own wrists. It was also sad in a way. The haughty nobleman had clung to his family pride even after squandering most of his wealth, but when Ishop came to kill him he had been blubbering and terrified, sobbing Keana's name as the assassin forced him to write a suicide note. On his Vielinger estate, he'd probably engaged in mock duels for his own amusement, but when Ishop killed him, he had fought back no better than a half-asleep child.

Not much of a nobleman, certainly not of the caliber that Ishop intended to be once he reclaimed his own heritage. Soon.

But in the meantime, he still served the Diadem. Ishop would not be surprised if Michella instructed him to ensure that Carlson Goler had similar "suicidal thoughts," but not yet. Ishop merely kept an eye on the prison, noting those who came and went. Michella imagined traitors and spies in every shadow, but Ishop knew she had real reasons for concern, because General Adolphus had sympathizers salted throughout the population.

That morning, Ishop paid attention when one of the regular servers called in sick. That was not in itself unusual, although any change in schedule regarding the territorial governor warranted careful scrutiny. When the replacement server arrived at the prison with proper identification papers, wearing the right uniform, he passed through security without incident. But Ishop directed the surveillance feed so that he could watch exactly what happened next. The replacement server spent some of the morning cleaning the halls, rearranging boxes in a storeroom. At lunchtime he delivered Goler's tray of unremarkable food and arranged to pick it up after the meal.

But when Ishop tried to learn the server's identity, he was surprised at how difficult that turned out to be. . . .

When the man left the prison at the end of his work shift, he eluded security, changed out of his gray uniform, and discarded the clothes, which were found later. That told Ishop he had stumbled upon something important.

Rather than reporting his suspicions to the Diadem's guards, he asked Laderna to help him dig deeper, and she applied herself with great enthusiasm to the problem, displaying her utter devotion to him, as usual. He had no intention of replacing her.

The server's real name was Burum Elakis, which did not match the name on his prison ID badge. Ishop learned that Elakis had served in the old military but registered as a conscientious objector during the General's rebellion; he had refused to be deployed as part of Riomini's Army of the Constellation, and was instead reassigned to a polar survey station.

Elakis originally came from Orsini, the Tazaar homeworld. He was also a collector of memorabilia from the General's rebellion, before such hobbies had been proscribed. A few years earlier, Elakis had sold valuable military memorabilia to an off-world collector . . . someone from planet Hallholme, as far as Ishop could tell.

Very interesting. Ishop knew there was more here to be learned. Though they were alone in his private office, Laderna lowered her voice to a conspiratorial whisper. "Are you going to expose him to the Diadem?"

Ishop shook his head, ran his fingertips along his smoothly shaved scalp. "No. I'll just hold the information for now and keep watching . . . in case it proves useful."

49

When Ian Walfor interrupted her meeting in the Saporo admin tower, Tanja knew it was something important, even dire. His face bore a dismal expression, didn't even show a smile upon seeing her; he looked haggard.

Tanja had been sitting on one of her office terraces with a group of her military advisers, where they had a magnificent view of the harbor with its floating buildings and heavy boat traffic. Seated around an outdoor table, they were discussing planetary defenses, including the six new ships placed in orbit. She looked forward to returning to Theser soon, to have a dinner with Sia Frankov and thank her for helping to make the new hub secure. Tanja also had patrols in the air and defenses on the ground, not to mention the shadow-Xayans, who had promised to defend Candela with their telemancy. She felt much safer—but the expression on Walfor's face changed all that.

With shaking hands, he poured himself a glass of water from a pitcher on the table. Though he had rushed here, he now seemed reluctant to say what was on his mind. Finally, he put down the glass. "Theser has been wiped out. Riomini did it—left one of his flags where the capital city used to be. All of Eron is only charred remains."

Her advisers gasped, one of them lurched to his feet, while others sat in stunned silence. Tanja felt cold, then feverish, as emotions surged over her. "And Sia Frankov? Any word that they took prisoners?" She felt uprooted, reminded of how she and her friend had planned their joint commercial empire, trade routes, dreams. "Any survivors, witnesses?"

"There's nothing recognizable anywhere." Walfor slumped into a chair. "Not so much as a blade of grass."

Tanja slammed a fist down on the table. "The Constellation is going to drown in all the blood they've spilled."

In her noisome cell, Marla Undine was obviously convinced she would never get out of this place alive. She sat brooding on the edge of her cot; as far as Bebe Nax could tell, that was all she ever did.

The harsh conditions seemed medieval, but Tanja Hu insisted on the humiliation, for reasons of her own. After hearing Ian Walfor's appalling news about Theser, which he had delivered yesterday, Bebe was inclined to agree that any representative of the Constellation should be treated like an animal.

Bebe doubted the captive territorial governor would show any remorse, nor would she be any more cooperative. Bebe stood outside the cell with Jacque at her side; she let out a heavy, impatient sigh. "I can improve your conditions here if you will just record the message for Sonjeera. It's the best way to resolve the situation."

Tanja had demanded that Governor Undine record a message to be sent to the Diadem, which Tanja would include along with her own condemnation of the Diadem's actions on Theser. But Undine did not seem tempted at all.

"I refuse to be part of your propaganda."

Jacque was visiting from his boarding school, and Bebe wanted him to see this. Although she had explained the Theser massacre to him, the boy didn't understand the significance of the events now; nevertheless, he had a front-row seat for history, and she hoped he would remember.

The boy always seemed fascinated by Governor Undine, as if he viewed the captive as a specimen in the zoo. Back in Saporo, Tanja had told Jacque many horrific tales about the Constellation's crimes, and he continued to regard Undine through the bars and gray mesh of her cell as if she were a monster.

"Why doesn't she want the war to end, Mother?" the boy whispered, as if Undine couldn't hear them clearly. The cowlick in his hair was more pronounced today than usual.

"Maybe she enjoys the killing." Bebe had brought a copy of the images Walfor had transmitted, showing the utter devastation of the verdant crater city. Blood, fire, destruction . . . the deaths of hundreds of thousands of DZ settlers.

The guard unlocked the cell door and smiled at Jacque, dangling a leech he had peeled from the wall, amused. Bebe entered the cell, holding a small, flat projection screen that showed the devastated landscape of Theser. "Let me show you what you're condoning, Governor. Is this truly a government you wish to support? Why do you owe them your loyalty?"

"I will not record a statement for you." Undine's eyes flashed, and she remained immobile on her bench. "The Constellation will come for me."

Bebe snorted. "The Constellation believed you were still being held on Theser—and they obliterated everyone and everything. They do not intend to rescue you." Sloshing across the pooled water on the floor, she pressed the horrific images closer, forcing the prisoner to look. "Don't you have anything to say to Diadem Michella after she tried to murder you?"

She glanced over at Jacque to make sure the boy was watching.

Suddenly, the listless Undine exploded into enraged motion like a released spring. She lunged forward, lifting a metal support strut she had secretly disengaged from her cot. Bebe didn't have time to cry out, could barely lift the projection screen as a meager defense.

Undine struck Bebe hard across the temple, crushing her skull. As she fell, a second blow broke open the back of her head; Bebe was dead before she dropped into the standing water on the floor.

Jacque saw it all, and he screamed.

Wild and suicidal, Undine charged out of the cell, swinging the metal club from side to side. Astonished, the guard protectively knocked the boy behind him. The governor managed to strike the man on the shoulder, but he was a fighter and slammed her into the wall with the full weight of his body. He broke Undine's arm when he wrenched the metal club free; when it clattered to the floor, he punched her hard in the stomach. She crumpled, choking, sobbing . . . then laughing.

Jacque ran into the cell and dropped to his knees in the filthy water, propping his mother's dripping, battered head on his lap. He wailed for her, but she didn't answer.

50

Sophie Vence sat on the front passenger seat of a Trakmaster while her son drove the overland vehicle across the rough terrain. It was deceptively like old times, before Devon had joined himself with an alien personality. She, Devon, and Antonia headed out to the lush valley that had drawn the attention of the mysterious ships.

Sunlight filtered through the dirty, streaked windshield. Antonia sat in the front between them. Her alien companion Jhera sometimes shared a veiled telepathic dialogue with Birzh, and sometimes Antonia conversed with Devon in her own voice. Sophie cherished the moments whenever the two showed flashes of their original personalities.

All three were curious about what they would find in the isolated, awakened valley. From a purely commercial sense, Sophie looked forward to inspecting the new native forest, which might provide useful raw materials. More importantly, she hoped to learn more about the strange ships and what had drawn them to the outburst of plant life.

She held on to a side rail as the Trakmaster rolled over boulders. When Devon brought them to more level ground, he picked up speed, driving the way he used to. Even Antonia had a smile on her face.

For Sophie, life had been full of surprises, some bad and some good. She'd had more than her share of hardships, but everyone on Hellhole could make that claim. She had never been destined for a normal life anyway, and this place had made incredible things possible for her. She'd met General Adolphus, and Devon had found real love with Antonia, along with their Xayan counterparts. Sophie had to keep reminding herself of their newfound joys.

She glanced sidelong at her son. Such a handsome, compassionate young man. She could not be more proud of him or hopeful about his future, but she was also worried about him. Despite his reassurances, Sophie did not know what would happen to his human side when the Xayans ultimately achieved *ala'ru* and "ascended."

The Trakmaster rumbled over the last line of hills, and Devon brought the vehicle to a halt so they could all stare at the mysterious verdant valley. Until now, the rugged terrain had shown only a few splashes of color, thorny scrub brush, and weeds . . . but the valley that stretched below them took their breath away. It was magical—the landscape exploded with life, a vibrant blue forest of feathery trees, sweeping meadows of spiky green and orange grasses—a different palette from the fast-growing red weed.

Devon and Antonia smiled at each other, and the spiraling sheen of Xayan amazement sparkled in their eyes. Birzh said through Devon, "After the impact, we lost hope that we would ever see so much life here again!"

Antonia unsealed the hatch of the vehicle, eager to emerge. "Our world is coming back . . . all of it is coming back!"

Sophie reached out a hand to caution the young woman. "We need to put on our air masks—you never know what pollens or allergens the plants might contain."

But Antonia disregarded her and bounded out of the Trakmaster. Devon followed, saying, "We know, Mother, and there is nothing to worry about."

Sophie hesitated, then gave a snort. "Well, as long as I have my own experts here." Stepping out onto the new growth, Sophie could smell freshness in the air, a heady humidity, and lush vegetation.

The three of them waded through waist-high, fernlike vegetation. Everything was so *alive*, Sophie could almost see plants sprouting and expanding before her eyes.

"So many different species! What caused such a surge—and why *here?"* The seeds or spores of native vegetation must have been dormant for centuries since the impact. Why had they all germinated now? And the large animals had been considered extinct.

The feathery blue trees bounded a sunlit, grassy glade with a narrow stream. They stopped to stare at a herd of grazing antelopelike creatures that had mossy green hides and antlers like tentacles. Startled, the creatures bounded away and vanished into the lush forest of ferns.

Devon and Antonia were quiet and contemplative. "Those animals are fern deer, but Birzh doesn't understand how the creatures could possibly be alive."

"This is strange, but wonderful," Antonia said in a voice that was only half her own.

Sophie followed the antelope prints to the narrow brook, then pushed her way through a stand of twitching ferns to gaze upon a broad expanse of orange grass.

She was startled to see that the meadow was dotted with the remnants of artificial canisters, like mechanical eggs. They lay scattered across the ground. She bent close to one, nudged it with her fingers. It was empty, weathered. "Did those strange ships drop canisters here? For what purpose?"

Devon stepped up beside her. "I don't think so, Mother. The canisters were deposited at least a month ago."

"Unless the ships have been coming here for some time," Antonia said.

Cautious but curious, Sophie turned over one of the empty canisters, but it bore no markings. "And what are they for?"

Wandering around the meadow, Devon discovered several bright, new canisters that were still sealed, freshly dropped onto the ground. "These are recent. The ships must have dropped them."

As they watched, one of the new canisters opened, followed by another, and another. Sophie stepped back as small larval creatures emerged and crawled away from the canisters and into the ferns. She was reminded of the stored embryos she had delivered to the rancher Armand Tillman.

Devon used Birzh's knowledge to identify them. "Those are nymphs, the larval stage of the fern deer."

Sophie straightened, unable to deny the evidence before her eyes.

"Are those strange ships restoring species to Xaya? Using embryo canisters to reseed the planet?"

Devon seemed fascinated. "The slickwater database is allowing us to restore Xaya's lost history and civilization. Now it appears someone else wants to return this world to what it once was."

Sophie thought of her own efforts to tame Hellhole, planting vineyards, erecting greenhouses, establishing the fishery, distributing livestock embryos. "The General needs to know about this."

As they made their way back to the Trakmaster, the spiky grasses rustled behind them, and Sophie heard a huffing sound. Turning, she saw a large creature bound through a clump of ferns that had been concealing it. The beast had long tusks and a ridge of spiny scales; its claws tore divots in the ground as it charged toward them.

"Run!" Sophie raced for the protection of the Trakmaster, although she knew they could never reach the vehicle in time. The predator closed the distance fast.

But Devon and Antonia merely turned and placed themselves in front of the animal. Sophie yelled for them to save themselves, but the two held hands. With placid expressions, they created a shimmer in the air around them.

The creature was only ten meters away when the energy crackled and intensified in the air. The charging beast struck the barrier, and telemancy repelled it. The thing threw itself forward again, and was deflected.

"We trained ourselves to fight armies with our telemancy, Mother," Devon said mildly. "We can protect against a predator without harming it." Ignoring Sophie, the hungry creature circled the pair of shadow-Xayans, looking for an opening but finding none. Finally, it stalked off toward the blue tree forest and a nervous group of fern deer.

Shaken, Sophie brushed herself off and urged the two toward the Trakmaster. "We need to head back to Elba. I've got a lot to tell Tiber."

51

The alien museum vault contained as many secrets as shadows. Cristoph de Carre and his team had spent months inspecting and documenting the items, listening to explanations from Lodo and from Keana's counterpart Uroa. He had marveled at the remnants of a glorious, lost Xayan civilization, admiring the fantastic works of the exotic race, their free-form buildings, their epic yet incomprehensible history, their philosophers, like Zairic, and their struggles to survive by any means when they knew the asteroid was coming.

Constellation archaeologists and scholars would have given anything for this opportunity. In his former life, Cristoph would have been astonished to visit such a place even once; now he practically lived in the vault, spending his days trying to unravel mysteries.

Cristoph had been trained as a manager and businessman at the iperion mines on Vielinger. When his father shirked his hereditary duties, squandered the family fortune, and dallied with the Diadem's *married* daughter, Cristoph had fought to keep the de Carre operations running, despite sabotage and scandal. After his family holdings were stripped and he was sent out to the worst planet in the Deep Zone, Cristoph had assumed his life was over.

And now he was here. Ironically, against all odds, he found that he liked what he was doing, and he was even coming to respect Keana Duchenet.

Though the Constellation fleet had vanished, Cristoph and Keana both knew that Diadem Michella would never give up so easily. She would still try to attack Hellhole. And they had to find some unexpected and effective way to protect the planet.

Keana-Uroa and Lodo activated a set of beautifully carved crystal chimes that made musical tones as they rearranged them. Cristoph found the artifacts wondrous, but unless they could be converted into some kind of sonic weapon, they would do the General no good.

Cristoph turned his attention to the five sarcophagi that had preserved the Original aliens for centuries after the impact. One of the five, Allyf, had died because the preservation systems burned out, but the other four had emerged from the tanks.

Cristoph walked around Allyf's sarcophagus now. The other four chambers were empty, the gelatinous protective fluid gone. Shortly after the Originals awakened, during one eerie night spent in the museum vault, Cristoph had seen the four Originals slip their soft hands into the fluid that contained Allyf's body, and they had worked together in an odd telemancy ceremony to *absorb* their companion.

Lodo showed no superstitious fear of Allyf's coffin, but in all the careful searching and inventorying of the vault's contents, Cristoph realized that very little attention had been paid to these sarcophagi. While the rest of the team continued their work, he knelt to examine the intricate hieroglyphic-style markings along the side of the container. The shadow-Xayans could draw upon their ancient memories to read and understand the language, but the symbols meant nothing to him. While poking around, Cristoph discovered a gap between the base and the floor, a seam beneath the blocky chamber. He pushed against Allyf's sarcophagus, and it slid aside with a dry, grating sound.

Underneath, he discovered intricate mechanical and hydraulic systems, crystals connected to tubes and shining designs that looked like gelatinous circuit patterns imprinted on sheets of metal. "Keana, look what I found," he called. "Uroa and Lodo, can you tell us what this is?"

She came over, followed by the slithering Original Xayan. The retractable feelers on Lodo's forehead waved in curiosity. Cristoph could not read the alien's large, dark eyes, but Keana still had enough human in her that he could understand her intense expression.

"This is Allyf's shield system," she said, straightening and looking at Lodo. "From within the sarcophagus he used his telemancy to provide added protection, sealing off this vault from the worst of the impact."

"It is true," Lodo said. "We knew the size of the incoming asteroid. Even this deep in the mountain we feared the strike would cause great destructive waves, and we could not be confident that our vault would remain intact."

Keana bent beside Cristoph and extended her fingers into the kaleidoscopic gel circuits, as if she knew what to do. "Yes, this device allowed him to focus and enhance his telemancy," she said in the eerie voice of Uroa. "Allyf must have remained conscious while the other four were suspended. Drawing upon his reserves, he used this telemancy amplifier to create an impenetrable shell around the vault."

"But it drained him too much," Lodo said, "and he did not recover from the effort. He might have saved everything here, but he did not survive the centuries."

Keana's breathing intensified, and she spoke in her own voice again. "If this is a telemancy amplifier, and one Xayan could shield this vault, what if many shadow-Xayans joined together? We could use this equipment to project a barrier around the planet, or at least above the main settlements! It would save us from an attack. Lodo, why didn't you tell us about this?"

The Original thrummed and swayed from side to side, as if disturbed. "It would not be wise to use it."

But Keana and Cristoph pushed the sarcophagus aside to expose the large device beneath the chamber. He immediately saw the possibilities. "Can we remove it? Take it to the shadow-Xayan colony? We couldn't crowd enough of them here inside the vault."

Lodo shouldered them aside. "It is very fragile."

Cristoph couldn't wait to report this to General Adolphus. At last their work in the vault might pay off, if the situation and the equipment were handled carefully.

Lodo extended his soft hands into the swirling patterns of translucent, not-quite-solid circuits. Then, in a flurry of movement, he tore his fingers across the filmy patterns and scrambled them like a child with a finger painting.

"Stop!" Cristoph cried. "What are you doing?"

With an invisible shove of telemancy, Lodo bent the metal plates, shattered the crystal components. He reached in and uprooted the flexible tubes. Sparks and pressurized droplets spurted up.

Keana reeled. "You ruined it!"

Cristoph felt sick. "That was the best chance we had for defending ourselves! Don't you want to save us? Don't you care about protecting this planet?"

"The device would have summoned far too much telemancy," Lodo thrummed. "Such a tremendous surge would have attracted attention to us, and we cannot afford that, especially now, when we are not close enough to *ala'ru*."

"How can you say it would attract too much attention?" Cristoph said. "We *wanted* the Constellation fleet to know—and be intimidated."

"Not the Constellation fleet," Lodo said. "There are other enemies. And they are alert."

"What the hell are you talking about? What others?"

Lodo regarded them with his alien face. From her own shocked expression, Keana didn't understand what the Original was talking about either, but Uroa was not forthcoming inside her mind.

Then a chill shot down Cristoph's back as Lodo said, "The original asteroid impact was *not* an accident."

52

Sia Frankov had been Tanja's friend and valued business associate—now wiped out along with the rest of the Theser settlement, hundreds of thousands of people slaughtered.

Bebe Nax was one of her closest, most devoted companions, sounding board, confidante, true *friend*. And Marla Undine had murdered Bebe right in front of her own son!

Yes, the Constellation—and especially Undine—would pay dearly for what they had done. They had unleashed the blood and fire.

Tanja found it hard to breathe, reeling from the shock and pain. Emotions roared around her like the mudslide that had wiped out Puhau and killed her uncle Quinn and his entire town, all because of Diadem Michella.

It seemed as if every bright spot of happiness, every close companion who had *humanized* Tanja despite her hatred toward the Constellation, was being taken away from her. She still had Ian Walfor, but he had already raced off to Hellhole to inform General Adolphus about the Theser disaster, and she didn't have the emotional strength to seek refuge in him. She had only her rage, and as it developed inside her she wanted to keep it. She *needed* to keep it and let it loose.

The General would retaliate for Theser in his own time, but here on Candela, it was up to her to avenge Bebe Nax. This was personal. And a dark part of her wanted to take action before anyone could advise restraint.

After his horrific experience, Jacque remained sedated in a Saporo medical center, although he kept crying out for his mother. Tanja went to visit the boy, though she could barely see through the fog of her fury. She doubted the groggy young man heard or understood her, but she swore to him that Undine would pay blood for blood. "I am the planetary administrator," she said, "and I will see to it."

Traveling alone, Tanja flew her own aerocopter out to the prison on the Puhau mudflats. She felt an arctic coldness settling over her, and terrible sorrow hung in her thoughts like a shadow that would never go away. Tanja felt outraged on Jacque's behalf, but she had also loved Bebe herself. She could never do enough to soothe the boy's deep wounds, to dispel the nightmares that would haunt him forever. Nothing could bring his mother back, and no amount of suffering by Marla Undine would make up for the loss.

But some things *had* to be done.

With her thoughts in a blur, she felt the intensifying acid of hatred. As if in a trance, Tanja walked through the dank prison corridors to Undine's high-security cell. When the guard opened the cell door, Tanja found herself staring at the governor's defiant, smirking face.

"Have you hired a new assistant yet?" Undine laughed. She was shackled to the wall. "I hear the one you had will be hard to replace."

Tanja's rage boiled over, and she did not try to contain it. Her fingers found the projectile pistol in her jacket pocket, and she drew it. "That is true, but you have no such value." Marla Undine barely had time to sneer before Tanja shot her.

The guard shouted, but it was too late. Tanja fired six more times before the weapon was drained, and then stood staring at what she had done. Moving with great care, the guard removed the weapon from her trembling hand, but his voice held no implied criticism as he said, "Saves the trouble of a trial."

Initially, Bebe had come to the prison to record a statement from the hostage governor; Tanja intended to use it for a message to Diadem Michella. Now she would send an entirely different sort of message.

"We are at war," she said, her voice tight. "What the Constellation did to Theser proves they mean to wipe us all out. I was justified."

"You'll get no argument from me, Administrator."

Staring down at the body slumped in the dirty, bloody water, Tanja felt no remorse. The dead governor had been a puppet of the Diadem, whose hands were covered with innocent blood. Michella's massacre on Ridgetop had been exposed not long ago; what happened to Theser was worse.

Yes, Tanja needed to send a very clear message to the monster.

As long minutes passed and she continued to glare at the lifeless, *worthless* body of Undine, she realized that General Adolphus might have wanted to ransom the political prisoner, but it was too late for second thoughts. Tanja had never killed anyone before, but as Candela's ruler she would stand by what she had done—and make it *count*.

The message would make the old Diadem choke. As she stared at Undine's bleeding body, a plan formed in her mind.

In a cool, controlled voice, she commented to the guard, "The Diadem thinks we are all savages out here anyway, so I'll show her what *savages* do."

53

shop paced his private office in a seedy part of Council City's government district, waiting for Laderna to arrive. His assistant had buried herself in research and investigations, and now she said she'd made an important new discovery. Ishop never underestimated the magnitude of her discoveries. Maddeningly, since it was Laderna's habit to draw out the suspense, she had provided no details.

He glanced at an ornate chronometer, a gift from Diadem Michella, and noted Laderna was running late. Not like her at all.

Maybe she had found a way to kill the Diadem's sister, Haveeda, or received confirmation of the death of Keana, so they could tidily finish up the list. He could keep his hopes up. He felt it was important to see a task through to its end. But if he was about to become a nobleman, then he had to leave his murderous days behind; better to keep his hands clean. One more month until he could reclaim his heritage.

Until then, he would continue to serve the special needs of Diadem Michella. He had advised and protected the old ruler over the years; he performed many of the necessary and unpleasant tasks that kept her rule strong. In return, Michella had rewarded him with tremendous opportunities, much more than a mere streetwise commoner deserved. When he finally revealed his true heritage, the Diadem would be his greatest champion.

He was glad he didn't have to kill her, just to complete his list. That would have put him in a quandary, confusing his priorities. . . .

After two quick raps on the door, followed by a pause and two more, their private signal, he let Laderna into the office and sealed the entrance behind her after a quick scan of the corridor. Her information was supposedly private. Flushed with excitement, she carried a leather briefcase, which she set on the desk. "Sorry I'm late, boss."

She expanded a filmscreen, turned it in his direction, and displayed a detailed surveillance report. "This is a summary from the Diadem's special team of guards, marking all identified security threats. Nothing particularly serious, everything being handled through normal channels." She smiled. "But they missed one."

Ishop knew what she was going to say. "Burum Elakis, the man who communicated with Governor Goler in the prison."

"We have to take all the information and surveillance into account. No actionable evidence against Elakis, but he has been engaged in highly suspicious activity. You know how good I am at making connections, boss. He's from Orsini, clearly an Adolphus sympathizer, and I believe he's up to something big, connected with both Governor Goler and General Adolphus—and I think it involves the Diadem." Laderna was not a person to waste time, and she continued in a rush. "Do you remember a few years ago when a palace butler was arrested on suspicion of stealing the Diadem's jewelry?"

Ishop had only a vague memory of the event. In the immense palace there was always one scandal or other. "A minor incident, if I recall correctly."

Laderna's eyes shone. "Supposedly the butler co-opted one of the Diadem's ladies-in-waiting to steal the gems, and then the two of them ran off to a resort town on Orsini. The butler was found dead in his cell afterward—a suicide, supposedly. But I think we know that's not true."

"I have some . . . experience in the true causes of prison suicides." He couldn't help but smile.

"The man's name was Willis Elakis, the older brother of Burum Elakis." She paused. "And Burum, it seems, still holds a grudge. That's probably why he requested reassignment from combat during the General's rebellion when everyone else was gung ho to fight."

Ishop scratched his head, scanned more details of the report. "Michella probably was responsible for his brother's death. She wouldn't let any-one get away with stealing from her."

"And there's more, boss. Burum Elakis is rather patriotic about his planet Orsini, and the Tazaars. It's a complicated situation."

Ishop wondered if Laderna had dug so deeply, looking for connec-tions, because they were considering Enva Tazaar as a possible noble wife for him.

"We'll watch him, see what he's up to, but keep this to ourselves for now. No one else needs to know. If we end up saving the Diadem, why dilute her gratitude toward us by letting anyone else participate?"

While Ishop continued the careful, albeit tedious, surveillance of the mysterious man, Laderna tracked down clandestine images and record-ings of Elakis's former activities on Orsini, before he came to Sonjeera for an utterly trivial job. Very puzzling. It could be a discreet cover.

They intercepted a message that Elakis sent in a seemingly innocent package to an old friend on Orsini, but Laderna traced it to a rerouting system that delivered it to the Tazaar estate. Even more puzzling. Laderna managed to extract the message and copy it. The words were coded gib-berish, but that was merely another layer of opacity to the problem. It took the combined skills of Ishop and Laderna to decipher the message, and when they finally stared at the translation, both grinned.

"Good thing we told no one about our suspicions," Ishop said. "Let's bide our time now and see how this complicated assassination plot un-folds."

Flushed in the face, Laderna said, "You're not going warn the Diadem about the bomb he's going to plant?"

"Not until I can figure out how to rescue her at the proper time and take full credit—along with you, of course. We can always arrest Elakis later, at our convenience."

She was so excited that she kissed him, and he was pleased to let her. In fact, he even suggested celebrating, for old times' sake.

54

I 've been doing this for a long time," mumbled the Commodore, feeling weary rather than joyful. Then louder, for good form, he added, "Strike fast, strike hard."

In his old uniform, Percival Hallholme stood straight and tall inside the stringline hub. For the quiet send-off, they had all gathered before a titanium framework studded with windows for viewing the stars and space traffic coming from the Crown Jewels.

Beside him, Diadem Michella gazed out at the assembled vessels that Commodore Hallholme would lead on a sneak attack against General Adolphus. The thirty warships had been crewed with personnel that Percival selected personally, based on their competence rather than pedigree. He did not need a crowd of useless, medal-hungry nobles.

"The ships are waiting for my order to depart," Michella said. "But with no fanfare this time, no announcement whatsoever. No one but your own crew will know where they are going, so the General's spies cannot warn him."

Percival nodded. "Thank you, Eminence. I will conduct this operation in the utmost secrecy." His very presence had attracted some attention regardless, and someone might have noticed the discreet reassignment of decommissioned trailblazer ships loaded with more iperion than the Crown Jewels could properly spare. But no one would suspect he'd venture along a dangerous and long-decommissioned route to Buktu.

Michella smiled. "We are hosting planetary celebrations for Lord Riomini's great victory on Theser, with a very powerful loop of images for all the public to see. We're even distributing the package to schools as educational material. I wish you could stay for the festivities."

Percival kept his expression neutral. "A shame, Eminence, but it provides the perfect distraction for our departure. My ships will be gone before anyone can put the pieces together. I shall attend an even larger celebration when General Adolphus has been defeated."

She smiled, touched his collar affectionately. "That's a promise, my old friend. Your son tried to take care of the mess, but it appears we've lost him and the battle fleet. Lord Riomini showed his bloodthirstiness on Theser, but he has more interest in the Star Throne than in being a true war hero. You're the only commander I can really trust for this mission. The fate of the Constellation is at stake."

He tried to hide the hint of impatience on his face. Percival served his Diadem, but he did not dare let Michella realize how much he disliked her personally. He would fulfill his responsibility and do her bidding—and do it extraordinarily well—but no more.

He saluted her, then, favoring his bad leg, hobbled into the boarding tunnel to his flagship, which already hung aboard its hauler. The string-line hauler was ready to begin picking its way along the intermittent iperion path to Buktu. By the time the raucous Riomini celebrations started, he intended to be far from the Crown Jewels.

⊷⊷

Diadem Michella spared no expense in celebrating Riomini's decisive victory against the "well-armed and dangerous" rebels on Theser. She would give the Black Lord all the glory he wanted, and for once he deserved it.

Fortunately, Riomini had launched his strike before Governor Goler came to the Crown Jewels with his naïve ultimatum from Adolphus. The Theser strike demonstrated to everyone how vulnerable any individual Deep Zone world was—the rebels couldn't possibly mount a large defensive force around so many frontier planets! And if the Diadem chose to call the General's bluff and devastate another colony, she didn't believe even a power-hungry madman like him would sever all their lifelines.

But she wouldn't risk it—she didn't need to. She would bide her time while Commodore Hallholme took care of the matter. The imminent death of Adolphus—drawn and quartered, perhaps, or slowly vaporized—would go a long way to restoring peace and harmony in the Constellation.

In the capital city, the festive mood had captivated the populace. She provided free food and drink, commissioned bands, scheduled breathtaking fireworks displays. The beloved Diadem and the brave Black Lord would symbolize strength and prosperity.

At the climax of the celebrations, she was due to present Riomini with a medal that was specially designed for the occasion. Her security detail took her by royal carriage to Heart Square, and the crowd noises became thunderous when she made her way to the central stage. This would be an important speech.

Due to the Deep Zone troubles, grumbling had increased across the Crown Jewels as well. Without the DZ tribute payments, many of the gentry were denied the luxury items they had grown so fond of, as well as the profits of certain business operations. More and more, they blamed *her* for not resolving the situation, and she'd been forced to arrest some nobles and businessmen for making seditious statements.

When shadows cast by the setting sun stretched across the plaza, dazzling torches were lit to enhance the spectacle. Michella crossed the stage and raised her arms high. Behind her, and on screens across Sonjeera, flashed gruesome and victorious images of Theser, accompanied by patriotic music. "Strike fast, strike hard!" she shouted repeatedly, and the crowd took up the chant.

In a firm voice, the Diadem gave one of her usual speeches about how ruthless the rebels were, how they had taken political prisoners, shirked their financial responsibilities to the Constellation, and more. The Deezees had practically forced the Diadem to attack them.

"It is what the traitors deserve," she announced. "We do not negotiate with such people. After what Lord Riomini accomplished on Theser, they are fleeing for cover. Our forces will meet very little resistance when we restore order to the Deep Zone." She needed to be vague, because she had not admitted the full debacle of the original fleet, despite Governor Goler's comments to the Council.

She motioned toward Riomini, who waited at one side of the stage. Puffed with pride, the Black Lord made his way to the podium. While he grinned beside her, the Diadem spoke lofty words and pinned yet another golden medal on his chest, to the resounding cheers of the onlookers. Then she released the crowd to continue their celebrations.

As she stepped down from the platform with Lord Riomini and headed back to the interior of the building, she felt relieved. When they entered the secure corridor and the doors closed to drown out the noise of the crowd outside, she saw Ishop Heer, surrounded by her own security team. They had gathered in the echoing hall to await the end of her speech. Michella noticed that they all stood around a diplomatic message pod.

"Eminence, this just arrived from Candela—sent directly from the planetary administrator." Ishop lifted the package, a cube less than half a meter on a side; it seemed heavy. "It's unopened, but we've scanned it for explosives, poisons, or dangerous biologicals."

"Candela? That's a Deep Zone world, isn't it? Bring the package along." Michella gestured for her guards to clear the way. She couldn't remember the name of the Candela administrator; no face came to mind at all. "Find us a place of privacy." She glanced at Riomini, made her decision, and said, "Join us, Selik. Maybe it's a surrender document after your attack on Theser. They know they have no option but to capitulate."

The Black Lord frowned. "Then Administrator Hu should have sent a tribute payment as well."

"The box isn't *that* heavy," Ishop said.

When they were inside a small, empty office, Michella commanded Ishop to unseal the pod and remove its inner wrapping. Impatient and dismissive, Riomini pushed him aside. "Allow me to present it to the Diadem." He removed the last layer and tipped the box onto its side, then recoiled.

A human head rolled onto the table—Governor Marla Undine's.

And yet she knew she had made the situation far worse.

Watching the activity in the harbor, Tanja stood alone. She was not a military leader, and if she could give her own life instead and resolve the conflict, she would do so. But she had already crossed the line . . . or plunged off a precipice.

A tiny voice inside her head suggested that even Bebe would have chided her for such a brutal, poorly considered act. And General Adolphus would be furious over the moral and tactical issues, but Tanja could not retract what she had already done. She accepted responsibility for her action.

Tanja had sent an urgent but professionally worded message to General Adolphus, explaining what she had done and why, then requesting him to send more DZDF ships so she could stand against an expected attack by the Constellation.

Closing her eyes, she tried to focus, tried to find the inner strength she needed now. Her head pounded. She might very well have brought down the full force of the Diadem's wrath on her beloved world.

⌘

Tanja Hu's shocking message reached Adolphus while he studied preparedness records in Elba. Ian Walfor's report about Theser had arrived only the day before, and the General was already scrambling for reports from all the other DZ worlds, placing every planet on high alert, prepping them to blow their stringlines. Apparently, Governor Goler had not been convincing . . . or maybe just too late.

With the turmoil and uncertainty caused by the vanished fleet, the plans of Adolphus had been unraveling; now Tanja's impetuous provocation was like a planet-sized monkey wrench thrown into the works.

He looked up from the message, saw Sophie's somber expression as she stood next to him at the desk. She had read the communiqué as well. She had reported the wondrous discovery of the old Xayan species being reintroduced by the mysterious ships—which would have fascinated him and demanded his attention for full investigation, but the Theser massacre and now this crisis with Tanja Hu had thrown a big steaming mess into his lap.

"I fear I have been overconfident," he said. "Long ago the Greeks of

55

As Tanja stood on her balcony outside the Saporo Harl building, she gazed out at the military drills in the wat the armed patrol boats ready to defend the government comp six orbiting warships were on high alert for a Constellation resp

She had no doubt a retaliation *would* come, and no amount o or second thoughts would change that. Tanja had sent Govern dine's head to Sonjeera in an ill-advised fit of pique, and the ol dem would have no choice. An attack was inevitable, but she wo ready.

Tanja's migraines had come back, like a military attack insid head. She remembered with a sharp pang that Bebe had always good at soothing the pain. . . .

She felt numb and on fire at the same time, deflated and adrift. ter the loss of Bebe, and before that Sia Frankov, and before that Ur Quinn—not to mention the entire town of Puhau, all the people Theser—Tanja had no desire to exercise restraint. She had not asked permission, had chosen not to overthink what she had done. Too la now. All the ghosts of her dead friends and loved ones had demande action, and Tanja hadn't looked for any advice or instructions befor she made up her mind. This was *not* a time for calmness, or for overcon-sidered acts.

Earth warned of hubris, and somehow I forgot the lesson. I may have overplayed my hand."

She looked at him with her gray eyes, and he drew strength from her. She rested her hand on his shoulder. "Then you'll just have to pull off another miracle—you've done it before. Maybe Goler can still find a way to resolve this diplomatically."

He shook his head. "By destroying Theser, Lord Riomini threw fuel on the flames, and now Tanja Hu sparked an even bigger blaze. There won't be any peace settlement." After thinking for a moment he said, "I have to go to Candela."

On another occasion, the thought of leaving Hellhole for another world would have gladdened him. This would be only the second time he had been off-planet since his exile.

Putting together the pieces of his plan, Adolphus used the secure codecall to contact Craig Jordan aboard the sixty patrol ships in orbit. "Mr. Jordan, I have reason to believe that Candela may be a target for a major Constellation retaliatory strike. Prepare fifteen of our most heavily armed battleships and load them aboard a hauler for immediate departure. I intend to deliver the ships myself."

Jordan sounded shocked. "Fifteen ships, sir? That'll leave us vulnerable!"

"Right now, Candela is more vulnerable, and I believe there's a credible threat there. You'll have to make do with forty-five ships at Hellhole."

Even without the Constellation conflict, he had numerous crises to deal with here on Hellhole. Rendo Theris had sent an update that his engineers were preparing to blast and drain away the slickwater aquifers beneath the Ankor spaceport. Seismic reports from across the continent tracked the increasing quakes; numerous aftershocks triggered eruptions in the volcanic area of the impact crater—and they were getting worse.

"I'm going with you," she announced.

He paused for a few seconds, because he would have liked her to accompany him, but then shook his head. "I need you here. Now, more than ever, I've got to be sure our operations run smoothly, and I can count on you."

Sophie squeezed his shoulder. "Then at least I'm going to Ankor to see you off."

With that, he didn't argue.

56

The General's fast flyer arrived at Ankor in late afternoon. The sky over the spaceport complex was a sickly shade of green mixed with sulfuric yellow from the volcanoes. For some time now, increasing eruptions had spewed lava from numerous active zones. Smoke tinged the air all across the continent. The troubled planet remained restless.

When he and Sophie disembarked, Adolphus felt a warm, dry breeze against his face, smelled the acrid sulfur of volcanic activity not far from the spaceport basin. Shuttles and upboxes were thrust into the sky from the paved fields, and passenger pods came down from stringline ships. A busy commercial day, hinting at how the Deep Zone could thrive . . . in normal times.

The new spaceport was undergoing expansion to accommodate the traffic, and now it was a maze of landing areas and one-story buildings. Rendo Theris hurried up to them, busy with his constant obligations. He was accompanied by the large, pale form of Encix rolling along beside him. Adolphus was surprised to see the Original alien out here.

Theris looked flushed, as always. "Sorry, General, it seems like there's one disaster after another. We are preparing your stringline hauler for immediate departure to Candela, including the fifteen warships you requested to be loaded aboard. It's a frantic day! The engineering team on the spaceport construction project is ready to blow release-channels to drain the slickwater aquifers. Afterward, the site will be stable for expansion—or so they say—but that alien goo keeps welling up. Our geologists used seismic probes to locate the aquifers, and they're drilling down to release the slickwater into a subterranean void, away from the spaceport. Safe and sound." He shook his head. "But Encix here has concerns. . . ."

The Original alien moved forward on her caterpillar legs, and her voice carried a warning tone. "You were not wise to build a spaceport here in the first place, General Tiber Adolphus. It should be moved."

He shook his head, adamant. "We don't have time to relocate our whole operation and start again from scratch. We're at war."

The Ankor operations had been mostly complete when the four Originals awakened in their deep vault. The second, hidden spaceport complex linked to a major new stringline hub was the heart of the General's plan for independence. Encix had urged Adolphus to abandon the entire facility and begin elsewhere, but that was something he would *not* do.

"I expressed warnings before. Now, however, you intend something else. If you use explosives against the reservoirs, you may provoke the slickwater and the Xayan lives within it."

"Provoke the slickwater?" His eyebrows drew together. "We're trying to drain it away."

Theris let out a long sigh, shaking his head. "See what I mean, General? If the slickwater can survive an asteroid impact that wrecked the whole planet, how can we bother it with a few mining charges? We can release the pressure and run the problematic reservoirs out where they won't cause any more trouble."

Encix thrummed. "The slickwater has ways to protect itself . . . but that does not allay my concerns."

"Your geologists confirmed the preparations, and we are ready to go." Theris sounded exasperated. "It's your call, General."

"My first priority is to protect this planet, and the Deep Zone," he said, looking at Encix. "And right now, the Army of the Constellation poses the greatest danger. For the defense of the Deep Zone, we need new landing areas and launchpads to keep the stringline network operating. This is a crucial time."

"And a crucial time for us as well, General Tiber Adolphus," Encix said. "My priority is to see that our race finally achieves *ala'ru,* and we are very close. To succeed, we require the slickwater."

Adolphus knew he was being stubborn, but he had no time to discard so many preparations. Enough of his overall plan had already been tangled and disrupted, and he had to keep the rest from falling apart. "The slickwater can well up anywhere else it likes—just not here."

After a long silence, Encix bent her flexible neck and did not object further. Looking relieved, Theris led them to a white groundcar that would carry them across the landing zones. "Your passenger pod is due to depart within the hour, sir. We can watch the drilling blast while we wait—it's just on the perimeter fields."

Encix surprised them by climbing aboard the open vehicle to join them. They rode over to a perimeter landing pad, near a group of uniformed workers who were watching monitors on mobile units. After disembarking with her companions, the alien stood there, swaying her soft body and murmuring to herself. Encix seemed disturbed, which troubled Adolphus.

Theris touched the codecall on his collar and deferred to the General. "They are ready whenever you give the word, sir."

He looked at the alien, tried to read her smooth, strange face. "We mean no harm to the slickwater," he said to her.

Encix swayed, and her soft feelers retracted into her forehead. "I understand that. And I will try to make the slickwater understand it as well, if necessary."

Adolphus glanced at Sophie, whose brow was also wrinkled with concern. "We need the spaceport, Tiber."

Adolphus nodded to Theris, and the spaceport administrator transmitted brief instructions to the geology teams. A moment later, they heard the dull thuds of a series of detonations, and felt the ground vibrate beneath them. One of the mobile monitoring units fell over.

Theris said, "That should have created an opening deep below. The slickwater can drain away into a new subterranean void, where it won't bother our operations here."

As the tremors died away, Encix suddenly twisted her upper body, then let out a strange moan. "No . . . the slickwater is coming back here."

Cracks began to spread across the expansive paved landing zone, fissures that ran like lightning bolts, zigzagging in all directions. A swath of pavement in the adjacent empty landing zone subsided. Some of the workers tried to take readings from their implanted monitors, while others simply fled. The cracking sound grew louder.

Silvery slickwater oozed up through the openings like spilled blood. Amebalike tendrils oozed out through drainage lines and flooded the landing pad in a mirrorlike pool. As it was exposed to the air, ghostly images manifested, shimmering electrical shapes and helixes that swirled about like static storms.

Adolphus stared at them, and Sophie frowned. "We've never seen anything like that at Slickwater Springs."

Then, in a burst of released energy, a group of the spectral shapes struck two of the spaceport workers hard and knocked them flat. A glowing cord of lightning lashed the ground like a bullwhip. More slickwater bubbled up, frothing and angry.

"Stay clear of the flood! Back to the vehicle!" the General yelled, and Theris did not need further encouragement.

Encix, though, remained where she was. "All this telemancy is like a scream in the air. I did not wish to exert so much power, but I will do what I can. The slickwater needs to understand . . . needs to be quiet." The alien moved forward to the advancing flood that percolated up from the ground. With no hesitation, she waded into the slickwater. "I can feel the flood of stored memories and history. To tap into the telemancy reservoir and quell this reaction, I require as much contact as possible."

She settled her sluglike abdomen into the quicksilver fluid and bent forward to immerse her upper body as well—torso, arms, even her face.

As the liquid pooled around Encix, the General felt an energy and pressure increasing in the air, static sparking everywhere. Guided by the Original, the combined telemancy accumulated and mounted, and Encix linked with the lost Xayans stored in the fluid. She soothed the reservoir and urged the slickwater to withdraw, as if it were a single living organism. The static and shimmering manifestations faded in the air as the slickwater responded to her.

As Encix nudged and controlled the liquid, the angry pools receded, dropping back through the cracks in the launchpad pavement, draining back into the ground.

Theris received word through his codecall headset. "Monitors say the slickwater is flowing into the subterranean void."

Encix turned her alien face toward Adolphus and Sophie. "Although the shadow-Xayans may practice telemancy to defend this planet, I can still do some things better than they can. I am reluctant to exert so much power, but it was the only way to utilize these defensive measures."

The pavement was badly damaged from the upheaval, but completely dry now that the slickwater had retreated. The shimmering, luminous manifestations had vanished, as the alien fluid returned to quiescence.

Standing alone where the slickwater had once been, Encix raised her humanoid hands to the sky. Her facial membrane vibrated with indistinguishable words, as if she were rejoicing.

Sophie was relieved. "Good. The slickwater is no longer a threat."

"No," Encix said. "The threat is not the slickwater."

Adolphus turned toward Theris. "Have the geologists run deep seismic tests to make sure, but the spaceport should be stable enough now for continued expansion."

Sophie remained troubled. "Encix, why would you need such a defensive mechanism in the first place? You said the Xayans were a peaceful race, what did they have to defend *against?*"

"We have long had enemies—dangerous enemies," the alien said. "Your Constellation is not the only threat to this planet."

Theris touched the codecall receiver in his ear. "General, your passenger pod is ready to depart. Mr. Jordan has fifteen warships loaded in docking clamps aboard the stringline hauler."

The General was troubled, but anxious to get to Candela. Knowing Michella's temper, she could already have attack ships on the way. He strode toward the launching gantry with his passenger pod, throwing a glance back at the Original. "The Constellation is my more immediate concern."

57

Aboard the *Diadem's Glory*, a pair of rangers donned spacesuits, took cutters, bypass toolkits, and weapons, and prepared to go outside along the hauler framework to the isolated pilot's blister.

Bolton addressed the two men as they suited up, while Escobar remained silent, watching them. "If you find any food supplies up there, you'll both get a double ration. We need to find out what happened to the pilot." Through a porthole in the spacecraft's ceiling, he glanced up at the domed enclosure high overhead in the immense framework.

Pilot Suri Dar had sealed herself away up there and refused to respond to any communications. Bolton felt little confidence they would find good news, and he dreaded another disaster.

The day before, a major tragedy had taken them all by surprise. The pilot of the second military hauler, carrying twenty fleet warships, had suffered a psychological breakdown. In a thin, hysterical voice, the pilot announced that he would find his own way to planet Hallholme, declaring it the only way to save himself. His hauler veered away from the other four carrier ships and activated stringline engines, plunging into the unexplored vastness with no iperion path to follow and no chance of reaching the destination.

Bolton had been astonished. Twenty warships, gone! All the

personnel . . . as well as all their supplies. A fifth of the Constellation fleet now forever lost. Madness!

He reeled from the magnitude of the foolish loss (and their failure to safeguard against it), although some members of the remaining crew expressed an irrational relief that at least the mad pilot had *done* something rather than just sitting there and waiting to die. Some even believed that if all the stranded haulers were to try finding their way to planet Hallholme, even without a stringline to follow, maybe at least one would make it.

In a calm voice, showing his charts and numbers, Bolton made it clear that the odds of success were infinitesimal. He insisted that they wait for Zabriskie and Caron to return. Rationally, it was their best chance.

But the crew hated their inaction.

The Redcom issued orders for the other hauler pilots to stand down and join the rest of the crew. Only Suri Dar had not answered.

"We'll find out what's happened to her, sir," said the first ranger. They sealed their suits and entered the airlock.

Stringline hauler pilots were, by their very nature, loners, even misfits. After Suri Dar isolated herself, a rumor started among the skeleton crew that she was hoarding an undocumented supply of food that should be shared with the conscious crew members. Even Escobar began to wonder if that might be true, although if the pilot had a large personal stockpile, it would amount to only a few mouthfuls when distributed across the twenty-five hundred crew members who were still awake.

The growing despair throughout the stranded fleet made each day like a barefoot walk across razor blades. Constant fights broke out; crewmen killed each other or committed suicide. The crewmembers remaining at their stations were so thin and jittery that they looked like real skeletons.

The food supplies were reaching critically low levels. Bolton could not sleep, and while he was awake, he could think of little other than the sharp teeth of hunger chewing in his stomach. More than 80 percent of the remaining crew was now sedated, surviving on minimal life support, kept at the lowest possible metabolic rate. Part of him envied those who were comatose, seemingly peaceful yet completely helpless. He didn't know which was worse.

Through it all they kept waiting for word from the trailblazer ship—waiting, *waiting*, and watching the calendar.

In order to give them hope, Bolton had calculated the absolute best-case scenario. Once the trailblazer arrived at Hallholme and dropped the terminus ring, the pilots could rush back here at stringline speeds in only a day. That meant two more weeks at an absolute minimum before the fleet could expect any sign. But even that estimated time, Bolton knew, was extremely optimistic.

Sheer boredom enhanced their fears. An effort to discover the fate of pilot Suri Dar would normally have been watched with great interest by the remaining crew, but Bolton had advised keeping it secret. The rangers weren't likely to discover good news, anyway. Lately he and Escobar had been forced to keep a lot of bad information secret.

Because the giant hauler was just a framework to carry twenty Constellation warships suspended from docking clamps, there was no easy access to the pilot's blister from the ships. Outside, the two spacesuited rangers worked their way along the flagship's hull, climbing to the docking clamp and traversing a structural girder. "We'll reach the pilot's blister in ten minutes, sir," the first ranger transmitted across the scrambled codecall.

The warships hung silent around the *Diadem's Glory*, many of them shut down and dark; even the inhabited vessels showed only minimal illumination. The air was stale. The ships were cold. The bridge of the flagship was a quiet and somber place.

"We've reached the hatch to the pilot's blister," said the second ranger. "Still no response to our signals."

"Use the tool kit to force your way in," Escobar said. "We need to know about her, one way or the other." He lowered his voice to Bolton. "I can't take the risk that she might power up the controls and take us on a joyride." The comment hung in the air like a guillotine blade.

"We're inside the first airlock door, sir," came the codecall.

"Can you see anything through the viewport?" Escobar asked.

"Just the interior of the cabin, and it seems empty."

"All right, access the pilot's blister. Have your weapons ready, in case she's violent."

Because the stringline hauler was a military vessel, the rangers had the proper override codes. They made their way through the second airlock door and into Suri Dar's small but comfortable quarters.

"Nobody's in the cockpit, sir. Moving toward her private cabin now. The door is sealed, both the electronic and some kind of manual lock."

"Force your way in if necessary."

Bolton stood nervously, waiting for the report. "Why would a stringline hauler captain need to lock her quarters? She's always alone up there. Why do they even *make* a lock?"

"Some pilots are paranoid," Escobar said.

"We're getting through," said the second ranger. "Door's open. What a stench!" He uttered a string of curses.

Bolton knew the answer even before the rangers reported.

"Captain Dar is dead, sir. She took her own life, at least a few days ago."

"I expected that," Escobar said quietly to Bolton, then transmitted to the rangers, "See if there are any nutrient supplies we can confiscate."

"Nothing left, sir. Just wrappers and empty containers. Medical packages scattered around, too—I think she took an overdose."

Bolton looked at the haunted expression on the Redcom's face, saw his jaw muscles ripple as he ground his teeth together. Escobar ordered the rangers to return to the *Diadem's Glory*. Bolton felt as if he had just suffered another blow to the gut.

"Review the records of our conscious crewmembers, Major," Escobar said. "Find someone we can train as a substitute stringline pilot."

58

shop and Laderna maintained their close surveillance on Burum Elakis. The man was a clever operative and gave very few indications of his plans, but he was no match for Ishop Heer.

As he stepped out of a lap pool at the exclusive private gymnasium building, he saw Laderna coming toward him with her usual brisk, businesslike step. Ishop preferred to swim at midmorning, when few others were around. He hated the smell of perspiration and the thought of other users on the equipment, so he sterilized each item before using it and checked the disinfectant levels of the pool water prior to stepping in. Michella had recently encouraged him to improve his physical condition. The old Diadem insisted that all her closest aides be as fit as she was, and Ishop couldn't disagree; he would be a noble soon, and he had expectations to meet.

Laderna grinned at him as he took a towel from the middle of the stack to be sure no one else had touched it. "I have confirmation, boss. Elakis has assembled and planted the bomb to assassinate the Diadem. We have to act right away to save her."

Such news was sufficient to cheer him, but he didn't feel any rush. "The Diadem did call an emergency Council session this afternoon. I suppose receiving a severed head is an emergency, although I daresay Governor Undine would have preferred preemptive action instead. Did

Elakis plant the bomb in the Council Hall? Now that I am a noble myself, I feel an obligation to save them all."

"It's more targeted than that. He planted the bomb in the Diadem's
autocarriage—more people will see the explosion out in the crowded
streets, though it'll play hell with traffic in Heart Square."

"I'd better not ride with her, then," Ishop said with a wicked smile as
he went to get dressed.

Laderna beamed with pride. "I have the names of the coconspirators
in the palace, a gardener and a driver in the motor pool, all of them
clandestine supporters of General Adolphus."

"Excellent work, as usual," he said. "Now I should shower, get dressed,
and go rescue the Diadem."

She touched his arm, made him pause. "Or . . ." Laderna let the word
hang for a moment. "We could remove the Duchenet name from our list,
finish the job that we started."

It would bring perfect closure, he realized, but he shook his head.
"The Diadem can still help us. She's too valuable an ally. But maybe
later . . ."

While Laderna waited outside, Ishop dressed hurriedly in an infor-
mal suit and rubbed ointment onto his bald scalp. Not fine clothing, but
under the circumstances, it would have to do. Time to be a hero.

At the palace he used his exclusive access codes to let himself into
the gardens, where Michella was taking a brisk walk; Ishop knew she
would be rehearsing her speech to the Council. She wore a dark exercise
suit with the oval, star-studded Duchenet crest on the shoulder. Seeing
him, she did not slow, and he had to jog to keep up with her. "Care to
join me?"

"I already did my exercise today, Eminence." He smiled, relishing
the surprise. "I thought you'd like to know—I discovered an assassination plot, and I suggest we take a different vehicle to the emergency
Council session this afternoon."

That was enough to make her pause in her exercise. He provided
details about the bomb plot and the network of Adolphus sympathizers
he had uncovered.

She paled. "And why didn't my own security team find out about
this?"

"Because I'm better at it than they are."

Michella sniffed, still trying to recover from the shocking news. "I'll call out my full guard staff, make widespread arrests—"

"Or, Eminence, we could wait and choreograph a more dramatic event. Let the assassination plot play out. Place a bureaucrat or two in your autocarriage, while you take a different route yourself. Make it look like a minor change in your plans . . . a case of indigestion perhaps? A serving of pâté that was off? You'll miraculously survive the attempt on your life, but the bomb would still go off."

"And what would be the point of that? I'd lose a couple of good government workers—"

"I didn't say to choose *good* bureaucrats, Eminence. You have plenty of extraneous ones. If you foil the plot ahead of time, the people will forget about it in a day. However, if there is a deadly explosion, public outrage will flare against the General. We can already blame the rebels for Undine's severed head, but this is much closer to home."

The old woman nodded slowly. "You are my most insightful adviser, dear Ishop. Very well, I will send my regular carriage ahead, and travel in a different vehicle." Her gaze hardened. "And *you* will accompany me in the second carriage. Just to make certain you have no plans of your own."

I always have other plans, he thought, but he was genuinely surprised by her comment. "I have never failed you, Eminence. Of all the people in the Constellation, who has served you better?"

Her expression softened. "Very few, Ishop. Very few." She ran her gaze up and down his street clothes. "My butlers will find you a more elegant outfit. I want you to sit beside me in my private box."

Ishop could not hide his broad grin. *Exactly where I belong.*

⤙⤚

An hour before the scheduled Council meeting, the Diadem's ornate autocarriage rolled along the normal route, pulled by six older horps from her stables. All for show.

Believing they were being honored with a special medal for exceptional botanical service, the Diadem's two court florists rode inside, behind darkened compartment windows. Ishop wondered what the florists must be thinking as they watched pedestrians cheering their carriage as it rolled past.

As for himself, he was pleased to ride with Diadem Michella in a less ornate carriage that took a roundabout route to the rear entrance of the Council Hall.

They arrived without fanfare, which seemed to disappoint Michella, but she understood the priorities. As she and Ishop emerged from the carriage and a security detail whisked them inside, he heard the explosion a block away—a blast so powerful that he felt it under his feet. A column of smoke rose over the building tops, and the distant crowd noise took on a fearful tenor.

He met Michella's gaze, saw a flash of anger in her eyes, along with deep gratitude toward him. Now she would trust him even more. He couldn't wait to present the papers to reclaim his noble title. Maybe she would give him an important cabinet appointment.

"You saved my life, Ishop," she said, staring at the smudge of smoke. "You have proof that Adolphus loyalists did this?"

"How much evidence do you need, Eminence?"

Security troops and rescue personnel rushed toward the site of the explosion. Alarms whooped through the streets, and emergency responders hurried the other Council members to safety, but Ishop knew there was no longer any immediate threat.

Michella's cheeks were flushed with anger. "I want the conspirator arrested immediately. My interrogators will wring every detail from him!"

Ishop could not allow that to happen. "If I may, Eminence? Your personal security staff already proved their incompetence. Let me do this myself, and I'll find out everything."

Michella dug in her heels. "But I must make an immediate response or else I look weak. That bomb could have killed me, and that insane woman on Candela beheaded one of my territorial governors! We won't just sit back and fume!"

"I thought Commodore Hallholme was already on his way?"

"Yes, but that could take weeks before we announce anything publicly—I need to do something *now*."

Ishop shrugged. "It's all simple enough, Eminence. To retaliate for the murder of Governor Undine, have Lord Riomini attack Candela, just as he did against Theser. How much more provocation do you need? In fact, send him to several DZ worlds—I'm sure he'd like that."

The old woman frowned. "But Adolphus threatened to blow all the stringlines if we move against the Deep Zone. Originally, I thought he was bluffing, but . . ."

"If we don't announce which planets Lord Riomini will attack, how would he know we're coming? He couldn't possibly send a message to all fifty-four worlds before our fleet launches."

Michella cleared her nostrils. "At least that's something. I'll have Selik move right away. If this is a war, we may as well intensify it."

Ishop's excitement built as more ideas came to mind. "But if you want to do something more immediate, Eminence, may I remind you that you do have Governor Goler in custody right here on Sonjeera." He smiled.

"Yes . . . we do, at that."

59

Hellhole was living up to its name.

Each day, seismic upheavals struggled to release internal pressure within the planet, like restless memories from the ancient asteroid impact. Out at the shadow-Xayan colony where Devon and Antonia continued to conduct telemancy sessions, the severe quakes triggered alien memories from Jhera and Birzh—images of the last days of their doomed world as the gigantic asteroid had hurtled toward them on a collision course.

As the ground jolted and spasmed in the worst tremors they had experienced, Devon and Antonia clutched each other near the free-form alien structures, which swayed but did not shatter. The nearby red-weed forest writhed and thrashed, reflecting the planetary unrest.

Joining their minds together, they attempted to use telemancy to quell the increasing tremors, to force down the upheaval. Devon and Antonia called on the nearby converts to add their mental strength as well.

When the quake finally ended, Devon looked at her and smiled. He spoke in his own voice, "I promised I'd keep you safe."

With a flash of her old personality, Antonia said, "Such a gallant hero."

Their fellow converts drifted out of their structures, unsettled. They inspected for damage, then used their united telemancy to shore up the distorted walls. But the ground beneath them still thrummed like a struck bell, restless.

Encix glided among the shadow-Xayans, studying their reactions and their mental strength. By now, an Original alien was a common sight to all the converts. After quelling the slickwater flood at the Ankor spaceport, and now riding out such a large quake, Encix seemed very disturbed. She turned her large dark eyes to Devon and Antonia, then around at the settlement. Her voice vibrated through the facial membrane. "That small fix does nothing to repair the wound in Xaya. Beneath us, and in the air and water, the planet's pain grows greater . . . and the pressure mounts. We need to stabilize it. Xaya is awakening, but painfully. It is restless."

From the seismic reports his mother had shown him, Devon knew that the increasing pressure was centered on the huge bull's-eye impact crater from the original asteroid strike. Though he had studied tectonic geology in his earlier years, he didn't understand the reason for the upheavals; inside him, Birzh sensed and communicated a different concept, envisioning a swelling energy within the heart of the planet.

Birzh said aloud to Encix, "There is great danger. We must mitigate this before it grows irreparable."

Jhera's presence had risen to the surface in Antonia's mind as well. "We have the telemancy to do it. We are strong enough, Encix—you can feel it. We will gather the shadow-Xayans, thousands of us, and use our mental powers to release the world's pressure. We can heal the wound before it breaks open."

Devon felt determination and excitement. "If we go to the impact crater, we can concentrate our powers, reach down through the crust to save the planet before the eruptions grow too great."

"Such a large number of telemancers working in concert is dangerous," Encix said. "It would be like a shout of telemancy."

"It is far more dangerous to do nothing," Antonia-Jhera said. "Centuries ago, we could not save our world from the asteroid strike, but with the vigor we draw from our human companions, we are closer to *ala'ru* now than we were then. We can prevent this disaster, Encix. And you will be the catalyst to draw us all together."

Devon was completely convinced they would be successful. With volunteers continuing to immerse themselves in the slickwater pools, more and more Xayans were being awakened. And with constant testing and practice, the numerous converts had increased their combined abilities.

Yes, they definitely had a chance.

60

Diadem Michella could have invited dozens of advisers and military experts to her strategic planning session, but she already knew what she wanted to do. She needed only the Black Lord, who would see the larger picture and the immediate need to move forward. And Ishop Heer, for his special advice.

The three sat at a table on one of the palace's outdoor patios, with a view of the ornamental vegetable gardens. It was a deceptively serene environment, yet the Constellation was anything but serene. Riomini ate his omelet with distracted efficiency; Ishop had not yet touched his food. Michella watched one of the assistant chefs out in the garden, directing a kitchen worker on the herbs and vegetables to gather for the evening meal.

She set down her teacup, sloshing the hot liquid onto the delicate saucer. "We cannot take weeks to respond, as we did with the first Constellation fleet. Candela must be punished. When will your ships be ready to launch, Selik?"

"Within days, Eminence. The force I brought back from Theser is still mobilized, and we are running final checklists on all operating systems and armaments right now. Now that we've tasted the blood of the enemy, my fighters are enthusiastic. We'll trounce Candela, destroy Administrator Hu, and avenge the barbaric murder of Governor Undine—"

Ishop interrupted. "That doesn't answer the question of why Undine was on Candela at all. She was arrested on Theser—that's why Lord Riomini chose that planet as his target in his first place. In fact, my Lord, didn't you assume that *your attack* already killed her? It seems a little disingenuous to be outraged that the rebels murdered her afterward. Why would General Adolphus move a political prisoner to Candela?"

Riomini puffed up, angry at the comment, and Michella knew there was no love lost between the men. Nevertheless, she scowled at Ishop. Was he trying to be funny? She said, "There must be something important on Candela. Another reason to strike there as soon as possible."

Riomini's annoyance began as an affectation to impress the Diadem, but he grew genuinely angry as he continued. "General Adolphus won't be content with merely securing the independence of the Deep Zone. According to Governor Goler, Adolphus has captured our hundred warships, and now his operatives tried to assassinate you, Eminence. Mark my words, he will try to conquer the Crown Jewels next if we don't stop him."

Ishop's husky voice sent a chill down Michella's spine. "And he also has the aliens with their telepathic powers and their . . . their pools of slime! He could be massing them for a full-scale invasion. The contamination has already subsumed his population, including Keana Duchenet. The aliens could have spread throughout the Deep Zone to Candela, for all we know."

Riomini pushed his plate aside and leaned forward. He seemed to be having second thoughts. "Eminence, we've already lost the main fleet, and Commodore Hallholme took his strike force. If I launch yet another large group to Candela, I fear the Crown Jewels won't be adequately defended."

Michella sipped her favorite black tea slowly; it was an expensive imported brand, with enhanced caffeine to give her energy in the morning. "I'm more worried about the rebels than about my own nobles."

Riomini shook his head. "I wouldn't be so sanguine, Eminence. While I'm away on the battlefield, some other noble might make a move against you. Perhaps I should stay behind to organize the defenses?"

Michella had not seen Riomini's hesitant side before. Maybe his level of aggression and "courage" depended upon how heavily the odds were stacked in his favor. "Selik, have you lost your stomach for the fight? This is wartime, and no leader can rest on old laurels. I thought you would embrace the opportunity for more battlefield glory, to give you an edge over Enva Tazaar and your other rivals."

He looked insulted. "How much more do I need to do to prove myself? What is Enva Tazaar doing for the war effort, compared to my contribu—"

Michella cut him off. "I don't need to compare. It is my perception that matters, not yours." He straightened in his chair as if he had been slapped. Her smile was no smile at all. "Selik, you're a skilled battlefield commander, but you'll have to be more than the equal of General Adolphus."

The Black Lord composed himself. "We don't know what truly happened to the original fleet, Eminence. And Governor Goler has given few details."

Ishop snorted. "I doubt if we could believe him even if he was more forthcoming."

"We can hope that Redcom Hallholme inflicted severe damage on the rebel defenses before he was captured—if he was captured at all," Riomini said. "I had my own operative aboard the fleet to see that errors were not made. I don't believe she would have let me down. It's possible the fleet is simply unable to report to us."

Diadem Michella frowned. "Then those ships are no help whatsoever. We'll make our own statement. Wipe out the colony on Candela, but don't stop there. Send simultaneous attack teams against five additional DZ worlds and scorch them to slag before the rebels can cut the stringline. Then return here for a new assignment. Such a decisive show of force should take care of the rebellion as well as silence any unrest here in the Crown Jewels."

"It will be my pleasure, Eminence. The breakaway planets will fall like dominoes."

"I don't want to play the General's game," she said, "I want to smash his entire game board."

"After hitting Candela and five other DZ planets," Ishop Heer said, "maybe they should try to head for planet Hallholme immediately, rather than returning to Sonjeera. Supposedly, each stringline terminus is mined, but maybe one group will get through."

"I don't like it," Riomini said, hesitant again. "After we crush six planets, our ships may not have the firepower to proceed against Adolphus."

The Diadem sniffed. "Then don't lose any ships, Selik. Commodore Hallholme is going after Adolphus, and your ships would help ensure a victory."

Riomini saw he would not win the argument. "Very well, Eminence. I shall do my best."

Michella smiled and sipped her tea. "Meanwhile, I have a nice send-off for Selik's battle groups. Since the rebels executed a loyal territorial governor, it seems only fitting that we do the same here."

61

General Adolphus felt uneasy and angry as he arrived at Candela with fifteen of Hellhole's warships. He did not want to reward Tanja Hu for the trouble she had caused—her brash action had destroyed any chance of reasonable negotiation, and she had likely put Carlson Goler at extreme personal risk on Sonjeera. He told himself that by devastating Theser, Lord Riomini had already destroyed any chance of peace, but that did not excuse the barbarity Tanja had done.

With his achievement of the new stringline network and rallying the planets against Sonjeera, Adolphus had led the Deep Zone to independence, but he was not a dictator. In fact, he had steadfastly refused to be crowned a supreme ruler, holding up the corrupt Diadem as a terrible example. In the brief time since cutting themselves off from the Crown Jewels, the frontier planets had not established a formal government with a constitution and rigorous procedures; even though the other planetary administrators looked to him for leadership, they had not agreed to accept his rule. And he had not tried to impose it. He could not afford a constitutional battle at the moment, or defections from other DZ planets.

Even so, Tanja had not made his task easier.

When the stringline hauler arrived from Hellhole, the fifteen warships dropped from their docking clamps and peeled off to take up stations in Candela's orbit next to her other six warships. He considered sending a scout ship down the line to Sonjeera to blow the mined substations after all, severing Candela from an attack.

But he decided to speak with Administrator Hu first, hear her explanations, and reprimand her if necessary. Most importantly, he had to do damage control; this could not become a catalyst that made the Deep Zone alliance crumble.

As his passenger pod descended to the landing zone near Saporo Harbor, Adolphus requested an immediate meeting with the planetary administrator. Tanja Hu was not at all surprised that he had come. She answered on the codecall screen, "I am at the iperion mines, General. Meet me out here."

In a safe zone near the mine entrance, Adolphus paced back and forth, waiting for the administrator. His arrival here did not at all mirror the joy and freedom he had felt upon visiting Ridgetop, his only previous excursion away from Hellhole.

When she emerged from the tunnel, she had removed her protective hooded suit and scrubbed herself clean of the ultrafine, toxic iperion dust. As she walked toward him, smoothing her dark hair, she looked fiercely independent, concerned but unapologetic.

Her resentment toward the excesses of the Constellation government had grown over the years, and she blamed her planet's hardships on the Diadem's greed, with good reason. But since the beginning of DZ independence, her personality had taken on an increasingly hard edge.

He faced her and spoke preemptively. "You've lost perspective. Candela depends on your thoughtful, reasoned leadership. You let your people down and put them in danger."

Tanja looked strong but shaken, and she replied, "General, hear me out. I may have made a harsh symbolic gesture, but Undine committed murder. As Candela's administrator, I was within my rights to impose a sentence of death." She raised her chin. "I executed one person. Lord Riomini murdered every single person on Theser. If Diadem Michella is willing to annihilate an entire planet, how can we ever reach meaningful peace terms with her?"

He shook his head. "There was a glimmer of possibility before, but now it's gone. You changed the entire nature of the war."

Her hard gaze met his. "With all due respect, General, *Theser* changed the nature of the war. The Deep Zone no longer has the option, under any circumstances, to forget that atrocity. Thanks to your reinforcements, I have twenty-one ships to guard Candela. I plan to fight."

Quelling his anger, he chose his words carefully. "You are the administrator of this planet, but your actions endangered the entire Deep Zone. The lawyers and philosophers can debate it at great length, but right now our main concern is to prepare for an attack. I share your conviction that Candela is likely a target for the Diadem's retaliation. The question is, are you willing to cut the Sonjeera stringline? It's the only way to be certain."

"It's not so simple, General." She led him into the mine administration shack outside the shaft opening. "I just received an emergency message pod sent from a secret loyalist who works in the Constellation military. Someone named Dak Telom? Not good news at all. There is indeed an attack planned against Candela—as well as five other DZ worlds. They intend to create a complete bloodbath. Scorched earth, no survivors . . . just as they did to Theser."

When Tanja gave him Dak Telom's report, he read with growing alarm—not just Tanja's gruesome delivery of Undine's head, but also the arrest of Governor Goler and the assassination attempt on the Diadem. The events had pushed her into a frenzy of reaction.

"Which five worlds?" he asked, scanning the report again.

"Unknown, General. Apparently, they'll be chosen at the last minute." She gave a grim nod. "So, you see, even if we cut the Candela stringline, that wouldn't help the others."

The General's mind spun. Despite their frantic buildup of ships, the DZ Defense Force could not provide enough ships to protect all the frontier worlds. "Even if we cut *all* the stringlines, there isn't time to spread word throughout the Deep Zone and instruct them to blow the substations. If Lord Riomini is ready to launch, we'll never accomplish it quickly enough."

Tanja had obviously thought this through. "And if any one of those target worlds loses control of their terminus ring, then Riomini's task force can get onto *our* stringline network and find their way back to Hellhole. Unless we can stop those ships, the Deep Zone could fall."

Adolphus paused to consider the magnitude of the problem, the unraveling of the DZ network and the failure of his plans. He looked over at Tanja. They did have one other chance. "Take me out to the shadow-Xayan colony."

⤙⤚

The seed colony of shadow-Xayans on Candela had only a hundred people. The prefab buildings were supplemented with exotic, organic shapes constructed through the combined mental powers of the awakened aliens. The shiny surfaces of the colony structures gleamed in hazy sunlight.

Expecting Hellhole to be the target of a devastating retaliatory attack, the volunteers had come here for safety. Now they were directly in the crosshairs.

The alien Tryn glided forward on her long caterpillar body, accompanied by slender, quiet Tel Clovis. After Adolphus described the crisis and asked if they could use their telemancy to help, Tryn spoke with pride, her voice vibrating. "I hoped you would call upon us, General Tiber Adolphus."

Clovis said, "We have all seen the images of Theser. We established this satellite colony to keep us safe from the Constellation fleet. We promised to help defend this world—and all of you."

The General said, "We can cut the stringline from Sonjeera and isolate Candela, but it won't protect the other worlds under threat. We can't warn the rest of the DZ in time—we don't even know which planets are targeted. I am out of conventional options. Mr. Clovis, I am hoping you have some ideas."

Tryn wavered back and forth as she pondered. Beside her, Clovis seemed to be connected with the alien, sharing thoughts with her. More shadow-Xayans emerged from the settlement buildings and came in from the thick surrounding jungles.

When she spoke, Tryn's voice became even more eerie than usual. "Your stringline network is similar to our web of telemancy. The principles are . . . somewhat parallel." She turned to face him, and shimmering spiral patterns appeared in her polished black eyes. "We understand that severing the one stringline to this planet would still leave all other Deep Zone worlds open to attack." She paused. "Why not simply eliminate the central stringline hub at Sonjeera? If you destroy it, then all the Diadem's avenues of attack would be incapacitated."

Tanja had a hard, eager grin. "Destroying the Sonjeera hub would throw the Crown Jewel network into chaos and give us the time we need."

The General began imagining ways to send a large force hurtling back to Sonjeera to attack the hub. But the hub had substantial military defenses in place, and Riomini's attack forces would also be gathered there. He shook his head. "I don't have the military power to do anything like that. We don't have enough ships." His eyes lit up. "Ah, I think I see where you're going with this."

"Correct," Tryn said. "We might do it with telemancy. From here."

"We can go on the offensive, General," Clovis said. "We send a blast along the iperion line, like a power surge. No battleships would be able to stop it."

Tryn shifted on her wormlike lower body. "To do so would require more telemancy power than anything we have attempted before. It will therefore be necessary for us to draw upon our comrades back on Xaya. We can touch them with telemancy even over such a distance."

Adolphus remembered that the shadow-Xayans on Hellhole had known immediately when Diadem Michella executed Fernando-Zairic and Cippiq. Tryn's idea was making some sense. Maybe it could work.

"It is *possible*, General Tiber Adolphus, even though we have not previously made such an attempt. Perhaps the challenge will teach us to increase our powers and take us closer to *ala'ru*."

Clovis sounded like his old self again when he said in a bright voice, "Sir, we would like to try. This is an emergency situation where we don't have time for more training. And it could save six planets."

"Or more," Tanja said.

The General nodded, even daring to feel a glimmer of hope. "We need to try—and we've got to do it immediately, before Lord Riomini can launch his ships."

62

Within three days, the bulk of the remaining Constellation warships returned to the Sonjeera hub from standard deployments throughout the Crown Jewel worlds. In peacetime, the ships were used to emphasize the Diadem's strength among the core worlds. She realized that unruly nobles needed the occasional reminder.

Now Lord Riomini gathered all those vessels for his dramatic retaliation against the "vile Deezees"—Candela, specifically, and five additional rebel planets as frosting on the cake. Diadem Michella knew the Black Lord would be ruthless; she did not need to encourage him in that regard.

With frantic preparations, the six-pronged assault would be ready to launch in less than a day. Riomini would spearhead the destruction of Candela, and he had chosen the other five DZ target worlds, in consultation with Lora Heston, his chief security operative. Heston had damaged her lungs and vocal cords saving him from a clumsy assassination attempt with an incendiary that dispersed acidic smoke. He had never forgotten that, and trusted the woman completely.

Commodore Percival Hallholme had departed more than a week ago for his backdoor strike on Hellhole, but with the uncertain condition of the Buktu stringline, no one could make an accurate estimate of when he might arrive at his target. Riomini had to undertake his own operation without regard to the old Commodore's timing.

While the ships gathered at the stringline hub, Riomini took every chance to rail against the rebels, pounding his fists, raising his voice. His face reddened in outrage as he decried the barbaric execution of the respected, talented, and *innocent* territorial governor, Marla Undine. In reality, neither he nor the Diadem had paid much attention to the appointee before—Riomini couldn't recall if either of them had ever met her—but the public didn't know that. They responded with predictable fervor.

When he reported his ships were almost ready for departure, the Diadem felt giddy. "Excellent! I shall now announce Governor Goler's execution as a traitor to the Star Throne. I'll arrange for a—" She tapped her fingers on the polished desktop in front of her as she pondered. "I think a firing squad is most dramatic. I wish I could pull the trigger myself, but that would not be seemly."

⊷⊷

Goler felt sick dismay but little surprise when the prison guard delivered the gloomy pronouncement. "When?" Goler asked.

"Within the day." The guard did not sound overjoyed; he glanced away from the governor.

"I shall appeal." The words came automatically, despite how absurd they sounded.

"To whom? The Diadem herself pronounced your sentence, and she is the highest authority in the Constellation. Lord Riomini's fleet is ready to depart on a major offensive to the Deep Zone, and your execution is scheduled to coincide with the launch."

Anger outweighed the sick fear in Goler's chest. "Did she not hear the General's warning? He will cut all the stringlines!"

"You won't need to worry about strategy or tactics much longer, sir. If I were you, I'd be more concerned with making your peace with God, and with yourself."

Goler balled his fists. "I've had almost four weeks to make my peace with all that. I knew the risks when I came here to deliver the message, and I still volunteered for the job." He looked up at the guard. "Because it's what is right."

But Goler thought, *I only wish it weren't so soon.*

Up until the moment the armed escort came for him at sunset, he kept waiting for a message of clemency, or at least a delay. Yet, he did not believe the Diadem was bluffing—she had too much pride and bullheadedness for that, and she would never change her mind once she'd made her announcement.

Goler clung to his only lifeline, a thin thread of hope that Enva Tazaar might take swift and secret action. He suspected she had been behind the recent assassination attempt on the Diadem—General Adolphus would never try to solve the problem with a hidden bomb. Lady Tazaar had already suggested she could eliminate Michella and take her place, but though she might want to help him, he doubted she had the connections or the time to plan his rescue.

When the guards escorted him out of his cell, Goler walked with his back straight and head held high. He had only his pride and confidence in the justness of his cause; this was the last service he could do for General Adolphus.

From the moment the dying trailblazer captain Ernst Packer had arrived at Ridgetop, Goler had understood that he needed to choose sides . . . and he also knew that the Diadem would never forgive him for picking the wrong side. His only remaining option was to make a good accounting of himself, to stand out as a man willing to die for Deep Zone independence and the downfall of the corrupt Constellation government. His dignity and legacy were all he really had left.

They brought him out to Heart Square in front of a carefully selected crowd; the viewing stands were filled with the most powerful nobles. Projection screens showed Riomini's huge military ships gathered at the Sonjeera hub, ready to fall like hammers on a half dozen DZ planets. Goler felt deep sorrow for all those innocent colonists. Obviously, the Diadem wanted him to see this.

When he stepped out into the fading sunlight, the crowd howled and hissed, as they had been primed to do. The nobles in the stands raised their fists and shouted, like wolves scenting blood. He recognized some of them, noblemen and ladies who had once been friendly toward him, but no longer.

Goler did not cringe, didn't look down at the ground; instead, he swept his gaze across these people who were pouring out hatred for him and decrying what he stood for. To his dismay, he saw Enva Tazaar among them, her face red as she joined a chorus of "Kill the traitor!"

Knowing her overtures to General Adolphus, he could have revealed her plans, perhaps earning himself a reprieve by doing so. What was such information worth to the Diadem? But when he saw the hatred on Lady Tazaar's face, he knew it was an act to divert suspicion. He forgave her for it—and he hoped that she did, in fact, find a way to bring down Diadem Michella and open the door of peace to the Deep Zone.

A blank wall had been erected as a divider in the center of Heart Square. The guards marched him to it, and Goler saw five uniformed men wearing the colors of the Diadem's personal guard; they all shouldered projectile rifles and stared at him without expression.

Riomini stood beside the old Diadem, who sat on a portable facsimile of the Star Throne. When Goler faced Michella from below, she did not rise, did not grant him the smallest gesture of respect. Instead she spoke into a voice amplifier. "Carlson Goler, former territorial governor, you have traitorously aided our greatest enemy, General Tiber Maximilian Adolphus. I was merciful before to the General, and that small benevolent gesture cost countless lives. I have learned my lesson and shall not show mercy again."

Goler stood with his lips pressed together. It was exactly what he'd expected her to say.

"As a convicted traitor, you are hereby sentenced to death, the execution to be carried out immediately so as not to delay the departure of our fleet." She looked around at the audience. "Lord Riomini is anxious to secure the rebellious Deep Zone worlds."

Although she had not invited him to issue any last statement, Goler shouted out. He needed no amplifier. "I am the formally appointed ambassador from the independent Deep Zone! Whenever *you* send your own envoy to meet with the General, I only hope the Deep Zone receives him or her with more courtesy and honor than you have shown me."

The Diadem looked annoyed and impatient. "Oh, don't speak to me of *honor*! I dispatched you to oversee eleven Deep Zone planets, and you turned against us. You were never an important person. Do you think anyone I would assign to the frontier is that important?"

The guards placed him against the flat wall, then walked away. Goler continued to stare at her as he shouted back, "You aren't the one who made me important—General Adolphus did!"

The Diadem gave the order, and her personal guards raised their projectile rifles, all the barrels pointed at him. Goler didn't close his eyes. He saw the bright flash of muzzle flares, and the bullets struck him before he even heard the sound of gunfire.

63

Bolton Crais had always been good at solving problems, but his definition of a "problem" had changed dramatically. It had been a major crisis when Keana fled to Hellhole in an ill-advised quest to find Cristoph de Carre, and then she'd joined the bizarre alien cult. Bolton had been ready to do anything to save his wife from her own foolishness.

Now he didn't know how many more days he would be *alive*, or if it was even possible to rescue his wife.

Keana had long been disappointed with their marriage. She and Bolton kept their distance from each other, and he interfered little with her activities, even her romantic dalliances. Keana hadn't flaunted them, and they'd had an "understanding," as she often said, though it was more *Keana's* understanding than Bolton's. He had accepted it, so as not to lose her completely.

Once, at the private lakeside cottage, she had hosted a garden party, inviting the sons and daughters of many noble families. However, in her self-centered way, Keana hadn't bothered to study the schedule, and her party conflicted with a major anniversary parade for Lord Selik Riomini. Since Riomini appeared to be the heir apparent to the Star Throne, most of the guests opted to attend the Black Lord's parade rather than her party.

In preparation, she had spent a fortune—Bolton doubted Keana even knew the cost—to buy four new watercolor paintings by Enva Tazaar, whose artistic aspirations were evident to everyone in the Council (though her artistic talent was not). Enva's father, the powerful Azio Tazaar, one of Lord Riomini's greatest rivals, had dragged his daughter to the anniversary parade, just to make certain they were seen.

Keana had displayed the paintings proudly outside in the open garden terrace, and her party was an embarrassing failure. She was so upset when her guests did not arrive that she ran inside, inconsolable.

When Bolton learned how much money his wife had spent on the poorly planned event and on the paintings, he worried how they would pay for it all. Even the Diadem's daughter and the oldest son of the Crais family did not have infinite wealth. The situation became even worse when a rain squall passed overhead while Keana was inside the cottage crying, and the downpour ruined the new paintings. . . .

Angry at her own foolishness, and spiteful toward the nobles who had snubbed her, Keana did not even understand the magnitude of the disaster, nor did she understand why she still had to pay for the wrecked paintings, which had no salvage value. Bolton had realized that if Enva Tazaar learned how her new artwork had been so carelessly destroyed, her noble family would take great offense, which might start a bitter feud between the Craises and the Tazaars—a feud that Bolton's family could ill afford.

So, he had taken the damaged paintings (along with photographs of what they were supposed to look like) to the best art restorer on Sonjeera, agreed to pay double to keep the work secret, then went to his father Ilvar and asked for a loan. Ilvar Crais had looked at his son, pressing his lips tightly together. "And how would our family benefit from *that* investment, Bolton? You and your wife seem to have no understanding of finances, and your prospects of making it on your own are restricted. You've already achieved the highest military rank that you're likely to manage." The old lord's tone had conveyed his disappointment.

Bolton had straightened and said, "It would save us great embarrassment, Father—and embarrassment to me has a ripple effect on my brothers and on you. The other nobles will wonder if every Crais is as big a failure as I am."

Ilvar stared at him for a full ten seconds before smiling thinly and nodding. "A reasonable argument. I will loan you half. Get the rest from Diadem Michella. She must be just as disappointed in her daughter as I am in you."

"She is. The Diadem makes no secret of it."

Now, aboard the stranded fleet, Bolton finished his calculations and stepped out of his dim, barely tolerable quarters. This crisis was so much worse than any concern over paintings or finances or noble family feuds. He shivered. The biting cold affected him with every breath.

The food supplies and fleet power requirements had finally forced the Redcom into holding another kind of lottery. At random, two hundred names of soldiers and crewmen would be chosen from the anesthetized thousands who lay connected to life support and nutrient drips. That group would be deactivated, the power shunted to other vital systems, the nutrients prioritized to keep others alive for a few more days. It was necessary. By now, the trailblazer was close. It had to be.

When Bolton presented Escobar with his list, he said, "These are the names you asked for, Redcom, selected at random. If you prefer a merit-based selection, I can run a different algorithm."

The Red Commodore looked as if a thunderclap had exploded behind him. "I will not do that, Major. I will not stoop to Carrington's level."

"We've all reached a very primitive level, sir." Bolton swallowed hard. He felt the jaws of hunger in his gut again. "The sedative stockpiles are running too low for us to put as many people into comas as I would like. As macabre as it sounds, there is another plan we must consider seriously, now that we've reached the point where we are taking steps to let crewmen die. We have the bodies—as well as the two hundred on this list. We have the automated means to process all that flesh into . . . usable protein. We don't even need to tell the rest of the crew what we're doing—in fact, I suggest we do not. Just provide their rations and give them what they need to survive."

Escobar looked as if he wanted to vomit. "We can't keep a secret like that. They'll find out, and kill us!"

"At least most of them will be *alive* in ten days when Zabriskie and Caron return. *If* they return. Or would you have more die because you refuse to cross a moral line?"

The Redcom drew a deep breath. "Six weeks ago, I might have given you a different answer." He scanned the list of names and froze. His bloodshot eyes widened. "Lieutenant Cristaine?"

Bolton had already noted her name on the list. "It was a random selection, sir. I can get another name. We'll classify her with us, as key personnel."

Escobar straightened. "That would entail killing someone else. If I abide by this, then I have to abide by it *all,* to the letter. If we survive, Major Crais, we are going to be judged by what we do."

"We will be judged, most certainly," Bolton said.

Escobar passed the list back. "Do what you need to do. Divert the nutrients and make the protein. Take away the life support for these people, and list them as casualties of war. There have already been deaths, and now we have more. Do everything possible to keep the crew from discovering the details." Escobar lowered his head. "When will you need to select another two hundred names?"

Bolton stood at the Redcom's door; he had not yet run the calculations of how much protein the bodies would provide. "Very soon, sir. I'm sorry."

64

Flying en masse by telemancy, the group of shadow-Xayans streaked across the battered landscape of Hellhole. Thousands of human forms, along with Encix, levitated themselves into the sky and cruised on a mission to the gigantic impact basin where an asteroid had struck Xaya five centuries ago, leaving a weak spot in the planetary crust. Devon hoped they could perform mental surgery with their innate alien powers and ease the world's festering wound.

From the height of the flying telemancers, Devon and Antonia could look down and see the curvature of the northern crater wall, a high line of broken swells so vast it looked like a mountain range, with the deep floor shattered and oozing lava in places. Hundreds of kilometers across, the impact crater swallowed up all sense of scale. The opposite rim was beyond the horizon, and the complete bull's-eye could only be recognized from orbit.

Within him, Birzh could feel the simmering turmoil deep beneath the surface, like a blister rising up, growing more dangerous.

In a mass migration, thousands of shadow-Xayans gathered on the northern rim, where they had the best vantage of the upheavals in the center of the crater. Encix landed next to Devon and Antonia, and the entire group—minds joined—knew what they had to do. Directed in a symphony of mental powers, the converts began to concentrate, and Devon could feel their strength and stability adding to his own.

Far below, in the expansive impact valley, a volcano spewed a scarlet stream of lava and dark smoke into the air. The wind carried a sulfurous stench that burned his nose and eyes. As if drawn by the turbulence, thunderclouds congealed in the sky, and static electricity built up in a cauldron that created a huge growler storm.

As the telemancers concentrated, the ground trembled, poised on the verge of another large quake, fighting back against them. The crater felt like a struck tuning fork, Hellhole's crust throbbing and vibrating. Out on the floor of the impact zone, slabs of stone cracked, split apart, and heaved up. Devon felt a jab of pain inside his head, and the shadow-Xayans murmured restlessly. Birzh gave him strength.

Encix writhed next to him, in pain but fighting.

"It's spectacular," he said, gazing at the incandescent lava rivers, "but we'd better do more than watch. And we should be quick about it." As if to emphasize his statement, the ground shuddered, and a steep section of the crater wall sloughed off in a rockslide half a kilometer away.

Many months ago, a group of new converts led by Fernando-Zairic had used psychic abilities to divert a powerful static storm and save Slickwater Springs, but this was an exponentially greater danger. "We've got to use our telemancy to release the pressure from this wound!" Devon shouted as the chaos grew greater.

Until he had actually seen the scope of the seismic buildup, he had not comprehended the magnitude of the challenge his group faced; this would be greater than any telemancy exercise the converts had previously attempted. As he stood with thousands of shadow-Xayans, he felt connected with his companions—and Antonia, closer than ever before. Their combined power increased as the whole group concentrated, but Devon knew it wouldn't be enough. They needed to accelerate their abilities. "Encix, you have to help!"

"You are not alone," Birzh said in his mind. "Gathered here, we are strong—strong enough to save the planet as it struggles to awaken."

With the intense expression of telemancy, drifting luminous afterimages appeared in the air, manifestations of their exertions. The shapes swirled and crackled around them, shooting off bright, bursting flashes of color. Devon could barely breathe.

The impact zone had a visceral significance to the Xayans. From the alien thoughts that flowed across his consciousness, Devon had clear memories of a sea of the soft-skinned, sluglike aliens standing together, faces turned to the sky moments before the asteroid impact. They'd had no hope for themselves, knowing they were doomed, but praying some portion of their race would survive. *Here, in this place.*

Out in the crater valley, the impact zone was rising higher, and the mouths of more volcanoes vomited geysers of fiery orange lava and smoke. The writhing growler storm darkened the sky and increased the wind to a ripping howl. The ground beneath them bucked and heaved.

But they kept concentrating. Their telemancy energy also continued to rise. Strengthened and focused by Encix, Devon and Antonia took the lead and directed the combined psychic front into the heart of the crater.

An enormous jet of molten magma belched into the sky, and a series of jagged rifts tore open at the bottom of the crater, but the telemancy served as a smothering blanket on the impact zone, dampening the violence, and releasing pressure.

In his mind's eye, Devon saw the combined telemancy tear into the erupting crater, smothering the storm overhead, and dissipating the angry energy. The lava geysers sputtered, turned dark, and fell back to the scorched landscape, sealing the rifts and fissures. Moment by moment, the growler storm faded, dissipated with only a few last gasps of wind and discharges of lightning. The tremors became quiet, the sky cleared, and the planet seemed to breathe easier.

Exhausted and exhilarated, Devon released his hold on the telemancy, as did Antonia, allowing the other shadow-Xayans to pull their powers back into themselves.

Though exhausted, Encix seemed impressed and relieved. "With your hybrid vigor you have taken us to a more powerful and effective telemancy than we Xayans could ever have achieved on our own." But she did not sound at all exuberant. "Perhaps it even lifted our race closer to *ala'ru* . . . if we can survive that long."

Devon's ears rang, and he had a ferocious headache. This had been a much more difficult exercise than any of their combined military maneuvers. "After succeeding here, defending against the Constellation fleet should be no trouble at all."

Deep in his consciousness, like something rumbling up out of Hellhole, he felt Birzh stirring, reading his thoughts, but his alien companion seemed unable—or unwilling—to give further explanations.

Encix had promised that all the shadow-Xayans would use their abilities to protect against the Constellation before letting the converts achieve their racial ascension. Both sides could be satisfied. When he looked at beautiful Antonia, Devon thought she might be thinking the same thing.

Encix seemed strangely reticent. "We stopped the pressure buildup in this planet, but with that demonstration, we shouted out our existence to the entire universe, a declaration that we are close to achieving *ala'ru*." She hesitated, her facial membrane thrumming. "But the last time our race was this close to our destiny, Xaya was nearly destroyed."

65

As the shadow-Xayan seed colonists gathered with him at Saporo Harbor, Adolphus felt hopeful, yet uneasy. If Tryn's claims were correct, they could use their combined mental powers to send a powerful burst along the iperion path, enough to scuttle Riomini's attack fleets. He had seen Devon and Antonia demonstrate the telemancy maneuvers on Hellhole, so he knew how effective they could be.

Nevertheless, as a military strategist, he preferred to rely on his own prowess, conventional ships and armaments, things he could *understand*. In this case, however, he had no option that would likely be effective against what the Constellation would throw at them. He had to depend on the eerie powers of the shadow-Xayans—and he relished the surprise. This, more than anything else, would show Diadem Michella that she didn't know what she was up against.

Moving with sinuous ripples, Tryn led the group of converts, acting as a catalyst for their telemancy. Her humanoid torso was erect, her retractable antennae twitching, and her soft, jointless fingers splayed as she and the shadow-Xayans gathered on the shore, some whispering, most silent. The capital city's buildings floated in the middle of the harbor, surrounded by steep jungled hillsides. Even though this was not yet the monsoon season, Candela's skies were cloudy, pregnant with rain.

High overhead were terminus rings to the DZ and Sonjeera string-line networks, as well as Tanja Hu's own new hub. The end of the line from Sonjeera was the vulnerable spot. That, the General knew, was how the Army of the Constellation would approach Candela. Tanja's six warships, along with the fifteen new ships he had brought from Hellhole, would put up a good fight against whatever the Constellation sent here, but the other five unidentified DZ targets wouldn't even have a warning.

Unless telemancy could stop the enemy at home.

Tanja Hu stood next to him, watching the shadow-Xayans. Her expression was angry and pinched. "I love my planet, General. I don't want to see those bastards wipe it out."

Tryn raised herself up on her caterpillar body. "We will not allow that to happen. We promised to help you when we came here. We can draw strength from the others on far-off Xaya, and stop the ships of the enemy faction before they depart."

"Then you need to act quickly," Tanja said. "They could already be on their way."

"We will do it now," Clovis said.

"If you save the Deep Zone, I will do everything possible to help you achieve your ascension," Adolphus said. "First, let's show the Constellation that we have defenses far beyond anything they imagine."

At a signal from the Original alien, the converts gathered closer around Tryn, shoulder to shoulder on the shore, while the General and Tanja moved a safe distance away. Tryn positioned herself and raised her hands into the air. The group fell silent, connecting their minds, then began to emanate a whisper-hum.

Water from the harbor grew choppy with a brisk breeze, and sprinkles of rain began spitting down. The tall floating buildings rocked and swayed in the harbor.

"We are not all telemancers, but we all have Xayan minds and memories," said the Original, her facial membrane vibrating. "Every one of us is connected as a race."

Next to her, Clovis lifted his face and closed his eyes. A louder humming sound came from his throat, and the other shadow-Xayans joined in, an eerie unison that built into a crescendo.

Adolphus felt static electricity prickling his skin. Goose bumps rose on his forearms. The wind circulated, stirring the harbor waters, agitating.them so that the Saporo buildings swayed even more.

Overhead, the clouds parted, and the ascending blast of rising telemancy tore away the rainstorm. The General's hair stood on end. The vegetation along the shore writhed and twitched as if stirred by a large invisible hand.

"We are linked with our comrades on Xaya!" Tryn's words sliced through the silent storm. "This is how we pull together in a single, grand mind to create a psychic weapon. Wait . . ." She faltered. "They have already been drawing on their telemancy, releasing Xaya's pain, tapping into the planet's wound. They are weak, drained—"

"We need the power here!" Clovis insisted. "Send it into the stringline."

"It is coming!" Tryn said. "They are responding, building our combined psychic energy. This will take more than I anticipated."

As the brooding static electricity built upon itself, the General's vision grew blurry. The objects around him were surrounded by shimmering halos, as if he could suddenly discern auras. He saw a transparent ripple in the air as the shadow-Xayans seized all the power they could grasp and sent a mental blast of energy to the overhead terminus ring, which then ricocheted outward and hurtled along the iperion line toward Sonjeera.

❧

After witnessing the execution of Governor Goler—which Lord Selik Riomini found to be a satisfying but somewhat anticlimactic act—he took a command shuttle up to the main stringline hub, where his six battle groups prepared for launch to the Deep Zone. Even if General Adolphus managed to sever one or two of the DZ stringlines in time, he couldn't possibly cut all of them. Riomini's battle groups would fall on the rebel planets like ravenous wolves. He looked forward to it.

Aboard the same flagship he had taken to Theser, Riomini settled into the command chair, fidgeting against its hard surface. Command chairs were not meant to be comfortable, yet the Black Lord adapted himself without much effort. While his security chief Lora Heston arranged her own attack force that would strike Komun, and his skilled operations officer Lucinda Ekova helmed the group headed for Ridgetop, the other three battle groups aligned themselves for departure to the DZ worlds of Atab Abas, Darenthia, and Ueter. As far as Riomini was concerned, those other worlds were mere names on a list, nothing remarkable whatsoever. He would take care of Candela personally.

Before the recent Theser action, he hadn't commanded a task force operation in a very long time, not since an early battle in the General's rebellion some sixteen years ago. As that war intensified, he'd relinquished operational command to Percival Hallholme—a risky choice considering the black marks on the man's early military record, but in retrospect it was the most fortuitous decision Riomini had ever made. He had sensed that Hallholme possessed the right sort of backbone and necessary ingenuity to make him formidable, and enough loyalty to toe the line when necessary.

Even now, the Commodore's unexpected military strike via Buktu might well put an end to the current DZ rebellion, if he did manage to pick his way along the decaying iperion path. Meanwhile, Riomini would make a more showy expedition, possibly even taking care of the matter before the old Commodore arrived.

This time, after his operation crushed six frontier worlds without mercy, even the most slow-witted or intractable Deezees would come crawling back to beg the Diadem's forgiveness. And everyone in the Constellation would know that *Lord Selik Riomini* had cemented the victory. Given the swell of popularity, he might just seize the Star Throne without further delay.

His attack ships hung at the Sonjeera hub, six different clusters ready to depart along six different stringlines. Lora Heston checked in from her own battle group. Speaking in her rough, damaged voice, she said over the codecall, "All battle groups are ready to depart, Lord Riomini."

The sleek, efficient woman reminded him of Gail Carrington in her prime. But since Escobar Hallholme had obviously failed in his mission and lost a hundred ships, then Riomini decided that Carrington must have failed him as well. He expected better from Heston.

"We've already had our fanfare," Riomini answered on the open channel. "Now let's go do a day's work." The six framework haulers at the Sonjeera hub interfered with the normal flow of space traffic, and he decided to demonstrate his leadership abilities by showing how efficiently he could bring normalcy back to the Constellation.

Riomini's stringline hauler was the first to disengage from the Sonjeera hub, gathering speed along the line to Candela. The other five haulers eased away, fanning out on separate iperion paths. Riomini heard inspiring military music over the fleet-wide intercom.

Suddenly, with the force of a bottled hurricane, a rippling distortion hurtled toward them. Riomini sensed it only a fraction of a second before the surge slammed into the hauler, derailing the heavily loaded framework ship and rocketing past—directly into the Sonjeera hub.

Sparks flew from the control panels aboard the flagship. Screens exploded from the overload. Screaming, bridge officers tumbled from their chairs. Riomini lurched to his feet, but as the deck tilted and the flagship broke from its docking clamp inside the hauler, he fell to his knees. "What the hell was—"

The screens flickered with static; two had gone dead. One showed a low-resolution, grainy image of the hauler's exterior. Riomini was shocked to see that most of his battleships had been shaken loose from their clamps and were drifting in space like debris.

"It was like a flash fire along the iperion line, sir!" the exec officer said. "The stringline is damaged, maybe destroyed."

"But what caused it? How could this possibly—" He caught himself, knowing it had to be the General's doing.

The comm-officer had torn the top panel from her unit and reconnected the circuits, routing paths until finally she made contact with the nearby Sonjeera hub. Short-range radio transmissions were sufficient.

From all around, alarms began to sound. Dozens of reports poured in from the drifting ships. Regaining his dignity, Riomini climbed back into the command chair. "Comm-officer, give me an assessment."

"The Sonjeera hub is in chaos, sir. That shock wave slammed past us and blew out half the nodes on the main hub. It's a disaster!"

They began to receive reports from the other five attack groups. The power surge hurtling along the stringline had not only torn apart their attack group and damaged the Sonjeera hub, the pulse had then ricocheted along the *outgoing* iperion paths. All five attack groups were torn from the stringlines. The pulse raced throughout the entire Crown Jewel network, spreading like shatter lines in a pane of glass and damaging some of the other routes.

"My God, what has Adolphus done now?" Riomini said.

66

Discouraged that his work in the museum vault seemed futile, Cristoph nonetheless continued to search and document the artifacts with the archaeology team. Encix and the remaining converts had all traveled out to the main impact crater to quell the seismic pressure, and Lodo had willfully destroyed the one Xayan item that might have helped protect Hellhole, and now Cristoph didn't know if he could trust the Original alien. Did Lodo really intend to help? What was his priority?

And how could the asteroid impact not have been an accident?

The Original gave no explanation, and even Keana could not pry information from her mental companion Uroa. As if grateful for a distraction, Lodo remained intrigued by the strange black artifact.

Cristoph watched as the alien levitated the obsidian object with his telemancy, tilting the oblong artifact this way and that, spinning it, turning it over, examining it from various angles. He tried to penetrate it with his mind, as if it were a complex puzzle box. Squiggles and sparks of illumination danced in the air around him, glinting off the nested, inverted curves.

Cristoph remained uneasy about what the Xayans knew but refused to reveal. He asked Keana, "Has he made any progress?"

"Lodo knows nothing more than when he started," she said. "It remains impenetrable."

Lodo looked up. "Encix is guiding the shadow-Xayans at the crater . . . and they have lanced the planet's wound." His head swayed from side to side. "And on Candela, Tryn is also . . . ah, she and her companions are drawing telemancy from all of us, using it to—" His feelers quested.

"They are sending a strike down the iperion path to Sonjeera," Keana said. "A telemancy blast."

"Too much telemancy," Lodo said, his voice a low moan. "Too much at once!"

Around them the walls of the vault trembled again, a shiver rather than the sharper crack of a quake. Keana looked up at the ceiling with a distant expression in her shimmering eyes. "It brings *ala'ru* closer."

"And worse," Lodo said, but Cristoph didn't know what the alien meant.

The shivering in the air intensified, and even he could feel it thrumming through his thoughts. Lodo fumbled with the suspended black artifact. Keana seemed troubled. "The pulse keeps growing . . . there is something else."

Lodo said, "This is very dangerous!" The alien cried out, an eerie, warbling wail, followed by a piercing scream. Keana buckled and fell to her knees, struggling with the inner Uroa presence. The black artifact rose up, seemingly borne on its own telemancy, and began to thrum.

"What's happening?" Cristoph shouted. The shadow-Xayan workers in the vault clutched the sides of their heads, dropped to the cave floor. The black artifact screeched out a signal that warbled high up out of the range of his hearing.

All around him, Cristoph saw numerous other artifacts in the vault begin to glow, the carved patterns in the stone walls, the crystalline figures, the spheres of enclosed jewel-tone liquid. . . .

As suddenly as it had begun, the mysterious black artifact fell silent and tumbled to the stone floor, as if drained of power. Lodo struggled to right his caterpillar body; he stared, his large black eyes spiraling like whirlpool galaxies. His facial membrane emitted murmuring sounds.

"What was that?" Cristoph gripped Keana's hand, pulled her back to her feet. "Are you all right? Lodo, are you hurt?"

Keana didn't seem to understand him. "Uroa . . . ," she muttered, then focused on him. "His presence swelled up inside of me, but now it's like an opaque net. He is silent."

Cristoph picked up the black artifact from where it had fallen to the floor. It was silent and cold, as if it had expended all its energy. Sending some sort of signal? Triggering an alarm?

Lodo stood motionless, as if in shock. "Our combined telemancy is stronger than I had hoped . . . but not strong enough. Not yet. And we have more problems than you realize."

67

After the telemancy blast down the stringline to Sonjeera, Tryn and the shadow-Xayans stood reeling and drained on the harbor shore, as if stunned by what they had done. Thunder rippled across the sky, and the air smelled of ozone.

Adolphus looked at all the alien converts, searching for a sign that the effort had worked.

Tel Clovis finally found words. "We succeeded, General! Our surge traveled down the iperion path like a telepathic tsunami. We knocked out the Sonjeera hub, overloaded the endpoints, disrupted the string-lines, and damaged some of the other Crown Jewel routes." He was breathing hard. "From what I could tell, sir, we seriously damaged the Diadem's transport capabilities."

Tanja Hu threw her head back and let out a throaty laugh. "That means Candela and the rest of the Deep Zone are safe!" Though she was grinning, her anger remained palpable. "The old bitch got what she damn well deserved."

Adolphus felt relieved to the point of exhilaration that the bold gambit had worked after so many things had gone wrong. Even without stringline travel, the twenty core planets were close enough to remain connected with normal FTL ships, but the Deep Zone worlds were much farther away and virtually inaccessible without long voyages. "We should be safe for months now, maybe even years. Plenty of time to get our defenses in order."

The clouds had regathered over the harbor. "A downpour will begin soon," Tanja said, turning her face to the sky.

Adolphus wasn't worried. "At least rainstorms are just rainstorms on Candela, rather than horrific static storms." He felt hopeful again, and he wished Sophie were there.

Tryn and the gathered converts remained linked on the harbor shore, and together they attempted to sever the psychic connection with the others on Xaya. The Original's voice was heavy, her energy level low, exhausted from the effort. On each side of her the hybrids continued to hold hands, communing in their paranormal link . . . struggling. Adolphus sensed no exuberance in the group at all, and he began to realize that something was wrong.

Tanja kept talking, as if she had forgotten the recent bloody darkness. "After that blast, the Constellation will be terrified of us from now on. It's time to go on the offensive, General. Fight this war the way it should be fought, and finish it! While they're weak and reeling, we could take over Sonjeera."

Adolphus drew his eyebrows together. "I don't want to conquer the Constellation. I just want them to leave us alone."

A sudden loud boom sounded in the fabric of the air, and a flash of light shot down from what must have been the terminus above. A beam of energy slammed into the telemancers and illuminated them. They let out an eerie, combined scream.

Adolphus backed away from the shadow-Xayans, tripped and fell as the shock wave throbbed in the air. His ears rang, and he could barely see. He staggered back to his feet, wiped his eyes, and tried to focus.

Tryn and the converts writhed, emitting a terrible combined sound that made the air pulse on the edge of the harbor. Trying to focus his vision, Adolphus saw the crowded shadow-Xayans collapse like harvested stalks of wheat, dropping one by one. The Original alien threw her rubbery arms around Tel Clovis, who stood nearest to her. She began to ooze, losing her bodily shape, softening, slumping. She collapsed with Clovis to the ground.

Adolphus ran toward them, but didn't understand how to help.

Tanja dropped beside one of the fallen shadow-Xayans. "General, they're . . . leaking!"

The converts' skin was gray and slimy; thick, mercurial water drained from their pores, mouths, eyes, and ears. Tryn continued to moan, unable to hold herself up, and Clovis grappled with her—or embraced her—but both were in severe distress.

Around them, other converts were dying, struck down by an invisible blow and strewn in awkward, impossible positions, as if their bones had become gelatin, their bodies horribly twisted, their faces distorted. A few survivors made mewing sounds of pain; somehow, they remained connected through telemancy, focusing their thoughts and appearing to send *strength* back to Tryn. Saving her.

Leaning over Clovis, the Original spoke comforting words to him, even though she herself had been severely injured. Her once-smooth face was half melted away, and one of her oversize eyes was gone, having merged into the alien skin.

Tryn was using all her concentration, which seemed to be keeping her and Tel Clovis alive, even as the other converts died around them. Weak sounds thrummed through her facial membrane, forming words. "We broadcasted more telemancy than we expected. Synergy . . . ricochet. Not *ala'ru*, just . . . death."

Clovis calmed as he drew strength from Tryn, like clinging to a lifeline, and the Original kept herself intact as the other shadow-Xayans shared their scraps of remaining energy, offering what remained of their telemancy for her. Tryn held Clovis to her bosom as if he were a child, and continued to comfort him. She managed one more burst of comprehensible words: "We did not consider the ramifications. We may have attracted . . . unwanted attention."

"Unwanted attention?" Adolphus demanded. "What do you mean?"

Around them, several dead shadow-Xayans collapsed into soft, oozing puddles. Tryn used all her concentration to preserve her integrity, keeping herself and Clovis alive.

As General Adolphus and Tanja Hu stared in shock and loss, the dying shadow-Xayans continued to twitch, then finally fell silent. Their bodies lay scattered on the ground, covered with a thick pearlescent film, dissolving.

68

The destruction at the Sonjeera stringline hub was unimaginable. Lord Riomini's six battle groups had been knocked off the iperion path, many of the vessels dislodged from their docking clamps. Thousands had been killed in the turmoil.

Explosions continued to ripple through the hub station, while power surges shut down life-support systems. Sudden decompression had caused automatic isolation of whole sectors of the complex. Stringline traffic throughout the Crown Jewel worlds was shut down, with ships en route unable to reach Sonjeera. Commerce reeled. Heavily traveled routes were blocked.

Fortunately, Riomini's six battle groups had not yet left the system, so the ships were able to limp home under their own engine power, while the large and empty hauler frameworks plodded back at much slower speeds.

It was total chaos.

Lord Riomini took the better part of a day to return to Sonjeera, where he presented himself, disheveled and agitated, to the Council Hall as ordered. His uniform was rumpled and torn, even the black trousers were ripped on one side. Usually vain about the way he dressed, Lord Selik Riomini didn't seem to notice it now. He appeared to be stunned, no longer looked like a hero reveling in his accomplishments, the heir apparent to the Star Throne.

Diadem Michella was looking for someone to blame. She demanded explanations, but he had none to give.

Riomini could not hide his anger and confusion when he mounted the speaking platform and faced the bombardment of questions from the nobles. "We are still assessing the damage," he said, his tone sharp. "As soon as we know what sort of appalling weapon General Adolphus used against us—and make no mistake, this had to be an overt attack from the Deep Zone!—we will do our best to counter it."

"It was an alien weapon!" Michella said, her voice shrill. "That was no technology we've ever seen. The General is preparing his alien allies for an invasion. I'm sure of it."

Riomini continued in a forcibly calm voice, dodging what sounded like paranoia in the Diadem's voice, "In the meantime, repairs and reconstruction efforts are being staged. I have placed every qualified orbital work crew on notice. All Crown Jewel resources will be devoted to reestablishing our defenses." He squared his shoulders and tried to project an air of confidence. "I have everything under control."

"What if the General attacks us in the meantime?" called old Ilvar Crais. "He says he's already captured our main fleet!"

The youthful but regal Enva Tazaar shouted out, "I think Lord Riomini has mucked things up enough already." Tazaar had a classically beautiful face with large blue eyes and a patrician bone structure; her long blond hair was perfectly coiffed. Her face showed well-pronounced indignation. "General Adolphus took no action against us until Lord Riomini's barbaric attack on Theser. Riomini *forced* this retaliation." She sniffed. "If I, and other noble members of the Council, had been consulted in the matter, we would have disagreed with such a foolish and unnecessary provocation!" The Black Lord tried to interrupt her, but Tazaar continued with rising vehemence. "Lord Riomini, you are a ham-handed, inept military leader. Your 'glorious triumph' destroyed a defenseless Deezee world and ruined significant industrial and technological capabilities that could have benefited the Constellation after the current difficulties are resolved."

Rolling his eyes, Riomini looked to the Star Throne, but Diadem Michella did not seem inclined to come to his defense. Then other nobles began shouting, pouring out their ire upon him. Riomini struggled to gain the upper hand, but Tanik Hirdan drew the attention of the audience. "You sent a hundred of our finest warships to planet Hall-holme. That was supposed to be an easy victory, too, and instead those ships are lost. Another bungled decision, obviously."

Enva Tazaar was not yet finished, but this time she turned her sharp gaze to the Star Throne itself. "And you, Eminence—you executed the official Deep Zone ambassador in a fit of pique. Another bad decision! How will the General respond when he learns about *that?*"

Michella rose to her feet, looking like a furious harpy. "I will not listen to this—"

Lady Tazaar pointed at the Star Throne, but directed her words to the increasingly restless audience. She said in a poisonously sweet tone, "Michella Duchenet has served the Constellation for many decades, but now perhaps she should go into a quiet retirement and relinquish the throne to someone more capable of leading in these trying times. We cannot afford to let her or Lord Riomini commit another blunder." Her voice grew even harder. "Because of them, our once-glorious Constellation teeters on the edge of annihilation. I call for a vote of no confidence."

The Black Lord heard a mounting swell of agreement among the nobles. A vote of no confidence? Riomini could not imagine what had gotten into Enva Tazaar. Something must have emboldened her.

Diadem Michella snapped, "Lady Tazaar, we are in the middle of a war, and I will not allow you to take advantage of the turmoil to advance your own political agenda. No one here will tolerate your petty games—we have work to do. This meeting is adjourned!"

The old woman stormed off before the complaints could grow any louder. Riomini stood reeling, until he departed, too, not certain what would happen to him next.

69

Their progress along the decayed iperion path to Buktu was painstaking and slow, but Commodore Hallholme quelled his impatience. His soldiers believed in his legendary military prowess, and he was determined not to fail. Thus, he had to be cautious.

"It's been two weeks already—and it should have been a five-day journey!" said Duff Adkins. He ran a hand through the streak of gray hair on one side of his head. "This damnable waiting is the hardest part."

"It always is, before battle. You know that, my friend."

"I just hope we don't lose too much momentum. When we left Sonjeera, every crewmember was full of adrenaline and bloodlust."

"When soldiers are too gung ho, they get stupid." And, though he didn't say so aloud, the old Commodore feared that his son had fallen prey to that mistake. Aboard his ships, Percival chose not to play the pulse-pounding military theme. His fighters all understood who the enemy was, and were spoiling for a rematch and a fresh victory.

The commando fleet limped along the fading stringline like a heavy man tiptoeing over thin ice. The string of quantum breadcrumbs had grown faint and diffuse. As the hauler moved forward, Percival dispatched small scout ships two at a time to leapfrog along the path. They would shoot ahead, adding extra iperion to shore up the route in the weakest spots, while the main battle group followed.

Three scouts had vanished already, losing the faint stringline. Retracing its path and starting again from the last certain point, another scout went ahead more cautiously, taking conservative leaps through space and mending the iperion path. It seemed to take forever, but a few weeks to an assured victory was not such a long time to wait, Percival told himself. He just hoped he could get there in time to save Escobar . . . whatever had happened to him.

The Commodore banked on the assumption that Adolphus had not bothered to booby-trap the abandoned path to outlying Buktu. As Lord Riomini had proved on Theser, the rebels did not have sufficient defenses in place on the main lines. Given time, Percival knew the General would realize he needed to bottle up the Buktu point of vulnerability, but with fifty-four DZ worlds to protect, he would not give this route top priority.

If Percival and his commandos could seize Buktu and use the new stringline to reach planet Hallholme, perhaps they could rescue the captured fleet after all. Though he did not admit it to anyone, he worried about his son. Despite Escobar's numerous shortcomings, the old man had always had high hopes for him, had tried to instill a moral compass in him when he was growing up.

More than a decade ago, Diadem Michella had ordered Percival to overstep the bounds of honor and commit what might be considered war crimes: torturing hostages and threatening to murder them so that he provoked a fatal moment of hesitation in his enemy. Percival had defeated Adolphus with those tactics once, and he knew the General would never make the same mistake again.

What if the situation were reversed? Assuming Adolphus had in fact captured the Constellation fleet, what if he did the same in reverse? What if he used Escobar and those innocent soldiers as human shields, maybe even threatening to murder the hostages—including Escobar—on-screen? The Commodore didn't know if he would be strong enough to make the correct decision. . . .

One of the scout ships returned along the stringline, transmitting a message. "The next segment is verified and reinforced, Commodore. We can now proceed to the following system."

Duff Adkins called up a chart, and marked another segment along the stringline path to Buktu. "That's excellent progress, Commodore. We might get there sooner than anticipated."

"Let's not get cocky," Percival said. "I want to be as fast as possible and as cautious as necessary."

The stringline hauler blurred forward along the line, but in less than half an hour, they reached the next endpoint. "Dispatch the scouts again to forge forward," Percival ordered.

The pilots lined up on the faint remnants of the abandoned line, collimating their stringline detectors and venturing ahead, repairing the iperion path as they went . . . starting, stopping, backtracking, starting, stopping.

And yet it was progress.

"This waiting is the hardest part," Adkins said again.

"As you've said before."

Adkins pursed his lips, looked down at his old friend. "Doesn't make it any less true."

70

With all the turmoil caused by the damaged stringline hub, and the embarrassing dissent Lady Tazaar expressed during the emergency Council session, Ishop Heer decided it was time to give Michella good news. Ever since the bomb had detonated the Diadem's auto-carriage, he and Laderna had continued their surveillance of the would-be assassin and his associates. Now it was time to move.

Ishop hired private security men to close the trap, not trusting any team Michella might choose. He wanted credit for the entire operation, and most importantly, he wanted to have the information first before revealing it to the Diadem. Laderna asked to accompany him, and since she had already helped him kill many victims on his long-standing list, he trusted no one more.

Along with six armed private security guards, they burst into a small, run-down apartment in the slums far from Heart Square. The small dwelling was cluttered with discarded food packaging; a filthy mattress lay on the floor. Ishop found it disgusting. Two men had been playing a game with cards and chits; another man sprang off the mattress, grabbed a weapon as Ishop's men moved forward.

The private security team tackled the situation with smooth efficiency, breaking a few bones—not necessarily by accident—and seizing

Burum Elakis. The other two were mere secondaries, and Ishop didn't care what happened to them.

The private guards stunned and dragged the two irrelevant men away, while taking great pains to keep Elakis conscious. With wires and adhesive strips they secured him to a chair so he could barely even squirm. Ishop inspected their work with a satisfied smile. "Thank you. You may deliver the others to the Diadem's security team and demand your reward. I'm sure Michella will be generous."

"But you've already paid us, sir," the head guard said.

"I don't begrudge you a bonus. Excellent work. Meanwhile, leave us alone here." He turned to grin at the silent Burum Elakis. "My assistant and I have a few polite questions for this gentleman." Laderna was smiling, and Ishop thought she looked quite attractive today. He was glad he had kept her around after all.

When the security detail left, Ishop put on gloves to avoid the mess of what he intended to do next. Elakis watched his every move, looking defiant and brave, but that didn't last long. Ishop was a professional.

The information the conspirator provided was unexpected and enlightening. Burum Elakis did not survive the interrogation, but Ishop had never intended him to do so anyway. The results were for Ishop's use alone.

The tools of his expertise lay strewn around the body: a razor knife, a small pair of pliers, injectors, even a few household items that Ishop and Laderna used for impromptu encouragement. Before they left, Laderna would clean up all their equipment and organize it in the carrying case again; when they returned to his private offices, she would sterilize every instrument. There was so much blood, and Ishop did not like the prospect of germs and infection.

While he found the traitor's revelations astonishing, the interrogation process itself was so stimulating that he had not wanted it to end. Still, he did not forget his professionalism. He was thorough with Elakis to the end, noting as he worked that Laderna stood right behind him, smelling of perspiration and excitement.

Splashes of blood made primitive artwork on the walls of the torture room. The scattered fingernails, five of them—any more would have been excessive and unnecessary—lay among the discarded wrappings on the floor. The man's body was still upright in an attentive pose because of the wires and adhesive strips, though he was quite dead, and mangled beyond recognition.

"That's all I have," Elakis had said at the end. He begged and swore and pleaded.

"We believe you," Ishop said with a hint of disappointment and pity. From the expression of relief on the captive's face, he misheard it as compassion.

Laderna stabbed him quickly in the heart, not wanting to waste any more time. Both of them were now very aroused, and each knew what would come next. No one would deny this was cause for another celebration. Finding the shower enclosure in Elakis's small apartment, they removed their stained clothes (planning ahead, they had brought new garments, sealed in plastic packages) and shared an invigorating shower, followed by lovemaking after placing a sterile plastic sheet on the floor.

Their pleasure was heightened by the remembered echoes of pain in the air of the apartment and the interesting information they had just learned. Laderna scratched his back at the height of passion, even let out a scream—but since no one had responded to Elakis's screams during the torture, Ishop did not expect her cries would draw any attention. He enjoyed himself, enjoyed being with her. Yes, he and Laderna made an excellent team.

They already knew Burum Elakis was an Adolphus sympathizer, but to discover that the man had been recruited into the assassination plot by Enva Tazaar—now, *that* was unexpected!

As he lay beside Laderna on the crinkling plastic film that was now moist with their perspiration, Ishop mused, "Why would Lady Tazaar have anything to do with the General?" Perhaps that explained why the Orsini noblewoman had been so outspoken against the Diadem during the last Council session.

Laderna stroked his smooth scalp. "Lady Tazaar is obviously making a power play. She'd love to remove Michella and set herself up as the next Diadem. She's probably just using General Adolphus as a means to an end."

"It'll be her own end, and we'll see to it." Still, he couldn't keep the admiration from his voice. "What a fascinating woman, a real risk-taker. Perhaps a good candidate as a noble wife for me."

For her own part, Laderna was disappointed by the discovery. "If Enva Tazaar is tarnished, that complicates her selection as an appropriate marriage prospect for you. It may be for the best, anyway. Lady Tazaar is a bit too attractive to make me completely comfortable."

"Now, don't be jealous." Ishop felt elated. Either way, this explosive information would help him regain his noble title, and the Diadem would shower rewards upon him. Soon he would have his own planet, his own domain.

With a long sigh, Laderna lifted herself from the sterile sheet. They still had a lot of cleaning up to do. She stood naked by the uncovered window, not caring if anyone looked in. "As soon as we're done here, I will set about compiling a list of less beautiful candidates for you."

71

Tension had frayed her nerves for weeks, and though Tanja Hu attempted to find her personal center again by focusing on administering Candela, the tragedies would not let go of her. Piled upon the tragedies she had already endured, now she had to add the horrific loss of the shadow-Xayan colony. The brave group had unleashed too much telemancy to strike the Sonjeera hub and protect Candela . . . and they had died from the unexpected ricochet. Only Tryn and one convert, Tel Clovis, had survived, both seriously injured.

Their seed colony, sent here for safety, was devastated, and according to the grievously wounded Original, the painful surge had been felt by the thousands of other converts back on Hellhole.

But as a result of the telemancy strike, the Deep Zone just might—*might*—be safe from further attacks by the Diadem. The boomerang of energy had caused some damage to the stringline terminus here, but her crews had completed the necessary repairs quickly. Regardless, *normal* was still a distant dream.

Uneasy teams in hazard suits had cleaned up the gelatinous remnants of the dead converts; hospital crews did their best to tend Tryn and Clovis, though they were at a loss about what to do for them. The man was twisted, his bones curved and bent at absurd angles, and the Xayan seemed distorted, her pale, translucent skin stained and her face

half gone. But both of them remained alive, held in a distant safety net
of telemancy from the rest of the converts on Hellhole.

When Tanja went to see the victims, tears burned her eyes. If not for
their sacrifice, Candela might now be a smoking ruin like Theser. And
five other DZ worlds as well.

As soon as the patients stabilized, she would arrange to send Tryn
and Clovis back to Hellhole, where they could rejoin their people. Maybe
the combined telemancy would strengthen or even heal them.

General Adolphus had already returned home and dispatched a full
alert to all the other DZ administrators. Spy probes sent down several of
the stringlines into the Crown Jewels confirmed that the Sonjeera hub
was offline, but they had no way of knowing how extensive the damage
was, or how long it might take the Constellation to complete repairs.

When Ian Walfor's small ship arrived on his run from Hellhole,
she was comforted just to know that he was back. She went to the landing zone with the boy Jacque, whom Tanja had taken under her wing
after Bebe's death. By staying together, she hoped to ease her own hurt
and his. She looked forward to seeing Walfor; though she had often
been aloof around him, the man was a stable point in her life, a reminder of her humanity. She didn't think Jacque would ever rest easy
again, but the boy clung to her as if she were an anchor.

Tanja and Jacque stood outside the Saporo Harbor terminal, shelter-
ing themselves from a light rain under an overhang as they waited for
Walfor's ship to land. Her heart was heavy as she realized a bitter truth,
that Ian Walfor was the only adult friend she had left in the Deep Zone,
the only one still alive. With a pang, she recalled that she and Bebe had
often gone together to meet him, and that Bebe had been skeptical of
Walfor, considering him a charming rogue. . . .

The thought of Bebe's terrible murder made anger bubble up inside
Tanja again. Looking down at the boy, she felt devastated, understanding his hurt; she squeezed his shoulder, wanted to make him feel better
somehow. Even though she didn't know what to do, had never imagined
herself as a mother, she would not let him be alone. She was a business-
woman, a planetary administrator, and for years had cut herself off from
her own irresponsible, unreliable relatives. In sharp contrast, Bebe Nax
had been a woman after her own heart. . . .

Jacque still seemed shell-shocked, and he suffered from continuing nightmares, but didn't like to talk about them. Now she tried to give the boy a hint of a normal day. "Let's see what Mr. Walfor brought. He always has interesting things in his cargo hold."

The boy nodded.

As he usually did, Walfor had disengaged his ship from the stringline once he reached the Candela system. With his experience as a black-market trader, as well as the resource scavenging he did on Buktu, he liked to scout the outskirts of the star system, surveying the outer bodies for possible resources or outposts.

The silvery ship came down through the patchy clouds, and sunlight glinted off its hull. Walfor had good enough piloting skills to land anywhere, and now he set down among the shuttles on the paved area at the harbor's edge.

Tanja grinned as the hatch opened, feeling a great sense of relief just to see his rugged, familiar face; she knew his warmth, his good humor, his easygoing nature. Walfor looked in her direction, but did not grin as he often did. His wavy black hair was longer than usual, and rippled in a gust of wind. She realized just how much she looked forward to having him back.

When he stepped onto the ramp, glancing around in the hazy Candela sunlight, his face had a haunted look. She ran up and surprised herself, and him, by giving him a hug. "Ian, I'm so glad you're here! We've been through . . . through so much here." She shuddered, heaved a sigh. He was aware of the destruction of Theser, but perhaps not the rest. "Maybe it's a good thing you missed it."

Holding him close, she spoke in a rush, with a hitching voice, not sure how much he already knew. She felt feverish as she talked, and her heart ached. She confessed, commiserated, and tried to remain detached, but failed in the attempt. Finally she ended with a sigh, forcing strength back into her voice. "At least Candela seems safe for the time being." She looked up at him, her eyes red and shining with tears.

But his expression said otherwise. "No, it's not."

She finally saw past her own turmoil to see his grim expression. He had not smiled since arriving, gave no hint of flirtation, put no innuendo in his words. "The whole Constellation fleet is a trivial nuisance compared to what I found."

She drew back, not sure that she could take any more devastating news. "What? What is it?" Instinctively, she drew the boy close.

"I need to take you inside my ship, show you the projections." He glanced at Jacque. "Maybe we could do this in private?"

She put a protective hand on the boy's shoulder. "No, he stays with me."

"He'll know soon enough anyway." Walfor led them into the cockpit, where he sat down and called up his navigation records. "As you know, I'm always scouting the nearby asteroids and the comet cloud for easy resources to extract. Any time I find something, I can ask Erik Anderlos to send in the Buktu crews."

On the cockpit projection screen, a starry field showed a bright planet in the distance. "I cast out a scattershot web of sensors to iden-tify and target nearby asteroids. Here's what I found." He displayed one image, then another, and another—a chaos of bright star points, some highlighted with crosshairs. "Look at these images, taken six hours apart." Many of the blips had moved noticeably. "Now, when I eliminate known asteroids in stable orbits—" He waved his hand, selecting an algorithm so that most of the dots disappeared into the darkness. "Only two re-main."

Jacque stared intensely, drinking in the data, but asked no questions.

"Extrapolating the remaining orbits gives us this." Walfor selected another projection, then stared at her, waiting for Tanja to see what he saw. "This is an exact science, and my instruments are very accurate." The ellipses of asteroid orbits painted themselves across the screen, and then the view panned out to highlight the star system, the sun and its five planets, including Candela itself.

"Look at the intersection point." He zoomed in. "*Both* of the aster-oids are on a collision course with Candela. They'll strike this planet—at the same time."

Tanja stared. "How can that be? The odds are inconceivable. This is ridiculous!"

"Yes, it is ridiculous—and the asteroids have actually accelerated. They are moving at a thousand times the ambient velocity of other as-teroids in the system. It's as if they've been diverted, and shoved toward Candela like cosmic cannonballs."

Tanja was speechless. Considering all the recent crises, it was no surprise that her outer system survey probes had not kept a close eye on cosmic debris. "But what could have caused this? I'm no astronomer, but I don't think that asteroids would just change course like that and pick up speed."

He zoomed in closer to the point where both of the asteroid paths converged on the planet Candela. "As crazy as it sounds, I don't think it's a coincidence. Someone targeted your world. Either one of those asteroids would cause an extinction event, and *both* of them are going to strike. You're fortunate I caught them on my instruments when I entered your system, or we wouldn't have known about the threat."

"But what the hell do we do about it? How do we stop the asteroids from hitting Candela?"

"There's nothing we *can* do about it. We have to evacuate the planet."

"Evacuate?" Tanja felt her thoughts whirling. "But hundreds of thousands of people live here! We couldn't possibly move them all!" She looked up sharply. "How much time do we have?"

"That's the worst part," Walfor said. "Those asteroids are shooting toward Candela like bullets. We have a week at the outside."

72

Escobar leaned over the life-support bed, reminding himself he was the *commander* of this fleet, or at least what remained of it. A shiver ran down his spine that had nothing to do with the flagship's bone-deep cold.

Next to him, Bolton made a strange comment: "Carrington looks so calm and peaceful. One might almost think she is harmless."

"She's not harmless," Escobar said, "just neutralized. I wish she'd been killed when she fought my guards—that would have saved us the trouble of all this."

"You are the Redcom," Bolton said with steel in his voice. "The decisions fall on your shoulders. You have to do what's right and what's necessary. Feeling good about it isn't part of the job."

Surprised at his hard tone, Escobar flashed him a sharp glance. This glorified supply officer had lived a pampered life, married the Diadem's daughter, and never had a trouble in the world. "What would you know about difficult decisions, Major?"

"I know that I chose not to be in your position. Don't you think I could have advanced beyond my current rank? My father could have bought me a command position—in fact, that was what they expected of me. But I had no interest in it."

"You aren't qualified for a command position. Your personality doesn't strike me as . . . leadership material."

"Maybe that's true, and maybe it isn't. In any event I refused, intentionally, much to my father's disappointment. After the end of the General's first rebellion, there were so many leftover military ships, and all of them needed captains. Heaven forbid that we reduce the size of the Army of the Constellation just because of an inconvenient peacetime! Ranks were sold like commodities, instead of earned. Do you know the fleet has an average of two officers to command every enlisted soldier? For economics and efficiency—not to mention military capability—the Diadem and Lord Riomini should have culled out a large percentage of the middle ranks." He narrowed his gaze, glanced down at the comatose Gail Carrington. "Just as we have to cull more people now, Redcom."

Three times in the past week, Escobar had approved the cessation of food and life support to groups of randomly chosen sleepers, two hundred at a time. The lists that Bolton compiled were just names, mostly people he had never met, and the bodies were quietly delivered to improvised coffin ships in the fleet. As far as most of the haggard, still-awake skeleton crew knew, their comrades were still sleeping.

The rations had been increased for those who remained conscious, and everyone ate their increased meals without comment; some of them consumed the new protein paste, assuming that their commanding officer had released all the remaining supplies, now that the trailblazer was due. The wiser crewmembers did not ask where the food came from. Escobar had been sick the first time he'd eaten the macabre protein paste, but ultimately he felt stronger because of it . . . strong enough to survive another day.

Escobar tried to hide his grief over the death of Lieutenant Cristaine—such a bright and cheerful bridge officer, a woman with a fine future in the Army of the Constellation, not one of the "unnecessary" officers Major Crais had mentioned. Rationally, he knew that her death should mean no more and no less than the hundreds of other victims, but he did feel the pain more keenly about her. She was not just a name.

And neither were the others. The energy requirements and nutrient solutions that would have kept those six hundred alive were distributed among the others, as well as the protein itself . . . but it still might not be enough to bring anyone out of this alive.

Some of the abandoned frigates, now cold storage ships, held thousands of comatose crewmembers, including the first squadron of fighter pilots who had volunteered for sedation. At some point, he would have to consider disconnecting them from life support as well, but so far he had not done that. He needed to separate the heroic, useful volunteers from the grudging ones. It would take some sorting.

For the time being, Escobar could lie, blame the hundreds of deaths on accidents, technical malfunctions in the onboard oxygen scrubbers of some ships, but he doubted many would believe it. The conscious crew were weak and listless anyway, and asked few questions. No one seemed to care where the extra food might be coming from.

"We're just prolonging the inevitable," Escobar said.

"And that's what we have to do," Bolton replied. "Prolong our lives as much as possible, keeping as many members of our fleet alive until the last possible moment—in case the trailblazer ship does arrive, and then we get our chance."

Escobar looked down. "Zabriskie and Caron should have been back two days ago."

"Optimistically speaking, not realistically," Bolton said. "We shouldn't give up on them yet."

"Many of us have."

Bolton's voice was sharp. "*You* cannot, Redcom! You are the son of Commodore Hallholme. As the leader of this fleet, you are responsible for getting us to our destination." He lowered his voice. "To Keana."

The scolding hit Escobar hard. Inwardly, he reminded himself of who he was, imagining what his father would say if he could see his son now. The pompous old Commodore would lecture him on everything he'd done wrong—and the old man would be absolutely correct in his assessment.

"We'll survive as long as possible," the Redcom finally said. "And the next two hundred will buy us more time. And Gail Carrington will be among them."

Until now, he had been reluctant to disconnect Carrington, even though he despised Lord Riomini's special operative and her secret mission. He had feared the wrath she could bring down on him and his family.

Increasingly, he missed Elaine and their two boys. He longed for a quiet afternoon sitting on a terrace in the sunshine on Qiorfu, gazing out on the Lubis Plain shipyards. He remembered how the boys liked to dress up in child-size military uniforms and play soldier, pretending to fight evil rebels. He had been amused at their flamboyance. Now, though, if Escobar ever had a chance to talk with them again, he would tell the boys to choose a different career; he would try to explain the realities of commanding a military operation.

Gail Carrington had once clung to the belief that it was better for them to be lost entirely than to arrive in failure. It was easy to make high moral decisions in a warm, well-lit room with a full belly—a luxury he didn't have now. Civilization imposed artificial realities, but that façade fell apart in desperate times.

"We lost twenty percent of our crew when one of our haulers flew off into the unknown," Escobar said aloud, as if Carrington could hear him "We lost six hundred more crewmembers in the name of preserving other lives. Two hundred and thirty-four have been killed in brawls, accidents, suicides, or from starvation. How I wish we could all have died as heroes in a blaze of battle, fighting for the Constellation, blasting the General's ships . . . instead of dying by sad degrees like this."

He looked down at Carrington, no longer afraid of her. What could she do to him now?

Dr. Hambliss came in, looking gray and beaten. "On this voyage I've lost more people than I've saved in my medical career. I wonder if there's some sort of balance sheet, a form I have to fill out?" He heaved a shuddering sigh, then looked at the motionless form of the dark-haired woman on the life-support bed. "This one, though, genuinely deserves death. She's ruthless and has enough blood on her hands to be sentenced to death in a Constellation court."

"We are the court now, Doctor," Escobar said, "and as the Red Commodore I am the judge of her war crimes. Disconnect her. Add her body to the protein vats, and let's hope her flesh doesn't poison us all."

Next to him, Bolton Crais swallowed audibly.

The ship-wide intercom crackled with a wild warbling alarm so loud he thought it might awaken the comatose patients. A breathy, panicked voice flooded through the *Diadem's Glory*. "Redcom, we just received a signal from the trailblazer! It's back!"

Escobar stumbled, falling against the bulkhead. His vision fuzzed with gray, and he thought he might black out. A chorus of cheers echoed up and down the corridors of the flagship, a weak and ragged sound.

Dr. Hambliss glared at Gail Carrington, as if he wished the signal had come five minutes later. Like a prisoner on death row, she had received a last-minute reprieve.

Feeling like a commander again, Escobar strode to the wall intercom. "I'm on my way. I want to meet Sergeants Zabriskie and Caron the moment they arrive."

⌘

The trailblazer pilots were so weak they needed to be helped out of the small vessel. Caron, the smaller of the two, said, "I hope you have a steak dinner for us, Redcom."

"We're fresh out of steaks, Sergeant, but I think the General has some on his world. A victory feast for everyone as soon as we reach planet Hallholme!"

"And now you *can* get there, sir." Zabriskie, gaunt now on his large frame, swayed on his feet and settled to the deck, sitting on the cold metal plates because his legs simply wouldn't support him anymore. "We reached the edge of the system yesterday and dropped our terminus ring, but not too close to the planet . . . then we turned around and shot back here following the new iperion line."

Dr. Hambliss was animated, pleased to be treating a real patient again. "They both show signs of prolonged iperion exposure. These men need medical care."

"We all need medical care, Doctor," Escobar said. "They'll receive all the supplies and treatment once we reach our target. Meanwhile, we've got to get the four haulers moving and prepare for a surprise attack. We might not have much time."

Bolton cleared his throat and said, "Sir, we still have to revive eighty percent of the crew. And once they're brought out of their comas, they'll be disoriented and weak, in no condition for battle."

Escobar whirled on him. "You want us to *wait* here? Are you saying we should delay? We're out of supplies!"

"We should start reviving them as soon as possible," the doctor agreed. "I have enough stimulants."

The Redcom nodded. "Then awaken our crew and get them ready to man their stations. Even with the loss of one stringline hauler, we still have a tremendous fleet of warships. We'll conquer Hellhole and confiscate their supplies." He drew a deep breath. "At last I have hope again. The whole crew will have hope again." He felt stronger once more; his voice was louder, his shoulders squared. "It's the difference between failure and success, Major Crais. We are *back*! And once we're finished, the Constellation will greet us as heroes."

"Maybe not the families of those who were lost," Bolton said quietly.

But Escobar would not hear anything negative. "A strong victory will comfort them in their grief." He clapped his hands for attention among the crewmen who had come to the landing bay. "Prepare for departure. As for this hauler, get our new stringline pilot up to the hauler controls." He turned back to Dr. Hambliss. "And now that we're finally able to strike General Adolphus, it would be a good time to wake up Gail Carrington."

The disappointment on the doctor's face was palpable.

73

Following the disaster at the Sonjeera hub and the increasingly blatant unrest among her nobles, Michella needed to make unchal-
lenged decisions. Unless she could lead properly now, the stability of the
Crown Jewels and *human civilization itself* would be lost to the barbarians
from the Deep Zone.

Now was the time to rule with an iron hand, without wavering, insisting on cooperation from the nobles, not letting them grow unruly.
She had to control Selik Riomini—stoking his ambitions just enough
to keep him strong as her heir apparent, yet reining him in enough to
keep him from overstepping his position.

Everything must be done for the good of the Constellation. And *she*
was the Constellation.

Early in her reign, to increase the power of the Star Throne, the
orbital hub over Sonjeera had been designed as a bottleneck; all fast
interstellar transportation had to pass through there, with no other alternative. Even though it would have made stringline transportation
more efficient, she refused to allow other worlds to build secondary
hubs. She wanted to control the network.

The usage fees had long since paid for the construction of the entire Crown Jewels stringline system as well as the extended lines out to
the Deep Zone, while the DZ tribute fees had easily paid for the rest of

the construction. No one but Michella and her highest-level accountants understood just how much wealth poured in because of the fees on all ships that passed through Sonjeera.

But that one central point for all transport also created a crucial vulnerability. By using some incredible power—alien technology, perhaps?—General Adolphus had brought the Crown Jewels to a standstill. Non-stringline ships could still travel slowly among the core worlds, delivering emergency supplies and messages, but all normal commerce had ground to a halt. The Diadem had armies of workers scrambling to repair the orbiting hub.

Lord Riomini's battle groups were stranded over Sonjeera, but perhaps that was a good thing. They could protect her against a more traditional military attack, should Adolphus make that move. What other alien powers did he have? How many of those sluglike creatures had he found on his hellish planet?

She shuddered at the thought. The very idea of how the slime-covered aliens took over human minds was repugnant to her. The creatures had to be stopped before they got loose and invaded the Crown Jewels.

Lord Riomini reported to the palace at midmorning, swollen with importance. She was indulging his request for an immediate meeting, although under normal circumstances she would have imposed a pro forma delay; it was a matter of principle that others must wait for the Diadem. But not today.

The Black Lord brought five men and women with him as he marched down the corridor to the conference chamber Michella had selected. While his companions remained out in the hall, Riomini entered and gave a perfunctory bow to the Diadem, impatient to speak with her. "Eminence, I brought a group of scientists with me to advise us on the . . . alien matter. After the attack on our stringline hub, it is imperative that we understand the threat those creatures pose."

"I couldn't agree more," she said, then turned to the blank wall and added in a normal speaking voice, "Ishop, join us." She knew he would be eavesdropping on the conversation from a clandestine observation room. In this crisis she valued his advice more than ever; after all, he was the one who had convinced her to impose extreme quarantine measures on the alien emissaries trapped in the spaceport hangar. Now she explained to Riomini, "Ishop and I are the only ones present who have actually come close to those . . . *things.*"

Hearing her summons, the large man emerged from his hiding place and walked into the conference chamber with a curt bow to the Diadem, ignoring Riomini as he glided into a seat beside her. Michella gave an impatient gesture to the scientists standing by the doorway. "Do you intend to present your findings from out in the hall? Come in and tell me how to solve this!"

Agitated, she looked at the art piece suspended from the ceiling: a strange aerogel sculpture Enva Tazaar had given her. Despite her anger at the outspoken younger noblewoman, Michella could not help admiring the exquisite tangles of the sculpture's form, which splashed rainbows of color across the walls.

As the five experts filed in, Riomini began, "Eminence, it's vital that we understand what sort of weapon General Adolphus used to strike at us through the stringline network. The power surge we received was unlike anything we have ever encountered." He folded his hands in front of him on the table, speaking as if he had already come to a conclusion and was merely issuing a pronouncement. "The obvious answer is that the aliens were somehow responsible. We have to understand their abilities and develop defenses. That's why I gathered this team, the finest scientists in the Crown Jewels. Under my guidance, they have come up with a suggestion that has great merit."

The scientists stood side by side on one end of the room, two tall men on one side, a pair of short, dark-haired women on the other side, and a pudgy, red-cheeked man at the center. The pudgy man bowed. "I am Tobner Mayak, Eminence, spokesman for the group. We are specialists in various disciplines that may help us understand the potential abilities, and dangers, of these aliens. *Xayans,* they call themselves."

A knot twisted in her stomach, and the Diadem feared the return of a nightmare. The last time she'd been in the vicinity of the aliens she had come close to being contaminated herself. Even now, her brain and body could be infested with their inhuman presence. "I spoke with one of the things, before I understood the danger they pose. If I hadn't taken immediate action, the contamination might have gotten loose on Sonjeera. Even now we must remain vigilant that not a single microbe escapes the sealed hangar."

Mayak fidgeted. "Yes, Eminence. Lord Riomini asked us to accumulate all data about the Xayans, looking for clues about how we might defend against another onslaught like the one that destroyed the stringline hub."

She shook her head. "The hub is damaged, not destroyed. We expect it to be functioning again within days, at least for the Crown Jewel lines." From the skeptical expression on Riomini's face, he seemed to know that was far too optimistic.

"The next alien assault might be worse, however," Ishop pointed out. An oily sheen of perspiration covered his pale skin. "And those monsters might come in person." Ishop seemed to be the only person who feared the Xayans as much as she did.

Michella struggled to maintain her composure as Mayak scanned a report. His companions looked at him, expecting him to continue. "Frankly, Eminence, our information doesn't amount to much. We have too little data to begin planning our defenses. Lord Riomini gave us access to the unedited records of the Xayan representative and his contaminated human companions who attempted to infiltrate Sonjeera, but that was little help."

Michella narrowed her eyes, looked at Riomini. "I ordered those records sealed. No one should have had access to them."

The Black Lord spread his hands in a quick, flippant apology. "It was necessary, Eminence. It is vitally important for us to understand the alien threat—I couldn't hamstring my scientists."

Mayak continued, "Those images were instructive in demonstrating the mental powers the Xayans can wield. Even as they were being poisoned in the sealed chamber, one alien caused severe damage to the pod, using only his mind. One can only imagine how much destruction they could cause if they acted in concert."

The Diadem shuddered again; the creature had very nearly escaped, but fortunately the poison gas had killed him in time. She did not want to think about a whole army, a whole *swarm* of such things, coming to civilized worlds.

"Obviously, they had enough power to destroy Sonjeera's stringline hub," Riomini said.

"The hub is severely *damaged*," Ishop corrected, though no one paid attention to him.

Michella's throat went dry. "What if the General controls a full alien army, along with countless humans who have been contaminated by them? What if the Xayans control *him*? He was formidable enough when he was a mere human, but now what are we facing?"

The chief scientist smiled. "Ah, so you understand, Eminence. We must learn how to prepare ourselves. How can we shield against those mental powers?" He shook his head. "We questioned anyone who escaped from planet Hallholme, anyone who witnessed the possessed humans that emerged from slickwater pools. We reviewed the frightening reports from Mr. Heer." He nodded to Ishop. "But we don't understand the most basic information about the alien biology, and we have to start there to discover if the human brainwashing is a virus or some kind of mental enslavement. It's vital that we have more data. We need cellular samples."

Ishop frowned. "I hardly think we can go to Hellhole to collect a sample!"

Picking up from there, the Black Lord said in a calm voice, "Actually, there's no need for that. We already have samples available right on our doorstep, Eminence—if you are willing to use them. My scientific team advocates examining the remains of the dead Xayan sealed in the quarantined hangar."

The Diadem's tone was cool. "Too dangerous."

"Our only specimen has been preserved in resin, and the cells may still be viable . . . or at least instructive," Mayak said. "Using proper decontamination precautions, building a larger sealed containment around the hangar, we should be able to safely conduct tests on the alien remnants, and on the remains of the possessed humans."

"Our very survival might depend on it," Riomini added. "We are in a race against time. General Adolphus could be gathering a full-fledged alien army against us. Therefore, the team requests permission to break into the hangar and unseal the pod to examine any and all evidence that might be trapped inside."

Turning pale, Ishop blurted out, "We don't dare take that risk. The slightest error, and all of Sonjeera could succumb to alien contamination! We might all be infected!"

Riomini ignored him and spoke to the Diadem with patient logic. "Eminence, we have no other leads! That alien stringline blast caused incredible damage to our hub *from light-years away.*" Now his voice became excited. "We need to know what the Xayans can do to us, and we can't make good decisions without information."

The Diadem was too deeply disturbed by her one close experience with the sluglike alien. She was sickened at the thought of the insidious contamination spread by those disgusting creatures—and all the deluded humans like her own daughter who allowed themselves to be taken over by it!

Ishop's voice cracked. "Eminence, I urge you *not* to take such a risk! We could all be—"

She didn't need to be further convinced. "I won't hear of it, Selik. I refuse to breach the quarantine and allow dangerous organisms to escape."

Puffing as if from great exertion, Mayak continued to explain his plan, even though he had already lost his case. "Eminence, I brought diagrams of the network of tunnels beneath the sealed hangar. We can drill an access from underground, with several layers of interlocks. I assure you, there will be no chance of contamination escaping."

Her stomach roiled as she thought of an alien intrusion into her own mind. "I won't allow it!"

Mayak and Riomini exchanged uneasy glances.

Angrily, Michella sent the scientists away, after which the Black Lord stood up and said, "With all due respect, Eminence, we must not ignore this opportunity—for the good of the Constellation. It is imperative that we understand our enemy. Otherwise how can we fight back?"

"I've made my decision, Selik. Now leave." She barely moved, maintaining her icy demeanor, but she knew it could crack at any moment. He probably considered her irrational, but he hadn't seen the things she had firsthand. He had not felt the insidious mental presence trying to get to her and her people.

Riomini paused as if to continue arguing, then left with a haughty, disrespectful air, which only angered her more.

❧

When they were alone in the conference room, Ishop Heer nearly hyperventilated in an effort to control his panic. He poured himself a glass of water from a pitcher in the center of the conference table. "You made the wisest possible decision, Eminence. No one else understands the real threat, as we do."

Unsettled, Michella paced the room, burning off nervous energy. "At least you realize the dangers, dear Ishop. You are able to see what others cannot. What would I do without you?"

He gave a somber nod. "It is my duty to protect you, Eminence—to see the dangers and intercept them." He knew it was time to tell her his other revelation, a more comprehensible one, at least. "And there is another danger, closer to home."

She sat, looking pale and old, obviously fearing what he would say. "What is it now?"

"As you asked, I found those responsible for the assassination attempt. My interrogations produced very disturbing information." Taking care to conceal his glee, Ishop handed her his report on the information extracted from Burum Elakis. Without giving Michella time to read it, he told her that the operation had been instigated and bankrolled by Enva Tazaar herself. "Lady Tazaar planned to murder you and set herself up as the next Diadem while cooperating with General Adolphus to form an alliance with the Deep Zone."

Michella's expression transformed into disbelief. "One of my own nobles in league with the General?" It was just the two of them in the conference room, and she remained greatly agitated by Lord Riomini's proposal. She stared up at the twisted aerogel sculpture. "Enva Tazaar?"

"Yes, Eminence. The evidence is incontrovertible."

Michella picked up the water pitcher and hurled it at the dangling sculpture, shattering the art piece and causing fragments to fall onto the table and the floor, leaving only a chunk hanging from a wire. "Time to extinguish any hint of unrest," she said. "The Constellation has to be absolutely united behind my rule in this time of crisis. We will arrest Enva Tazaar, present the evidence to the Council, and strip her of her noble titles and fortune. That should snuff out any other plots."

Ishop hid his satisfaction. "I am your eyes and ears, Eminence." It pleased him that Riomini had been tarnished, and now Enva Tazaar would also be removed from the equation. Ishop's earlier ambitions had been simply to regain his noble title—which he could triumphantly do in only a few more days—but perhaps he should be thinking even bigger. "It seems the choice of who will be the next Diadem is no longer clear," he said.

Michella blinked at him, as if wondering where that comment had come from. "Given the current state of affairs, I don't see anyone on the horizon who can competently assume my duties. I'll just have to live forever."

"Oh, I'm sure someone will emerge."

The Diadem let out a long sigh. "It's not like you to be so optimistic, Ishop. Usually, you are a pragmatist and realist."

He bowed, so she wouldn't be able to read his expression. "I've always been your most faithful supporter, your loyal expediter, and I hope you will remember that . . . and reward me appropriately."

Michella laughed. "You have certainly proved yourself in recent days, Ishop. And over the years you've been indispensable, more valuable than any ten nobles. No one deserves my generosity more than you do!"

"I am glad to know I have your complete support, if ever I need to ask."

74

After more than two interminable months of deprivation, the last step of the fleet's journey would take only a day. Ironically, after so much waiting, Escobar knew his troops weren't ready, but he didn't dare wait any longer. Strike fast, strike hard!

It was a balancing act to get the four remaining stringline haulers in place as thousands of groggy crewmembers returned to consciousness. Though the revived soldiers were weak to the point of starvation, gaunt and jittery, the supply of stimulants kept them functioning, as did their own adrenaline. They were heading for planet Hallholme at last!

What had once been a well-organized military operation, however, devolved into confusion and disbelief as word spread about what had occurred while they slept in blissful unconsciousness—the suicides, the brawls and killings, the disappearance of one full stringline hauler containing twenty battleships. Escobar managed to keep secret the source of the remaining rations—for the time being.

Another 157 crewmembers died of medical complications while being revived from their comas. Though distraught by the deaths, Dr. Hambliss was not surprised. "This was an experimental procedure in the first place, Redcom. We didn't have the proper monitoring equipment or nutrients, or the beds to keep so many in induced comas. The Sandusky stasis drug was never meant to be used for such a prolonged time. That many casualties out of almost ten thousand sedated people is an acceptable loss by any measure."

"We already have a long list of casualties, Doctor," Escobar said. "So long as we still have enough fighters and firepower to defeat General Adolphus."

Invigorating military music played over the intercom to keep the fighters inspired and moving for just one more day. They were like scarecrows returning to their posts; many were ill, nauseated and dizzy. Nevertheless, the Redcom did his best to whip them into shape. Escobar would have preferred to spend days drilling everyone and going over a concise battle plan, but there wasn't enough time. They would face the enemy soon, and he needed to focus them on their imminent goal.

Many fighter pilots had perished in the random cutbacks, and he had fewer to join the attack than he would have liked. With the twenty warships lost on the vanished stringline hauler, four more ships that were still loaded with frozen bodies, and six that had been damaged in mutinous uprisings, he was left with seventy capable warships. Despite the diminished force, Escobar hoped that his arrival would be such a shock to the rebels that he would overwhelm them and cause the General to surrender.

Seven hours after the return of Sergeants Zabriskie and Caron, the stringline haulers lined up on the new iperion path and launched for planet Hallholme. Escobar counted on making the rest of the preparations during the last day of flight. It was all the time they had.

Medical teams, assisted by growing ranks of revived volunteers, continued to awaken the sedated soldiers. As the four haulers hurtled down the stringline toward the target, Escobar walked the corridors of the *Diadem's Glory*. Bolton gave him quiet reports of conversations overheard. "The crew is only beginning to grasp the magnitude of what's gone wrong on this mission. They're growing angry, sir, and they blame it on you."

"I knew they'd blame it on me, Major. As you told me before, a commander's decisions aren't always easy, but if we can achieve this victory, I'll keep the rest of them alive. We'll feast on the General's stockpiles, and all will be forgiven."

"A true commander doesn't need to ask forgiveness from his men," Bolton said, "if the decisions he makes are warranted."

Escobar was annoyed. "Thank you for dispensing your command wisdom, Major Crais."

"It's not mine, Redcom. It's a direct quote from your father."

Gail Carrington returned to the bridge, looking wan and weak but with a fire in her eyes. She paused to give Escobar an accusatory glare, then nodded to him and to Bolton. "Although I expressed my doubts, Commodore Hallholme, it appears that your harsh plan did work. I accept the necessity of what you did, but the victory is not won yet."

"Thank you, Ms. Carrington. Include that in your report to Lord Riomini when we come home victorious." Despite his professed confidence, Escobar remained concerned. Each time he glanced at Lieutenant Cristaine's empty station, he was reminded of all they had lost.

His task force was not exactly the well-oiled machine it had been when it departed from Sonjeera. Power reserves were low, and they had barely enough energy to activate their primary weapons—not the impressive punitive force that Diadem Michella had wanted to throw against General Adolphus—and they were arriving two months later than expected . . . but they should have the element of surprise on their side—even more so than before.

Escobar ground his teeth together. If they were victorious, the Diadem and the Black Lord would be satisfied enough.

He delivered an impromptu speech over the fleet-wide channel, telling his crew he knew they were upset over the horrific losses they had endured, but General Adolphus was the real enemy, not their commanding officer—not him. *Adolphus* had cut the stringline and stranded them all; *Adolphus* had caused their misery.

He knew he was pushing the troops hard, and realized they were weak, reeling and disoriented from the aftereffects of long sedation, and the shock of the deaths. Some struggled to find their focus, but most were good enough soldiers that they fell back into their routine.

They had been drilled and trained before leaving the Crown Jewels, and they understood the simple and swift initial plan to overwhelm the enemy, striking fast and striking hard. They had never dreamed they might lose; failure was not part of any plan.

Escobar had painted himself into a corner and he had only one chance to redeem himself, but he feared this crew was not ready. "It feels like a disaster waiting to happen," he whispered to himself.

Carrington overheard him and responded in a brittle voice, reminding him of his place. "I disagree, Redcom. It feels like a *victory* waiting to happen."

A signal came from the stringline hauler's replacement pilot. "Approaching the Hallholme system, sir. Arrival at the terminus ring is imminent." Her voice carried an undertone of disbelief.

Escobar sat in the command chair, drew a deep breath, and prepared himself. "It's about damned time."

He ordered everyone to battle stations, and the surviving pilots rushed to their fighter craft, ready to engage the rebel forces. The four stringline haulers decelerated and appeared, one after another, at the discreet terminus ring that Zabriskie and Caron had deposited at the edge of the Hallholme system. As soon as the haulers were in position, Escobar ordered all warships to disengage from their docking clamps and prepare to move forward in a full aerial assault. He would leave the hauler frameworks at the terminus ring.

"It won't be long before the General's sensors spot our four haulers," he said. "We have to be on the move before he can take action."

A shudder ran through the *Diadem's Glory* as the docking clamp released them from its months-long grasp. The flagship's in-system engines guided it forward to join the other ships. They would swoop down upon planet Hallholme and open fire, disrupt whatever defenses the rebels had in place, and secure a swift victory. He had to overwhelm General Adolphus before the man could see just how weak the Constellation fleet truly was.

The familiar, rousing theme played. If everything went right, the Redcom was creating a stirring tale to tell his sons—if he survived long enough to return home and see them again.

Leaving the new terminus ring behind, the Constellation task force began its final approach toward the hellish world. Seventy warships flew in, an impressive force, but the formation was too loose for Escobar's liking; the crews lacked discipline. He had hoped for precision, a model operation, but it was all he could do to get the attack ships to engage the same target. It would have to do.

He broadcast a final rallying cry across the secure fleet codecall channel. "Our first priority is to disarm the General and destroy his defenses. After that, we send immediate recovery teams down to the colony cities to secure their food stockpiles. We'll take what they have and make ourselves whole again. I promise you, we'll have all we can eat tonight!"

He heard a ragged cheer from his bridge crew, and it was echoed throughout the fleet. It pleased him how readily they believed his promise. It meant they still had faith in him. According to Constellation propaganda, Hellhole was a squalid and miserable place where the people could barely survive, but now, somehow, the warship crews imagined a wealth of supplies, stockpiles of food.

Long-range scanners displayed detailed images of the planet; everyone gazing at their screens felt sickening dismay at the same time. To their astonishment, they saw dozens of rebel warships circling the planet, along with smaller weapons platforms. The reconditioned battle vessels looked formidable, along with FTL attack ships that bristled with weapons, all positioned to defend their DZ stringline hub. A much larger force than Escobar—or anyone in the Constellation fleet—had expected to see.

"Not so defenseless as we've been led to believe!" Escobar growled.

Bolton said, "The General has had two extra months to prepare."

Gail Carrington added, "We still outnumber them. We are not going to turn back now."

"I wouldn't think of it." Escobar opened the command codecall line. "Forward! Engage the enemy before they even know we're coming."

Discipline in the Constellation fleet was lax and morale at rock bottom; the formations were ragged, the ships wove about like drunken birds. He could see by the clean lines and tightly regimented formations, however, that the rebel defenses were much better drilled, much more alert.

"Maintain course. We can outgun them."

He watched as the General's ships lit up and began to move, turning their glowing weapons ports toward the oncoming fleet.

"They've spotted us," reported his female tactical officer. At first, Escobar thought her voice sounded just like Lieutenant Cristaine's . . . but it was someone new.

"Open codecall to the public channel, but without visuals. I don't want the enemy to see how we look, or he'll realize that we are in a desperate situation."

After verifying that the system was voice-only, he spoke directly into the voice pickup. "This is Red Commodore Escobar Hallholme, representing the Constellation. I hereby seize this planet in the name of the Diadem and demand your unconditional surrender. Turn over the criminal Tiber Adolphus for proper punishment—or you will be destroyed."

75

The alarms in Elba rang in the middle of the night, a private emergency signal from the *Jacob* patrolling the skies over Hellhole. Adolphus was immediately awake, as if gunfire had echoed overhead. He knew this was no minor call, no false alarm. Sophie groaned as she roused herself and hurried to dress.

Craig Jordan, who operated the flagship while in orbit, shouted over the direct codecall link, "General, a large force just appeared in our system!"

"A large force?" Adolphus said. "How many ships?"

"More than fifty, sir. ETA, less than an hour."

Adolphus shook his head. "How could they *appear* in the system? Are you monitoring both stringline networks?"

"They didn't come in on either line, sir—not from the DZ and not from Sonjeera." Jordan sounded flustered, trying to keep control of the situation. "They came in on some other path. We're checking."

Sophie, bleary-eyed, reacted with shock. "A *new* stringline?"

"I'm going to my war room, Jordan. I want a full report when I get there."

After his nerve-racking expedition to Candela and the alarming events at the Ankor spaceport, Adolphus was glad to be back at Elba.

On his first night at home, he had looked forward to sleeping in his own bed, comforted to have Sophie beside him. He drew strength and stability from her; she made him feel he could keep all the myriad cogs and gears in place, moving along. . . .

Now, as if the two of them moved in a well-choreographed dance, Sophie pulled out his appropriate clothes while Adolphus dressed rapidly; in less than ten minutes he cut an impressive figure.

Adolphus entered Elba's conference chamber, where screens on the walls were linked to the *Jacob's* bridge and to other primary ships guarding Hellhole. Although he had sent fifteen vessels to Candela, he still had forty-five armed ships here to defend the DZ stringline hub. He would have to make the best of them.

As soon as the General activated the screens in the war room, Craig Jordan's image appeared from the *Jacob's* bridge. He gave his report without being asked. "Here's what we know so far, sir. Seventy warships are heading this way under standard in-system propulsion."

"But where did they come from? And are there more in hiding?"

"With our high-res scanners, backtracking the route of the inbound warships, we found four stringline haulers on the edge of the system, military-size carrier vessels."

Standing at his shoulder, Sophie interrupted. "We don't have a stringline terminus so far out—how did they get here?"

"Somebody placed another terminus ring outside the system," Adolphus said, his thoughts spinning. "It means a trailblazer laid down a new iperion path, just like we did with our own DZ network."

"But a voyage from Sonjeera would have taken years!" Sophie handed him a cup of steaming kiafa from Elba's kitchens.

"We'll ask for details once we've defeated them. Battle stations, Mr. Jordan!" He turned to Sophie, frustrated. "I can't stay down here. I need to be on the *Jacob's* bridge, at the front of the attack."

Sophie put her hands on his shoulder to keep him in his seat. "If those ships will arrive in less than an hour, you don't have time. Stay here in the command center and manage our response. Take a breath. Do it right."

He looked around, anxious to be in the thick of the fight, but he had established this Elba war room as a satellite administrative chamber. It contained the equipment he needed. "You're right."

"You don't need to remind me," she said with a smile.

Jordan reported, "Message coming in, sir. It's from—" He caught his breath. "He says he's Red Commodore Escobar Hallholme."

Adolphus remained motionless as the pieces fell into place. "So, the missing Constellation fleet finally got here." Somehow those ships had found their own path to Hellhole, though it had taken them months. Was this an ingenious surprise maneuver, or an act of desperation? Had they somehow kept the true nature of their mission a secret even from Dak Telom? Adolphus felt beaten by the very idea, the *audacity* of such a risky plan.

He muttered under his breath, "I will not surrender to a Hallholme again."

Sophie's voice was hard. "Damn right."

"Put him on, Mr. Jordan."

A male voice spoke over the connection, but there was no visual. "This is Red Commander Escobar Hallholme. I repeat, surrender and turn over the criminal Tiber Adolphus—or you will all be destroyed."

Adolphus switched to a private line, said, "He's blocking his image, Mr. Jordan. I want to know why. Can you break through the codecall blocks he's placed on his warship?"

"Already working on it, sir. Getting close. When we get the visual line, we should be able to hold it open for maybe ten minutes before they find a work-around and it goes dark again. Here it comes, sir!"

In the seconds it took for the images to appear, the General's pulse raced. Then, as the screen came into focus, he found himself face-to-face with the son of Commodore Hallholme. As soon as he saw the Redcom's face, Adolphus understood much more: Escobar Hallholme's bluster was diminished by the haunted, desperate look on his emaciated face. He didn't seem to know yet that he could be seen.

"You have five minutes before we open fire," the Redcom said, glaring ahead. "We await your response."

Adolphus looked carefully at the man. He had similar facial features to his legendary father's, though his light-brown hair was neatly trimmed, and he did not sport the old Commodore's distinguished muttonchop whiskers. Escobar's hard eyes stared ahead like weapon beams. He looked confident, arrogant, completely in charge. But he had hollow shadows under his eyes, a gaunt and shaky look. Despite his bravado, he carried an aura of desperation, like brittle glass. Everyone on the enemy bridge was thin and stooped over, with haunted eyes, like images he had seen of torture victims.

Sophie saw it, too. "Look at him, and the other officers on the bridge! They're all starving."

Without activating his own codecall, the General stared and pondered. This revelation changed everything. "Let them eat silence for a few minutes."

The answers now crystallized, and Adolphus guessed what must have occurred. This surprise ambush was not part of a long-standing, devious plan at all. When the iperion path was cut, the lost fleet had indeed been stranded—just as the Urvanciks had determined. But they had gone so far astray that the General's search parties had not been able to locate them. They had limped their way here, using the last gasps of their resources; only four of the five stringline haulers had made it.

Although he admired the younger Hallholme for the impossible decisions he must have made just to keep his fleet alive for so long, Adolphus realized that every person aboard those ominous battleships had to be weak from malnutrition, desperate, at the ragged end. Before his ships fired a single shot at them, Redcom Hallholme had already lost 30 percent of his fleet.

Adolphus could use that.

Before he responded to the ultimatum, Adolphus made preparations. He had the kitchen staff deliver a platter of pastries, cheese, and hard-boiled eggs, an impromptu breakfast feast. Only when he had the extravagant food spread out before him did he activate his own codecall screen; for good measure, to make certain everyone aboard the seventy attacking ships saw him, he expanded the signal to include all standard Constellation military frequencies.

When he finally answered, he gave a bright grin. "Greetings, Red Commodore. You are a long way from Sonjeera." He picked up one of the pastries, took a slow bite.

"Your actions forced us to come, General," Escobar said. "I have orders from Diadem Michella to accept your immediate surrender. All of your assets are forfeit."

"You don't look well, Mr. Hallholme."

The Redcom jerked back, looked around. A female officer whispered in his ear, apparently telling him that their enemy could see the inside of their ship. Hallholme scowled, stared straight at the screen. In the background, his officers struggled to find the work-around to shut off the images.

"In fact," Adolphus added, "your entire bridge crew looks ragged and hungry." He casually nibbled on his pastry. "You have intruded upon my territory and I'm afraid it won't be possible for us to surrender." He took a sip of kiafa, leaned forward. "I will, however, accept *your* surrender."

"Don't be foolish, General. We have twice as many ships as you do!"

Adolphus's gaze did not waver, nor did he quibble with Escobar's exaggeration. "I see your ragtag ships, and I'm convinced you're out of supplies. How long has it been since your crew has had a decent meal? And how are your power supplies? Life-support reserves? Are your weapons at full capacity? Your fuel levels must be very low."

"After we take over this planet in the name of the Diadem," Escobar said, struggling to find his defiance, "we'll confiscate what we need from your stockpiles."

"You are welcome to try," Adolphus said with a shrug. "Although I'd rather you saw reason. You may have a handful more ships, but my well-armed fleet is more than a match for yours. We have plenty of weapons, all systems fully powered, and we're on our home territory." He smiled again, twisting the verbal knife. "And my people are well fed, well rested, and well trained, at the peak of their abilities. Can you say the same for your crew?"

He raised his eyebrows. When his rival fumbled for words, Adolphus continued, "I promise we'll put up a hell of a fight, and we'll wear you down. We can hold you off, and it'll be a stalemate for at least a week or two. Are your crewmembers prepared to wait that long?"

Adolphus picked up a wedge of trimmed melon, took a bite, then tossed aside the half-finished slice. "I was a military officer in the Constellation, Redcom—just like you. I went through the Aeroc Academy, excelled in my training. I only turned against the corrupt government when they cheated me out of my rank and tried to kill me and other second-string nobles, just so someone could steal our holdings. How is my family estate on Qiorfu, by the way, Redcom? I hope the Hallholmes are taking good care of it for me."

"The *Hallholme* estate is doing well, General, and I look forward to returning to it after we wrap up this matter. You are a traitor to the Diadem, a condemned rebel."

"Actually, I'm a man of honor," Adolphus said, calmly. "No matter how Constellation propaganda distorts what happened during the rebellion, the most inept historian can study my pattern of decisions and the ethical basis on which I made them. I gave my word, and I abided by it, and now I have an obligation to my people. Allow me to extend a generous offer to your crew. We will feed all of you and keep you safe. Those who need medical attention will receive it. You will be accorded fair treatment as prisoners of war until we resolve this conflict with the Constellation."

Escobar's angry laugh held an undertone of anxiety. "If you won't surrender, General, I'll order my forces to destroy you."

"Go ahead and try if you think you can pull it off," Adolphus said as he ate another pastry. "All of our ships have full larders, and we can wait you out. In a week or two I *might* extend my offer of food and shelter again."

He switched off the codecall.

※

Escobar was shocked when two of his Constellation frigates, the most desperate warships with the most unruly crews, surged past his flagship. They opened fire without orders, strafing the General's defensive vessels in orbit. The attack was sudden and unplanned, but vigorous.

"Hold your fire! Return to position!" Escobar shouted. "I gave no command—"

Two of the Hellhole defenders were damaged in the initial flurry, but the rest opened fire on the advancing frigates. Within minutes, the impetuous Constellation ships were gutted, leaking air into space. Their fuel chambers reached critical levels, and engines detonated in chain reactions, destroying both vessels.

Carrington snapped, "The die is cast, Redcom. Are you going to just stare at the screen?"

Escobar lurched to his feet. "Advance! Full attack formation! We need to cripple the General's defenses."

His fleet spread out to engage independent targets, but it was a pell-mell effort, following none of the plans they had reviewed. Fighter craft dropped out of the warship launching bays and swept like tiny hornets in frantic attack sorties.

Carrington watched with sour displeasure on her face. "This is sloppy, Redcom. Very sloppy."

The DZ Defense Force formed a neat line to face them and opened fire, concentrating their weapons on one incoming ship after another. A dozen previously unnoticed automated weapons platforms targeted the Constellation vessels. As the front lines surged forward in a chaotic scramble, two more of Escobar's ships were ripped apart in space.

The Constellation soldiers had suffered months of deprivation, and most of them had just been revived from induced comas; they'd had little time to assess their situation. Five of the Constellation ships raced forward, and they suddenly began transmitting messages—to the planet. "We accept your offer, General Adolphus. We will not fire on your ships, if you accept our surrender and provide food to our crews."

In shock, Escobar called to the rest of his ships. "Stop those vessels! Cripple them, destroy them if you must! We can't let the General seize any portion of our fleet!"

Like the wind shifting abruptly in a sudden squall, four more Constellation warships broadcast their surrender and raced toward the DZ Defense ships, their own weapons systems shut down. A few loyal Constellation vessels opened fire on the deserters, who shot back. The General's well-disciplined defenders were careful to target only the aggressors while protecting the surrendering enemy vessels with their own shields.

Escobar yelled across the fleet-wide channel, "Remain at your posts! Anyone who communicates with the enemy will be court-martialed and executed in the name of the Diadem."

The General responded over the open codecall. "Any member of the invasion fleet who surrenders to me will be given amnesty and sanctuary in the Deep Zone. Under our protection, you have nothing to fear from the Crown Jewels."

"They need to fear *me*," Escobar said.

On the bridge, Bolton said privately, "Our crew is mad with hunger, Redcom. They've waited too long and can't stomach the possibility of a long siege, if that's what it takes for victory."

In arrogant response to Escobar's threat, one of the deserting frigates took a potshot at the *Diadem's Glory,* penetrating the hull and venting one deck to space. Then the frigate accelerated away, broadcasting its surrender.

Escobar watched his ships desert, one after another. His commands sounded desperate and pathetic to his own ears. No one even seemed to be listening to him. Ship after ship deactivated their weapons and accepted the General's offer. His fleet was crumbling!

Standing next to him on the flagship's bridge, Bolton stated the obvious. "There is no way we can win this engagement, Redcom. It's your job to salvage the situation and save as many of us as you can. Perhaps Keana can help with the negotiations?"

Escobar glared at him, sputtered, "I will never surrender, Major! I have orders from—"

"We've *lost,* Redcom."

Gail Carrington pushed Bolton's comment even further. She spoke in a withering, disgusted voice. "It's worse than a loss. You've *failed.*"

76

When the secondary attack group finally reached Buktu after a painstaking progression, the old Commodore was impressed with what the remote colony had accomplished.

The stringline hauler decelerated at the end of the last verified segment of the fading iperion path. Scouts had already informed Percival that this next jump would be the final one, and they would reach the frozen planetoid.

Percival's recon pilots had delivered surveillance images of Buktu's industrial facilities, the strip-mining operations on the small frozen moon, the fuel stations, the ice-extraction factories, and the storage depots in orbit. Such intelligence allowed the experienced Commodore to develop an attack plan, which he distributed to every subcommander. His warships were ready to move; the fighter pilots drilled in their simulators, anxious to launch as soon as they arrived at the terminus ring of the long-abandoned iperion path. It was going to be a textbook operation.

As the hauler slowed at the end of the line, the battleships detached from their docking clamps; launching bays disgorged two hundred small fighters, which soared like angry wasps toward the Buktu facilities.

Duff Adkins stood next to the Commodore, shaking his head at the screen. "If I were stuck trying to eke out a living in a squalid place like that, I'd *welcome* an invasion from the Crown Jewels. I would have been on the first ship back home—but these people stayed."

"Buktu is no man's idea of a paradise," Percival admitted. "That's why the Diadem decommissioned the stringline. But that doesn't mean they're happy to see us."

The old warrior stared at the extensive operations, the half-repaired ships in spacedock, the giant orbiting cylinders filled with spacedrive fuel extracted from the isotope-rich glacier fields.

Very little information about Buktu had been available over the past several years. The Diadem had expected the icy settlement to be no more than a ghost town, a desperate tragedy of colonists who could never survive in such an inhospitable place. But he realized that Diadem Michella had been oblivious to the unorthodox and illegal methods that pioneers would utilize under harsh enough circumstances.

"One must admire what they accomplished, Duff. It seems a shame that we have to ruin everything they've built over the years."

Adkins frowned. "But we have our mission, sir! You're not having second thoughts?"

"Regrets, Duff. Not second thoughts. This is just a stepping-stone on our way to General Adolphus, and a victory we are obligated to achieve." He scratched his muttonchop whiskers and gave orders for the operation to commence.

Comm chatter from the Buktu facilities erupted in surprise and panic as soon as the military hauler arrived at the long-abandoned terminus. By then, Percival's warships were already en route to their designated targets. Thirty small attack craft arrowed toward the strip mining operations on the small moon, buzzing the giant machinery on the lunar surface. Another twenty fighters seized the orbiting fuel depots and the construction spacedocks full of half-finished spaceships.

The rest of the attack craft skimmed low over the planetoid's surface, dropping thermal incinerators that exploded on the glacial expanse, melting circular craters into silver lakes that froze quickly. Giant columns of steam rose, and the heat radiated outward in ripples like a stone thrown into a pond. The spectacular explosions were meant to intimidate the people below rather than cause casualties.

Cruising around the planetoid, his scout ships located the stringline path that led to planet Hallholme. Several desperate Buktu ships rushed in to destroy the terminus ring, but the Commodore's fighters cut them off. His first priority was to seize the new stringline connection—his back door to the enemy.

His strike force tightened the noose around Buktu and its moon. Gunners took their stations, all weapons ports loaded with high-powered energy projectiles. Percival knew his gunners were eager to take part, but he hoped they wouldn't have to open fire with their more devastating weapons.

He reminded them over the codecall, "Target carefully. Keep collateral damage to an absolute minimum. This is just a way station—save your firepower for the General's stronghold."

Adkins looked at him. "You haven't even called the Buktu facilities to request their surrender, sir."

Percival shook his head. "Give them another few minutes to understand their situation. It'll be easier to negotiate once they've given up."

The fighters dropped more thermal incinerators onto the lunar facilities, which cracked the rock and ice. Percival had ordered the detonations to be targeted close enough to the industrial operations for the colonists to feel them, but no one should have been killed—or so he hoped.

Finally, he activated the broad-channel codecall and made his formal announcement. Earlier in his career, Percival had worried about the precise verbiage of his surrender demands. During the initial battles against Adolphus, he had scripted his words carefully, aware that the Diadem would replay his speeches for vast audiences. Now, although he was committed to accomplishing his mission, he didn't give a damn about advancing his career. He just wanted to get the job done, and get it done well.

"This is Commodore Percival Hallholme. I warn you to take no aggressive action. Anyone who opens fire on our forces will be destroyed—and you can see that we have the firepower to back up our threat. Please do *not* make this any more difficult than necessary. I now control all Buktu facilities. No one will be harmed, if you cooperate."

A string of defiant curses and insults rippled across the codecall channels. A small mining shuttle from the lunar operations accelerated toward the Constellation battleships and dumped its cargo of ore. Momentum carried the dispersing rocks toward Percival's ships, but their shields deflected all but the largest projectiles.

Before the Commodore could give the order, one of the slightly damaged battleships blasted the mining shuttle. It was overkill, like firing a nuclear warhead at a fly, but he knew the response was necessary. Still, the small explosion was not frightening enough, so he issued further instructions to his fighters. "Blow up one of the fuel depots. Maybe that will shake some sense into them."

High-energy projectiles detonated an orbiting cluster of tanks, and the volatile spacedrive fuel erupted like a nova. Waves of light rippled outward.

He waited a few moments in silence, then said, "Now, let me speak to Administrator Walfor."

A blond man with a rectangular face and severe Nordic features appeared on the screen. "Ian Walfor isn't here—he's on another run. I'm Erik Anderlos, second in command." He puffed out his chest. "You have no claim here. We're an independent settlement. The Constellation cut all ties with us years ago and abandoned this colony—we can show you the documentary evidence. Diadem Michella washed her hands of us. And now she sends an invasion force?"

"You are allied with the rebel General Adolphus, and as such you stand charged with treason against the Constellation. We hereby commandeer these facilities for the Diadem's war effort. Within the hour, you will submit a full list of personnel, military assets, and industrial operations."

Anderlos crossed his arms over his chest and lifted his chin. "I will not!"

Percival sighed. "You're fortunate I'm a man who believes in second chances, Mr. Anderlos, so I'll give you the opportunity to reconsider. And if you still refuse, I will instruct my ships to blow up something else. Then I'll ask again, and again, and each time, I'll punctuate my demands with more destruction—and the regrettable deaths that will be associated with it. The process may take a bit of time, but we both know the end result. It all depends on how much destruction and death you want to witness before you give up."

On the screen next to his chair, Percival received a quick summary from his scouts: seven FTL ships were in the spacedock facilities in various stages of repair, none of them ready to launch. He doubted General Adolphus would have left *all* of his worlds so unprotected, but Buktu was an outlying facility with no direct iperion path from the Crown Jewels, and his defenses were spread thin across the Deep Zone. A commander with limited resources had to relegate his assets to the most vulnerable points, and Adolphus would have concentrated his defenses on the most likely targets, including planet Hallholme. Under similar circumstances, Percival would have made the same decision himself.

He drew his thick brows together, making his next calculation. The spacedrive fuel might prove useful, but he didn't think the Diadem would want those old patchwork ships. He glanced to the gunner on the bridge. "Target one of the vessels in the repair dock and destroy it."

"Yes, Commodore!" The gunner fell to the task with eager efficiency.

Erik Anderlos began yelling on the open codecall line, but Percival did not rescind his order. High-powered projectiles tore apart one of the bulky vessels that hung in the orbiting framework. The explosions destroyed the ship and damaged the spacedock, causing it to reel out of orbit.

"Damn you! I had a repair crew aboard that ship! Ten men and women! Why didn't you—"

"But I did, Mr. Anderlos. That was your third chance. I'll pick another target if you force me to. Perhaps one of the settlements beneath your planetoid's ice sheet? We have deep-penetrating explosives."

From the tracking grid on the screen, Percival knew that was the location from which Anderlos was transmitting. After another fifteen tense seconds, the Buktu administrator capitulated.

❧

In regimented formation, personnel transport ships landed on Buktu to gather up the prisoners. Considering the ambitious extent of the operations, the colony had a surprisingly small complement of workers. Only a few hundred people in charge of all these facilities!

Meanwhile, the military hauler that had carried the attack force along the rough path from Sonjeera now repositioned to the DZ terminus ring, ready to depart for planet Hallholme.

Ian Walfor had apparently gone on his own run, delivering supplies and equipment to Candela. Other captives informed Percival's interrogators that the direct journey from Buktu to planet Hallholme would take three days. Percival had expected a shorter transit, but the time was acceptable; at least now they were on their way to the endgame.

Percival did not leave the bridge to accept the formal surrender of Erik Anderlos; he didn't consider that necessary. Duff Adkins took care of the administrative details, crowding the prisoners into empty mess halls and auditoriums. As the last captives were loaded aboard, Percival felt a sickening sense of déjà vu.

Adkins noticed his concern. "Do you really think you'll need all these hostages, Commodore?"

"I might, although I doubt the General will make the same mistake twice."

Once the Constellation warships returned to their docking clamps, the stringline hauler prepared to depart. The Commodore stared ahead at the starfield as they began to accelerate out of the Buktu system.

"We're on the road to Hellhole," Adkins said, in a poor attempt at humor.

"That we are, Duff."

77

No time to lose.

Within an hour of when Ian Walfor showed her the images of the incoming asteroids, Tanja Hu dispatched an emergency message pod to the main Hellhole hub, describing the asteroid crisis and requesting help. "Send evacuation ships fast, General—as many as possible. We have to move our entire population off the planet."

But even a message pod would take two days to reach the Hellhole hub, and he would need some time—a day?—to gather vessels, then another two days for them to return. The rescue vessels would barely arrive before the asteroids slammed into Candela, and the physical process of shuttling thousands of people to orbit and loading them aboard ships would itself take days.

She couldn't imagine how she could possibly do it.

For backup, she dispatched another message pod to Cles, to which she had just connected via her new stringline, but Cles had almost no ships. And she could not send a direct communication to any other DZ planets without going through Hellhole. There wasn't enough time!

Nevertheless, she had to do what she could with the ships she already had available at her planet. *Her* planet. Thanks to the fear of Constellation reprisal, the General had left another fifteen guardian ships at Candela, and she had the six ships she had recently received from Theser. They were vessels large enough to hold tens of thousands of people. It was a start.

"We don't have time to hold meetings and dither about a decision," she told Ian Walfor in her office. "If we really do have less than a week, there's not going to be enough time to round everyone up and evacuate, even with perfect cooperation. According to our most recent census, Candela has about three hundred thousand colonists, but that information understates the numbers."

Walfor was surprised, since he knew every single person on Buktu—all three hundred of them. Tanja shook her head in dismay. "We didn't bother to find everyone and count them because the Diadem would just tax us more if we did."

Next order of business, she transmitted the crisis announcement across Candela, requesting everyone's help. Tanja went to her office's largest viewing window, gazed out on the blue-water harbor and the floating high-rise buildings; right now, everyone went about their daily business, crossing the linked walkways, taking ferries to shore. That would all change soon enough.

Although Walfor admired her businesslike reaction, he lifted his eyebrows at the planetwide broadcast. "This could start a panic."

"If I hide it from them, it'll start a panic, too. I'll opt for trusting my people instead." She knew that was what Bebe would have counseled. "We need their help."

Motioning to him, she led the way up a spiral staircase that emerged on the rooftop of her administration building, and they sat at a table in hazy sunlight, with a gentle, warm breeze blowing. It was so pleasant here, and so illusory.

"Many of the distant hill villages might not get the message at all, and the people won't know they're in danger until they see the asteroids bearing down on them. And even if they do find out in advance, they won't be able to get to the spaceport in time. But even if everyone makes it to the spaceport in time, we don't have enough ships to carry everybody."

Walfor shifted uneasily next to her. A black stubble of beard covered his lower face. "In the meantime, let's worry about the ones we *can* save, take care of them, and then see how many more we can reasonably round up."

Tanja felt hot under the hazy sunlight of the rooftop gardens. The breeze picked up, carrying a dash of warm sprinkles, but the brief rain shower passed. Oddly, she began to feel energized again, gaining the strength she needed to face yet another problem. She had erased the dark bitterness that had caused so many painful repercussions, but even so she couldn't believe how things kept getting worse and worse. Each time she dealt with a crisis, a bigger one arose to take its place, as if they were all lined up waiting for their turn to strike. Now she had to find a way to save her people.

Walfor slumped in a chair on the rooftop, showing his exhaustion. "More than three hundred thousand! Where are we going to put them?"

"We'll scrounge as many ships as we can," Tanja said. "Anything to get people off the surface of Candela, even if it's just to hold them in orbit, because nobody will survive the impact shock wave."

She had already looked at first-order simulations: The double strike would be a hammer blow on the landmasses, enough to flatten forests, shatter mountains, and pulverize any creatures on the ground, followed by flash fires that would sweep across the landscape; plumes of ejecta would rain down on the surface. Then would come storms, volcanic eruptions, quakes—years of incredible upheavals. No one left down there would survive.

"Once we leave Candela, we leave for good," she said.

They went together to the administrative records section of the building, where Tanja and Ian scanned the inventory of Candela's ships, *all* craft of any kind that could fly out of Candela's gravity well, even just to low orbit. "How many passengers can your ship hold, Ian?" They stood at a table with papers strewn across it.

"Twenty-five in a pinch, but not comfortably."

"How about fifty if they stand shoulder-to-shoulder? Can you get off the ground?"

He nodded. "We can put thousands in your stringline hub. They'll just have to last for a little while after the asteroids hit—and hope rescue ships arrive."

As she considered the disheartening numbers, Tanja fervently wished Bebe Nax was back at her side. She paused as a shudder of grief went through her. Outside, she saw the calm waters of the harbor, the steep forested hills, and the ruins of the funicular rail that had been built by the previous administrator.

She felt as if a trapdoor had dropped out from under her. "We're on our own, aren't we, Ian?" she said in a quiet voice.

"We live in the Deep Zone, my dear." He rubbed her shoulders. "We've always had to survive with the resources at hand. But I agree, this is more challenging than usual."

She straightened, focused her attention, driving away all her distractions. "I want a constant stream of humanity out of here, shuttle after shuttle filled with people for the next seven days."

"More like six days and fifteen hours," Walfor said.

"We evacuate Saporo first, because the people are already here. Order everyone to the spaceport—I want our first shuttleloads of refugees to head up to the military vessels within the hour."

At her urgent summons, district administrators began to arrive at the headquarters building, one by one. Tanja did not delay the meeting for any stragglers, simply gave instructions to each man and woman as they arrived. Because of her initial emergency broadcast, thousands of people had heard of the imminent crisis, although the reality had not yet sunk in.

"We need organizers," Tanja said, "and security personnel to crack down on unruly crowds and riots. Anybody who causes trouble, damages facilities, or slows down our operations can cost lives. I hate to say this, but authorize security to shoot if necessary." She presented the calculations, after studying how many ground-to-orbit vessels they had available, as well as questionable fuel supplies for the operation.

Young Jacque came into the records section, looking for her, clearly alarmed. "This is an emergency," she told him, sweeping the boy into her arms. "We're sending you up to orbit, where you'll be out of danger." She lowered her voice and held him close. "I've got to make sure you're safe."

"Can I watch the asteroids come in from there?"

"Yes—a lot of us will."

"I'll make sure he gets off-planet," Walfor promised. "You have enough to worry about down here."

"Thank you." She touched the boy's shoulder, desperate to keep him by her side, wanting to be reassured that he was all right, but she needed to get him as far away from the cataclysm as possible, as quickly as possible. "Pack a bag as fast as you can, a small one. Take only the most important things, because it's going to be crowded. We'll find a new home."

"Will it be as nice as Candela?" Jacque asked.

"I can't promise that, but let's hope so." She kissed him on the forehead, surprising herself at the show of affection. "Now get ready. Everything is going to be frantic for the next few days."

"We also have cargo upboxes that are already vacuum sealed and can hold people," Walfor suggested. "We could add oxygen tanks, heaters, enough to keep people alive for a short time in orbit. And we have the big ore ships from the iperion mines. They've been delivering load after load up to your new stringline hub."

"They're contaminated with iperion! We can't use those ships to carry people."

He had a hard look on his face. "In that case, maybe we should have them haul up as much iperion as we can possibly extract from the mines."

"We can't worry about iperion—we've got to evacuate the people! Even now, we don't have enough time or ships—"

Walfor raised a hand. "I know, and I feel for them, too. But Candela is the Deep Zone's only known source of iperion. Without that, we can't maintain the stringlines. The whole DZ network will unravel, and that could lead to the collapse of our government."

She pondered this. "All right. They'll step up production for the next few days while we figure out the details of the evacuation plan." She shook her head. "In the final day or so, though, we're going to crowd the contaminated ore boxes with people, if there's any room. So long as they disembark in a relatively short time, most of them will recover from the iperion exposure, and it could save another few thousand people."

Walfor agreed. "If their only other alternative is to be dead, they'll take the chance."

Even with the expected wrinkles and snags of getting such a large operation under way, fifty flights went up during the first half day, carrying five thousand people to the orbiting military vessels. For the time being, the guardian ships carried only skeleton crews, so there were plenty of available cabins, common rooms, and even general cargo vaults. Tanja was willing to pack the vessels like old-fashioned sardine cans, if need be, and more people would be piled onto the stringline hub, anything to buy a day or two.

Tanja and her advisers determined that there *might* be enough time for one round-trip to Hellhole, if they left immediately, disembarked the thousands of evacuees there within hours, and returned at full speed to pick up more survivors. When two ships were completely packed, she sent them flying back down the stringline to Hellhole.

But afterward, when there was no possibility of later ships making a round-trip in time and saving more people, she declared that none of the military vessels would depart from the Candela hub until the last possible moment. Even when they were supposedly full, she would keep cramming people aboard, as long as the shuttles brought more refugees. She commandeered all the planet's fuel supplies and devoted them to the operation; she seized every functional ship and required that they operate constant flights with the shortest possible turnaround. When one captain complained about the draconian measures, Tanja ordered her vessel seized and the captain's name placed further down on the evacuation list. The others learned their lesson.

When she killed Governor Undine, Tanja had been ruthless and implacable; now her unwavering hardness would give the people of Candela a chance at survival.

She hoped General Adolphus would receive her emergency message in time. In the best possible scenario, his rescue ships would arrive with only a day to spare. If they arrived at all . . .

78

eneral Tiber Adolphus waited only an hour, after much of the Constellation fleet had already surrendered, before he transmitted his ultimatum to the *Diadem's Glory*. On the bridge of the flagship, Escobar cringed when he heard the brutal instructions.

"Redcom Hallholme, you are to direct your remaining vessels into low orbit, where they will wait to be boarded. All Constellation soldiers will be taken to the surface and processed. Those who cooperate will receive full rations of food and water, as well as medical attention."

On the codecall screen, the square-jawed Adolphus wore the familiar deep-blue uniform jacket Escobar had seen in the historical records of his surrender to Commodore Percival Hallholme. On the image now, the rebel leader looked freshly shaved, alert, implacable, and menacing.

He continued, "For the formalities, Redcom, and for history's sake, I must insist upon your unconditional surrender. You will come over to my flagship and present your ceremonial sword. I'm sure you're familiar with the procedure."

Escobar was enraged to hear this. He felt smaller now and more adrift than during those bleak days when his fleet was marooned in empty space. He could hear his father's voice scolding him from the pages of his military journals: "By the time your opponent feels confident enough to *ask* for your surrender, you have already been defeated." He didn't think even the old Commodore, with all of his legendary military genius, could have found a way out of this trap. On the other hand, the old man would never have made such blunders in the first place.

Escobar kept his transmitting system blank and turned to his bridge crew. "Options! How can we turn this around?"

"I don't believe we can, Redcom," Bolton said. "The numbers are clear. Nineteen of our ships remain loyal to us, but forty-six have already surrendered to Adolphus, and five were destroyed in skirmishes. General Adolphus still has forty-five of his own ships, all fully armed, fueled, and crewed, and he's quickly putting our own captured ships into service against us. A total of ninety-one ships against our nineteen. It's simply not possible, sir."

While Escobar kept his end of the transmission line blocked, General Adolphus began broadcasting his own images for everyone to see, real-time video of shuttle after shuttle of captured Constellation soldiers being taken down to the Michella Town spaceport. The prisoners of war were escorted to makeshift mess halls and received platters of rations. Nothing extravagant, simply preserved military meals—nevertheless, it looked like a feast compared with the rigors of starvation in space.

Before rebel technicians could punch through the codecall blocks on the *Diadem's Glory*, Escobar opened the connection himself to show his own image. He glared into the screen while Adolphus spoke.

"I am providing for every one of your soldiers, Redcom, but before we grant relief to the crews aboard your holdout ships, I require a formal surrender ceremony. You have been a worthy opponent, and I bear you no personal enmity, but I suggest you accept my offer before your own flagship crew mutinies."

"I refuse," Escobar said automatically and added with false bravado, "My remaining warships have ample supplies."

"Very well." Adolphus shrugged. "If you believe discipline trumps hunger, we can keep you bottled up for as long as you like. We're patient. Take your time."

Escobar realized he was hyperventilating; he could barely see or concentrate. He knew he would have to concede sooner or later. Adolphus's stringline facilities were too well guarded for Escobar's handful of loyal ships to capture one of them. And the new stringline had no value as an escape route, since it led to only a deep-space graveyard.

Thoughts sped through his mind like weapons fire. How many more deaths did he want on his conscience? He knew the General was not exaggerating: the threat of a mutiny, the constantly playing images of well-fed prisoners, the bounty of colony food offered to anyone who laid down their arms, were irresistible to starving crewmembers who could not endure for another day, much less weeks. General Adolphus could indeed wait as long as he liked.

Escobar turned to his rival's face on the screen. "All right, damn you! We'll come over to your flagship."

Adolphus gave a nod and a congenial smile. "I am glad you've seen reason. Shall I send a shuttle for you?"

"We can get there ourselves," Escobar snapped. He tried to end the transmission, but for several moments his opponent's codecall override kept it open, until it finally shut down.

⁓

Back when Gail Carrington was forcibly sedated, Escobar had read her private orders from Lord Riomini. He knew she had been instructed to kill him should he fail—and by any definition he had surely failed. Now, in his dim quarters where he prepared himself for surrender and shame, Escobar was half-convinced she would murder him in front of everyone. Perhaps that would be for the best anyway.

This defeat was entirely Escobar's fault, and because of him, a full fleet had fallen into the hands of the enemy. Because of him, the Constellation might well lose the war, thanks to all those warships he had inadvertently handed to the Deep Zone Defense Forces. The General would have enough military might to overthrow the Diadem and her government. And once word of the humiliating surrender ceremony got back to Sonjeera, even his father's legendary triumphs would be swept aside. Escobar's own sons would grow up in disgrace—if either of them survived this revolution.

Carrington and Major Crais entered his quarters. Escobar rose stiffly from his desk chair and looked at the ceremonial sword hanging on the wall. He remembered when the old Commodore had given it to him before Escobar departed on this mission. The library screen, where he had viewed so many of his father's exploits, was blank.

He turned to Carrington, his hands at his sides and fingers loose, as if to make it clear that he had no weapon. He tilted his chin up in a gesture that might have been interpreted as pride, but Carrington probably saw it as baring his throat. He remembered how she had slit the jugular of the naïve young comm-officer before he could send a distress message.

Maybe that was how she intended to kill him as well.

Before she could make a move, though, he surprised her by saying, "I understand that we must snatch these ships from the jaws of our enemy, at all costs. As Redcom, I have access to certain fleet command codes that are not in any standard manual. I . . . I still have a way to turn this around."

Carrington seemed surprised. "I'm listening, Redcom."

He looked away from the quiet Bolton Crais. "The majority of our troops have deserted us already, and the General demands our surrender. But I refuse to allow our remaining fleet to become part of his Deep Zone Defense Force. I'll destroy the ships first."

Bolton said, "He already *has* most of our fleet, sir. The ships are in low orbit, being boarded. What can we do about it now?"

"We can render them useless," Escobar said with a hard smile. He felt a chill go down his back.

"Continue," Carrington said, as if she were his superior.

"For logistical override, all of the command computers in this battle group are linked and accessible from the *Diadem's Glory*. Those systems were installed and recalibrated at Aeroc before the fleet departed for the Sonjeera hub."

"I know—I handled a lot of it," Bolton said.

Escobar drew a breath. "I can trigger a cascade shutdown throughout all of our ships. There is a command virus embedded deep in the operating computers, and I can render the engines useless. The ships will drop out of orbit and burn up. Those soldiers who can't get to the evac pods will die, but at least history will remember that we did the right thing."

"Acceptable, Redcom." Carrington nodded. "You have surprised me."

Escobar felt sick, though, after he had fought so hard to keep his soldiers alive, and now he would be the direct cause of their deaths. It was an ignominious way to end his own career, and his life. . . .

Bolton had paled, and he fidgeted as he wrestled with his own thoughts. "But if our goal is to prevent General Adolphus from commandeering our warships, it may not be necessary to slaughter our personnel as well. The deserters are being taken off, but those who remain aboard our ships are the most loyal fighters, the ones who refused to surrender. They don't deserve that."

"It is their duty to die," Carrington said, as if the answer were obvious.

"But it's not necessary!" Bolton said. "Allow me to modify the plan: I can add a delay to the virus trigger. Give the General enough time to evacuate our personnel, let him put his own people aboard—and *then* the virus can activate the autopilot. I can reprogram it. The result is the same: Our ships will still burn up in the atmosphere."

Escobar seized on the hope. "I have enough blood on my hands already. That seems like a good solution."

Carrington looked as if she would argue with the idea, but then her thin smile was like a razor slice on a bare throat. "And by that time, our captured ships will be infested by *his own people*. Yes, Major Bolton, I can see the advantage in that."

Escobar felt some of the weight lift from his chest. "And the General won't be able to do anything about it." He would still be a prisoner, but his plan would snatch the prize right out of rebel hands in a bold final gesture. "We will set the virus timer before we go to our surrender ceremony. It's not the victory I had hoped for, but it will deny the advantage to the enemy."

Carrington still looked dissatisfied. "We must do more than that, gentlemen. We have to eliminate General Adolphus himself, or all our other efforts will be irrelevant."

79

After so many recent setbacks, Diadem Michella's subjects had begun to grumble more loudly. The disruption of stringline traffic through the Sonjeera hub had been a disaster, and her engineers were working to exhaustion—and astonishing expense—to reconnect the iperion lines throughout the Crown Jewels. Also, despite vague excuses the government released to the media, the people knew the war against General Adolphus wasn't going well, and that the original fleet had been lost. Not-so-discreet mutterings among rebel sympathizers were mounting.

Ishop had provided her with an excellent distraction, and he knew he would be rewarded for it.

With great publicity and indignation, Michella would expose Lady Enva Tazaar's involvement in the assassination attempt and her collusion with General Adolphus. She was the perfect scapegoat.

By a stroke of good luck, Lady Tazaar had been on Sonjeera when the alien psychic blast severely damaged the hub and disrupted stringline travel. She could not go home to Orsini, and the Diadem's guards arrested her—in public, with many media imagers in place; they timed their operation well, bursting through the door during a lavish dinner party and evichord musical performance. The startled noblewoman was hauled away to prison—for effect, Ishop suggested she be placed in the same cell where Governor Goler had been held. Tazaar's party guests were questioned and eventually released, though under a cloud of suspicion. They helped spread the rumors.

The media played the story constantly, and Ishop arranged for the proof of Enva Tazaar's conspiracy to be released in several stages, each piece more damning than the previous, which kept the scandal alive and at the center of attention. The distraction gave the Diadem breathing space to have her crews restore commercial traffic among the core worlds.

Though Ishop knew Enva Tazaar was guilty, he felt a twinge of remorse, considering what had happened to the Osheers seven centuries ago. It was also a shame that Enva was so strikingly beautiful and intelligent; he felt sure they could have made a fine team, two aristocratic lines raising themselves to great heights. Even Laderna approved of his assessment. In fact, Enva's overall scheme to ally herself with the rebel General, assassinate old Michella, and reach an accord with the breakaway Deep Zone worlds had a great deal of merit. Secretly, Ishop and Laderna admired her large-scale planning.

But he chose to look on the bright side. With the Tazaars stripped of their family wealth, their holdings on planet Orsini would be ripe for the taking. And once the nobles accepted Ishop back into their fold, he was going to need a planet to rule. Yes, the timing would be perfect. . . .

The sentencing of Enva Tazaar was such an important event that Diadem Michella chose to officiate over the punishment herself. For the occasion Ishop wore his finest suit with gold buttons, part of his new wardrobe of expensively tailored outfits; Laderna said it made him look like the nobleman he actually was. As part of his reward for service, the Diadem had granted him a seat of honor in the front row for the proceedings. He sat there now, smiling and proud, gazing up at the old woman. But he was inexplicably nervous, and he felt perspiration on his smooth, clean-shaven scalp, as if he were the one accused rather than Lady Tazaar. Laderna sat in the general audience chamber as well, several rows back.

The immense entrance doors swung open, and a hush fell over the chamber as four soldiers in dress military uniforms escorted the prisoner in. Enva Tazaar attempted to walk with her head held high, but the heavy symbolic chains weighed her down. This once elegant noble-woman wore no gown or expensive jewelry, but rather a drab brown prison jumpsuit; her long blonde hair was matted, and she looked gaunt. Ishop saw the flicker of her gaze, the haunted aura of fear.

The evidence against her had flooded public broadcasts; all nobles in the chamber had seen the complete classified report (which had also been leaked to the media). Enva Tazaar's attorneys had filed protests and appeals, but they were merely pro forma gestures, not expected to accomplish anything.

As the prisoner shuffled forward, already ruined, the noise in the chamber increased; some nobles shouted insults, and Ishop noted that many of them were the same people who had been guests at her dinner party.

"Traitor!"

"Strip her naked and parade her through the streets!"

"Kill her!"

"Make her suffer!"

Enva halted at the foot of the Star Throne, and Ishop could not help but think of images from the much-publicized treason trial of General Adolphus more than a decade ago. She stared defiantly at the Diadem and did not plead for mercy. She had enough political savvy to know she had been caught in an unbreakable trap. As Enva held her head high, Ishop could not suppress his admiration for her.

Her father, Azio Tazaar, had been one of the early victims on Ishop's list; by murdering the dyspeptic old blowhard, he had been responsible for placing her in power. She was magnificent now . . . but he had also engineered her downfall.

Seeing this broken noblewoman made him ponder how *his* Osheer ancestor had reacted when he was hauled before the ruling council, disgraced and stripped of his noble titles and wealth, hearing the decree that his descendants were to be cast out of the ranks of nobility for seven centuries. His hands clenched into fists.

The Diadem maintained a long and hateful stare, then said in a measured tone, "Lady Tazaar, you attempted to have me killed, and now I shall return the favor. You wanted to seize the Star Throne for yourself, and worst of all, you plotted with the Constellation's greatest enemy."

The anger rolling through the nobles sounded like the threatening growler storm Ishop had endured on his first visit to Hellhole.

"Every member of the Council has had a chance to review the files, as well as the ridiculous rebuttals your attorneys submitted. As Diadem, I am ready to make my pronouncement." She sat back on the Star Throne, then surprised Ishop by looking directly at him. "I must express gratitude to my faithful aide Ishop Heer for offering a neat solution. His office discovered a useful and interesting clause in ancient Constellation law. We had all but forgotten about the provision, but it seems most appropriate now."

Ishop maintained a demure, respectful smile as everyone looked at him, but he had no idea what the Diadem was talking about. His heart pounded hard.

Michella continued, "There is an old proviso in the Constellation Charter that can be used in extreme circumstances, when a noble so significantly breaches acceptable standards of behavior that simple censure will not suffice." She squared her bony shoulders, made her voice more ponderous. "Enva Tazaar, you are stripped of your family wealth, including planet Orsini, but because your crimes against the Constellation are so extreme, your family must pay the price as well. Therefore, all members of the Tazaar family and their descendants are banned from the ranks of nobility for a period of *seven hundred years*."

Ishop fought down a gasp. He had not made the suggestion to Michella, but suddenly he knew that Laderna must have done it. He turned from side to side, looking at the faces crowded in the general audience chamber, until he spotted her. She was grinning at him.

Laderna was such a dedicated partner, devoting her energies to advancing his cause. Now he easily grasped her logic in making this revelation to the Diadem: By pointing out the forgotten proviso in the Charter that endorsed banishment for seven centuries, Laderna was setting the stage for Ishop to step forward with his own claim. Since the Diadem now used the proviso to punish Enva Tazaar, she therefore explicitly reaffirmed its legality. Thus, when Ishop presented his own case, the nobles would have no excuse not to follow the same proviso.

Even so, he had a knot in his stomach as he watched the heavy blow of disgrace fall on Enva Tazaar, and saw the dark, hate-filled expression she could not conceal. He knew this was exactly what had happened to his own noble family. At some point seven centuries hence, would a resourceful Tazaar descendant write a list of his or her own that included one of Ishop's family members? It was too far in the future to think about. Seven hundred years was a long time.

After the jeers and catcalls subsided, Diadem Michella continued, smiling now. "Prisoner Tazaar, criminal sentencing will commence within the week, after I consult with my trusted nobles." The old woman waved an arm dismissively, signifying that the soldiers were to remove Enva from the chamber. "You have stained Constellation history and poisoned your own bloodline for centuries. At least you can serve as a warning for anyone else planning treachery."

Amid cheering and clapping, Ishop knew that Michella's consultation with the nobles would be nothing more than symbolic. In fact, he was sure they would all endorse the Diadem's suggestion of a death sentence. Lady Tazaar's fate was a foregone conclusion.

But the odd displacement in his feelings gave him pause, and he made another consideration. Perhaps he should take a different stance himself, since he knew what his own family had endured for seven hundred years. Was it a twinge of conscience? Ishop wasn't certain, because he had never known what a conscience felt like.

❧

A day later, Sonjeera was shocked when "Adolphus loyalists" succeeded in removing Enva Tazaar from her cell and slipping her out of the highest security zone. It was a daring midnight escape, which showed extensive knowledge of the Council City prison system and secret-access passages in the bowels of the ancient building. The uproar and further scandal dominated the public's attention so much that the Diadem's announcement of several restored Crown Jewel stringline routes went unremarked.

Ishop had hired his freelance team with great care and briefed the operatives with every detail they needed. He had himself slipped in and out of the noble prison chambers many times before, most recently when he'd murdered Louis de Carre. This time he did not inform Laderna of his plans, though, still fearing she might have some innate jealousy toward Enva Tazaar. Instead, he took care of every detail himself.

He did not breathe a sigh of relief until he received word that Enva Tazaar had been slipped onto a small black-market trade ship and whisked away to the Deep Zone world of Tehila. The disgraced noblewoman never even knew the identity of her surprise benefactor, nor would she unless Ishop found a way to call in a favor. With a little rewriting of events and payoffs in the proper places, he might even find "proof" that Enva was innocent after all, and return her to prominence in the Constellation—when the time was right. If that ever proved beneficial.

With the task completed, he eliminated his well-paid operatives quickly and efficiently, tying up the loose ends.

Very soon, with Orsini and all the Tazaar holdings available, and with Diadem Michella fully convinced of his worth, Ishop Heer would formally enter the ranks of nobility and take his long-overdue place.

It was better than a fairy tale.

80

Within five hours of Escobar Hallholme's acquiescence, General Adolphus prepared to travel up to the *Jacob*, where he would meet with his enemy and accept his surrender. Though he knew the significance of what was about to occur, Adolphus did not relish the humiliation of Commodore Hallholme's son.

The General was not a vindictive person. He simply wanted the problem resolved and the Deep Zone planets kept safe from harm.

Escobar's task force had been overconfident, and so foolish in their assumptions that they did not adequately prepare for battle. Without doubt, the Redcom would have ordered *his* execution upon capture, or perhaps brought him back to Sonjeera in chains so the Diadem could make an even greater spectacle of him.

At Elba, as he put on formal clothing, Sophie seemed more satisfied by the impending surrender ceremony than he was, but she did not gloat, either. The DZ worlds had already suffered too much pain, and they both felt compassion for the haggard and malnourished soldiers aboard the Constellation fleet. When he'd cut the stringline, Adolphus had never intended to put even his enemies through miserable months of deprivation. He knew how much the soldiers must hate him. Nevertheless, he had defeated them, and they were now his prisoners.

Sophie's workers were already fencing off a large compound in the

Slickwater Springs valley, where the prisoners would be held. They quickly erected tents, supply stations, prefabricated shelters—watched over by a contingent of armed guards.

"Those pampered Constellation troops don't understand how rough Hellhole can be," she said as she helped him with his uniform. "They might try to escape into the wilderness, thinking they can live off the land. Ha! The fences and guards will be mainly to save those people from their own stupidity." She straightened his jacket, stepped back to appraise him. "You look so distinguished and handsome. I'm glad I bought back your jacket—it was worth every penny."

Craig Jordan transmitted from the orbiting flagship that the Deck 3 meeting chamber was ready. The surrender ceremony could have been held in the much larger all-hands auditorium with the General's loyal soldiers crowded in to watch the humiliation of the Constellation commander. Such an event would have twisted the knife, but Adolphus decided it was not necessary for Escobar Hallholme to suffer such indignity. Instead, he would broadcast the ceremony widely, and the inhabitants of Michella Town would watch and cheer the General's victory.

An hour before the shuttle's departure to rendezvous with the flagship, Devon and Antonia arrived at Elba, accompanied by Keana Duchenet. Along with all the shadow-Xayans here, they had been affected by the psychic backlash from the converts' horrific deaths on Candela, which had occurred only moments after their gigantic release of telemancy to stabilize the planet's seismic upheaval. Devon described the mental blow to all of them as an embrace of razors. The shadow-Xayans on Hellhole had been drained of energy and now struggled to regain their strength.

As they arrived, the General could tell from Keana's animated and worried expression that her own personality was back in control of her mind, rather than the alien presence. "My husband is with the captured fleet?" She looked confused. "Why would Bolton come here?"

"He asked about you," Adolphus said, "wanted to know if you are safe."

Keana bit her lower lip. "I thought he wouldn't even notice I had gone away. We've led separate lives for so long."

"He *is* still your husband, Keana," Sophie said.

The Diadem's daughter shook her head, looking puzzled. "I must have disappointed him so much. Bolton's not a bad man, and I didn't mean to hurt him. We were both trapped in a sham marriage that was just a token alliance of powerful families. He's done nice things for me before, but I didn't think he cared much."

"Well, he seems to," Sophie said. "If he came all this way."

"It does suggest an interesting opportunity for us," Adolphus pointed out. "If Bolton Crais is concerned about you personally, Keana, maybe the two of you could negotiate some sort of détente between the Deep Zone and the Crown Jewels. He might be able to make Diadem Michella listen."

"My mother listens to no one, but I'd like to attend the surrender ceremony nonetheless. I'd like an opportunity to speak with him."

Devon and Antonia had offered to represent the shadow-Xayans during the surrender formalities; Adolphus had considered inviting Encix as well, but didn't want to tip his hand about the aliens too soon. Keana Duchenet, a known convert, would be enough of a surprise.

Sophie sounded cheery as she hurried them to the Michella Town spaceport. "We can't finish the surrender ceremony until we start it. Let's get going. I'm sure Redcom Hallholme has other things to do today."

⁓

Only moments after the General arrived aboard the *Jacob*, an emergency message drone hurtled in along the stringline from Candela. The recorded message from Administrator Tanja Hu broadcast on all frequencies as soon as it arrived at the Hellhole hub. "This is Candela, declaring an emergency!"

The General felt an immediate chill, afraid the Black Lord had somehow managed to dispatch an attack fleet after all, despite the damage the telemancy blast had inflicted on the Sonjeera hub.

On the imager, Tanja's expression was drawn and urgent. "Two massive asteroids are on a collision course with this planet, with impacts to occur within a week. We are in the midst of a full-scale evacuation, but we don't have the capacity. Send evacuation ships fast, General—as many as possible. We have to get our entire population off the planet." Her voice hesitated, then cracked as she continued. "Please help us, General."

He sat up straight. Asteroids on a collision course? "That's not possible. Two at once, with impact in a few days?" But he knew Tanja Hu was not prone to wild fantasies. "We don't even have time to verify her message."

Craig Jordan was astonished and skeptical. "It could be a trick to lure away our defense ships, sir."

Sophie looked at him. "We have to send everything we can, Tiber. We've defeated the Constellation fleet. How could this be a trick?"

He spread his hands, standing on the *Jacob*'s bridge. "All our crews have their hands full here. Most of my personnel are heading over to the captured ships for retooling."

Jordan shook his head. "I still don't like it, sir. The story's not believable."

Sophie crossed her arms over her chest, and he had seen that stubborn expression before. "We won't be without ships. We've seized the enemy fleet and can convert them for our own defenses. Meanwhile, you have at least twenty large vessels you can dispatch right away—and you'll barely have time as it is. No other DZ world can send help in time."

Tanja's message pod contained images of the two oncoming asteroids, each one gigantic enough to wipe out most life on Candela. Adolphus reviewed the data, knew he had no choice. "I've got to help her. If it's a trick, then I will use my wits and resources to deal with it. If those asteroids really are hurtling in . . . I can't risk being wrong. We need to save as many people as possible."

Without further delay, he summoned two of the captured stringline haulers his military had just brought in from the new terminus at the edge of the system. "Load them with as many available ships as will fit in the docking clamps and launch—two hours maximum." He shook his head, feeling naked to send away so many ships, but he could not turn a blind eye to such a desperate plea from one of his own planets.

He focused attention back to the ceremony at hand. "Now let's get this surrender over with."

⨋

Aboard the *Diadem's Glory*, Bolton had a final meeting with the Redcom and Carrington before they departed for the General's flagship.

Bolton had little advice to offer his commander; his mind was exhausted from weeks of frantically seeking solutions to critical situations.

During their many weeks of desperate isolation, Escobar Hallholme had implemented the ruthless but necessary measures for survival. The Redcom would take the credit for them all, and the blame—with Bolton's blessing. Even if this had been a flawless operation, with a complete victory over the rebels, Bolton would not have wanted any glory when they returned to Sonjeera.

And this had most certainly *not* been a flawless operation.

At least they could take satisfaction now that the last-ditch computer virus had been transmitted, and Bolton had bought the Constellation soldiers enough time to get to the surface. When the captured fleet began to surge out of control, it would be a dramatic and satisfying blow.

After their formal surrender, Redcom Hallholme, Carrington, and all surviving crewmembers would be out of the conflict, held prisoner until someone else defeated the General, or until some sort of peace accord was negotiated. Bolton dreaded living on that hellish planet, but took comfort from the fact that at least he might see Keana again, if he could find her. He would look into her eyes, talk to her, and try to figure out whether she was truly happy with the strange alien cult. Bolton had been unable to give his wife what she needed, but he didn't begrudge her a chance for a contented life.

In his ready room, Escobar looked broken and miserable. "There is no way I can paint a cheerful picture of our situation. We've been soundly beaten, and I take responsibility as the fleet commander. But now I have to face facts and think about my soldiers. As the one in charge, my first duty is to keep the rest of them alive. I already have too much blood on my hands. Maybe saving them is one way I can earn back a glimmer of honor." He heaved a sigh, and his shoulders slumped. "I will be satisfied with the small victory of keeping Adolphus from using our fleet. Thank you, Major Crais, for your modifications to the scuttling virus."

"You are both fools, too willing to accept easy solutions." Gail Carrington's glare flashed from Escobar to Bolton. "Your first duty is to the Constellation and the Diadem, not to pamper your soldiers. They all knew the risks when they joined this expedition, and all were willing to die in order to make the mission succeed. We have a chance to cut off the head of the monster that threatens to devour our way of life." She raised her voice. "And we *must* do so!"

"I've already instituted our plan," Escobar said. "The virus will activate within hours of the surrender ceremony, and our ships will reel out of control and burn up in the atmosphere. The General will not have our fleet."

Carrington lashed out at him. "The enemy won't be able to use our warships, but neither will the Constellation fleet! Our forces will be crippled regardless, and we lose more than the enemy. We have the opportunity to hit back hard, and we can't let it slip away. We are not without other options."

Bolton and Escobar stared at her blankly.

Her face was stony. "If you complete the formal surrender ceremony, Redcom, the rebels will use it as propaganda throughout the Crown Jewels. We must deny them that. The General will surely broadcast the meeting to all of his followers. With what I have in mind, we can crush their spirit completely."

"And how do you expect to accomplish that?" Escobar asked. "We've been hamstrung."

Her voice had no sympathy, no forgiveness. "You two might be weaklings and cowards, but I am never defenseless, never defeated. I trained as one of Lord Riomini's bodyguards, so I know more than five hundred ways to kill a person, using any possible weapon." She shot Escobar a withering glare. "Or have you forgotten that I killed three of your best guards and crippled three more when they tried to sedate me?"

With a laugh, Escobar said, "If you intend to assassinate the General with your bare hands, let me be the first to wish you well."

"I will take the opportunities available to me," she said. "And you will cooperate."

Bolton glanced at the chronometer on the wall. "We have to depart soon. There is no time to put a complicated plan in place."

"I don't need any time," Carrington said. "I was prepared from the moment we boarded these ships on Aeroc."

She reached up to her face and, as Bolton recoiled, sickened, the woman poked her slender fingers into her left eye, gouging, fishing around until she popped the eyeball out of its socket and held it in the palm of her hand.

"This is an artificial biological replacement, connected to my optic nerve system. I can see through the synthetic gel lens, and it's not just an eye." She held it up and smiled cruelly. "This is a concentrated organic explosive, undetectable by any scans. By squeezing it, I can arm and detonate it in the General's presence. This should be enough to take out at least two decks of the flagship—and our greatest enemies at the same time."

"All of us will die?" Bolton asked, stunned by the plan.

Carrington said in a matter-of-fact tone, "Yes, we'll all die, but we'll die knowing that we have removed the greatest threat in the history of the Constellation."

To Bolton's dismay, Escobar nodded, accepting what the woman was saying. "We'll die with honor."

81

In the bedroom of Edwond House, Ishop and Laderna made love again—a strange reminder of their relationship that he didn't fully understand. She had come to understand and accept the political necessity of him marrying a noblewoman, but with the Enva Tazaar woman disgraced, sentenced, and a fugitive, Laderna seemed relieved.

He knew Laderna was fully dedicated to seeing him achieve his goal of being restored to the noble ranks, but neither of them were quite certain what would happen to her once he did achieve his rightful status. For now, Ishop was glad to have their relationship back to normal. That way, he could focus on his real priorities.

In four more days, he would appear before the Council, present his bold petition, and reclaim his family heritage.

Now in the early evening they lay together in silence, resting before the unusual mission they would face in a few hours. He studied Laderna's pale face, met her brown eyes, and they both smiled with anticipation. They had so much in common. Even though they had finished the list (except for confirming a Duchenet victim), this would seem like old times. It was something they could do together, and do well.

With Enva Tazaar secretly taking sanctuary in the Deep Zone, Ishop was glad he had continued to spy on Lord Selik Riomini. Diadem Michella thought she had gotten rid of a single note of dissent among the nobles, but she had more major internal problems than she knew about. Ishop wouldn't mind bringing down the Black Lord as well. . . .

At the appointed time, he and Laderna dressed in dark clothing and checked each other's equipment before heading into the coolness of the night. They arrived at a rarely used access gate on the outskirts of the main Sonjeera spaceport, used passcodes Laderna had stolen from supposedly secure government databases so that they left no record of their passage. In shadows, they stood within view of the quarantined, resin-encased warehouse.

Lord Riomini was going to attempt something very unwise.

"This is the best place to enter the tunnels," Laderna said. "We need to go five levels underground to make our way beneath the hangar. That's where the diggers have been working."

"So much for the Diadem's defenses," Ishop said. "She ordered all accesses permanently sealed."

"Michella thinks that just because she orders something, it automatically happens. Riomini's elite bodyguards worked for days to penetrate the tunnels. They did the hard part for us already. We just have to catch them at it."

In defying the Diadem, the ambitious Black Lord had made a dangerous decision; worse, he had not been careful about covering his intentions. Sloppy! Ishop was going to enjoy this. If the man suffered enough disgrace—again exposed by the dutiful, attentive Ishop Heer—maybe Michella would grant Ishop the Riomini holdings as well as the Tazaar holdings. It seemed perfectly appropriate. Knowing his worth, the Diadem was sure to be generous in her reward. But he didn't want to seem greedy by asking for too much.

Ishop broke the seal of a small access plate on the spaceport pavement, pried aside the covering, and then shimmied down a tube with Laderna. Once they were several meters belowground, they reached a thin metal ladder and followed green emergency lights to a larger subterranean passageway.

"From their previous movements, Riomini's workers should be congregating directly under the quarantined hangar about now, boss," Laderna said. "Drilling upward. I scouted it out, so I know the best place to observe."

Ishop's throat felt dry. "I'm almost ready to call in the Diadem's guard. We need to do it before Riomini's people breach the quarantine containment—can't take any chances. But the closer they are to the danger zone, the more I'll look like a hero."

Finding a good place to conceal themselves, the two settled into the shadows and watched the immense, long-empty storage chamber several stories beneath the resin-encased hangar. Despite the protective layers of rock, the thought of being so close to the contaminated bodies of the oozing alien and the possessed humans sickened him.

When they heard female voices approaching, the two retreated farther into the darkness, pressing closer together. Laderna gripped his arm, and he could feel her warm breath on his neck. He focused his dark-adapted eyes ahead.

As the sounds grew louder, he discerned stealthy shapes that glided forward. In the light cast from their headlamps, Ishop spotted a hole they had burrowed through the ceiling on previous nights, excavating an access tunnel up into the sealed hangar from below. He recognized one of the voices, the unmistakable gravelly tones of Lora Heston, Riomini's most trusted bodyguard.

The Black Lord must be so desperate to gain access to the alien specimens! In a logical sense, Ishop could understand his argument, that his scientists could learn vital information from the remnants sealed inside the passenger pod. But Riomini did not know what Ishop and Michella had seen. He was defying the Diadem's explicit command, and Ishop had little doubt of Michella's wrath when she found out.

Heston's throaty voice carried over those of her companions as she instructed the group. The women moved in the low illumination, efficiently assembling components of an article of machinery. Soon, Ishop heard a whirring motor, and then the construction telescoped upward, chewing into the ceiling.

Months ago, he had stood beside the Diadem in the hangar above, both of them fearful of the strange aliens. They had been wise to quarantine the monstrosities inside the passenger pod. Using complete isolation procedures, she had ordered the pod sealed and filled with poison gas to eradicate everyone and everything inside. The hideous, sluglike monster had died with its companions, then decomposed into a pool of crawling slime that seemed to be still alive. . . .

Now, as Riomini's machinery churned its way upward, Ishop felt the superstitious fear again, the deep chill that he might not be quick enough to protect himself. If these commandos did break into the encased hangar from below, the Diadem might decide to sterilize *him* as well—just to be safe. And Laderna. And the entire spaceport zone.

"We don't dare wait any longer," he whispered, hearing an edge of panic in his voice. "Let's retreat—and call in the Diadem's troops."

Laderna gave him no argument. They slipped back through the tunnels and hurried toward the surface access. Ishop was perspiring heavily when they emerged into the open night air. He wanted to get away from the contaminated place.

One advantage of being such a trusted aide was that he had a direct codecall link to the Diadem, to be used under only the direst circumstances. Such as now.

He wiped sweat from his forehead, caught his breath, and activated the codecall. "Eminence, there is an emergency situation at the quarantined hangar. Someone is trying to break in from the catacombs below— I suggest you call in your guards before they break the seal." He didn't need to identify Lord Riomini as the culprit; the Black Lord's guilt would soon be obvious enough.

He let out a long, slow sigh of relief and leaned against Laderna. "Now we wait."

⌒⌒

As expected, the Diadem did not underestimate the threat. More than a hundred members of her personal guard force met Ishop and Laderna at the edge of the security zone, then they swarmed down into the tunnels. Claiming that he did not want to interfere with their operation, Ishop declined to join them. He gladly allowed them to penetrate the catacombs on their own.

Ishop could hear muffled gunfire coming from below, and exchanged smiles with his assistant. On his own security codecall unit, he listened in on a barrage of reports and alarms from the assault squad, and soon people began to emerge from the tunnel access. Six bodies were brought up—four of the Diadem's guards, two of Riomini's—and then came the prisoners, each one bound and guarded by three of the Diadem's troops. The casualties and the captives bore no identification, no familiar items of clothing, but they would be named soon enough.

He recognized a battered Lora Heston being forced toward a waiting airvan. She challenged the guards in her husky voice. "I outrank you. I serve the Supreme Commander of the Army of the Constellation. My authority extends—" Noticing Ishop as he stood there watching, she struggled to step toward him. "Ishop Heer! Inform these guards they are making a mistake."

Keeping his distance, he merely smiled at her. "Yes, mistakes have been made. Diadem Michella gave explicit orders that this area is to remain sealed. I'm sure these guards will sort it out." He turned to the captain. "Place all the prisoners in extreme quarantine. We don't know how close they got to the danger zone, but we can't be too careful." In fact, he would recommend that all the Diadem's guards be placed in biological isolation cells as well.

He turned to Laderna and whispered, "Let's get ourselves away from here, too. Just to be sure."

82

The day resonated with memories. Aboard the bridge of the *Jacob*, Adolphus blinked in morning sunlight as the flagship orbited around from Hellhole's nightside. His old deep-blue uniform felt comfortable and *right*. Even after all these years the garment fit him like a second skin; it had always been a clear symbol of who he was.

More than sixteen years ago, he had been forced into his rebellion, when he and his fellow "second string" nobles were set up to be killed. Discovering the betrayal, Adolphus had rushed back to Qiorfu only to find his father conveniently dead and Riomini forces already occupying the Lubis Plain shipyards.

Disobedience had turned into outright rebellion, five years of bloody battles against the corrupt Constellation. The brave fight should have culminated in his conquest of Sonjeera and the defeat of the Diadem's forces, but for his own moment of compassion, his moment of *weakness*. And General Adolphus had lost everything.

Now, standing aboard the flagship he had named after his father, he knew this was his second chance, and he intended to get it right this time.

Mulling silently, he recalled how Commodore Percival Hallholme had used rebel family members as hostages in that earlier battle, placed them as human shields aboard the Constellation battleships, where they would die if Adolphus opened fire. The ensuing seconds had been critical. . . .

Sophie said to him, "You waited a long time for this victory, Tiber."

He tried to act dismissive. "This ceremony is just a symbolic gesture."

She gave him a disbelieving laugh. "Don't ask me to believe that for a second. I know how much it means to you."

Keana Duchenet stood close to Devon and Antonia, the three of them bound together by their alienness. Keana also wore a dress made of the red-weed fabric, and she seemed nervous and very human. "Because this is such a personal matter for me, Uroa will stay in the background. But I . . . I still don't understand why Bolton decided to come here."

Devon and Antonia held hands. Seeing the two so happy, the General doubted even Sophie could object to how her son had changed.

"The Constellation shuttle is entering our docking bay, General," said the comm-officer.

He nodded. "Mr. Jordan is there with the honor guard to welcome them?"

"He has a dozen armed soldiers, sir. Only three passengers are aboard the shuttle—they're all cleared."

"Mr. Jordan knows his business. He'll scan the three to make sure they're carrying no concealed weapons." Adolphus smiled at Sophie. She wore a brownish-red dress made of the fabric the shadow-Xayans manufactured from the red weed. The cut was perfect, showing off her figure, although the dress's color reminded him too much of dried blood. She was not a woman to wear much jewelry, but for this occasion she had selected an elegant necklace, and had taken the time to brush and arrange her wavy dark-brown hair. He smiled in appreciation. "This may be my moment, Sophie, but you're going to attract all the attention."

"I doubt it, Tiber." She laughed and took his arm. "Shall we go and prepare ourselves?"

He escorted her to the lift doors, feeling strong and victorious, but did not bask in his triumph. True, it was a historic event to have a Hall-holme surrender to him, and with the Constellation fleet now under his control, the Deep Zone would be much safer in its independence. But he still had large problems to resolve, including the eleven thousand prisoners taken from the captured ships, as well as the evacuation of

Candela before the two asteroids smashed into the planet. All the ships he could spare had rushed down the stringline toward Candela and should be arriving soon, but evacuating an entire population was no small matter. . . .

In the Deck 3 conference room, a banner with the blue and gold colors of the Deep Zone Federation hung on the wall next to a second one with the gold-and-silver Deep Zone Defense Force insignia. Adolphus had asked for no other trappings, no podium, no stage or chairs. The ceremony would be brief and to the point, without any social frippery. This was not supposed to be a party.

Craig Jordan spoke into the General's earadio. "We're coming down the corridor, sir." Adolphus clicked to acknowledge and took his place, standing at the head of the room. Imagers on the walls would record the event from different angles. Historians would comb over every instant of the ceremony, but he would not let that distract him.

Though they had no official role in the ceremony, Devon-Birzh and Antonia-Jhera stood with Keana, while Sophie remained off to the side, so the attention could fall on General Adolphus. He faced the door of the conference room as three guards entered and fanned out, two on either side of the door, and one behind. Red Commodore Escobar Hallholme marched inside the tight formation, with Craig Jordan close behind him.

The son of Commodore Hallholme seemed like a statue carved from glass. He stepped forward like an expertly manipulated marionette, moving mechanically as if his mind were willing him to be elsewhere. Remembering what it felt like when he himself had surrendered to Commodore Percival Hallholme, Adolphus hoped he had never looked so defeated as Escobar did now. The Redcom was skeletal, his eyes shadowy, as if he had been tossed into a hurricane and battered by winds he could not control.

Last came a man Adolphus identified as Bolton Crais, along with a lean, sharp-edged woman whom he did not recognize. A dozen more guards followed them and took assigned places along the walls of the conference room. They all wore projectile pistols as sidearms and kept their hands ready to draw and fire the weapons; Craig Jordan had two sidearms of his own.

"General Adolphus, sir," Jordan announced, "Red Commodore Escobar Hallholme is here to present his sword in formal surrender."

Adolphus kept his eyes on the Redcom, saw him swallow hard. His eyes were bloodshot.

Bolton Crais entered the room and froze; he seemed to lose his balance when he saw his wife. "Keana! You shouldn't—"

Keana looked disturbed as well. "You didn't need to come for me. I chose to stay on Hellhole. You would have been better off back on Sonjeera."

Adolphus cleared his throat to return to the formalities. "Who is the woman?"

Jordan answered, "She claims to be a representative of Lord Riomini from Aeroc. Her name is Gail Carrington. All three have been searched and scanned, sir. Other than the ceremonial sword, they are unarmed."

During the General's surrender, Percival Hallholme had insisted on more pomp and spectacle, knowing that the Diadem demanded it. For this occasion, General Adolphus preferred a more simple surrender ceremony, but one that still adhered to tradition. His focus remained on Escobar Hallholme, seeing so much of the father in the young man's appearance, but the old Commodore would never have found himself in this situation.

"Very well," Adolphus said. "On with the business at hand."

Bolton stared at Keana and felt his knees go weak—she shouldn't be here! His mind spun as he tried to think of what to do to keep her safe.

Though they had been distant from each other for some time, Bolton knew her moods and habits, her many flaws; doubtless, she could list dozens of things about him as well. He saw the changes in her expression from the alienness she carried in her body, and she did not have the impatient and dismissive look she often gave him. How many ways had she changed?

Keana Duchenet had always viewed her marriage to Bolton as a hindrance, although she knew that he had given her every possible freedom to do as she pleased without asking for anything in return. Perhaps she had finally come to understand that Bolton did love her in his own way, though more as a brother than as a husband.

Sweat prickled on his forehead and under his clothes, and he could not suppress his anxiety. Gail Carrington stood next to him, concealing the fact that she was, herself, a loaded weapon. He knew how dangerous she was, how driven. *I can't let Keana die!*

Going through the motions, Escobar stepped forward, his shoulders squared. He had donned his heavily decorated dress uniform, similar to the one the old Commodore had worn in the original surrender footage. The ceremonial sword hung at his side, and Escobar placed his hand on the glittering hilt, slipped his fingers through the hand guard.

The General spoke. "Red Commodore Escobar Hallholme, your Constellation ships came to my planet—my sovereign planet—to inflict great harm on our population. But you have been defeated. All your vessels are now forfeit to the Deep Zone Defense Force, to protect my people against further military aggression. In exchange for your surrender, I promise safety to yourself and every member of your crew. You will all receive food and shelter, and I will take no punitive action against any of you."

Bolton felt a heightened sense of urgency, even more than he'd felt when the fleet was stranded. It was easy to blame the rebels for their predicament, but he knew many of the things Diadem Michella had done to cause this situation herself, how she had forced the Deep Zone into an untenable situation, provoking them, taking too much while giving back almost nothing . . . until the frontier worlds sought their own solution. Was Adolphus really the monster here?

The General faced Escobar. "I will accept your sword now, Red Commodore."

As Bolton stood with his emotions writhing, his turmoil building toward panic, Keana looked at him, her eyes still dark blue and beautiful, but with a faintly spiraling shimmer. Her face had softened, and her expression showed puzzlement, as if she wondered why he was so upset. She shrugged, as if to ask him why.

Bolton had grown up a highly practical man, although his father would always be disappointed by his accomplishments. Marrying the Diadem's daughter was a political triumph for the Crais family, but Bolton had nothing to do with it. Keana had always been a dreamer whose expectations of a fairy-tale marriage were far different from his. He wished he could have been the husband she needed, and now he looked away from her in sorrow. It seemed so cruel for it all to end like this.

Escobar drew the ceremonial sword from its scabbard, then held it horizontally, the sharp tip in the palm of his other hand. "General Tiber Adolphus," he said, but his voice cracked. He started again. "General Tiber Adolphus. You . . . I—"

The tension in the air was like a cauldron of acid coming to a boil. Bolton thought of the Constellation, the future, the Diadem, his patriotism to the Crown Jewels . . . and most of all, of Keana.

He knew what Gail Carrington intended to do.

While all eyes were on the Red Commodore as he extended the sword toward the General, Carrington reached up, put her fingers to her eye—

Bolton's pulse leaped. The insidious command virus had already sabotaged the Constellation ships, and they would soon go rogue. The General could not use the captured vessels to cause any further harm. Wasn't that enough of a defeat? Bolton had come all this way, enduring months of deprivation and committing terrible but necessary acts just to survive so he could find Keana, and make sure she was all right. He could not tolerate what was about to occur.

Carrington did not have to murder the General, and Escobar, and him, and all these bystanders. And Keana.

Bolton's every instinct for survival shattered like a pane of glass breaking into infinite pieces. He hurled himself into the wiry woman, shouting, "Her eye—it's a bomb!" He had intended to knock her down and prevent her from activating the hidden explosive, but with her free hand Carrington struck a hard, stunning blow to his forehead, making him fall back against one of the guards.

Already tense, Craig Jordan and the nearest guard reacted like sprung catapults, crashing into her. Carrington lashed out like a wildcat and tried to leap back, but the guards seized her arms, wrestling her hand away from her face. She struggled, and Bolton saw her half-attached explosive eyeball dangling from its socket. Carrington tried to crush it in her hand to detonate it, but Jordan grabbed her wrist, jerked it away. The gelatinous artificial eye dropped to the deck, where it landed, staring up at them.

But it didn't detonate.

With the sudden outbreak of fighting, Escobar Hallholme thrust his sword toward the General, but Adolphus dodged and grabbed the hilt in an attempt to wrest it away from the Redcom. With his lips drawn tight, Escobar pushed and twisted, trying to drive the blade into Adolphus's chest.

The young man and woman standing next to Keana closed their eyes, and Bolton heard a loud humming noise coming from them. Their hair wafted upward in static electricity, and a whisper of breeze built up in the room.

Carrington broke free of Craig Jordan's grip and kicked hard sideways, breaking a second guard's knee. Then she whirled, driving her elbow under Jordan's jaw, crushing his larynx and breaking his neck.

Even before Jordan's body slumped to the deck, Carrington tore both sidearms from his hip holsters, slipped her fingers around the triggers, and shot two more guards surging toward her. Swiveling her lithe body, her eyes predatory, she aimed one of the weapons at Princess Keana Duchenet.

When Bolton saw the gun pointed at his wife, he struck Carrington's arm, deflecting her aim in the instant that she fired.

Hot projectiles struck Antonia in the center of her chest, driving the young woman into the metal wall, where she fell into the banner of planet Hallholme.

Next to her, Devon's intent expression dissolved, and the wind and static electricity died. As Antonia dropped to the deck, bleeding from the impact holes in her chest, he cried out in grief, his mouth open in horror.

Carrington was already swinging the second pistol at General Adolphus, but by now the remaining guards tackled her and tore the weapons from her hands. Bolton heard her wrist snap, but nevertheless she threw the two guards away from her in a superhuman effort, and she stood free of them.

⤜⥤

On the floor beside Antonia, Devon stared in total disbelief at the blood seeping out of her chest. Two bullets had struck her. She wasn't moving or responding, but she remained alive. The inner presence of Jhera gave Antonia strength, but the blood, the torn fabric of her blouse, the gaping wounds . . .

Devon felt a rage greater than anything he had experienced since he'd defended Antonia against her abusive stalker, Jako Rullins. The fury of despair, vengeance, and loss became a cyclone within him, creating a synergy with the similar horror of Birzh and building into a whirlwind of telemancy. Devon stood, clenching both fists, grinding his teeth.

With a wordless wail, he unleashed all the psychic power bottled up within him.

Gail Carrington was completely unprepared for the invisible hammer that drove her back and pinned her against the far bulkhead. Devon's telemancy continued to build, and her face reddened. She flailed, fighting against the invisible force; her remaining eye bulged, her mouth dropped open, gasping.

Then the telemancy smashed her, flattening her rib cage and breaking all her bones, crushing her body. But Devon wasn't finished. He continued to apply his mental force until the murderous woman was nothing more than a human-shaped outline of pulped flesh, tissue and splintered bits of bone, dribbling down the wall.

Then Devon knelt beside Antonia and cradled her in his arms.

83

Although Escobar Hallholme was driven by adrenaline and desperation, he was fighting against a well-muscled and well-fed man. General Adolphus slowly turned the sword away, then ripped it free from his grip.

In a smooth, potentially deadly motion he touched the swordpoint to the Redcom's throat and drew blood, but somehow Adolphus found the self-control not to kill him. He spoke through gritted teeth. "I will now accept your surrender."

His grip did not waver, and he did not take his gaze away from the Redcom's defiant eyes. If he had been a lesser man, he would have plunged the blade through him, but he controlled himself, reminded himself that he was a leader. He continued, "Long ago, I made the mistake of believing that your father was a man of honor. And now I see you are even less of a man. You are a liar, unworthy of any uniform. *You gave your word!*"

Escobar said, in a ragged voice, "But before that I gave my oath to the Diadem and the Constellation. Execute me now and get it over with. You've won—what more surrender could you want? How much more humiliation do I need to suffer?"

"I will not execute you," Adolphus said. "I will not break *my* word, but I've made a mistake again by agreeing to a promise I'll regret."

Keana confronted Bolton, face-to-face. "Why are you here? Was this all a trap?"

"I came to save you," he answered. "I couldn't let you and everyone be killed for a useless . . ."

Five of the guards lay dead on the deck next to Craig Jordan's body. Two of the survivors seized Escobar roughly by the arms. Adolphus finally lowered the sword. "Place Redcom Hallholme and Bolton Crais in bindings and secure them in the brig." As the guards dragged Bolton and Escobar out of the conference room, Keana followed, angry and distraught.

On the other side of the room, the terrible sound of Devon sobbing on the floor tore at his heart.

Sophie knelt beside her son as he held the young woman's bleeding body. "She's dying," Devon said. "I can feel their presence fading . . . both Antonia and Jhera."

Sophie shouted to the surviving guards, "Get her to sick bay! Call the doctors to prep."

"It won't be enough, Mother." Devon's hands were covered with blood as he pressed against the bullet wounds. "I'm using telemancy to help her cling for a few moments longer. I've slowed her metabolism, but she can't survive this. If only we had the slickwater."

Adolphus was there. "Go—now! Take her on a shuttle direct to Slickwater Springs, if that's what you need to heal her."

"It's too far away." A vast gulf of despair seemed to be inside Devon. "We're in orbit."

Sophie touched his shoulder. "You know not to give up hope, Devon. When have we ever given up?"

The dismay inside him seemed to be coming from the Birzh personality, because Devon struggled to the fore. "You're right, Mother. Her heart is still beating—we have to try. If Xayan telemancy can help her hold on for just a few minutes longer, we've got to take that chance!"

Adolphus spoke over the intercom. "This is a top-priority message. Prep a shuttle for immediate departure with the pilot who can make the swiftest flight possible to Slickwater Springs. *Go, go, go!* I want that shuttle ready now!"

Rather than letting anyone else carry Antonia's body, Devon used telemancy to lift her from the deck. He began to run with her body drifting in front of him, still dripping a bright intermittent trail of blood onto the deck, like scarlet breadcrumbs. Sophie ran behind them, breathing hard.

A lift tube took them directly down to the *Jacob*'s hangar bay. An alert young female pilot was waiting for them, and she rushed Devon and Sophie to a shuttle whose hatch was open. The pilot didn't give a second glance at the bleeding young woman who floated into the craft's passenger compartment.

The pilot was already warming up the shuttle's engines, and as soon as the passengers were inside, she activated the thrusters and lifted the craft off the deck even as the hatch sealed.

The gravely injured Antonia sprawled on the seat, her eyelids flickering. Devon propped her head on his lap, holding on to her. "I've slowed her heartbeat as much as possible. She's still with us, but only by the thinnest of threads." His face was drawn, the eyes wide and wild. He looked like a child again, and Sophie wanted to comfort him, but she didn't dare disrupt his concentration.

Antonia tried to whisper something, but Devon placed fingers on her lips. "Save your energy." He closed his eyes, touching her face with his fingertips and communicating silently with Jhera. He did not even react when the shuttle accelerated out of the open launch-bay doors and arrowed down toward the cracked surface of Hellhole.

Knowing the urgency, the pilot dispensed with the customary safety checks, and did not give them a gentle flight. She took the swiftest possible descent, burning through the atmosphere at such a steep angle that the hull heated to the limits of its tolerances. In the back compartment, Sophie was jostled from side to side, thrown off balance in the buffeting winds as the shuttle peeled through the cloud layers.

Somehow, Devon kept his balance, bracing himself and Antonia in a bubble of telemancy. He leaned close and whispered, "Just hold on. . . ."

"There's a growler storm between here and Slickwater Springs," the pilot said over the intercom. "I have to skirt it."

Sophie shouted back. "We need to land as soon as possible—every second counts!"

"Hang on. I'll try to find the best way through, but this is going to get rough."

The craft's reinforced framework groaned with the strain as the shuttle entered the immense static storm. Sophie heard the pelting dust and pebbles that slashed against the side of the vessel.

With his arms wrapped around Antonia, Devon closed his eyes and concentrated with such intensity that Sophie couldn't see him breathe. His eyelids did not flutter, nor did Antonia's. Their faces looked as if they had been carved out of marble.

When the shuttle passed through the growler and got beneath it, the sudden calm was shocking. "Smooth as glass. We'll be down in five minutes!" As the pilot accelerated into the clear air, Sophie was shoved back against the seat.

The pilot circled the basin and the mirrorlike alien pools that gleamed in the midday sunlight, surrounded by prefab tents, outbuildings, a lodge house, and the shelters Sophie had built for those who came to immerse themselves in slickwater. Nearby, a large encampment was being fenced in and workers hurried to set up the prisoner holding area.

The pilot set down hard, scattering spectators on the edge of the landing field. Sophie bounded to her feet and opened the hatch as dust swirled around them from the landed shuttle. "Come on, Devon! I'll help you—hurry!"

But Devon sat motionless in the seat, still holding Antonia. Her clothes were soaked with blood, as were his arms all the way up to the elbows. He hung his head and looked up at his mother. She saw no distant alien presence there now, just a terrible emptiness. "She died before we passed through the storm."

"Oh, Devon . . . oh, Devon, I'm so sorry!" Sophie reeled, clutching the side of the hatch.

Though he seemed to be drowning in grief, Devon gathered Antonia's body, held her in his arms, and buoyed her up with telemancy. He plodded forward on leaden feet.

Around the landing zone, other shadow-Xayans had gathered to watch them. Devon stepped into the dusty haze and walked forward carrying Antonia; he looked like a man approaching his execution.

Tears streamed down Sophie's face. "With the slickwater and all your telemancy—isn't there something you can do?"

"I'll take her to the pools," he said.

Nearly fifty shadow-Xayans were already there, recently converted volunteers. They formed a silent column, watching as Devon walked toward the nearest pool. Sophie remained close, matching her son step for step. The thick tears that rolled down Devon's cheeks were his own, not an alien's.

They reached the pool, and he stood on the boardwalk, looking at the placid but mercurial waters that held the preserved memories of a great ancient race. He glanced over his shoulder toward Sophie. "Thank you, Mother. I love you."

Then he stepped into the water, carrying Antonia's limp form in his arms. Sophie's breath hitched. Her son and the young woman he loved had merged with another romantic couple from a different time and a different civilization. Sophie would never be able to understand the depth of the loss that Devon felt now.

He waded forward until the sparkling alien water came up to his waist, then his chest, and Antonia was floating. He held her up and kept walking ahead until they reached the center of the strange pool.

The other shadow-Xayans gathered on the boardwalk, their gazes focused on him and his grief. No one uttered a word.

Devon submerged himself, pulling Antonia under the mirrored surface.

Sophie swallowed hard, sobbing, not knowing what he was doing. A moment later Antonia's body floated to the surface, drifting free . . . and beside her Devon rose up as well, facedown in the slickwater. Neither of them moved.

"Devon!" Sophie screamed, ready to jump forward, but she stopped herself. If she entered the slickwater, one of the shadow-Xayan lives would join her body. She didn't dare touch the alien liquid. Frantic, she looked from side to side, begging the shadow-Xayans. "One of you, please! Go retrieve my son! Bring him out! And the girl!"

Ten shadow-Xayans dropped into the pool and swam out to where Devon and Antonia drifted, side by side. Working together, they retrieved both forms and pulled them back to the shore. As the shadow-Xayans lifted the two out onto the boardwalk, the slickwater slid off them, curled away in living droplets and dripped back into the main pool, leaving the walkway dry.

But Devon and Antonia were lifeless and empty, their faces smooth and at peace. Sophie moaned. She turned to the slickwater pool and the distant reflections on its surface, and cursed it.

84

As the asteroids hurtled closer, Tanja didn't sleep for three days straight, but exhaustion finally made it impossible for her to function. She budgeted a few hours for a nap, although she was too heartsick about Candela to sleep.

Several generations ago, her family members had given up everything to journey here from the Crown Jewels and make a fresh start. They lived on this frontier planet, accepted the beautiful views and verdant landscape, even when it was offset by torrential rains and terrible mudslides.

Then the greedy Diadem had surprised them all with the arrival of an unexpected trailblazer and the establishment of an unwanted stringline connection back to the old core worlds—so much for their solitude and independence. As a flood of new and uninvited colonists poured in, all of them loyal to the Constellation, Michella Duchenet had "welcomed" the independent Candela colonists back into her taxable fold like prodigal children, and forced them to pay exorbitant tributes for the privilege.

General Adolphus's new Deep Zone network granted them independence again, with new dreams, a bright future. Tanja had expected a struggle against the Crown Jewels, yes . . . some pain and anxiety, probably bloodshed. She had fought back against the Diadem's depredations in every way possible—too harshly, she realized now—but she'd done it to give her people and her planet a real chance.

And now all of that was being stolen from them by a pair of capricious asteroids—a disaster that Tanja couldn't even blame on the Diadem or her corrupt government. But how could *two* asteroids target her planet simultaneously? Impossible! Survey ships and observation telescopes kept track of the incoming space rocks, each one nearly a hundred kilometers across. They hurtled forward on schedule, only three days from impact.

No one on Candela could stop them, and no one could survive on the surface in the aftermath of the impact. It was twice the disaster that had occurred on Hellhole five centuries before.

Her shadow-Xayan colonists had telemancy, but they were almost entirely wiped out from the backlash of their previous mental blast through the stringline. Only Tel Clovis and the Original alien Tryn survived, despite serious injuries, and they did not have enough power to nudge the asteroids onto a safer course. Even if the hundred shadow-Xayans remained alive, though, she suspected their telemancy would not be strong enough. Centuries earlier, the entire population of Xayans had not been able to push away *one* giant asteroid.

Tanja would have to save her population by other means.

⟿

The two stringline haulers arrived from Hellhole loaded with thirty-three rescue ships, which General Adolphus had dispatched from his military fleet. The first hauler pilot delivered his report in a breathless voice: "We were just attacked by the Army of the Constellation!" He showed Tanja Hu and Ian Walfor the images of Redcom Hallholme's ragtag fleet. "But the General defeated them! They surrendered—they were starving!"

"Are you sure it's not a trick?" Walfor asked. "Those ships disappeared months ago."

"I saw the look in their eyes, sir," the hauler pilot said. "They couldn't surrender fast enough after hearing the promise of a hot meal. The General is now configuring the captured ships for his own defenses, but he sent these available vessels to help you evacuate. I hope these thirty-three ships are enough."

"We're going to need every one," Tanja said.

The constant evacuation had continued for the past four days. Of the twenty-one main ships she had over Candela, eleven were completely loaded, their corridors packed with refugees, their life-support systems already beyond the nominal capacity. She needed to dispatch them to the Hellhole hub right away. The ships had never been designed to hold that many people, and certainly not for long.

Now that Adolphus had provided more ships, Tanja wasted no further time. She dispatched a codecall message: "All loaded refugee vessels—depart for Hellhole immediately. All passengers will disembark there, where they will be safe. Meanwhile, we will keep loading here until the last possible second."

Time was now the issue. They wouldn't have enough hours to make the shuttle flights needed to get everyone aboard the orbiting ships.

The pilot quickly returned to his hauler, ready to take the crowded refugee vessels into the docking clamps made vacant when the newly arrived vessels disengaged. Shuttles at the stringline hub kept dispatching evacuees onto the waiting ships.

Walfor had already done the calculations. Shuttles ran constantly, and now the main problem was arranging enough fuel for the upboxes and passenger pods. They had dispatched more flights in the past few days than Candela would normally have launched in a year.

"At least now we don't need to pack people aboard iperion cargo ships," he said, then narrowed his eyes. "And I'm sorry to be so blunt and pragmatic, my dear, but we've also got to keep extracting and shipping iperion ore until the last possible second. Candela is our only known source in the Deep Zone, and our network will unravel without it."

"Ian, I've got to get the people off this world before the asteroids hit! I can't ask miners to stay at work."

"It's not an either-or prospect," he said. "We must do both."

She drew a deep breath and let out a long sigh. "All right, we'll do both. We'll do everything we can."

85

To Diadem Michella, a large part of ruling the Constellation involved putting out fires, crushing flare-ups before they could cause
damage. Thanks to Ishop Heer, she was able to take care of many small
blazes before they became conflagrations—such as Selik Riomini's appalling scheme to break into the quarantined hangar and extract the
alien specimens inside. He might have unleashed contamination across
Sonjeera. Worse, he had openly defied her explicit command! She was
so thankful for Ishop's diligence.

She could assemble charges and destroy the Black Lord. Added to
that was his failure to understand the military implications when he
first learned that the stringline to planet Hallholme had been severed
and that their large fleet had been lost. In his initial analysis, he had
failed to realize that General Adolphus had set a trap, had assumed
only that the ships would not be able to return home by their traditional route. He had been so wrong, and if Governor Goler's report
was to be believed, all those ships had been captured by their greatest
enemy.

Despite her fury at what the Black Lord had done, however, Michella understood that she couldn't execute him, or even strip him of
everything, as she had done with Lady Enva Tazaar. Michella's detrac-
tors would turn the accusations on her, and make her look incompetent

for choosing Riomini in the first place, for relying on him so heavily. The uproar among the nobles would tear the Crown Jewels apart.

Or Riomini's supporters might fight back and start an uprising of their own to depose her. He controlled the Army of the Constellation (what was left of it). Michella had to tread carefully, or she might find herself facing a coup, and the Black Lord would probably find irony in sending *her* severed head in a message pod as some sort of peace offering to General Adolphus.

Most importantly, despite his transgressions, Selik Riomini was her only viable option as a successor. Michella was realistic, and knew that she could not rule forever.

But she was not ready to step down yet, and in order to maintain her authority she needed to punish the Black Lord for what he had done. Once again, Ishop Heer had come up with the perfect solution.

Responding to her crisp and annoyed summons, Lord Riomini stood stiffly before the Diadem's desk in the windowless war room of her palace. He wore his characteristic black clothing, but this time he chose not to adorn it with medals and braids. He obviously knew he was in trouble.

As usual, she had arranged for Ishop to observe from concealment, where special monitoring screens would display Riomini's body temperature, pulse rate, and perspiration. As she looked at the Black Lord, though, Michella didn't need any specialized images to see that he was sweating. She'd never seen him this way.

"Eminence, allow me to apologize, and explain—"

"I don't think I need any explanations." Her voice was cold and angry. "I want this lesson to *hurt*, Selik, so that you will remember it the next time you are tempted to get out of line."

"I acted only for the good of the Constellation." Now he didn't even look shamed! "We must defend the Crown Jewels against further alien attacks, and the only way to do so is to understand what those creatures can do. My scientific experts were quite clear in their assessment."

"And I was quite clear in my refusal! You *defied* me. Don't you see? General Adolphus wants us to dabble with the specimens and become contaminated by them. This could be part of his overall plan, an insidious way to spread the alien infection. Breaking open the hangar would have been like triggering a biological land mine, and once the alien influence spreads across the Crown Jewels, the rebels wouldn't even need to fight. They would defeat us from the first moment of contamination."

"I . . . did not consider that possibility, Eminence." He lowered his gaze, and at least had the good sense now to look cowed. "In warfare, it is always necessary to take chances. We cannot win if we do not accept some risk, even considerable risk."

"You don't understand the power those aliens wield. You weren't there in the hangar when Ishop and I saw that creature exert a mental hold upon the human passengers. No doubt the creatures have already done the same to the entire population of planet Hallholme, including my own daughter!"

"But didn't your man Ishop Heer journey there and interact with the inhabitants? Didn't he himself go to the strange pools that supposedly contain alien sentience? Is *he* contaminated, Eminence?"

Michella considered this for a moment, then said, "Don't try to turn this on me, Selik! Ishop is *not* infected, and we are here to discuss *your* actions, not his."

As her voice became more shrill, Michella realized she might be overreacting, even irrational on the subject, but once she had established her opinion she would never back down.

She could see the retreat on his face, and again he looked cowed. "Are you going to strip me of my rank and command?"

She leaned back in her chair, took a moment to compose herself. "No. I am not blind to your power and influence, and I won't risk another civil war on top of Adolphus's rebellion."

Riomini looked relieved. "I will not deny my ambitions, Eminence, but I serve you first. I would never call my supporters to engage in a civil war. I do hope to become your successor on the Star Throne, so why would I destroy the very Constellation I desire to rule one day?"

She nodded slowly. "Now, that is an answer I can believe." The Diadem took a deep breath to calm herself. "For your years of long service, Selik, I am going to be lenient—to a point. Therefore my reprimand will only be between us, no public scandal. My people need to view you as a bastion of strength. Publicly, I intend to support you as always, but I will not forget your poor judgment—nor do I want you to forget it."

She activated a screen on a side wall, which displayed a live image of

Riomini's bodyguards who had been captured alive during the raid at the hangar. The women looked disheveled, angry, and defiant, though not the least bit frightened. They were held in an impenetrable vault, a large white-walled cell with no windows and no furnishings. Michella's own uniformed guards, who had captured Riomini's team beneath the quarantined hangar, had been assigned to guard the women inside the sealed chamber.

She saw him swallow, then cover up the gesture with feigned defiance; that gave her a sense of satisfaction. Was he actually getting cocky? He remarked, "You must be afraid of my team, Eminence, if you need to place so many of your own people inside a locked cell."

She smiled. That had also been Ishop's idea. "Oh, Selik, my people may think they're guarding the prisoners, but they're *all* prisoners. I told you, one can never be too careful about contamination. The risk is simply too great."

Riomini's brow furrowed, but she pointed at the screen and transmitted a signal. "When you proposed your punitive strike on Theser, do you remember what you said to me? That the rebels needed to be taught an unforgettable lesson so they would never forget the consequences of defying my orders? It seems you need a similar reminder."

Nozzles opened in the white walls of the chamber, and jets of flame shot out. The inferno came from all directions. Both the prisoners and her own guards barely had time to scream, scrambling on top of one another, clawing desperately for shelter. Within moments they all caught fire.

Rather than watching the screen, the Diadem kept her gaze on the Black Lord while listening to the interesting sounds of death. As Riomini stared, wide-eyed in horror, the whole chamber was engulfed in fire—Lora Heston, the rest of his captured bodyguards, as well as the Diadem's own security staff. The flames continued to roar and swirl long after the screams had stopped; the bodies blackened, and the bones crumbled into ash, while the fires still filled the chamber.

"Was that really necessary?" His voice was hoarse.

Michella spoke as if she were a narrator. "Every speck, every shred of life, has been incinerated and sterilized in that chamber. For safety reasons." She studied his patrician face, saw anger and dismay there. Yes, she had hurt him deeply, and he would not forget. "You needed to understand the seriousness of the situation, Selik. For every bad decision there is a cost, and you have yours. For now."

The wall screen went dark. Riomini stared at it, as if he continued to see the cleansing flames and hear the screaming victims. Finally, his defiance had been incinerated as well. He bowed slightly. "As you command, Eminence."

Her voice softened, as if she were scolding a child she loved. "Never forget that you're not the Diadem yet. Don't make me consider other choices."

86

After days of disembarkations, the last stragglers of captured Constellation soldiers came down under guard in military shuttles to the large temporary holding area outside of Slickwater Springs. Even before the formal surrender ceremony, Sophie had assigned fifty of her best supply chiefs to prepare the camp using colony materials, and the town sprang up overnight. And filled up with prisoners.

Though Sophie remained crippled with devastation and disbelief from the loss of her son and Antonia, her well-trained work teams rushed to erect shelters that would protect the captives from the worst of the planet's mercurial weather. Site crews arranged for power, water, and sanitation. Eventually, the prisoners would be dispersed to other work sites and villages, but for now they had to be kept under tight control.

Despite her grief, Sophie insisted on being at the camp, and Adolphus felt compelled to join her. He remained sick inside at the debacle of the surrender ceremony and disgusted at Redcom Hallholme, all those good people dead, including Craig Jordan, Devon, Antonia, and the guards. A slow burn of anger continued to flicker within him, held in check only by adherence to his promise of safety to the enemy. *His* honor.

A tension headache twisted the wiry muscles in his neck, and he felt a dull pounding at the back of his head. If he had been a lesser, more emotional man, Adolphus would have executed Escobar Hallholme—just like Tanja Hu had killed Governor Undine—and no one would have criticized him for it. Now he felt he understood the Candela adminis-trator better.

But when Adolphus had attended the military academy on Aeroc, the underpinnings of military honor and acceptable civilized behavior were drilled into him. Tiber Adolphus had lived his whole life by that code, even after turning against the corrupt government. Commodore Percival Hallholme had beaten Adolphus only by threatening to mas-sacre innocent civilians. His son Escobar was worse, like a mad dog. It was clear to Adolphus that the Hallholmes had not learned their moral underpinnings in their youth, but rather on the battlefield, in their own desperate attempts to win at any cost.

Yes, if Adolphus had been a lesser man, he would have wrung Esco-bar's neck himself. But he was not an animal and would not commit such a moral breach.

Out at the prisoner-of-war camp, a dusty wind blew grit and rattled the thin walls of the prefabricated shelters. He had originally assigned three hundred well-armed guards to monitor the camp—partly to pro-tect the prisoners from any stupid ideas of escaping out into the perilous Hellhole wilderness—but Sophie demanded twice as many. Bitterness flowed like acid in her voice. "Just to be sure, Tiber. And I'm giving them orders to shoot to kill, if any of those bastards cause trouble."

He saw the depth of pain on her face and knew how hard she was try-ing just to make it through each day. So he gave her the six hundred troops without argument, reassigning them from other duties. He had sent all but ten of his own DZ Defense Force warships to help with the Candela evacuation, so he had plenty of active-duty personnel available on the ground.

⌁

When he arrived at the camp, many of the prisoners were outside, sitting listlessly in the afternoon air. Others slept inside shelters, recovering from their own ordeal of living for two months on the edge of starvation; they were only just learning the truth that many of their comrades had been sacrificed in order to keep the rest alive for just a few more days. Now that they were well fed, getting good medical care, and were at least temporarily safe, they cooperated.

Most of them had surrendered quickly and voluntarily; very few had been forced into submission. Every one of the prisoners had pledged an oath of nonviolence, accepting the terms of surrender. Adolphus had not asked them to promise loyalty, because that surely would have been a lie in most cases.

Desperate people would promise anything when they were starving and near death. Given a week of full bellies and calm, Adolphus knew some would reconsider their promises to him, and he took precautions.

Sophie met him outside the fence. Wind whipped the hair around her face. Dust grains stung her eyes, but her cheeks remained dry. Sophie Vence was not a woman to shed tears easily; she had cried for her son, then bottled the rest up inside, sealing her emotions with anger toward the Constellation invaders. Adolphus knew she wasn't finished grieving yet, although she pretended to be strong near him.

"Every hour, Tiber, I can barely stop myself from marching into the camp's headquarters tent to tear Escobar Hallholme apart for allowing what happened."

"Do you think it would do any good?"

Sophie still looked beautiful, but all the softness and humor had drained from her face. "I doubt it. After that treachery, he should at least have the decency to be ashamed, or express regret." She shook her head and looked away. "I wanted to do so much for Devon. I brought him to this planet when he was just a boy, and this was supposed to be his bright chance, his whole future. Then he lost himself to the slickwater, and now he's—"

Adolphus tried to console her. "You heard what he said, over and over. Because of the Xayans, he had a richer life with the Birzh presence than if he had lived a hundred lifetimes without him."

She finally allowed herself a wan smile. "Yes, he told me that more than once. He wouldn't have traded the experience for anything."

Encix arrived at the fenced-in compound from the nearby shadow-Xayan settlement. The Original alien glided in silence, her stubby caterpillar feet flexing and carrying her along in a sinuous rolling movement.

When the Constellation prisoners inside the fence saw her coming, they muttered in awe; some came close to the barricade, while others backed away in horror.

Adolphus knew that not many in the Crown Jewels even believed that the resurrected aliens existed; they thought the shadow-Xayans were nothing more than an odd religious cult that had seduced Princess Keana. But now the bizarre caterpillar-centaur creature stood before them, unmistakably not human.

Encix, Lodo, and the group of alien converts had been rocked by the destruction of the seed colony on Candela. The pain they felt through the ricochet of telemancy had damaged them collectively, setting back their progress toward *ala'ru*. All the mental power they had expended to quell the upheavals in the Hellhole impact crater, as well as the psychic blast that damaged the Sonjeera stringline hub, had drained the converts.

Encix turned her antennae toward the camp, then faced the General. "Are these your prisoners? Are you allowed to do with them as you wish?" He knew her voice well enough that he could tell she sounded anxious.

"I promised them safety and shelter."

Encix hesitated. "That is a strange commitment to make to a rival faction that means to destroy you."

Sophie's voice was laced with scorn. "And obviously, they don't all abide by those rules themselves."

Encix continued to gaze ahead, regarding the thousands of human prisoners. "You are aware of how powerful the shadow-Xayans have become, how close we were coming to our ascension. That is all-important— more so now than ever! But time grows short, and we have been weakened with our recent expenditures of great telemancy. There is danger to us . . . but if all of these humans were to enter the slickwater, then we would certainly resurrect enough telemancers for *ala'ru*."

"I'd be happy to dump them by the truckload into the slickwater," Sophie said. "But I promised it had to be voluntary. That was the deal, even for people like this."

Thrumming, Encix stared at the thousands of captured soldiers. "May I address the human who leads them? Perhaps I can convince them to make the choice themselves."

Adolphus considered. "If you like, but I doubt you'll make an impression. I'll take you there." He thought that maybe these prisoners could do something worthwhile after all.

Under guard, he and Sophie led the large alien to the camp's main gate, where guards stood with their weapons shouldered. Although the locals were familiar with seeing the Original, Encix still intimidated many of them.

"We need to have a word with Redcom Hallholme," Adolphus said. "I want twenty soldiers to come with me."

When the gates opened, the guards led them to the central tent that Escobar Hallholme had chosen as his primary residence. When they approached the fabric structure, the Redcom waited for them outside. He still wore his Constellation uniform, which was now dusty, rumpled, and bloodstained. He stared at the hulking alien, and his eyes widened.

Encix turned to the General. "This is the man who betrayed you? Who was responsible for the loss of Jhera and Birzh?"

Sophie answered before the General could. "Yes, he's the one."

Adolphus answered differently. "This is the man I defeated." He locked hard gazes with the gaunt Constellation commander. "Redcom Escobar Hallholme, may I present Encix, one of the Original Xayans who inhabited this planet before the asteroid impact."

The enemy commander seemed alarmed and did not know how to respond. Encix spoke loudly through her pulsing membrane. "Red Commodore Escobar Hallholme, the Xayan race has need of your humans. Thousands of our lives are stored within the slickwater pools, and they require human hosts to awaken them, bodies and minds to share. Your people will be content with us, and they will be useful."

Paling, Escobar turned to the General. "What is this . . . creature . . . talking about?"

Sophie explained, "They want you and the prisoners to immerse yourselves in the slickwater and take on a Xayan personality, so their race can ascend to a new evolutionary level. It is their holy grail."

"None of my people will submit to that sort of inhuman . . . brainwashing!"

Encix was puzzled. "But it would give us numbers sufficient for *ala'ru*. That was our agreement, General Tiber Adolphus. We make no claims on your planetary colony, provided that you help us reach our destiny.

These prisoners are defeated. Their faction is weak. You are their master."

"I could give the order, but I am bound by my own honor," Adolphus said, "and I *will* remain true to my word." His gaze cut like razor wire when he turned it on Redcom Hallholme.

"I only tried to do what was necessary," the Redcom said.

"And you failed." Adolphus was matter-of-fact. "Now your fleet has become part of the Deep Zone Defense Force to protect my worlds."

"Maybe so," Escobar said," but I will not allow alien access to my gallant soldiers. You may force it on them, but it would be taking dishonorable advantage of a defeated enemy."

Adolphus scowled. "Perhaps you are right, Redcom. I'll give it further thought."

Sophie's voice carried an acid bitterness. "We'd better rename the *Diadem's Glory*, Tiber. Let's call it *Hallholme's Folly*."

His heart ached to see her pain. Normally, he would have avoided a choice that seemed petulant, but he would grant her wish. "If you're serious about that, Sophie, I'll do it—for you. We'll talk about it later."

"I've already changed my mind," she said, "and I don't like any name that refers to the Constellation government—not the Diadem, and not the name Hallholme. We should come up with a more suitable name, a Deep Zone name."

"All right, Sophie." He turned about with a last glance at Escobar Hallholme. "I'm going up to supervise the final consolidation of your fleet. I'll go aboard your flagship myself."

Hallholme's eyes had an angry, defiant sparkle. "You do that, General. My flagship is yours. There's no way I can prevent it."

Adolphus paced around the bridge of Escobar Hallholme's flagship, but chose not to sit in the command chair. That did not feel right.

Many of the surrendered vessels remained empty in low parking orbits, waiting for cleanup crews and spaceship specialists to complete inspections. A dozen programmers and engineers were gathered on the bridge of the *Diadem's Glory*, working at control stations to download fleet data. Adolphus had already scanned some of the Redcom's log to get the broad strokes of their ordeal. He wondered how much Escobar Hallholme had left out.

Since the Constellation crews had been removed from their captured ships, most of those vessels were on standby, with the systems powered down. Some of them had Adolphus's inventory crews aboard, preparatory to reconditioning and refitting the craft. He'd also transferred over most of the personnel from the ten original DZ warships he still had, keeping only skeleton crews aboard, along with a handful of pilots for the onboard fighter craft.

The lights flickered on the bridge of the *Diadem's Glory*, and the humming background noise took on a deeper, grinding sound. He heard a distant vibration, the flagship's engines roaring unexpectedly, and the deck tilted.

"What's happening? Report!"

The techs scrambled at their stations. At nav-control, a flushed young programmer said, "The engines just activated, and I'm locked out of the system."

The other programmers reported being locked out as well.

Emergency signals came in over the comm. Another engineer looked at the flood of reports. "Same thing across the captured fleet, sir. The ships have gone rogue, setting their own courses and moving."

"How could that happen?" Adolphus said. "Most of the ships are empty—we haven't even finished sending engineering crews over!"

"Their autopilots switched on, sir." The nav-tech hammered at his panels. "This ship isn't responding."

Adolphus reeled through the possibilities. "Is the fleet escaping? Under some kind of autopilot?"

"No, General. The ships have all begun to *descend* into decaying orbits. They'll burn up in the atmosphere!"

87

The bridge of the captured *Diadem's Glory* felt very much the same as his own flagship, but different somehow . . . colder and haunted. Adolphus had never intended to make those thousands of soldiers endure months of starvation, but that was the fault of the Red Commodore's impetuous decisions.

The captured flagship was much newer than his *Jacob;* the systems seemed uselessly ornate. Not surprising; since his rebellion, the Army of the Constellation had paid more attention to trappings and unnecessary promotions. The last time he'd been aboard a ship like this was when he surrendered to Percival Hallholme. . . .

He felt confident now that he had plenty of extra vessels to disperse among the at-risk Deep Zone planets, guard dogs to protect against further depredations—and by removing so many ships from the Army of the Constellation, he had made it far less likely the Diadem would send further attacks against him. By the time Sonjeera completed repairs to its damaged stringline hub, maybe Diadem Michella would see reason. But he would not count on it. Undoubtedly, her warship-manufacturing facilities were running around the clock.

Or maybe someone would overthrow her. That would be for the best.

With the autopilots activated and guiding the Constellation warships down into lower orbit, the minimal crews he'd placed aboard had little effect.

Panicked comments filled the codecall lines. "Can't reassert control, General!"

"We're locked out. Command systems nonresponsive—the ships have a mind of their own!"

"It's not responsive, we can't get the engines to stop! It's a damned ticking time bomb."

"Navigation systems are down. Crash course is locked in!"

"Everything's dead. This ship is going down!"

Adolphus seethed as he listened to the cacophony of alarms and urgent messages. On the screen, he saw the green lines of the warships' former orbits, along with plunging curves in red for their new suicide courses into Hellhole's atmosphere. "Redcom Hallholme must have installed some sort of scuttling protocol before handing over his fleet." He turned to the comm-officer. "Send a signal. On my orders, dispatch crews from our own battleships and bring experts up from the ground if you need to. I want full teams aboard every one of those captured ships. How much time do we have?"

"Not enough, General. Depends on where the ships were in orbit, but they're all going down."

"Find some way to disengage the autopilots! Cut them off manually, shut down the engines if you have to." He stared at the dots on the screen.

He would not let all these newly captured ships slip through his fingers. He needed to get more people aboard the errant vessels and wrest control from the rebellious computers before they all burned up in the atmosphere.

"Other teams of programmers and engineers are heading for the nearest ships, General—our best people from the fleet. They'll be aboard our shuttleboats within twenty minutes, but they have to catch up with each descending vessel."

In a higher orbit, the *Diadem's Glory* was surrounded by numerous smaller vessels like a shark accompanied by remoras; they drifted along in lockstep, guided by no human hand as they headed downward.

"Don't waste a second," Adolphus ordered. "I won't let this whole fleet burn up before my eyes."

In the flurry of activity, shuttleboats pulled away from the Hellhole defense ships and raced off to the rogue vessels. It required an ambitious and well-organized effort just to dispatch appropriate teams to the appropriate ships. He watched two small unmanned Constellation frigates scrape into the planetary atmosphere and begin heating up. As they continued their plunge, the empty vessels turned into comets in the air.

One engineering tech was in charge of the small crew on his flagship. "We have some operational controls, General. It's only the engines, navigation, and control computers that refuse to respond."

"*Only?*"

A female programmer wiped sweat from her forehead. "Best guess, sir, is that we'll have to evacuate in half an hour."

"Then we've got half an hour to salvage the ship." Adolphus hurried toward the raw diagram on a status screen, where the display showed the alarming distribution of the out-of-control military ships.

The planet turned beneath them as the *Diadem's Glory* continued its decaying orbit. Hellhole's huge impact crater looked like a maw waiting to devour the ships plunging toward it.

Transmitting a ragged announcement, another team aboard a Constellation frigate abandoned ship, jettisoning themselves in evac pods before the craft burned up.

"Two more ships are entering the atmosphere!" one of the engineers called. "And three right behind them. They've got ten minutes left before the systems overheat."

Adolphus saw a red tinge around his vision. "Are there people aboard?"

"Small crews, sir, but they're having no effect whatsoever. Unable to reassert control."

A static-filled transmission spilled out of the loudspeakers. "Our lower hull is burning up, systems are shorting out."

Adolphus ran to the codecall. "Use the evac pods. Get out of there—there's nothing left for you to do."

Like spores ejecting from a mushroom, small lifeboats popped out of the dying vessels just before their hulls turned cherry red. One fuel tank exploded, spraying the wreckage in all directions. Within three minutes, the other three ships vaporized in the atmosphere.

By now, Adolphus could feel the bumpy turbulence as the *Diadem's Glory* entered the upper atmosphere. He went to the flagship's primary control panel. "Let me try something. I was trained in how these systems work."

The programmers stepped back, shaking their heads. "It's inaccessible, sir. We've got no way to get into the core programming."

Adolphus gave a noncommittal nod. In his academy training, he had risen to an officer's rank with a bright future ahead of him. He'd learned to fly battleships, with access to the control codes. He'd been the captain of a survey vessel in the Army of the Constellation, sent on a sabotaged mission that was designed to result in the death of him and his unwanted crew. In the intervening years, he was sure that Supreme Commander Riomini would have changed the codes, but maybe not all of them. At least it was a starting point in the options he had. "A lot of things have changed, but maybe I can override—"

The initial command string didn't work, nor did he expect it to. He tried a higher-level access code, but still the screen remained dead. The rogue autopilot responded to the tampering by pushing the thrusters, causing the flagship to take a steeper plunge. Shouting, the engineers tried to get their own stations to respond, but even the course-adjustment thrusters did little to halt the ship's death plunge, and then they, too, gave out.

Adolphus suddenly had another idea. "Dispatch our squadrons, get as many ships up here as possible, even small ones, anything with engines. Maybe we can shoulder some of the Constellation fleet back up into orbit by brute force."

"That might damage our own ships, General!"

"Then we'll have to be gentle. Do it—we could buy some more time."

Within five minutes, fighter craft and troop haulers dropped out of the remaining DZ Defense Force ships, seeking to match courses with the descending Constellation vessels. It was touchy flying, requiring the best piloting skill as the ships matched course and speed, then applied thrust, nudging the rogue vessels higher. Five Constellation warships were successfully deflected, to much cheering over the communication channels. One pilot struck too hard and breached the hull of the descending ship while damaging his own; he barely extricated his craft in time, backing out to a safe orbit as the damaged ship tumbled into the atmosphere.

The *Diadem's Glory* shuddered and rocked. The black starry sky now showed a faint haze as they skimmed the outer stratosphere. A bow shock of heat ripples surrounded the flagship as it carved its way down. Two bridge stations exploded in sparks, injuring one of the struggling programmers.

"We've got ten minutes left," said the lead engineer. "Barely enough time to make it to the evac pods. We have to *jettison*, sir!"

"Not yet." Adolphus keyed in the third code, one he barely remembered—and when that did nothing, he tried again and again, transposing digits, struggling to recall the exact sequence. And finally he was into the core programming, but still unable to override the virus.

The flagship rocked from side to side, the hull groaned with the strain. Another set of alarms began to sound.

"Heat loads are reaching maximum. The shields are going to give out in four minutes."

On the screen, another Constellation ship exploded in the atmosphere not far below them.

"As least I have access now," Adolphus said. "I broke in. Now, one last thing to do—a complete shutdown of all systems, including the main computer. That should drag down the peripheral nav-controls, killing power to the engines. Once we shut them off cold, then reset the computer, we should restore control."

"We're already dead in the sky, General," said the lead engineer.

"So it can't get any worse. Without downward thrust, this big ship might skip like a stone across the atmosphere." His voice remained quiet, but hard and implacable. "We don't have time to discuss this."

One of the programmers dove to a panel beneath the main control station. She dug her hands deep into the circuit grid to find wires, and at last she threw the manual switch that completely shut down the flagship's engines.

The bridge dropped into blackness for a second, and all the stations went dark, lit only by the eerie glow of plasma flares, sparks, and the sunlight scattered through Hellhole's upper atmosphere.

"Wipe the computer!" Adolphus shouted. "Start from scratch. We only need enough control to turn the rudders and navigation flaps, get us pointed upward again."

A large blast—some external tank rupturing from the heat—tilted them to one side. Another programmer restarted the power systems. "We have no computer control, General . . . but thanks to you at least the autopilot's dead and not fighting against us anymore."

As the power came back on, another station exploded in a spray of sparks. "That was the weapons system, sir."

"I'm more interested in the navigation flaps."

One of the engineer pilots wiped sweat from his face. "We've adjusted our altitude—at least we're no longer descending out of control."

"Transmit to all the other ships! Give them the code and tell them to shut down power, wipe the computers. Do what they can to save as many vessels as they can."

"There's not much left of this flagship, sir." The female programmer climbed back to her feet from the control access on the deck.

"It's one little victory," the General said. "I'll take it."

88

After traveling three days along the captured stringline from Buktu, Commodore Percival Hallholme's battle group arrived at the planet bearing his own name.

During the relatively quiet trip, Percival had interrogated the uncooperative Erik Anderlos, as well as the Buktu factory workers, ice miners, and ship refitters. Before he faced his nemesis again, he wanted to develop a clear understanding of how many frontline military vessels the rebels might have in their defenses—and if General Adolphus had truly captured his son.

The inhabitants of the frozen planetoid had no chance to plan ahead or coordinate their stories, but they all lied to him nevertheless. Some gave him ridiculously inflated numbers, while others claimed that the five half-assembled ships in spacedock were all they had ever worked on.

"Useless information," he told Adkins an hour before arrival. "We don't have any better intelligence on the General's defenses than we did before."

His old aide leaned against the bulkhead in the Commodore's ready room. "You didn't really expect them to spill every detail, did you? These are rebels, hardened to their cause, but you'd think *someone* would cooperate to gain better terms for himself or his family."

"That would certainly be the case if we weren't dealing with General Tiber Adolphus. We know from past experience that when people join his fight, their loyalty is extraordinary." Even his own crews did not bond with such tremendous allegiance.

Percival finished his sweet kiafa, straightened his uniform, and then glanced in the mirror to make sure his whiskers and hair were neatly combed. He gathered his formal cap. "Shall we go to the bridge? We're about to arrive."

Adkins had a jaunty step as they entered the lift. "Ready for your rematch, sir?"

Percival frowned; he had never viewed this as a game. "I defeated Adolphus the first time. I'll do it again."

His deepest worry was that Adolphus was holding Escobar as a hostage and would threaten to kill him. During the first rebellion, the honorable Tiber Adolphus would never have stooped to such tactics, but now . . . Percival wasn't so certain. He himself had redefined the rules of acceptable behavior in the Battle of Sonjeera. How far would General Adolphus go now?

When the Commodore and Adkins arrived on the bridge, every officer and enlisted soldier snapped to sharp attention, looking at the aged commander with great respect. He could tell they were on the verge of applauding him, but he didn't want that. "To your stations," he said gruffly and slid into the command chair.

"We begin decelerating in ten minutes, sir," the chief pilot said, sitting beside him.

"Very good." He laced his fingers together and looked at the viewscreen, which, as yet, showed nothing. "Mr. Adkins, separate Erik Anderlos from the other prisoners, in case we need to use him as an intermediary."

Both men knew that by "intermediary" he actually meant *hostage*. The Buktu deputy administrator had been tight-lipped and uncooperative throughout the entire journey. "Yes, sir."

"Sound battle stations."

Alarms reverberated through all thirty vessels hanging from the stringline hauler. "Pilots to your fighter craft, ready to launch as soon as we reach the hub. Every second will count." They had drilled for this, counted down the hours as they sped in from distant Buktu. During the last day, he had even allowed the intercoms to play the loud and optimistic

"Strike fast, strike hard!" fanfare, though he found it annoying. If there was ever a time to leverage their feelings of patriotism, it was now.

Percival had considered reviewing historical records of the final confrontation over Sonjeera years ago in order to gain more insight into the General's previous tactics, but that would be a waste of time. He already knew how Adolphus had outmaneuvered him before finally losing.

But in the following years Percival himself had changed. During that legendary final battle, when the Diadem forced him to use despicable means to win at all costs, Percival had seen the rot at the core of the Constellation. He had withdrawn into retirement, wanting none of the glory he could have attained based on his famous victory. All that bravado now felt hollow to him—but he would be a less formidable opponent if he doubted his own beliefs, and he could not allow that.

Percival was also certain that General Adolphus had grown stronger during his years of exile. This would not be an easy victory.

He gave his obligatory speech before engaging in battle. "We must use our element of surprise to its fullest advantage. The rebels will not know we are coming, but Tiber Adolphus isn't a man to let down his guard. We must strike quickly and shock them. Our battle group *will* seize this planet and its stringline network in the name of the Diadem!"

The hauler pilot's codecall transmission interrupted his broadcast. "Arriving in the system, Commodore."

"Very well," Percival said. "This is our moment in history."

As the impact-scarred planet appeared before them, growing larger by the second, Commodore Hallholme ordered the thirty warships to disengage. In a coordinated effort, like opening hands, docking clamps released the ships, all of which dropped down, engines igniting in the airless vacuum. They spread out in a deadly swarm, arrowing straight toward planet Hallholme.

Duff Adkins reacted as soon as the images and data poured across the viewscreen. "A lot of ships around the planet, Commodore! More than fifty."

"Zoom in, high magnification."

The ships appeared, many of them streaming along in orbit, others down in the atmosphere. "Those are *our* ships—the Constellation fleet!" The bridge crew let out a gasp as they watched a vessel burn up in the atmosphere. "It's total chaos, it seems to be some kind of battle."

Escobar's ships. So, his son had arrived here after all!

Then, as Percival watched, he realized that the Constellation ships were in a flurry; many seemed to be diving in suicide plunges. He counted ten of the General's warships, but they drifted along as if empty, not part of the engagement.

"What the hell?" He leaned forward in the command chair. "What could possibly be going on here?"

"They haven't even reacted to our arrival," Adkins said. "I can't believe the General would be so lax."

"He seems preoccupied at the moment. This is fortuitous timing." Percival flicked his gaze from side to side as he tried to discern flight formations or strategic patterns among the chaotic movement of the Constellation ships or even among the General's old refurbished vessels. "Everything is in disarray. Adolphus would never allow such a lack of discipline."

"Now they've spotted us, Commodore! Here they come!"

Five of the seemingly dormant DZ Defense Force ships shifted course and rose into higher orbit, activating their weapons; the other five still hung motionless.

"Dispatch fighter craft and tell them to fire at will. We've caught the rebels snoozing. Let's take advantage of it."

His attack fighters came in with weapons blazing, shooting projectiles at the nearest DZ ships.

One of the pilots reported: "We've identified the Constellation flagship, sir. The *Diadem's Glory* is just above the atmosphere, severely damaged."

"Contact their commander," Percival ordered. "Tell him help is on the way." He prayed that Escobar was still aboard, still in command. If this was the aftermath of a battle, then his own ships could rescue the remnants of the Constellation fleet. When his son departed from the Sonjeera hub, he'd led five full stringline haulers loaded with a hundred fully equipped vessels. Now, at a glance, Percival saw only a few dozen warships.

"Calling *Diadem's Glory*. This is Commodore Hallholme—I've

brought a full battle group from Sonjeera. I thought you might need some help." He looked at the screen, raised his eyebrows, and waited. "Please respond. My vessels and weapons are at your disposal."

But when the codecall screen shifted and resolved into a man's image, the last person Percival ever expected to see at the helm was General Adolphus himself.

89

Keana hurried along the dusty paths between the prison camp structures and tents, watching the sky as Constellation warships destroyed themselves overhead, tumbling unpiloted down through the atmosphere.

From his assigned tent, Bolton Crais saw her and rose to his feet, stepping out to meet her. He wore one of his confused, disarming expressions.

"Bolton, what's happening up there? Why are those ships out of control?" As she faced him in the camp, she noted his dirty, torn uniform, his unshaven, gaunt face. She hadn't had the opportunity to speak with him after the bloody debacle aboard the *Jacob*. He eyed her warily, but she wanted him to see it was *Keana herself* speaking to him, not some alien-possessed puppet. "Yes, it's really *me*. Did you do something to the fleet controls? Tell me!"

Showing a little pride, he said, "Yes, I helped program the ships to fall out of orbit and burn up in the atmosphere. We delayed by enough time for our crews to be off-loaded, but now . . . it was imperative that we not allow the enemy to capture our fleet."

Bolton had done that? She had never really looked at him like this before. For years she had been married to a lackluster and uninteresting nobleman, but now she saw a different man, a stronger one. She was surprised, and impressed, that he'd been able to wrest some kind of victory out of such a complete defeat.

He stood before her, straight backed, meeting her eyes. "Now ask me why I'm here."

Her shoulders slumped as she suspected the answer. "Did my mother send you to save me?"

"Your mother? No," he said, sounding surprised. "I did my duty as your husband. I came to . . . make sure you are all right."

"Why didn't you just let me go? I'm here because I want to be. You won't understand the marvelous changes in me, the life and memories I have. . . ."

He smiled thinly. "I came because I do care about you, and I worry about you."

Even with the chaos around, the patrols outside the fence perimeter and the restless prisoners, the crisis with the rogue warships burning up in the atmosphere, Keana felt as if the two of them were in a bubble of silence. Her thoughts would not form into words.

Inside her mind, Uroa reminded her that this man, along with Redcom Escobar Hallholme, had come here to devastate the planet, but Keana pushed the angry alien presence into the back of her mind. *This is between him and me,* she insisted silently. And though Uroa remained there, ready to exert his powers, she held him in check. She focused on Bolton, reassessing him, putting aside some of the assumptions she had made over the years.

"You ran away, Keana," he continued. "You disappeared—and then we learned you'd joined some alien cult. There was a time when you couldn't take care of yourself in the real world. Of course I worry about you."

Her expression softened. "That was before. I'm . . . different now."

With a collective gasp, the captive Constellation soldiers looked up to the sky where a high black smudge showed another ship tumbling out of orbit and burning up.

Bolton swallowed hard and said, "I imposed a delay in the shutdown virus for all autopilot and command systems. I didn't want to kill innocent crewmembers—not even rebels. After what I did to keep us from starving, I have enough blood on my hands."

Keana could see from the thinness of his face, his sunken cheeks, that he had been through a terrible ordeal. "The General did not intend for you to starve either. He wanted to capture your fleet without bloodshed . . . but you were lost. Scouts searched and searched, but couldn't find you."

"The Redcom refused to sit around and be captured."

Keana stared at him, saw that Bolton looked haggard and disappointed, but not beaten. "Do you even know what you're fighting for?" she asked. "The Diadem? You know what my mother is like."

"Yes, I know her well." Bolton hung his head. "But she is my legitimate ruler, and I'm fighting for the *Constellation,* for our noble tradition and way of life."

With the continuing disaster overhead, the prisoners grew unruly, shouting at the guards along the fences, taunting them. Keana flinched when she heard a peppering of sharp gunfire, but Adolphus's soldiers were merely firing into the air to intimidate them.

Bolton seemed more interested in their own conversation than in the turmoil in the camp. "Keana, you're my wife, but I know the circumstances of our marriage. I'm not imagining this will be one of those happily-ever-after romance stories. I have no delusions in that regard, and I haven't had them for a long time. But I still want to take care of you, as much as you will permit. It's more than an obligation."

She lifted her chin. "And *I* promised to protect this planet from Constellation attack. I'm not the old Keana anymore. I'm different, I'm . . . more significant here than I ever was as the Diadem's daughter." Uroa finally asserted himself in her mind, causing her voice to become harder, more powerful. "I can use my Xayan knowledge, which makes me far stronger than I was as an ordinary human being."

Bolton's hazel eyes glinted. "I can see that."

Red Commodore Hallholme stepped up to the two of them, interrupting. He seemed to interpret Keana's assertiveness as threatening. He looked disturbed and angry to hear the gunfire from the guards. "Your General Adolphus promised us safety."

She quelled the flare of Uroa inside her. "The General is always true to his word."

A ripple of disquiet passed through the camp as Encix returned, this time she was accompanied by Lodo, who had arrived from the museum vault with Cristoph de Carre. Although the numbers of shadow-Xayans had greatly increased, Encix, Lodo, and the badly damaged Tryn were the only surviving Original aliens. As the bizarre caterpillarlike creatures moved through the camp, the prisoners drew back.

But Escobar Hallholme seemed more surprised to see Cristoph.

With a confident air about him, the young disgraced lord came forward to join them. He met the Redcom's gaze. "Escobar Hallholme . . . the last time I saw you, your troops were stripping my manor house on Vielinger, plundering my family's possessions, leaving me little choice except to escape to the Deep Zone."

Escobar faced him. "I did as Lord Riomini ordered. Your father brought about your family ruin himself."

Cristoph shrugged. "I know, and I have begun to embrace the turnabout. The loss of my wealth and the unfortunate death of my father opened my eyes and made me see the rampant corruption in the Constellation. The question, Redcom, is whether *you* see it now."

"The de Carres got what they deserved. Your father was a disgrace." Escobar turned to Keana as if Bolton weren't there. "You and Louis de Carre behaved like fools, embarrassing yourselves—and look what's happened to both of you!"

Cristoph's smile had no humor. "But look what's happened to *you*, Escobar Hallholme."

The two Original aliens stood together, observing. Lodo spoke aloud to Encix, "These human factions are fascinating, and quite destructive to each other."

"I am not interested in their factions," Encix said. "We must convince these prisoners to accept the slickwater. You know why we have to hurry. You know what is happening at Candela. With these thousands converted, though, we can achieve *ala'ru*—before it's too late." The alien turned toward Keana. "Tell them, Uroa."

The alien voice swelled inside her, but Keana fought it back down. She gestured to the sky. "No, we're having a crisis of our own."

Sophie Vence marched into the camp, looking like a firestorm contained in a woman's body. She walked directly toward Keana and the two Originals.

"We need you and all the shadow-Xayans—now! It's time to use the telemancy you practiced to save this planet. Devon and Antonia showed you all how to do it." Sophie shot a razor-edged glare at Escobar. "We are under attack, and Xayan power can drive it off."

Bolton sounded fatalistic rather than smug. "My shutdown virus can't be stopped. You can't prevent the ships from spiraling down."

"Not the virus," Sophie said. "Commodore Hallholme just arrived with his own military force."

Keana knew that General Adolphus could defeat a fleet that size under normal circumstances, but he had sent away most of his DZ defense ships for the evacuation of Candela, and his captured Constellation ships had gone berserk. These were not optimal circumstances.

Hearing this, Escobar Hallholme swelled with pride. "I never wanted my father to come to my rescue, but . . . victory is victory." He turned to Sophie. "If you would like to discuss your surrender with me, we can negotiate the terms."

She looked at the man as if he'd gone insane. "Don't be an idiot, Redcom. I wasn't addressing you." All traces of softness had gone from her. "What we need now is Xayan telemancy. The shadow-Xayans practiced their abilities for exactly this situation, and they promised to help. Now is the time."

Lodo and Encix swayed, troubled. "The risk has never been greater. We don't dare use too much telemancy, especially now."

Sophie crossed her arms over her chest. "I don't know what you're talking about, but if you don't do this now and Commodore Hallholme takes over this planet, you can forget about your chance for *ala'ru*." She gave a sharp smile to Bolton and Escobar without seeming to see them. "And if you do save us—I'd dump every one of these soldiers into the slickwater as 'volunteers' . . . if it were up to me."

Encix and Lodo turned their inhuman faces toward each other. "Yes, planetary salvation is necessary," they said in eerie unison, their facial membranes vibrating. "We will summon the shadow-Xayans—immediately."

90

shop had been to many governmental proceedings in the Council Hall, during which he provided advice or delivered private messages to Diadem Michella. As her special representative, Ishop had addressed the nobles, delivered surveillance reports about Hellhole, and even raised the alarm about the General's insidious activities, although the nobles hadn't taken his warnings seriously at the time. In fact, they had never taken *Ishop* seriously—because he wasn't one of them.

Now, at last, all that was going to change. The long-awaited deadline had arrived, and Osheer descendants no longer had to remain in the shadows. Seven centuries was a long time, but these last few months of waiting had seemed even longer.

Before knowing his true destiny, Ishop had been content with his important, if nearly invisible, role in the Diadem's government. Michella Duchenet knew she could count on him to accomplish even the darkest of tasks. She understood his worth.

Today, though, he felt different inside, elated. Ishop had always been capable and ambitious, greater than any common man; he knew that because he had grown up with so many drab, sleepwalking people. He'd once believed he had achieved his destiny in becoming the Diadem's most trusted aide, but now he knew there was much more in store.

On the day of his grand announcement, he bounded up the marble steps of the Council Hall, buoyed by the feeling of *nobility* within him. Diadem Michella had agreed to grant him time at the podium. "I can give you ten minutes at the start of the session, Ishop. Just don't waste the Council's time, or mine."

"It's a matter of utmost importance, Eminence," he had reassured her, though she seemed preoccupied.

Arriving well before the Council session was scheduled to begin, he made his way past noblemen and ladies—his *equals!*—to his reserved seat near the Diadem's chair. Already there, Michella wore an elegant woven business suit, with her gray hair freshly cut and spangled with tiny gems. Today's session was only a business meeting, alas, rather than a grand spectacle, but Ishop didn't want to wait any longer.

Ishop looked up at the podium. So many times he had imagined what he would say if he was permitted to present his case here. He had rehearsed the speech in front of Laderna numerous times in recent days, but as the time approached, his heart fluttered. He'd never been this nervous before committing murder, but this *mattered* more.

Presently, the Council chairman called the session to order and turned the podium over to the Diadem for her introduction. Michella gestured to Ishop. "Many of you know my loyal aide, Ishop Heer." Her words blared, so the technicians turned the volume down quickly while she continued, "He has asked to address the Council, and in deference to his years of excellent service, I grant him ten minutes of my own time."

A restless and disrespectful murmur began in the audience, and other people paid no attention at all. The nobles had always treated Ishop as a trivial underling, but that would change once they knew his true heritage. He took this as a personal lesson and made a silent promise that he would be nicer to commoners as soon as he reclaimed his title.

"On what subject does he wish to address us?" a young nobleman called from his seat in the back row. "We've already got a full agenda."

"Yes, what is the subject?" a noblewoman shouted, her voice shrill.

"Something important, he tells me," Michella said and gave Ishop an indulgent smile. It made him think of a kindly pat on the head, like a master would give to a faithful dog.

Several seats down in the same row, the elderly Lord Tanik Hirdan made a rude noise. "Let the man speak and get it over with!"

Flustered, Ishop made careful note of the nobles who grumbled loudest as he walked to the middle of the polished stone floor. He felt alone out there, but he shored up his resolve. At the podium, he bowed toward the Diadem.

"Eminence, I have served the Constellation for years, providing you with able assistance, and my work has bolstered the stature and integrity of the position you hold. Now I've made a momentous discovery in the historical archives—and I have wonderful news!"

He had expected this to rivet their attention, but many of the nobles were chatting, not even bothering to whisper, showing him no courtesy or respect. He frowned, but continued in a firm voice. "Many centuries ago my family name was *Osheer*, not Heer. We were a respectable noble family that wielded great power. Two of my ancestors even served as Diadem in the early days."

At last, he was gratified to see surprise on Michella's face.

With a swelling heart, reaching his moment of triumph, he continued, "Seven hundred years ago, through a long-forgotten political scandal, the Osheers were stripped of their holdings on the basis of the same proviso that was recently used to banish Enva Tazaar. My ancestors lived as commoners for so many generations they eventually forgot who they were. But *I* haven't forgotten."

He waited to see the excited reaction he expected, but it was slow in coming. Maybe they didn't believe him yet.

He raised his voice to hide the fact that he was flustered. "I have copies of the old paperwork from the Constellation archives. I can provide extensive proof, including family trees and genetic markers. For formality, I will submit documentation to each of your offices. The dates are recorded, the details clear. As of two days ago, that long period of disgrace has passed." He smiled at the audience, panning from face to face. "According to the Constellation Charter, I now reclaim my heritage. Today, I formally rejoin the ranks of nobles!"

Before they could applaud, he continued in a rush. "Along with my title, I therefore petition for holdings appropriate to my status. The best and obvious solution, since it is available, would be to grant me the planet Orsini and the former holdings of Enva Tazaar." He looked at Michella and added, "Subject to the payment of proper taxes to the Diadem, of course."

Exuberant, he stood awaiting thunderous cheers of approval. Instead, the Council members just stared, either stunned or smiling disdainfully. Then, after a moment of silence, he heard chuckles, which gradually built into outright laughter.

In disbelief, he looked at Diadem Michella for help, but she gave him an indulgent smile tinged with impatient dismissiveness. "We'll discuss this further when there is time, Ishop." She glanced at her ornate personal chronometer. "That's the end of your ten minutes."

Ishop stood frozen at the podium.

"Next item of business," Michella said, addressing the assemblage. "Investigating the escape of Enva Tazaar. It is vital that we determine how best to root out any additional Adolphus loyalists who may be lurking among us. . . ."

Reeling, Ishop made his way back to his seat, unable to believe what had just happened.

91

For years, Tiber Maximilian Adolphus had dreamed of facing Percival Hallholme again. But not now, not like this.

Although he had saved the *Diadem's Glory* from burning up in the atmosphere, the General remained hamstrung, the bulk of his fleet gone, his captured warships out of control. He tightened his grip on the flagship's command chair, as if he meant to break off the padded arm. "Weapons systems?"

The distraught engineering teams looked up at him. One woman shook her head. "None, sir."

"How about propulsion?"

"Barely," said a second engineer. "Enough to keep us above the atmosphere, but we're not going anywhere. We can't escape Commodore Hallholme's ships."

"I don't intend to run away," Adolphus said. "I just want to know how much maneuverability we have."

The chief engineer lowered his chin. "Not much, sir."

His mind spun. According to a preliminary analysis, Commodore Hallholme's ships had come in on the stringline from *Buktu*! But how? The decommissioned iperion path from Sonjeera should not have supported any travel whatsoever, but the old Commodore was resourceful; Adolphus didn't doubt that. He wondered if the Buktu facilities had been captured or destroyed. An aggressive commander would have left scorched earth behind him, destroying all the enemy's resources and advantages. Or had he captured them for the Diadem?

"Do we still have the weapons platforms?" he asked. "Can they open fire?"

After checking, the engineer said, "Eleven of the twelve platforms are still functional, though their charges were diminished by the initial fight. We never had a chance to reload and reconfigure. We have fighter craft, too, but they're busy trying to keep the captured fleet from burning up."

Adolphus knew he had ten of his own DZ warships with full weapons systems, but their crews were minimal and he didn't know how much benefit they would be in a fight against such a skilled opponent. He folded his hands together as his mind raced through the worrisome details. At least he had something left. "I'll make the most of the few shots we have in our arsenal. Keep me linked with the firing crews for the weapons platforms."

The Commodore's battle group closed in, demanding his surrender. These unexpected reinforcements could not have arrived at a worse possible time, but maybe his old nemesis did not know how bad Adolphus's situation was. The Commodore could see confusion in the ranks, scattered ships, vessels burning up in the atmosphere. Hallholme could draw his own conclusions. . . .

Nevertheless, Adolphus would do his best to bluff. He was good at it. "Cover up our repair activities on the bridge. Put the imagers tight in on me, then respond to the Commodore's codecall." He mastered the emotions on his face, fell into his well-practiced routine.

One of the engineers made a quick adjustment. "Go ahead, General."

Adolphus said, "Commodore Hallholme, greetings from your son's flagship. I'm surprised to see you here at my planet. I don't believe I extended an invitation."

As he stared at the old man, he could not push aside the resonant memories from the last time, when he'd faced this man's vile tricks over Sonjeera. Adolphus had been in a much better position then, his ships far outnumbering the opposing fleet. The Diadem's forces had been backed into a corner, and that battle should have been their last stand.

Now the old Commodore stared back at him. His hair was silver now, his muttonchop whiskers bushier, and his eyes looked more tired than Adolphus remembered them. "Diadem Michella gave me orders to finish the job, General. You've tested her patience enough, and she has authorized me to end this conflict by any means necessary."

General Adolphus scoffed. "Any means necessary—as Lord Riomini did to Theser? As you yourself did to me on Sonjeera?" He made a sound of disgust. "What helpless hostages will you cower behind this time?"

On the screen, Hallholme looked queasy, as if he had bitten into a large sournut. "I do have . . . human leverage with us, General—as be-fore—if you force me to use it. The success of my mission is paramount." Hallholme's face looked grave. "I apologize for the tactic, but this is war."

On the screen, he displayed a group of captive colonists from Buktu, two hundred workers from the shipyards, ice fields, and fuel-processing facilities. Adolphus recognized Erik Anderlos. He remained rigid and cold.

"We captured Buktu," the old Commodore continued. "The facili-ties remain intact for the most part, and these hostages are unharmed. But you know what I am willing to do."

"Yes, I know, Commodore. Your lack of honor is deeply troubling. You are as bad as your son."

A flush of anger rose on Hallholme's face, but before he could reply the comm-network on the *Diadem's Glory* showered sparks. The Com-modore's image flickered to static and went blank. Adolphus yelled over his shoulder, "I need him back!" He had not wanted to let his rival see the damage to the Constellation flagship; unfortunately, that part of the bluff would no longer be effective.

When the old man again stared back at him on the screen, Adolphus said, "Sorry for the interruption, Commodore—we had a brief technical difficulty. Your son's flagship suffers from . . . maintenance issues."

"You should take better care of the Diadem's ships," Hallholme said. "I shall order full diagnostics and refurbishing after you surrender them."

Adolphus leaned forward on his command chair, his face a mask that belied the tense situation. "You taught me an entirely new set of tac-tics, Commodore Hallholme, so I'm sure you will appreciate the turn-about I have for you." He glanced over at the young, harried-looking software technician who had jury-rigged the comm-system. "Pipe up our images from the prisoner-of-war camp. Show the Commodore exactly who we have in *our* custody."

Although the new comm-officer took longer than expected, Adolphus continued to focus his gaze on Percival Hallholme. Finally the images streamed across the screen, showing the hastily erected tents and prefab shelters, and the crowds of crewmembers from the battleships he had captured. "*Thousands* of Constellation soldiers have surrendered to us, Commodore, including Major Bolton Crais. Eleven thousand prisoners, give or take. Oh, and we have your son Escobar."

The images showed gaunt and severely malnourished captives standing about in the dusty, miserable camp. One image even showed Escobar Hallholme, who stood outside one of the tents, looking defeated. Although the soldiers were starving when they'd been captured, the Commodore would assume that Adolphus had held them in squalid conditions for months. Let the old man draw his own frightening and incorrect conclusions; they made for a better negotiating position.

Adolphus did not react when a software tech, sweating over the half-dismantled weapons control panel, held up a display board on which he had scrawled: "WE HAVE TWO SHOTS—NO MORE."

The eleven automated weapons platforms were in position, ready for a surprise broadside, along with the ten original DZ warships, manned by skeleton crews. Adolphus would use the flagship's weapons only as a last resort, if Commodore Hallholme fired upon him. The desperately wounded *Diadem's Glory* could not endure the pounding for more than a minute.

❦

When Percival saw the images, the thunder of his own pulse echoed in his ears. After Escobar's fleet vanished months ago, the Commodore feared Adolphus had done something terrible. Now he knew that the rebel General was willing to ignore the line he had previously refused to cross—and the Commodore couldn't blame him.

"Sorry, sir," Adkins said after silencing the codecall line; they were alone.

Percival felt incredibly weary. "Are you going to advise me to open fire anyway, Duff?"

"I wouldn't dream of instructing the most talented commander I have ever had the pleasure of knowing."

Percival stared at the screen. "Your advice, please."

"Honestly, sir, I can't think of anything to do. We've never faced anything like this. They have your son, so I must defer to whatever you think is best."

"In other words, I'm on my own."

"I will support your decision, whatever it is, sir," his old friend said. "We all will."

In the harsh prisoner-of-war camp, the gaunt Constellation soldiers were obviously being mistreated. The old Commodore was surprised Adolphus would stoop to such appalling levels . . . but he himself had tortured civilian family members in front of the General, so he could not claim the moral high ground. He should have learned his own lesson from the General's previous failure. His decision should be clear.

But he has my son hostage!

Percival could never face the Diadem if he refused to do what was necessary, if he failed this crucial test. He needed to *win*, regardless of the cost. But how could he ever look at Elaine and his grandsons if he simply threw away Escobar's life as the cost for victory?

"Prepare to fire," he said. "Target the flagship—it looks damaged. But also prepare to cut loose a full barrage on those other ships. We outnumber them, and they don't appear to be in any shape to stand up to a heavy pounding."

"The General may just be tricking us," Adkins muttered.

"If so, it's a pretty damned sophisticated trick." When Adkins opened the codecall line again, the Commodore addressed his rival once more, "You should know one more thing, General. Call it a confession of sorts." Smiling, he exuded calm confidence. "During the Battle of Sonjeera, Diadem Michella obligated me to use barbaric tactics, and for that I am not proud. After she exiled you, however—when she sabotaged your supplies and equipment and tried to make you fail—my bruised and scarred conscience could not tolerate that. So I arranged secret deliveries to help you make it through that first year. Your colony might not have survived without me." He sat in silence for a long moment, letting the astounding news sink in. "General, *I* am your benefactor."

Adolphus reeled at the revelation. He'd never known who had secretly padded the shipments, sending lifesaving equipment and vital food-stuffs that kept them alive during those first months. That act of kind-ness had enabled his exiled refugees to survive until their residences were built and their greenhouses became functional, until their crops produced enough to feed the people. Commodore Hallholme's assis-tance had saved their lives.

Then he felt strengthened by a rigid determination. "And you think that will stay my hand? Once you have lost your honor, Commodore, you can't buy it back in a fit of conscience." He muted the audio and barked over the secure channel, "Ground crews, launch the first salvo from the weapons platforms! Thirty seconds after that, I want all DZ warship crews to open fire."

He saw a flurry of fire from the small unmanned defensive stations in orbit, and seizing his advantage, he turned to the engineer who had become the de facto weapons officer. "Fire our two shots now—and make them count."

The young officer didn't hesitate and launched the projectiles di-rectly toward Hallholme's flagship.

But even before the shots struck, before the General could see whether he had dealt a crippling blow to his enemy, a ripple of feedback explosions cascaded around the bridge of the *Diadem's Glory*. The weapons station, comm-station, and navigation panels geysered with sparks as if small explosives had been planted deep within the workings. The bridge viewscreen went dead and black, and then the flagship lurched downward again, plunging toward the atmosphere.

"What just happened?" Adolphus demanded. "Did our shots hit? Did the Commodore return fire?"

Frantically his officers struggled at the controls, but every system had been deactivated. "That wasn't return fire, sir—at least not yet."

In a leaden voice, the software engineer said, "It was another com-puter virus—tied into the weapons systems. One shot, and now this whole ship is dead, every system fried."

The flagship had been barely functional, held together with a string of jury-rigged emergency repairs. Now the deck rocked and trembled as the atmosphere buffeted the vessel, and it plunged back toward Hell-hole again.

"We're going down, General. We have no control whatsoever."

92

The guards around the prisoner-of-war camp remained tense as the battle continued overhead, concerned that the captives would stage an uprising. On the ground they had only hints of the drama skittering through the atmosphere, but everyone understood what was at stake, both the people of Hellhole and the captives from the Army of the Constellation. The prisoners had given their word not to resist when they thought they had no other chance, but now, knowing that legendary Commodore Hallholme had come to rescue them, many of them reconsidered.

Sophie was bitter as she looked at the restless captive soldiers and heard the increasing murmurs of their private conversations. Hadn't they caused enough pain already? It was time to put an end to this conflict.

After Lodo and Encix sent their telepathic summons, droves of shadow-Xayans began arriving in a matter of minutes, levitating themselves and flying swiftly from their ever-growing settlement. The Constellation prisoners of war stared in amazement while groups of people flew in from over the surrounding hills. As they stared, the alien-possessed crowds floated in the air and arrived in silence. They stood together, and their numbers continued to grow.

Sophie watched Escobar Hallholme, disgusted with him. He was arrogant, unrepentant, and now that he knew his father had arrived to rescue him, he had recovered his dignity and arrogance. With a sniff, the Redcom turned away from the eerie shadow-Xayans, and said, "Your General should just surrender now."

Sophie responded with a laugh and a snort. "You don't know Tiber Adolphus very well."

"I know the situation he's in." Escobar flashed a glance at Bolton. "Tell them, Major Crais."

Bolton looked at Keana, his expression apologetic. "The engine-shutdown virus is only the first part. As soon as anyone tries to fire a shot from our captured ships, an automatic feedback will destroy the weapons systems and melt down the engines. *Permanently.* There's no returning from that. If General Adolphus opens fire, even once, his flagship is wrecked."

Before she could warn Adolphus, Sophie heard a codecall report in her earadio, and any confidence she had vanished. A male voice said, "Too late. The General's ship has no power—the engines are destroyed. They were barely staying aloft as it was, and now the flagship is going down with all hands."

Bolton looked grave and said in a quiet voice, "I wanted to prevent our own ships from being used to open fire upon Constellation targets. Normally, the shutdown would have merely left the flagship helpless in space, but they were already in a low orbit."

Sophie whispered into her codecall, closing her eyes and trying to picture herself on the bridge next to him. "You'll get out of this, Tiber. I can't wait to hear about your brilliant solution when you're back home and safe." A tear trickled down her face.

Beside her, Keana straightened. "It is time for our telemancy."

~⌖~

Inside her mind, Keana felt Uroa awaken again, and the two of them joined together. All the shadow-Xayans had trained for this eventuality, too, and knew how to exert their power.

Lodo and Encix joined their primary telemancy and used it as a catalyst to guide the thousands of converts. Together, they all sent out a powerful, thrumming summons that sounded like a taut, plucked string.

The shadow-Xayans standing in ranks outside the prisoner-of-war camp straightened in unison. They had already demonstrated their abilities when they released the seismic pressure from the planet's crust.

Keana did not allow any twinges of fear to divert her own contribution with Uroa. This would be a grand display of their mental abilities, and a major step toward *ala'ru*. Stronger and stronger.

Lodo and Encix stood at the forefront of the converts, raising their pale arms into the air, guiding the psychic impulses.

Escobar Hallholme looked puzzled, but still arrogant. "Your rebellion is finished."

Keana took control of her voice and turned to look at him. "No, Redcom, we are not done yet."

⮹

Adolphus held on as the deck tilted at a steep angle, and caustic smoke swirled through the bridge, making him cough. The engines had exploded, the weapons systems had melted down. The *Diadem's Glory* was now just a smoldering projectile that tumbled into the atmosphere.

The General commanded the computer specialists and engineers to crowd into the flagship's evac pods.

"We have a seat for you too, sir," said one of the software engineers. "You're more important than any of us—you need to get away."

Adolphus shook his head. "This flagship is going down, and Commodore Hallholme will seize the rest of the ships, take over Hellhole, and impose Constellation rule. Even if he shows some glimmer of honor for my people, the rest of the Constellation will not. The only question is whether he will choose to execute me here or send me back to Sonjeera, where I'll be made into a public spectacle. I'm dead anyway. At least you all have a chance to live."

The viewscreen flickered back to life with a trickle of emergency power, although they still had no control over the flagship's engines. Commodore Hallholme's image appeared, wreathed in static. The flurry of shots from the weapons platforms and a few of his lightly manned DZ warships had damaged several of the Commodore's ships, but it was not enough.

Even Hallholme didn't seem to know what had caused the sudden shutdown of all systems on the *Diadem's Glory*. "General, if I could find a way to rescue your remaining crew, I would. My people are discussing options right now, but I doubt I'll be able to send a rescue craft in time."

Adolphus leaned into the field of view, hardening his expression. "You skipped a step, Commodore—I haven't surrendered."

When Sophie contacted him from the surface, he switched to the private channel and talked with her, ignoring the shuddering explosions, the buffeting blasts from the atmosphere. "I'm glad I didn't bring you aboard, Sophie. See if you can manage without me. Look up in the sky—I'll try to make a memorable flash as I go down."

"Save that for another time, Tiber," she said. "Let's see if our shadow-Xayan friends can pull off a miracle."

Before he could ask what she meant, an unseen force wrapped itself around the flagship and *shoved* against it like a hurricane wind.

One of his engineers yelped. "We're not doing anything, General!"

"It's telemancy." He smiled. "We still have no engines and no control, but we're gaining altitude."

Around them, on the few functioning screens, Adolphus saw dozens of doomed Constellation battleships being nudged away from their decaying orbits, lifted above the atmosphere, like an invisible hand moving game pieces on a board.

Increased acceleration pushed the bridge crew back against their seats, and Adolphus could feel the flagship rising above the fringes of Hellhole's atmosphere until finally, in a sudden stillness, the vessel hung in space, with the damaged planet far below. For a moment he felt safe, peaceful, and protected in an invisible cocoon, although sparks continued to sputter from the control panels. Although they were coughing, the remaining crewmen cheered.

Adolphus didn't point out, however, that now the old Commodore's ships would just round them up and capture every one of them.

⸙

Commodore Hallholme watched his son's flagship plunging toward the planet, burning out of control . . . and then he saw it *rise up*, along with all the other ships that had been spiraling into the atmosphere.

"How are they moving? I thought their engines were destroyed."

"No engine signatures at all, Commodore," reported the weapons tech. "Something else is happening—it's scrambling our sensors."

Then the psychic wave struck Percival's warship as well. Telemancy waves from the surface slapped the Commodore's battle group—but instead of scattering and pushing them out of the way, this psychic blast burned out their weapons systems, melted down the gun ports. The artillery batteries belowdecks exploded.

Alarms whooped throughout his ship and emergency signals came in from the other vessels in his battle group. With difficulty, Percival struggled to his feet. "What the hell is going on? What was that weapon?"

Adkins turned pale as he looked at the preliminary readings. "Our defenses, our shields, our weapons—all neutralized, sir. We're unarmed and helpless."

Then Percival knew. "The aliens did this! Do we have any functional weapons? Can we open fire at all?"

"None, sir." His aide seemed nonplussed and added with a splash of dry humor, "You didn't think victory would be easy, did you?"

"I never believed that, Duff, but the rebel ships are in disarray, the General's forces are about to collapse . . . and now we have no weapons?"

While his engineers scrambled with the systems, ripping out panels, trying to reroute, Percival had a feeling that there would be no simple fix. The initial report was as bad as he feared. "The weapons ports are completely *melted*, sir. There's no way we can reset them, no reprogramming. They're useless."

His voice was quiet. "And we are as defenseless as babes."

On the few remaining bridge screens, alarms began to signal. "Two big stringline haulers just came in, sir! Large vessels, military-capable—eleven of them are battleships."

"Where did the General get more *ships*?" Adkins asked.

Percival did not know the answer.

93

When General Adolphus saw the large haulers arrive, he jumped to his feet on the flagship's bridge. The man at the battered comm-station couldn't keep the excitement out of his voice. "They're from Candela, sir!" He scrambled to clear the static from the signal on the damaged codecall system. "Loaded with refugees, requesting safe haven and assistance."

"They are also warships, fully armed and ready to fight," Adolphus said. He had dispatched the ships himself to guard Tanja Hu's planet against an attack—and they were a very welcome sight now. Sophie had already informed him that the shadow-Xayans had neutralized Commodore Hallholme's weapons. "Connect me with the ship captains and the two hauler pilots." He coughed and rubbed his eyes from the stinging smoke in the air as he called the freshly arrived vessels to prepare for battle.

"But, sir!" one of the captains squawked on the secure channel. "We're crowded deck after deck with refugees! We can't go into military maneuvers!"

"If you don't, then you're going to have to ask Diadem Michella for sanctuary instead," Adolphus said. "The enemy can't fire back—all their weapons are offline. Time to make our move."

As the Candela refugee ships closed in, several more of the General's DZ Defense Force ships came around the planet's rim, their hulls glinting as they emerged from the shadow.

One of the remaining engineers on the bridge laughed. "The skeleton crews have finally rallied, sir."

The General smiled. "It looks that way."

The crowded Candela refugee vessels began taking potshots at the Commodore's damaged attack fleet, hammering with all the weapons they had, not asking questions. Hallholme's own flagship hung dead in orbital space, although the *Diadem's Glory* was in no better shape.

At least the General could use his own vessel, wounded though it might be, as a command center from which he could direct the still-functional ships. The automated weapons platforms managed another round of shots at Hallholme's strike force before their energy reserves were depleted.

He steepled his fingers and leaned over to watch, sensing a possible win despite the chaos. Finally, releasing a long breath, he sat up and activated the codecall to his opponent's flagship. "Commodore Hallholme, my aliens have demonstrated their capabilities. They rendered your weapons useless, but they could just as easily have shut down your life-support systems or even blown your ships apart. You have been defeated. Cease hostilities, and I will accept your sword." He paused, then added mildly, "I believe you're familiar with the proper surrender ceremony?"

"Let me get back to you on that, General Adolphus," the old man said in a clipped tone. "Thank you for your patience." The Commodore terminated the transmission.

⌘

"Immediate report," Percival demanded. "Does anyone have weapons? I need to know our ability to fight back."

The grim answers flooded in from the other stunned vessels. Duff Adkins stood at the Commodore's side, a sour expression on his ruddy face. "Nothing, sir. Every weapons system on every one of our ships is inoperative. No alternates available."

"How long until repairs are complete?" He tried to think of how he could stall. "*Can we fix this?*"

Adkins frowned at him. "No, sir. Our guns are . . . *ruined*. Lumps of slag."

The unexpected ships from Candela closed in, their weapons systems glowing as they prepared to fire. The scattered and mostly empty Deep Zone defense ships had begun to rally, also closing in.

"The Buktu hostages are the only gambit we have left, sir," Adkins suggested. "How would Adolphus react if we threatened to execute them one by one?"

A chill went through the Commodore's chest. He stared at the oncoming warships, and when he didn't answer, his adjutant pressed, "Last chance, sir. Shall I have Erik Anderlos brought to the bridge? He can be the first."

Slowly, Percival shook his head. "Not this time. I won't do it."

"The Diadem would demand that you do everything necessary," Adkins said. Each person on the bridge turned to the old Commodore, waiting for his decision.

"Michella Duchenet is not the one sitting in the command chair, Duff. The Star Throne is very far from here."

"Sir! You can't be contemplating surrender!"

Percival knew what he had to do. After a tense moment of silence, he rose to his feet, not thinking about his aching body. "Tell the stringline pilot to power up the engines of the hauler. Our weapons systems may be inoperative, but our engines still function perfectly well. Transmit my orders to every ship in the battle group: Return to your designated docking clamps with all possible speed. We will retreat immediately along the iperion line back to Buktu."

The armed ships from Candela continued to close in, and he raised his voice. "Do it, now!"

Like a released bowstring, the crew threw themselves into their assigned activities. The Commodore's thirty impotent ships pulled away from orbit and retreated to the stringline hub, where the empty hauler waited for them.

"I have never surrendered before, Duff, but I've never retreated either."

Percival knew all the logical reasons why he didn't dare let General Adolphus capture him, even if it meant leaving his son behind. The great Commodore Hallholme could not be taken prisoner by the rebels!

He could not allow Adolphus to capture his thirty ships, in addition to whatever the rebel leader salvaged from Escobar's fleet. Surely, the General would turn them loose upon the Constellation.

Adkins remained silent, although the bridge crew continued to bustle around them. After a long moment, the aide cleared his throat and said, "I agree that escape is preferable, sir. You can report back to the Diadem and fight another day."

"Believe me, this is not over." He vowed to find some way to rescue Escobar and all the captured Constellation soldiers in the Hellhole prisoner-of-war camp, but he could not do it now.

As the Commodore's ships began to retreat, General Adolphus shouted orders across the open channel. The refugee battleships from Candela raced in toward him, attempting to cut off his escape.

"We can't fight," Percival said. "We have to outrun them—all possible speed!"

They closed in on the giant stringline hauler, and the framework began to pull away along the iperion line where it had waited after dropping off the battle group. Now all those weaponless vessels raced back, trying to reach the hauler as the Deep Zone military accelerated after them.

Percival said over the fleet channel in a maddeningly calm voice, "I would prefer not to leave any ship behind. Therefore, I'm counting on all of you not to make that necessary."

The outlying ships reached the stringline hauler, and with admirable precision they all linked up to the docking clamps. Just like a well-choreographed exercise. Percival was impressed by their efficiency, even though they had never drilled for such a speedy and large-scale retreat.

Two guards arrived on the bridge of the flagship escorting Erik Anderlos in cuffs. The Buktu deputy looked rumpled, having worn the same clothes since Percival's raid on the frozen planetoid, but he no longer seemed tired and defeated. Apparently he understood that the attack on Hellhole had failed.

"So you're running back to Buktu," he said. "Why don't you leave us behind? The General might be more lenient with you."

"No time for that, I'm afraid," Percival said. "Adolphus is already after us, and I need to be out of here as swiftly as possible."

The flagship docked in its clamp on the stringline hauler. One by one, his warships acknowledged they were secure and ready for departure. "All vessels aboard, Commodore," the hauler pilot transmitted.

Closing in, the refugee ships from Candela fired, trying to damage the giant framework vessel.

"Get us out of here!"

Weapon strikes began to pepper the stringline hauler as it lumbered along the iperion path, accelerating until the hellish planet and the General's defense ships blurred in the distance and vanished. At unimaginable speed, the Commodore's ships headed back up the line toward Buktu. Percival suspected that General Adolphus would be on their heels as soon as he could rally his ships.

The old Commodore sat back in his command chair, feeling sick with the taste of defeat.

94

Tanja chose to ride away from Candela with Ian Walfor, since his ship was one of the last to depart as the pair of deadly asteroids bore down on their collision course. Jacque, who had been held safely at the hub, came aboard the vessel after it docked, giving Tanja a long, wordless hug. Now the boy stood silently at a porthole, his eyes wide in horrified fascination.

The first impact would occur within hours.

In the chaos of mass evacuation, she had initially insisted that he go with the first loads of refugees down the stringline to Hellhole, but she wanted him at her side instead. She had agreed to allow Jacque to be with her when the asteroids struck. It was something he would never forget, something she couldn't deny him. The death of a planet.

And being with the boy made her feel strong, too. The two of them had lost so much, and now they were like life preservers for each other. Besides her growing affection for him, Tanja saw the ten-year-old as an anchor to her humanity. Maybe it would drown out the other nightmare that haunted him.

Also aboard Walfor's ship was the recovered, though still damaged, Original alien Tryn and the only surviving shadow-Xayan from the seed colony. The two of them wanted to witness the final hours of Candela as well. Twisted and bent over, Tel Clovis had difficulty moving, but he had

leaned on the one-eyed Tryn as they boarded the craft together. They
would all be the last witnesses.

Thanks to the extra ships General Adolphus had sent from Hellhole,
shuttle after shuttle had loaded with passengers. Evacuees were packed
aboard every possible vessel, using every drop of fuel that could be
scrounged from Candela. Each person barely had room to move, and there
wasn't enough food or other supplies for so many. But they would have to
last only a few days until they all got back to the Hellhole stringline hub.

The operation never stopped. Another loaded stringline hauler
headed down the iperion line; the last few shuttles continued to climb
up from orbit bearing the final refugees. That was all—no one else was
going to escape. She had done her best.

Despite all her efforts, thousands of people remained down there,
trapped. Many out in the frontier had no idea of the imminent disaster.
Perhaps they were the lucky ones. The whole planet would be their
graveyard.

The asteroids were still on course to strike, close enough to be visible in space.

The last fully loaded iperion cargo ships reached orbit and headed
toward the partially assembled stringline hub with its lines to Cles and
Theser. A dozen loads of the rare mineral substance had been launched
from the mines; the workers had scrounged every possible scrap before
abandoning the operations six hours earlier.

Walfor was sweating. "We're cutting this close. Less than an hour
until the first asteroid strikes, and the other one will hit before the end
of the day."

"After the first strike, it doesn't matter," Tanja said, shaking her
head. "An impact of that magnitude won't leave anything for the second asteroid to destroy."

They stood in grim silence, and Walfor reached out to squeeze her
hand. "You saved most of the people, Tanja. I never would have bet
you'd rescue as many as you did. No one could have done better."

She couldn't feel good about her supposed accomplishment. Even so,
she knew the credit was not all hers. "I couldn't have done it without
you, Ian." Her eyes burned, and she closed her eyes to block the view,
but forced them open again to make sure she watched every last second of her beautiful, pristine planet. "You might think our effort would

matter . . . and it should. But rather than thinking of everyone who will survive because we led the rescue operation, I can't ignore those thousands who are unaccounted for. We'll never know how many we left behind." Tanja looked away. "It doesn't matter. I failed them either way."

Moving with her unsettlingly soft gait, the malformed Tryn came into the small piloting deck, accompanied by limping Clovis. The Original alien waved her drooping, retractable feelers in the air while Tel leaned against her. "It is almost time."

Walfor switched the ship's comm-system to play the flurry of reports over the speakers. "All but five loaded ships have departed on the stringline. One hauler is left, waiting for the last evacuees."

"They may as well stay and bear witness, as long as they're safe." She shook her head. "It's not as if I can command them anymore."

"You're still the planetary administrator."

"Not for much longer, without a planet."

Jacque came to her side, and he was shaking with fear. She put her arm around his shoulders, but the trembling did not subside. On the screen, satellite sensors displayed the two incoming asteroids, which were clearly visible against the starfield. Compared to the size of a planet, they were tiny pebbles; nevertheless, each terrible impact would send reverberations through the crust.

The shock wave alone would kill most creatures—just like on Hellhole. Forests would be leveled, engulfed in flames; earthquakes would rip the continents apart. Cubic miles of the surface would be vaporized, saturating the atmosphere with ash. Nothing would be able to live on the devastated world for centuries. It would be a mortal wound, no doubt about it.

The misshapen Original alien made a low humming sound, saddened and disturbed. "When Xaya faced a similar asteroid impact, five of us had already sealed ourselves in the museum vault. We never observed the end of our planet. And I am deeply saddened to witness this one."

"Here comes the first asteroid," Walfor said.

On the far right edge of the screen, one of the gigantic rocks rolled in, a cratered irregular lump almost a hundred kilometers in diameter. The asteroid looked graceful, even casual, as it tumbled toward its target.

"It's moving so slowly," Jacque said.

"Just a matter of perspective," Tanja answered. "It's heading for

Candela at fifty kilometers per second." Much faster than any natural piece of space debris. The second asteroid was farther out, coming from a slightly different direction, aimed at the bull's-eye of her world.

"Candela . . . I built a home here." She stared down at the familiar continents, the wispy clouds, the patches of green, the coastlines. "It was a new hope for us, a place where we could live by our own means and build a society that was our choice. I never expected it to be easy, but who could have anticipated a disaster of this scale?"

Jacque looked up at her with his big brown eyes. His trembling had diminished. "Will General Adolphus find us a new home?"

"Yes." Tanja tried to sound as confident as possible, but the dread was suffocating her. Why was this happening? Two asteroids coming in like bullets from a celestial firing squad—it had to be the work of an intelligence she could not fathom.

The first asteroid sailed along through the vacuum, then grazed Candela's atmosphere and tunneled a hole through the sky. Burning its way to the surface, it struck with a slow-motion impact. Scarlet and orange shock waves rippled along with hot jagged fissures as the dissipating energy set the atmosphere on fire, carved an enormous crater in the crust, and shouldered aside mountain ranges.

Tanja caught her breath. Even Walfor let out a shocked sound. Beside her, Jacque wept.

In that one instant, everyone who had remained behind, everyone who had missed the evacuation call, was now dead. The impact had leveled every structure the colonists of Candela had ever built. The majestic floating towers in Saporo Harbor, the villages in the hills, the shadow-Xayan seed colony, the rich iperion mines.

A thrumming ripple echoed through Ian Walfor's ship. Tanja couldn't believe it was a feedback or shock wave from the asteroid strike, but then she realized it was a telemancy echo, a vibration of despair emitted by Tryn and Clovis. "Exactly like what happened to Xaya five centuries ago," the Original said in a quiet, throbbing voice.

Tanja's throat was dry, and her heart pounded. She forced herself not to turn away and hide from the end of her world, but she could think of no appropriate response to what she had just witnessed.

Two hours later they watched the second horrific asteroid strike, which was even larger than the first.

95

shop's complete disbelief swelled inside of him like a gathering storm. The Council of Nobles had dismissed his legitimate claim! They had disregarded the law, the Constellation Charter—even though they had applied the same proviso when it suited their purposes. Even Michella had brushed him aside, after all he'd done for her, all the political messes he had cleaned up.

Because he was her most loyal aide, Michella had lavished praise upon him. She'd supported him, appreciated his work, trusted him with her life . . . so long as he knew his place. In her view, the most talented butler in the universe did not deserve even a minor seat at the master's table.

His ancestors had been Diadems—and the nobles had *laughed* at him!

Michella seemed not to give any thought to how much blood he had on his hands because of her. Wallowing in dark thoughts, he wondered what difference a little more blood would make. . . .

He paced the patio of his townhouse, seething. Laderna came up from behind and held him close, and he felt the comforting softness of her caress. "You're not alone in this—I'm still here," she said in a gentle voice. "And *I* know you're a nobleman, as good as any of them. Better, in fact."

She never denigrated him, never laughed at his dreams, and she supported him regardless of his title. As a lord, he had planned—strictly in a business sense—to marry an acceptable noblewoman and establish a Heer dynasty, rebuilding the family name after centuries of neglect. He had been willing to keep Laderna around, perhaps even as his own trusted assistant—like he was to the Diadem—to do necessary but unpleasant work. . . .

Now all that had been dashed, and still she was here with him.

It was a typical sunny Sonjeera day, and Ishop decided he had to leave Council City. He took Laderna on the hovercycle—one of several flashy gifts from the Diadem, though one he rarely used. Now, as Laderna sat behind him and held on tight, he streaked off on a cushion of air and followed a winding road out of the city, skimming so fast that he felt he could race away from the insults the nobles had heaped on him.

Ishop turned into a tree-lined sanctuary, the new Hirdan Wildlife Park, and stopped at a brass dedication plaque at the gate. Laderna laughed at the irony as she read: "'The land for this park was donated by Lord Hirdan, in honor of his deceased son.'" She chuckled. "One of our first accomplishments on the list!"

"Somehow I don't see the humor right now," Ishop said. "The list did me no good. All that work, all the terrible risks we took, for nothing."

"Not for nothing! You exacted your revenge, and don't tell me there wasn't personal satisfaction in that. Besides, now we can enjoy this nice park."

They rode the hovercycle to a lookout that showed off the grandeur of Council City. They absorbed the view in solitude, but were interrupted by a group of bicyclists, so they left. Continuing on the hovercycle, they found a grassy slope that overlooked a small blue lake; their only company was a flock of large white-winged birds.

Laderna reminded Ishop of what he already knew so well. "Remember, the list really isn't finished. There's still the Duchenet name. . . ."

He looked into her eyes, then kissed her, tasting a sweetness he hadn't noticed before. "And I always finish a job, once I've set my mind to it." He gazed down at the serene lake. One of the white-winged birds flew near them, flapping slowly as it rode a thermal, then glided back down to the water.

"What a lovely place to plot a murder," she said.

"You mean an assassination—a necessary political homicide. The Diadem made a point of explaining the difference to me, many times."

"She still trusts you, Ishop. You still have access to her. It should be a simple matter to poison an old woman, just like we did to that snotty socialite on our list."

"Evelyn Weilin," he said with a wistful smile. "The acid made her skull collapse and her face dissolve! Yes, that might be fitting for Michella. Reminds me of that alien creature dissolving in the hangar. . . ."

"Now you're thinking, boss." She raised her eyebrows, leaned closer. "Shall we make love to celebrate?"

He shook his head. Too many plans were already whirling through his mind. "She's not dead yet."

⬦

Ishop didn't waste any time. He had waited long enough already, months of planning, anticipating, building the case for reclaiming his noble name, putting all the pieces together. Only to be snickered at.

Slipping into the Diadem's office alone, he replaced her favorite black tea with a special mixture that he and Laderna had concocted, taking care to leave subtle evidence (which he would be sure to "find" later) that blamed one of the servants. Michella's favorite beverage was expensive tea imported—ironically, from Ogg, the planet where the Osheers had been exiled so long ago—and Ishop knew that Michella enjoyed several cups each day. Her special, private treat.

The following morning, with a carefully crafted humble demeanor that showed he was ready to get back to work, he arrived for a scheduled meeting with the Diadem. By now, the old woman had probably forgotten about his request, or at least she might pretend so. It took all his skill to drain the hatred and anticipation from his expression.

Michella sat at her desk reading a document. She looked up and greeted him with a warm, grandmotherly, and totally false smile. A maid-servant stood on one side, preparing the Diadem's tea as well as the sweet kiafa that Ishop always drank. He had never seen this particular maid-servant before, but old Michella went through employees quite rapidly, always finding something about each one that displeased her.

While the Diadem continued to read, forcing him to wait (not an accident, he was sure), Ishop watched the maidservant check the temperature of the teapot, arrange the Diadem's cup, and extend the silver tray as if she were performing an elaborate ritual. He tried not to fixate on the teapot.

At last, Michella gave him her attention, accompanied by a sweet smile. "Now then, Ishop, I wish you had consulted with me before revealing your silly story to the Council members. I could have saved you some embarrassment."

"It is not a silly story, Eminence. I have the legitimate paperwork to prove lineage." His pulse was racing. "My claim is valid."

"Your family story is very interesting, dear Ishop, but it's ancient history, and we don't want to dig up old bones, do we? Haven't I rewarded you enough? I had no idea you were dissatisfied. What more would you like?" Now she gave him her best warm smile.

"I would like my noble title restored," he answered, crisp and cold. "And I would like the Tazaar holdings as my due."

She fluttered her fingers, as if to brush the words out of the air. "Out of the question. Planet Orsini is an important bargaining chip, and right now, with the unrest brewing among the nobles, I will need to use it to buy absolute loyalty from one of the most powerful families. Other nobles are far ahead of you in line, don't you see? No, we'll have to reach a more sensible resolution for you. A villa or two would be realistic, but not an entire planet, and certainly not a Crown Jewel world!" She laughed, expecting him to laugh with her. He didn't.

Moving with efficient habit, the maidservant poured a small amount of tea in a second cup. Ishop held up his hand. "None for me, thank you. I prefer my usual kiafa."

"The second cup is not for you, dear Ishop," the Diadem said. "My special-blend tea is far too expensive for guests."

"Even a noble guest?" He felt tense, like an overtight spring ready to be released, then realized it was a stupid, impulsive thing to say. He didn't want her to offer him any tea!

"Ishop, if you were counted among the nobles, how could you continue to do your quiet work for me? That's much more important, for the good of the Constellation."

To his horror, the maidservant raised the second cup to her own lips and took a long sip. Knowing she only had a few moments to live, and seeing a quick way to conceal his guilt, Ishop said, "But your own maid can drink your special tea?

The Diadem primly arranged her hands on the desktop and pursed her lips as she pretended to consider. "Who knows what other assassination attempts might be brewing? General Adolphus still has many loyalists, and Enva Tazaar already turned against me, and Lord Riomini proved his defiance, and there was the bomb plot." She shook her head, then looked up at the maidservant. "I can't be too careful, Ishop—you know that very well. She has been tasting my tea and my food for three days now. Didn't you know?" Michella placed a finger to her lips. "Ah, you were preoccupied. At any rate, it seemed a wise precaution. Adolphus's traitors could be anywhere."

Though he cursed inwardly, he responded with a vigorous nod. "I was going to suggest a similar thing myself, Eminence." Trying to appear calm while his intestines knotted, he poured his own cup of kiafa from the second pot, letting it cool. It wouldn't be long now, and he would have to look genuinely surprised.

The Diadem extended a document toward him so he could comment on a new clause, when the maidservant cried out, first a gasp of pain and surprise, then a loud shriek. She fell backward as if her spine had unraveled and knocked the tea tray to the floor with a crash.

The Diadem recoiled from her chair, and Ishop sprang away from the desk. He made a point of dashing his kiafa to the floor, knocking the pot into the pile of debris as well. "The tea is poison, Eminence—and my kiafa, too! Don't drink anything!"

The maidservant writhed on the floor, her mouth opening and closing like a fish's. Her throat collapsed as acid ate outward from her esophagus. Then her face sagged as the roof of her mouth liquefied.

That could have been Michella. His disappointment felt palpable.

Ishop hurried the Diadem out of the room as he yelled for guards. After a brief panicked moment, he also remembered to call for medical attention, just to show his compassion for the maidservant, but knew it was useless.

"I will order an immediate investigation, Eminence!" He knew that he and Laderna had covered their tracks and planted appropriate evidence; none of the indicators would lead back to them, but Ishop was discouraged.

Wheezing, the Diadem wiped sweat from her powdered brow. "Look into it yourself, Ishop. There's no one else I can trust."

Maybe she would simply collapse from a coronary right now, but he knew he would never be that fortunate. She was a tough old hag.

"I will get to the bottom of this, Eminence. Remember, Enva Tazaar is still on the loose, and you're right—Adolphus loyalists could be anywhere."

96

As Percival Hallholme's battle group raced away from Hellhole along the stringline, he had three days to plan what to do next—but there were no decisions to be made, no commands to be issued, only contemplation over his retreat. And, worse, how he would report his failure to Diadem Michella and Lord Riomini.

When he'd been dragged out of retirement from Qiorfu, he had not accepted this command so that he could earn glory, or because he had any thirst for combat. He had been satisfied with his career, content with defeating General Adolphus in the first rebellion. But instead of acquiring another bright badge of honor for his legacy, Commodore Percival Hallholme now had a large stain.

The Diadem had been naïvely confident in his ability to solve the problem and clean up the mess. Percival realized now that he never should have accepted the mission, and instead should have convinced Diadem Michella of the magnitude of the challenge. His opponent was *General Tiber Maximilian Adolphus,* who had lost the first rebellion only because of treachery, not through any lack of command skills.

In his quarters, with the lights dimmed, Percival faced his own thoughts, wondering if he really *had* wanted the taste of glory again, and he thought that might be true. The earlier victory in orbit over Sonjeera had seemed so hollow from a military standpoint, leaving the

Commodore with nagging doubts about his own abilities. To help erase the guilt for his part in the situation, he had secretly helped General Adolphus survive on the hellish planet, when he felt the Diadem acted dishonorably against a defeated foe.

This time, Percival had hoped to defeat the General in an honorable way—the right way.

As the stringline hauler hurtled back to the Buktu end of the DZ stringline, he spent hours at his desk, writing and rewriting his formal letter of resignation. That went without saying. He had not managed to stop the rebellion as ordered; he had neither defeated nor captured the enemy. He had not recovered the captured Constellation fleet, and he had not rescued the thousands of prisoners of war. Or his own son.

He had been forced to retreat.

Percival had, in fact, succeeded only in damaging thirty more of the Constellation's finest warships, rendering them weaponless. And undoubtedly that would embolden General Adolphus.

No, Michella would not be pleased at all. He hoped his resignation would be sufficient, but he realized that the old woman might require his execution as well. He looked down at the letter:

Eminence, it is with great pride that I have devoted my life to the Constellation and the Star Throne. And it is with even greater regret that I must end this service. My abilities have proved inadequate during the Constellation's greatest crisis. It is clear that I was not the right commander for this operation. I will lend my support to any better officer who can lead the Army of the Constellation to victory. Regrettably, I am not that person.

He signed it with a flourish, stared at the document for a long time, then sealed it in his private locker. Now that he had attended to the distasteful matter, he could turn his mental focus to the next phase of the operation. He was not finished, by any means.

During the three-day flight to Buktu, the best Constellation engineers worked at the damaged weapons systems, trying to cobble something together. All the primary batteries and controls had been melted into slag, but Percival ordered his chemists and engineers to build explosive projectiles from scratch. Be resourceful. Even customized catapults would do, if used properly.

"When we reach the facilities at Buktu, we'll find much more that we can use," he said to Duff Adkins.

"If the General pursues us, he will bring those aliens to attack us again. How can we possibly fight them?"

"We can't afford to have a face-to-face battle. The idea is to not conduct a military engagement, but to leave chaos in our wake. Buktu will not be a last stand, but a primary line of defense. We will prevent any pursuers from getting through. No telling what's on our tail, or how far back they are."

He had met again with Erik Anderlos, trying to convince the hostages to cooperate, promising leniency when they reached the Crown Jewels. Percival requested an inventory of the planetoid's fuel-processing facilities, the supply and fuel depots, and the ice cave settlements, but no one would speak a word. Percival hadn't really expected them to.

"We'll do our best to map out the facilities ourselves when we get there," he told Adkins. "Our demolition crews can determine how to destroy them all, and we'll make Mr. Anderlos and his companions watch."

The Buktu captives were kept in well-guarded chambers. They would be taken back to Sonjeera, paraded before the Diadem, and no doubt used for propaganda purposes. In old times—actually, not so long ago—Michella would have exiled them to the Deep Zone, but that was no longer an option.

When the hauler reached the terminus at Buktu, the pilot disengaged from the iperion path and moved to the repaired stringline that would take them back to Sonjeera. The old Commodore intended to leave nothing behind that the rebel General could use. As the first order of business, he sent a team of commandos over to the DZ terminus ring. The demolition specialists planted their compact explosives and returned to the flagship in time to watch the detonations rip apart the docking facility, thus cutting off easy transport back to planet Hallholme.

When this was accomplished, he breathed a little easier. "Now the General will have a harder time coming after us."

Afterward, Percival refueled his thirty warships and loaded all the fuel stockpiles he could take aboard the hauler.

"Do we occupy Buktu as a beachhead?" Adkins asked. They were standing on the bridge of the flagship, waiting for the refueling to finish. "Reinforce our defenses here and use it as our primary base? We could bring more war materiel from Sonjeera and use this as our foothold into the Deep Zone."

"We can't hold Buktu with what we've got, Duff—we have to get back to Sonjeera and regroup there." He scratched his head. "It's best to use a time-honored military tactic. If you can't hold a strategic asset, destroy it and prevent the enemy from using it as an asset."

"We'll all be happy to see an explosion or two," Adkins mused. "It'll ease tensions among the crew."

Percival smoothed his muttonchop whiskers. "I wish we could accomplish something more significant than that."

He summoned Erik Anderlos to the bridge under guard and made the Buktu deputy observe the demolition operations. Anderlos reddened. "You already captured us, and you cut the stringline to Hellhole. Why destroy it all? Are you just proving your barbarity?"

"We're implementing a scorched-earth policy," the Commodore said.

As they watched, one of the fuel depots exploded, then a second, and a third as the demolition teams triggered explosives from storage silo to storage silo.

He never should have left Qiorfu. He wanted to tend his grapevines, spend time with his grandsons, drink in the tavern with Duff and tell war stories, embellishing them and chuckling when he was caught doing it. That was what an old military officer should do with his remaining time.

He dispatched squadrons of fighter craft to saturate-bomb the lunar mining operations with crude new explosives, wrecking Buktu's excavating machinery and stockpiles of materials used to rebuild ships. The remaining vessels in spacedock were also triggered to explode.

With explosion after explosion, Percival became numb to the parade of devastation, but he didn't let Anderlos leave. "You have to watch all of this."

"Why? I can already see how mindlessly destructive you are."

Percival looked at the man. "It's not mindless. It's necessary."

The large settlements beneath the ice sheet were buried, the entrances vaporized, the tunnels shattered. This was not a military attack, but a thorough deconstruction process. And when the last orbiting fuel tanks had erupted like small supernovas against the black, starry sky, Commodore Hallholme regrouped his vessels. The fighter craft landed in the launching bays, and the detached frigates locked onto their docking clamps.

"If and when General Adolphus ever returns to Buktu, he'll find that we've left nothing for him. Nothing at all."

As the stringline hauler departed for the Crown Jewels, the Commodore knew that he had nothing left either. He tried to tell himself that this made him even with General Adolphus, but he knew it was not true.

97

Commodore Hallholme had fled, leaving Hellhole safe—for the moment.

While he was stranded aboard a damaged, nonfunctional enemy flagship, General Adolphus watched the Constellation task force escape. Though he knew the *Diadem's Glory* wasn't going anywhere, he signaled his other ships. "All functional vessels, head off in pursuit! They have no weapons, thanks to Xayan telemancy. Follow them to Buktu before they destroy the outpost there."

The captains of the refugee ships balked at the General's order. One said, "Sir, we're overloaded already, and we don't have the food or life support for this many people. We need to start off-loading immediately. We won't last the three-day voyage to Buktu."

Another captain said, "More Candela ships are due any minute now, and there are more behind them. Some will be in worse shape than ours. Half the vessels don't have systems to keep people alive for more than a day or two."

Adolphus stared at the stringline hub, not willing to let his enemy get away, but unable to justify the pursuit. His adrenaline made him want to run the Commodore down anyway, to the ends of the universe if necessary; Percival Hallholme would either set up an ambush back at Buktu, or he would keep running all the way back to the Crown Jewels.

Either way, the General realized that it would be foolhardy to chase him.

"We're not going after him," he said. "Now that Hellhole is secure, we need to save the evacuees at Candela. Dispatch more emergency ships to assist Administrator Hu with the rescue operations, retrieve anyone in orbit who couldn't get onto a stringline evacuation vessel." Yes, that was his priority.

Another hauler arrived on the stringline, carrying ships overloaded with refugees. One of the ships had a badly compromised life-support system, and many passengers had already lost consciousness after standing shoulder-to-shoulder for days. Although some had died, most survived, but they were hungry and gasping. Adolphus thought of the gaunt Constellation soldiers he had retrieved from Escobar Hallholme's fleet.

One of the new captains issued a breathless report. "General! When we left Candela, the asteroids were coming in. Impact was only a few hours behind us, so by now, the planet is destroyed. I hope Administrator Hu got more people off. She stayed until the very last minute."

Right now, his own recovery crews were boarding the remaining ships in the captured Constellation fleet, assessing damage, replacing ruined parts, reinstalling computer systems, or scuttling ships that could not be repaired. None of those vessels were in any shape to rescue evacuees from Candela, but Adolphus scrounged other craft to transport the ragged remnants of a whole planetary population down to Hellhole.

While the operation was ongoing, the General looked around the battle-scarred bridge of Escobar's flagship. "Now, somebody get me to a functional shuttle to take me back to the surface. I want my feet on solid ground, at least as solid as Hellhole can be. Time to get back to business."

Once he returned to Michella Town, grimy and exhausted, he was met by Sophie, who had rushed there from the prisoner-of-war camp. She threw her arms around him, and he responded in kind, pulling her close and feeling how real she was. They kissed, and he didn't care who saw them.

"I knew you'd find a way to win, Tiber." She pulled back to look at him. "You've engineered a final flash of glory."

He shook his head. "The Xayans proved themselves. Without their telemancy, Commodore Hallholme would have won."

Shipload after shipload of refugees landed in Michella Town, and as the magnitude of Candela's disaster sank in, the General concentrated his efforts on organizing the retrieval of the refugees, with Sophie's assistance. He had already dispatched urgent message drones throughout the Deep Zone, requesting aid and sanctuary for the evacuees; Hellhole certainly couldn't support so many thousands of additional people, and they would be distributed among the other frontier worlds. Sophie took the challenge to heart and managed the resupply and redistribution, providing food and shelter for the shell-shocked survivors.

Next morning, General Adolphus and Sophie Vence worked in his study at Elba, receiving reports from the orbital hub and his ship commanders. At midmorning another flurry of vessels arrived from Candela, all of them filled with panicked evacuees. By noon, a final ragtag group of salvaged ships and loaded iperion ore boxes reached the Hellhole hub, apparently the last survivors who had gotten away from Candela, including Tanja Hu and Ian Walfor, who were on their way down to meet with him.

Adolphus told Sophie, "We need to debrief them as soon as they arrive. And I also want Encix and Lodo here, along with Keana-Uroa, and maybe Tryn, too, if she can make it. Can you arrange it?"

Sophie had already anticipated his request. "They can all be here, including Tryn, as well as Tel Clovis. I want to review the images from Candela—and I hope somebody can explain how two giant asteroids decided to smash that planet at the same time. . . ."

Cristoph de Carre drove a Trakmaster from the camp near Slickwater Springs, bringing Keana-Uroa as well as Encix and Lodo. They emerged from the overland vehicle, and Adolphus invited the group into his residence. Both Tanja Hu and Ian Walfor came down from the refugee ships in orbit, accompanied by Jacque Nax and the malformed Tryn and Clovis. The alien Tryn glided along and touched soft-fingered hands to Encix and Lodo, telepathically sharing everything she had witnessed. Tel Clovis shambled along behind her, a severely injured man who could not stand straight; he took halting, erratic steps, as if learning to walk all over again.

"It was a hell of a show, General." Walfor uploaded recorded data into Elba's screen and displayed it on the wall of his conference room. In silence, the group watched the last images of Candela: the first asteroid scooped through the atmosphere and shattered the surface, erupting in smoke, flames, and great clouds of dust. Shock waves flattened everything on the continents. Ripples of seismic fury shot across dry land; tidal waves roared kilometers high into the atmosphere.

The second impact was even bigger, and dumped enough debris into the atmosphere to obscure the entire planet. On Hellhole, just one impact had nearly wrecked the entire ecosystem. Given what Adolphus had just seen, there could not be anything left alive on Candela.

He paced the room, addressing Tanja. "If Ian Walfor had not accidentally spotted the threat, *everyone* on Candela would be dead now. "

"The asteroids were not on a natural path," said Tanja. "We had less than a week."

"That doesn't sound right to me," Cristoph said. "An asteroid orbit is *years* long, maybe decades. The chances of a celestial impact like that are vanishingly small—and for two of that size to strike a planet simultaneously is *just not possible*."

"It obviously wasn't an accident," Sophie said. "But that still doesn't explain what happened."

"It's what happened to Xaya," Lodo said. "The death of a world. Now they did the same to Candela, because of Tryn and the shadow-Xayans, because of the huge telemancy burst they used against the Sonjeera stringline hub. It made Candela a target."

Encix's thrumming voice reflected her alarm. "It is as I feared. We used great telemancy here to quell seismic unrest from the impact crater as well. Now our presence is known, and we will be targeted next . . . just as we were five centuries ago. Since we exhibited such telemancy, we cannot hide how close we are to *ala'ru*." She and Lodo turned their smooth alien faces toward each another, sharing a thought.

On the screen, Keana watched the replay of the slow and devastating impacts; a haunting horror was plain on her face. "What is it?" she demanded aloud, but spoke to the presence inside her. "Uroa, what are you hiding from all of us?"

The Originals conferred with each other in telepathically linked unison. Finally, Lodo faced the General. "We have much more to tell you, General Tiber Adolphus."

Encix spoke: "The Xayan race has long had its factions. In a bygone time Zairic showed us the path to enlightenment, explaining that our racial destiny was to ascend and become more perfect than any other. But another group, the Ro-Xayans, refused to hear the truth, refused to follow that sacred vision. They vowed to prevent our race from achieving *ala'ru*. By any means possible."

"Why would they want to do that?" Sophie said.

Encix turned her blank, alien face toward Sophie, and Lodo let out a humorless chuckle. "Could any of you explain your human factions and your wars in a sentence or two?"

Keana was struggling with herself, and the voice of Uroa emerged from her throat. "We Xayans were close to achieving our potential. In another two generations, more or less, we could have been superior beings in all ways, our souls liberated from the material universe. But the Ro-Xayans were powerful as well. After arguing with our political and religious leaders, they left our planet and ventured among the stars. Eventually, they used their combined powers to divert a large asteroid. They *aimed* it, sent it toward Xaya."

Encix said, "The disagreements were so severe that the Ro-Xayans decided to destroy our race and our world, rather than allow us to ascend."

Lodo said in a sad voice, "Our mortal enemies are still out there, even after all these centuries. They always watched Xaya. When we awakened again from the slickwater, and this damaged planet began its rebirth, something alerted them. And our use of telemancy showed them how far we have come . . . and that we are a potential threat to them."

Keana struggled with the revelations from her mental companion. "I think they're trying to reclaim this world, seeding it with the genetic material of creatures they took before the impact."

Sophie blinked in surprise. "That's where the large animals came from? Those embryo canisters dropped in the isolated valleys? The herds crossing the plains?"

"This also explains the strange visiting ships," Adolphus added.

Tanja Hu hung her head. "And when the shadow-Xayans protected

Candela with their great blast through the stringline network, it was like a shout to the Ro-Xayans? Did *they* send two asteroids to destroy my planet?"

"They snuffed out Candela to make sure we did not reawaken further," Lodo said.

Encix was grim. "What they did to Candela is just a start, General Tiber Adolphus. They know that the greatest concentration of reawakened Xayans is here on this world. We have very little time. Unless we achieve *ala'ru* soon, we are all lost. The Ro-Xayans will come back to destroy the planet."

98

Under gray clouds that were uncharacteristic for Sonjeera, the Diadem stood with Lord Riomini and a group of leading nobles at the Sonjeera spaceport. Commodore Hallholme's strike force descended from orbit, thirty large warships settling like a flock of birds on the paved expanse. Around the Diadem, Riomini and the Council members spoke in low tones. She wasn't the only one to notice that Hallholme was not returning with a hundred rescued battleships from his son's fleet. Disappointing.

An hour ago, upon returning to the partially repaired stringline hub, the old Commodore notified Michella by codecall that he would bring in all of his ships, rather than take a shuttle down. As she watched now, she had to admit that it did make for an impressive show.

When she'd demanded a preliminary report on what had occurred in the Deep Zone, he was not communicative, not even evasive. He simply didn't answer. A hard knot had formed in her stomach, and she hurried to the spaceport. She hoped he was here to declare a victory of some kind, *any* kind. That would be best for all concerned.

A small-statured woman in a red jacket and white slacks emerged from the spaceport administration building and hurried toward Michella and the official observers. The spaceport bureaucrat spoke in a small voice, like that of a child. "Eminence, Commodore Hallholme notified us that he has several hundred prisoners. His mission must have been a great success!"

Michella felt a chill of relief. "He'll have a grand story to tell for sure, something to add to his legend." She prayed that General Adolphus was one of his prisoners.

"I knew we could count on the Commodore." Lord Riomini looked stony but imposing in his dress army uniform. He had been cool to her since her strong reprimand, probably still shaken, but she knew it was only a matter of time before he tried to find a way back into her good graces. Maybe she would see signs of his old personality today, and she would be receptive to it. The prospect of a big victory over Adolphus had put her in a good mood.

Hallholme's flagship set down closest to the noble reception party, and two exit ramps dropped. The distinguished Commodore walked alone down a ramp, limping as he always did from an old war injury. His silvery muttonchop sideburns looked unbrushed; his antiquated uniform appeared as worn as the man wearing it. His shoulders drooped as he marched toward the Diadem.

Though she continued to smile, Hallholme's body language told her that he had bad news.

With a crisp salute, the old war hero said, "Eminence, I regret to inform you that I did not complete the task you gave me. I will present a full report of our operation's failure at planet Hallholme, and I am prepared to tender my resignation."

Alarmed, she stared at the landed warships. "Commodore—your battle group appears to be intact. Did you even engage the enemy?"

"We were about to, when General Adolphus's alien allies destroyed all of our weapons systems. We had no way to protect ourselves. In addition to his own formidable defenses, the General has captured the ships in the Constellation fleet led by my son, whom he now holds in a prisoner-of-war camp, along with Major Bolton Crais, and thousands of loyal soldiers."

Michella paled. Lord Riomini stepped forward. "Were you able to inflict any damage at all?"

"Many of the captured Constellation ships were disabled when we arrived, burning up in the atmosphere. Most of Adolphus's fleet was nowhere to be seen, and I could have defeated him handily if the aliens had not struck."

Deeply concerned, Michella said, "Commodore, shortly after your ships departed, a powerful energy surge traveled along the stringline from Candela and seriously damaged the Sonjeera stringline hub. Many ships were lost, and transportation across the Crown Jewels was disrupted."

Hallholme gave a somber nod. "Probably the same energy they used against me. They would have seized my entire battle group if I hadn't made a tactical withdrawal. We returned via Buktu and used special teams to destroy as much as we could. We took the rebel population of Buktu as our prisoners."

Breathing hard beside the Diadem, Riomini said, "Eminence, I feel vindicated that I took this alien threat seriously! We must learn how to fight them, or they will defeat us. Our only connection, our only clue, is sealed within the quarantined hangar. We simply *must* break into that passenger pod and analyze the alien bodies."

The Commodore remained at attention. "I concur, Eminence."

Michella snapped, "That is not for either of you to decide!"

Hallholme looked down. "Indeed, it is not." He reached into his uniform jacket, withdrew a folded sheet of paper. "In my entire career, I have never suffered a defeat of this magnitude. Because I have utterly failed you, I no longer deserve my rank. This is my letter of resignation." He extended the letter to her.

Michella was furious about the Commodore's defeat, but she knew that none of the lesser commanders serving in the Army of the Constellation could hold a candle to his abilities. She would be a fool to get rid of a proven war hero, even with his embarrassing "tactical withdrawal." She needed to play up the fear of the aliens and make the populace even more terrified of an invasion.

She tore up the resignation letter in front of him. "On the contrary, Commodore Hallholme—when faced with no other acceptable options, you made the right decision and retreated, keeping these valuable warships out of enemy hands. You will regroup and fight another day."

He looked at her silently, sadly, and then lowered his head.

She pressed him: "Do you think I can do without you in times like these? I'm still counting on you to defeat General Adolphus! Even after this misfortune, you are my best military leader. The Constellation needs your wisdom and experience. You will retain your rank and your position, and you *will* continue to serve me—that is my explicit command."

She couldn't understand why the Commodore did not look pleased. She was saving him from disgrace! Was the old man actually looking forward to retiring and being forgotten in his dotage? With a slight bow, he replied, "As you wish, Eminence."

She looked long and hard at the Commodore. "I want you to work with Lord Riomini to bolster the defenses of the Crown Jewel worlds. Prepare us for every possible type of attack. I want to be ready for anything."

"Eminence, we've got to open that passenger pod and analyze what's inside!" Riomini insisted.

She whirled on him. "You idiot, as I've told you, the pod *is* one of their points of attack! They *want* us to open it, so that everyone on Sonjeera will be contaminated by the Xayan body inside. And once we are all possessed by alien organisms, they will sweep across the Crown Jewels—just as they must have done in the Deep Zone."

Riomini seemed to wilt under her unrelenting glare. Commodore Hallholme, though, cleared his throat. "It is difficult to defend against something we do not understand."

"Defend against it anyway!" Glaring, Michella stalked away. On the landing field behind her, hundreds of defeated Constellation soldiers began filing out of their landed ships.

⤙⤚

Too many things were spinning out of control. Diadem Michella's daughter had been lost to alien possession, and the entire Constellation was vulnerable. The weirdly powerful aliens that General Adolphus had awakened now threatened to overwhelm all of her planets.

Here at home, she could not forget about the two recent attempts to assassinate her. A bomb and poison! She was convinced that murderous rebel sympathizers were everywhere. . . .

When the Diadem returned to the palace, she fired her kitchen staff and most of the servants, and ordered that replacement personnel be brought in; Ishop Heer was responsible for vetting dozens of applicants. She didn't know whom else she could trust.

He joined her for an evening meal, and she sat with him at an improvised dining table in her private suite. Ishop had personally watched every step of the meal's preparation, but even so she made him taste each dish before she put it on her plate.

"You are one of the few people I can rely on," Michella said, hearing the anxiety in her own voice. They had just finished a course of roast sonji pheasant, and were waiting while the plates were cleared and the next course was brought in from the kitchen.

"From now on, my food will be tested even more carefully than before, each item double-checked," she said with a sigh. "The meals will probably be cold by the time I get to eat." Michella squared her bony shoulders. "A stronger security force will accompany me on even the most trivial of outings. I will depend on you more than ever, Ishop, my good friend. You are worth so much more than one of those petty, selfish nobles. Don't worry—I'll see to it that you are richly rewarded."

"You are safe with me," he assured her, but she thought she caught a flicker in his eyes—a hint of hostility? She shivered and looked away, then felt ashamed of herself for seeing assassins and traitors everywhere! It was mere paranoia.

They continued their meal while studying an array of security screens. After Commodore Hallholme's frightening news of the Xayan telemancy attack, and Riomini's obsession with the alien contamination in the hangar, she now focused on a live surveillance image of the Sonjeera spaceport. Behind numerous security barriers, the resin-encased hangar formed a rounded profile against the night sky, illuminated by floodlights.

She scowled at it. "The alien presence is trapped inside there."

"And it is neutralized," Ishop said.

"How can we be sure?"

As they watched, the sealed hangar began to glow.

Appendix A

THE 20 CROWN JEWEL WORLDS

Aedl
Aeroc
Barassa
Cherby
Fleer
Indos
Jonn
Kappas
Klief
Machi
Marubi
Noab
Ogg
Orsini
Patel
Qiorfu
Sandusky
Sonjeera
Tanine
Vielinger

Appendix B

THE 54 DEEP ZONE PLANETS

Aimerej

Ankheny

Argyth

Astervillius

Atab Abas

Balkast

Bija'dom

Blythe System

Boj

Brevor

Brezane

Buchad

Buktu

Candela

Casagan

Cles

Cobalt

Darenthia

Ehemi

El Kuara

Enesi

Erebusal

Eviticu

Haiasi

Hallholme/Helhole

Hossetea

Karadakk

Karum and Kanes

Kirsi

Moloch

Nephilim

Nicles

Nielad

Nomolos

Ondor's Gambit

Oshu

Osian

Qolme

Qotem

Ridgetop

Rinthi

Ronom

Salm
Setsai
Signik
Tehila
Teron
Theser

Thiop
Triol
Ueter
Umber
Vytr
Xodu

Consolidated Glossary

ADKINS, DUFF—retired sergeant in Army of the Constellation, served under Commodore Percival Hallholme during General Adolphus's rebellion.

ADOLPHUS, GENERAL TIBER MAXIMILIAN—leader of a failed rebellion against the Constellation, now the exiled leader on the planet Hallholme. Commonly called the General.

ADOLPHUS, JACOB—father of Tiber Adolphus, patriarch of the Adolphus family on Qiorfu.

ADOLPHUS, STEFANO—brother of Tiber Adolphus, now dead.

AEROC—one of the Crown Jewels, ruled by Lord Selik Riomini, main headquarters of the Army of the Constellation.

ALA'RU—Xayan evolutionary and spiritual ascension. In translation, the Constellation word "soar" comes closest to the Xayan *ala'ru*, a word not easily expressible in other languages. Depending upon how *ala'ru* is pronounced (and to whom, and by whom), the word can mean various degrees of sacredness in the actions of the Xayan individual as he progresses toward a state of perfection and merges his psyche with those of his fellows. In its ultimate form, *ala'ru* refers to the ascension of the entire Xayan race, a word that is uttered with a great exhalation of passion, from the deepest portion of the alien soul.

ALLYF—one of the five preserved Xayans in the museum vault; he did not survive the long sleep.

ANDERLOS, ERIK—deputy administrator of Buktu.

ANKOR—launch center and spaceport on Hellhole, linked to the new DZ stringline hub.

ANQUI, ANTONIA—young Hellhole colonist, girlfriend of Devon Vence. A shadow-Xayan whose alien counterpart is Jhera.

ARMY OF THE CONSTELLATION—space navy and ground-based military that was consolidated during Adolphus's rebellion, commanded by Lord Selik Riomini.

ATAB ABAS—Deep Zone planet.

BARASSA—Crown Jewel planet.

BATTLE OF SONJEERA—final space battle in General Adolphus's first rebellion, in which he was defeated (some say tricked) by Commodore Percival Hallholme.

BIRZH—Xayan telemancer preserved in slickwater, lover of Jhera; became the counterpart of Devon Vence.

BLACK LORD—nickname for Lord Selik Riomini, based on his penchant for wearing black.

BOJ—Deep Zone planet.

BUKTU—isolated Deep Zone planet, administered by Ian Walfor; cold and frozen, previously cut off from the Constellation stringline network.

BUREAU OF DEEP ZONE AFFAIRS—government bureau administering the five territorial governors, located on Sonjeera.

CANDELA—Deep Zone planet administered by Tanja Hu. Secret source of iperion for the Deap Zone rebels.

CAREY, LUJAH—leader of the Children of Amadin group on Hellhole.

CARON, SERGEANT ARBIN—trailblazer pilot for Army of the Constellation.

CARRINGTON, GAIL—special attaché to Lord Riomini, former head of his bodyguards.

CARTER, ANDREW—one of Sophie Vence's line managers.

CELANO GEESE—waterfowl native to Sonjeera.

CHERBY—Crown Jewel planet, original home of Franck Tello.

CHILDREN OF AMADIN—isolationist religious group from Barassa that has come to settle on Hellhole.

CIARLI, TANN—one of the victims on Ishop Heer's list of noble descendants.

CIPPIQ—one of the Original Xayans, volunteered to be emissary to Sonjeera; he was murdered by Diadem Michella.

CLES—Deep Zone planet.

CLOVIS, RENNY—former Ankor site administrator, partner of Tel. He was killed in the collapse of a slickwater-filled sinkhole.

CLOVIS, TEL—former Ankor site administrator, partner of Renny; after Renny's death, Tel immersed himself in slickwater and became a shadow-Xayan.

CODECALL SYSTEM—Encrypted communications system used throughout the Constellation.

CONSTELLATION—stellar empire of 74 planets, comprising 20 core worlds called the Crown Jewels and 54 frontier worlds in the Deep Zone. Capital is Sonjeera, ruled by the Diadem.

CONSTELLATION CHARTER—primary binding document that defines the government of the Constellation.

CORI, ELWAR—Vielinger physicist who discovered how to use processed iperion to mark a path in space, defining a constrained route that the new stardrives could use.

COTTAGE—private residence at the Pond of Birds used as a discreet retreat on the grounds of the Diadem's Palace.

COUNCIL CITY—government center on Sonjeera.

CRAIS, ALBO—elder member of Crais family whose political ambitions were thwarted by Michella.

CRAIS, BOLTON—husband of Keana Duchenet, logistics officer in the Army of the Constellation, rank of silver major.

CRAIS, ILVAR—current head of the Crais noble family, father of Bolton.

CRAIS, NOK II—former Diadem, Bolton's great-great-grandfather; the Council City Spaceport building was constructed during his reign.

CRISTAINE, LIEUTENANT AURA—first officer of the *Diadem's Glory*.

CROWN JEWELS—twenty core planets in the Constellation, the most closely packed worlds and most civilized.

DAR, SURI—pilot of one of the Constellation's military stringline haulers.

DARENTHIA—Deep Zone planet.

DE CARRE, CRISTOPH—exiled son of disgraced Lord Louis de Carre, now works for General Adolphus on Hellhole.

DE CARRE, LORD LOUIS—disgraced leader of Vielinger, lover of Keana Duchenet.

DEEP ZONE—the 54 frontier worlds in the Constellation, recently opened to settlement.

DEEP ZONE DEFENSE FORCE—the ships, veteran soldiers, and volunteers General Adolphus pulled together to defend the frontier worlds.

DEEZEE—derogatory term for a Deep Zone settler.

DELAYNE, MARIA—planetary administrator of Nephilim.

DESTINATION DAY—the completion date of the new DZ stringline transportation network.

DIADEM—the leader of the Constellation government.

DIADEM'S GLORY—flagship of the Constellation fleet sent against General Adolphus.

DOWNBOX—cargo boxes dropped from a stringline hauler down to the surface of a destination planet.

DOZER—large construction machine.

DUCHENET, DIADEM MICHELLA—leader of the Constellation.

DUCHENET, HAVEEDA—Michella's younger sister, rumored to be a witness to the murder of their brother Jamos as a child; she has not been seen in public for many years.

DUCHENET, JAMOS—Michella's older brother, murdered when he was young (Michella is rumored to be responsible).

DUCHENET, KEANA—only daughter of Diadem Michella, now on Hellhole, accompanied by Xayan presence Uroa.

DZ—Deep Zone.

EDWOND HOUSE—building where Edwond the First, the Warrior Diadem, held war cabinet meetings. Now Ishop Heer's residence.

EDWOND THE FIRST—former diadem of the Constellation, also called the Warrior Diadem.

EKOVA, LUCINDA—operations officer for Lord Riomini's strike force.

ELAKIS, BURUM—secret Adolphus supporter on Sonjeera, also connected to Enva Tazaar.

ELAKIS, WILLIS—brother of Burum Elakis, who died in prison.

ELBA—Adolphus's estate outside of Michella Town.

ELBERT, WILL—one of Sophie Vence's line managers.

ENCIX—female Xayan, leader of the three surviving Originals.

ENGERMANN, OLV—owner of a machine repair shop on Orsini, former boss of Vincent Jenet.

ERON—capital city on Theser, located in a deep crater.

FEN, ELDORA—planetary administrator of Cles.

FERNANDO-ZAIRIC—joined personalities of Fernando Neron and Zairic.

FIRTH, JACKSON—leader of diplomatic team accompanying the Constellation fleet against Hellhole; he is a historian of the General's first rebellion.

FLEER—Crown Jewel planet where Tel and Renny Clovis served a prison term, homeworld of the Duchenets.

FRANKOV, SIA—planetary administrator of Theser, close friend of Tanja Hu.

GAXEN—draft animals native to Sonjeera.

GAVO—one of Tanja Hu's cousins.

GOLDENWOOD—valuable trees native to Ridgetop.

GOLER, CARLSON—administrator of Ridgetop and territorial governor of eleven planets, including Hallholme and Candela.

GROWLER—colloquial term for a static storm on Hallholme.

HALEY—climbing goat Tanja Hu used to ride on Candela.

HALLHOLME (PLANET)—formal name for Hellhole.

HALLHOLME, CORAM—younger son of Escobar.

HALLHOLME, ELAINE—wife of Escobar, grandniece of Lord Selik Riomini.

HALLHOLME, EMIL—older son of Escobar.

HALLHOLME, RED COMMODORE ESCOBAR—son of Commodore Percival Hallholme, assigned to lead retaliatory strike against Hellhole.

HALLHOLME, COMMODORE PERCIVAL—retired leader of the Army of the Constellation; he defeated General Adolphus the first time and quashed his rebellion.

HEART SQUARE—central square in Sonjeera's Council City.

HEER, ISHOP—Diadem Michella's confidential aide, spy, and hatchet man.

HELLHOLE—hellish frontier world, considered the most inhospitable of the Deep Zone worlds, colloquial name for planet Hallholme.

HELLTOWN—colloquial name for Michella Town.

HERALD, PETER—former lieutenant in General Adolphus's rebellion.

HESTON, LORA—leader of Lord Riomini's bodyguards.

HIRDAN—noble family.

HIRDAN, TANIK—head of the Hirdan family.

HORP—Sonjeeran racing animal.

HU, QUINN—Tanja Hu's uncle and mentor, killed in a mudslide caused by overmining on Candela.

HU, TANJA—administrator of Candela, one of the first coconspirators with General Adolphus on Hallholme.

IPERION—rare mineral used to mark stringline paths across space. The Constellation's primary source of iperion is found on the planet Vielinger.

J-PALM—flammable, explosive fluid.

JACOB—General Adolphus's flagship, named after his father.

JACQUE—adopted son of Bebe Nax.

JENET, DREW—Vincent's ill father.

JENET, VINCENT—Hellhole colonist, sentenced by Enva Tazaar to live there as punishment after he was convicted of a crime; friend of Fernando-Zairic, killed with emissaries to Sonjeera.

JESSUP, ROLF—shadow-Xayan, originally from Ridgetop.

JHERA—Xayan telemancer preserved in slickwater, lover of Birzh; now the counterpart of Antonia Anqui.

JONN—Crown Jewel planet, ruled by the Hirdan family.

JORDAN, CRAIG—Adolphus's chief of security, now managing part of the Hellhole defense forces.

KAPPAS—Crown Jewel planet, ruled by the Paternos family.

KEATS, HUME—worker on Buktu, as well as a pilot who flies with Ian Walfor.

KERRIS—linerunner ship operated by Turlo and Sunitha Urvancik, named after their dead son.

KIAFA—popular hot beverage.

KLIEF—Crown Jewel planet, former home of Sophie and Devon Vence.

KOMUN, GEORGE—planetary administrator of Umber.

KOUVET, CAPTAIN—security officer at Council City Spaceport.

LASSEN, OWEN—representative from Teron.

LINERUNNER—maintenance ship that travels along the stringline paths to check iperion integrity.

LODO—male Xayan, one of the three surviving Originals, assigned to studying the museum vault.

LUBIS PLAIN SHIPYARDS—large military shipyard on Qiorfu.

LUMINOUS GARDEN—one of the spectacular gardens on the grounds of the Diadem's palace.

MACHI—Crown Jewel planet.

MAGEROS, LADY OPRA—noblewoman, descendant of one of the families that brought about the downfall of the Osheers.

MAIL DRONE—small automated packet that travels along the stringlines.

MALIBU, HENRY—deacon among the Children of Amadin, former doctor.

MARUBI—Crown Jewel planet.

MAYAK, TOBNER—scientist on Sonjeera.

McLUHAN, EVA—a linerunner who committed suicide in deep space between destinations.

MERCIFULS—secular order of nurses.

MICHELLA TOWN—main colony town on Hallholme; referred to colloquially as Helltown.

MORAE, ELWYN—first administrator of Candela.

NARI—drilling supervisor on Hellhole.

NAX, BEBE—Tanja Hu's administrative assistant on Candela, mother of Jacque.

NEHL—young orphaned girl, a member of the Children of Amadin.

NELL, LADERNA—assistant to Ishop Heer, also his lover.

NEPHILIM—Deep Zone planet, supposedly the site of a fountain of youth.

NERON, FERNANDO—Hellhole colonist, first man to immerse himself in slickwater and take on an alien personality, Zairic. Fernando-Zairic served as spokesman for the shadow-Xayans, until he was murdered on Sonjeera along with other emissaries.

NICLES—Deep Zone planet.

NOAB—Crown Jewel planet, home of the Crais family.

NOABY—valuable jewel mined on Noab.

NOMOLOS—Deep Zone planet.

NOORMAN, CAPTAIN FELIX—captain of a scout ship aboard the Constellation fleet.

OBERON, LANNY—supervisor in iperion mines on Vielinger.

OGG—Crown Jewel world where Osheer family was exiled.

ONGENET, ARIA—beautiful wife of historical Diadem Philippe the Whisperer, known for her numerous lovers, which she often entertained at her Cottage on the Pond of Birds.

ORIGINAL—one of five Xayans preserved in the vault against the asteroid impact: Allyf, Encix, Cippiq, Lodo, and Tryn. Only three remain alive.

ORSINI—one of the Crown Jewels, ruled by Lady Enva Tazaar.

OSHEER—centuries-old variation of Ishop Heer's family name.

OSHEER, LORD ELMAN—Osheer patriarch at the time of the family's disgrace.

OSHU—Deep Zone planet.

PACKARD, ERNST—one of Adolphus's trailblazer captains who died establishing the line to Ridgetop.

PARRA, ZINN—noble descendant of one of the families that disgraced Ishop Heer's ancestors.

PASSENGER POD—cargo container with life support and amenities, used for transporting people along stringline network.

PATERNOS—noble family from Crown Jewel planet Kappas, rivals of the Tazaars.

PATERNOS, LADY JENINE—ruler of Crown Jewel planet Kappas.

PENCE, TORII—trade representative of the Hirdan family from Jonn.

PHILIPPE THE WHISPERER—historical diadem, husband of Aria Ongenet.

POND OF BIRDS—small body of water on the grounds of the Diadem's Palace, site of the romantic, luxurious Cottage.

PRINIFLOWER—medicinal plant native to Ridgetop.

PRITIKIN, LUKE—one of the Diadem's inspectors on Hellhole.

PUHAU—isolated mining village on Candela, wiped out in a mudslide.

QIORFU—Crown Jewel planet, site of the Lubis Plain Shipyards; original home of the Adolphus family, now ruled by the Riomini family and administered by retired commodore Hallholme.

QUIRRIE, TONA—real name of Antonia Anquie.

RAPANA—iperion-processing center on Vielinger, site of an industrial fire.

RICKETTS, COLONEL—representative of the Army of the Constellation.

RIDGETOP—forested Deep Zone planet best known for its goldenwood groves, administered by Carlson Goler, site of a massacre that was covered up by Diadem Michella.

RIDGETOP RECOVERY—massacre that occurred when Constellation forces razed an existing colony on Ridgetop to clear the way for new settlement; the truth was covered up by the Diadem.

RIOMINI—powerful noble family headquartered on Aeroc.

RIOMINI, GILAG—former Riomini lord who helped Michella establish her power base.

RIOMINI, LORD SELIK—head of the Riomini family, Supreme Commander of the Army of the Constellation; he is also called the Black Lord.

RO-XAYAN—rebellious Xayan faction.

ROLLER—small all-terrain vehicle.

RONOM—Deep Zone planet.

ROYAL RETREAT—one of the Diadem's seven official residences.

RUE DE LA MUSIQUE—the Street of Music, run-down section of Council City where Ishop Heer has his secret office.

RULLINS, JAKO—abusive man, former lover of Antonia Anqui.

SANDUSKY—one of the Crown Jewel planets, known for biological research.

SAPORO—harbor city on Candela.

SETSAI—Deep Zone planet.

SHADOW-XAYANS—humans who have accepted a Xayan personality from the slickwater pools.

SLICKWATER—Xayan liquid database of lives.

SLICKWATER SPRINGS—settlement out at the three original slickwater pools.

SMOKE STORM—meteorological event on Hallholme.

SONJEERA—capital planet of the Constellation, heart of the Crown Jewels, seat of power for Diadem Michella Duchenet. Also, site of the central stringline hub for all travel throughout the Constellation.

SONJI PHEASANT—game bird native to Sonjeera, considered a delicacy.

SPENCER, LIEUTENANT JOHAD—former weapons officer during Adolphus's rebellion, now his staff driver.

STAR THRONE—the Diadem's throne on Sonjeera.

STATIC STORM—dangerous electrical-discharge storm that occurs on Hallholme; colloquially called a "growler."

STRINGLINE—ultrafast interstellar transportation system that follows quantum lines of iperion laid down across space.

STRINGLINE HAULER—large-framework ship that is loaded with cargo containers and passenger pods; travels back and forth from Sonjeera to a designated stringline terminus.

STRINGLINE HUB—central point from which all the transportation lines radiate; the Constellation's only hub is on Sonjeera.

STRINGLINE TERMINUS—endpoint of a stringline, a station in orbit over a destination planet.

SUZUKI, RANDOLPH—chocolatier, member of a fallen noble family.

SVC-1185—blue-giant star, site of a stringline power substation on the route to Ridgetop.

TANINE—Crown Jewel planet, site of a brief uprising.

TASMINE—Governor Goler's old household servant, only survivor of the Ridgetop Recovery.

TAZAAR—powerful noble family headquartered on Orsini, rivals of the Riominis.

TAZAAR, LADY ENVA—head of the Riomini family, also an aspiring artist.

TEHILA—most distant Deep Zone planet, home of semi-intelligent herd animals.

TELEMANCY—Xayan telekinetic power.

TELLO, FRANCK—officer in the first rebellion, General Adolphus's best friend, killed during the Battle of Sonjeera.

TELOM, DAK—officer in the Army of the Constellation, secretly a spy for General Adolphus.

TERON—Deep Zone planet.

THERIS, RENDO—administrator of the Ankor spaceport complex.

THESER—Deep Zone planet, administered by Sia Frankov, home of eccentric spacedrive engineers.

TIER, DOM CELLAN—planetary administrator of Oshu.

TILLMAN, ARMAND—cattle rancher on Hellhole.

TRAILBLAZER—a ship that lays down a path of processed iperion to create a new stringline route.

TRAKMASTER—heavy-duty overland vehicle used on Hellhole.

TROMBIE, BUXTON—Duchenet family attorney.

TRYN—female Xayan, one of the three surviving Originals.

UETER—Deep Zone planet.

ULMAN, LIEUTENANT RICO—test pilot at the Lubis Plain shipyards.

UMBER—Deep Zone planet.

UNDINE, GOVERNOR MARLA—one of the five territorial governors of the Deep Zone, arrested and held as a political prisoner.

UPBOX—cargo container launched into orbit, where it is picked up by a stringline hauler.

UROA—Xayan leader whose presence now shares a body with Keana Duchenet.

URVANCIK, KERRIS—son of Turlo and Sunitha, killed in military service shortly after the end of Adolphus's rebellion.

URVANCIK, SUNITHA—stringline runner, married to Turlo.

URVANCIK, TURLO—stringline runner, married to Sunitha.

VENCE, DEVON—son of Sophie Vence, boyfriend of Antonia Anqui. A shadow-Xayan, his alien counterpart is Birzh.

VENCE, GREGORY—former husband of Sophie Vence, father of Devon.

VENCE, SOPHIE—powerful merchant woman in Michella Town, in a relationship with General Adolphus.

VIELINGER—Crown Jewel planet, source of iperion, formerly ruled by the de Carre family, now a holding of the Riomini family.

VOBBINS, JALUKA—head of the Theser spacedrive engineers.

VOJA TREE—a type of willow common on Vielinger, whose bark is said to have medicinal (and some say spiritual) qualities.

VONDAS, CAPTAIN—expedition leader on original colony ship to Buktu.

VUARNER, PRIEMA—last noble victim on Ishop Heer's list.

WALFOR, IAN—administrator of Deep Zone planet Buktu, with shipyards and ice mines. Previously, he was a black-market runner who delivered supplies to DZ planets without using the stringline.

WARRIOR DIADEM—Edwond the First.

WEILIN, EVELYN—socialite woman from a noble family fallen on hard times; descendant of one of the twelve nobles who caused the disgrace of the Osheer family.

XAYANS—original race of inhabitants on Hellhole.

YARICK—Constellation noble family.

ZABRISKIE, SERGEANT FRANCONE—trailblazer pilot for Army of the Constellation.

ZAIRIC—Xayan leader who originally proposed the slickwater preservation plan; his presence joined with Fernando Neron, both killed by Diadem Michella.